FULL
SHARE

ISBN-10: 1-940575-02-8
ISBN-13: 978-1-940575-02-5

Second Edition: August, 2013

For more information or to leave a comment about this book,
please visit us on the web at:
www.solarclipper.com

Publishers Note:

In the memory of my aunt, Patricia Wallace Whitney Lane

When I was a kid, Aunt Pat would bring over large grocery bags
filled with paperbacks about once a month or so.

Many of them were odd little books called "Ace Doubles"
which I devoured.

Without her, I might never have become the fan
or the writer
that I am today.

The Golden Age of the Solar Clipper

Quarter Share
Half Share
Full Share
Double Share
Captains Share
Owners Share

South Coast
Cape Grace*

Tanyth Fairport Adventures

Ravenwood
Zypherias Call
The Hermit Of Lammas Wood*

* Forthcoming

FULL SHARE

NATHAN LOWELL

Durandus

All children, except one, grow up. Recent events had proven to me, again, that I wasn't that one, not that I'd ever considered I might be. The other issue is that "growing up" isn't a destination the same way as "grandmother's house" is. It's not a condition you arrive at, like "growing bored" or "becoming hungry," but rather a process that ends—as the Bard might say—gravely. I was reflecting on that idea while on the afternoon watch and, to be truthful, more than a little bitterly. Three days out of port, the *Lois McKendrick* clawed her way out of Dunsany's gravity well bound for Betrus. Our stay at the orbital had been so surreal and bizarre that I wondered if the air supply had been laced with aerosol hallucinogens.

The console jarred me out of my reverie by initiating an Automated System Integrity Check. The status message blinked *Running* for less than a tick before changing to *Air Systems Nominal* and under that *Water Systems Nominal*. I acknowledged the messages and went back to my funk.

The rollercoaster of the previous week had left me emotionally exhausted. It started with my self-absorbed exhibitionism at Chez Henri, continued with a rendezvous with the second mate of the *Duchamp*, and ended with pathetic debacles with three of my shipmates. The fact that they were, as Henri Roubaille had said, "three of the most delightful and strikingly beautiful women on this end of the galaxy," made me feel even more like a mooncalf. I was left with the singular and distinct impression that whatever else might have happened I had been an idiot. Given my gender—male—and my age—eighteen—that should have come as no surprise, but I had hoped for better from myself.

In spite of all that, I had to admit it hadn't been all bad. I think

I helped the new mess deck attendant, Sarah Krugg, come to grips with years of abuse she had suffered on St. Cloud. She was shaping up to be a crackerjack cook and might very well be the best natural born salesperson in the galaxy. As for her practicing a little South Coast shamanism on the side, well, everybody needs a hobby.

Pip—that's Philip Carstairs, cargo genius—and I had made a tidy profit on our last leg and we had some interesting cargoes for Betrus. The McKendrick Mercantile Cooperative, a trading club for the crew that I helped to setup, was going great guns. The group of crewmen known as the co-ed crochet team was seeing fantastic success. They bought yarns in one port, crocheted their goods in the Deep Dark, and sold the completed products at our next destination. They'd just been getting started going into Dunsany Roads and I was glad to see my little idea was working out so well for them.

The chrono clicked over to 1600 and I realized I hadn't done my Visual Site Inspections yet. I slaved my tablet to the watch station and pulled up the sensor overlay.

"Hey, B," I called to Specialist One (Environmental) Brilliantine "Brill" Smith, "I'm going on VSI now."

Brill was in her office with the door open. "Stay on the path. Write if you get work," she answered back. This was one of those silly ritual responses we all used. She'd just told me to check the sensors in the specified order so that if something unexpected happened they'd be able to find me quickly. The last part was an instruction to notify her if I found something that needed attention.

"Aye, Chief," I replied. I couldn't help but smile. Brill had that effect on me. As one of the aforementioned "strikingly beautiful women" she had other effects on me as well. I sighed again.

I headed out to check each environmental sensor package by working my way down the two hundred and sixteen meter length of the ship. It was a good hike and helped to break up the monotony of a watch. The other advantage was I couldn't carry that heavy funk all the way. It got too heavy and began to flake off along the passageways.

By the time I got back, there wasn't a lot of the watch left, but I settled in with my spec two environmental lessons and worked on that awhile. The test was in a few days, and if I passed, I'd be promoted to spec three and finally qualify to fill the slot left when Gregor Avery took a new berth on the *Audrey Moore*. I had just enough time to run a practice test and scored a whopping ninety-six when Francis, Spec Three Francis Gartner, showed up to relieve me.

Francis was a good guy. He was a tall, skinny drink of water who held a Ph.D. in astrophysics but worked in Environmental just so he could get out into space. Seeing him made me consider that notion. For all the time we spent in the Deep Dark, we actually saw precious little of it. Sometimes it seemed like we got on board, sealed the locks, sat confined for some specified number of weeks, and when the doors opened again we found ourselves in a remarkably similar orbital. I supposed the bridge crew must get to experience it on a different level, but for most of us, we could have been on a really long subway ride.

"Hey, Francis," I said as he stepped through the hatch right on the dot of 1745.

"Hey, Ish. How goes?"

Francis and I had had our differences, but that was in the past. Wind through the sails and all that. "Good. Looks like I'm ready to take the test," I said. "Did you have a good time in Dunsany? We didn't see much of you."

A kind of silly smile formed on his face. "Oh yeah, very good." Francis didn't elaborate, and I was beginning to smarten up enough not to ask.

"You ready for duty?" I asked him.

"Let's do it."

"Mr. Gartner, all ops normal. No maintenance scheduled or performed. You may take the watch."

"I relieve you, Mr. Wang. I have the watch," he said, returning the required response.

With that I was off for the next twelve stans—free to sit in my bunk and stew all I wanted. Brill stepped out of her office then and smiled at us. "Hi, guys!"

"Hi, B," Francis said.

I just waved.

"You headed up to dinner, Ish?" she asked.

"Yup. Wanna join me? My treat."

"Cheapskate!" she said and even Francis laughed.

The thing to remember about Brill is that she's tall. Not like what you think of as tall, I mean really, really tall. In a galaxy of people who seldom break the two meter threshold, Brill tops out just above two and a quarter. She's also beautiful, smart, and sexy. Brown eyes, a willowy build, and the fierceness of a Valkyrie when she puts her mind to it. Like the rest of us, she was currently zipped into a shipsuit, and she even made that look good—really good. Heart-achingly good.

We set out and I held the hatch for her while she ducked carefully through it. I suspected that being so tall on a ship had to be a headache, quite literally, although she never complained about it. She never complained about anything.

"You don't look good, Ish," she murmured after the hatch closed.

"Aw, you know. I'm still adjusting. That was a rough ride through Dunsany. I need to pace myself a little more when we get to Betrus." I tried on a smile to see if I could distract her.

"You need to do more than that," she said, brow furrowed.

"Like what?"

"If I can offer some advice, you need to figure out who you are and then go for it."

"I know. I'm working on that."

She shook her head. "No, I don't think you are. You've made a start on Dunsany, but you need to do more."

"What are you talking about?"

"Look, you're still young, but you can't afford to waste it."

"Waste what?"

"Time, Ish, time. Do you want to be like Francis and slop sludge until you're fifty?" She was serious and, what's more, she was right.

The realization slid down my back like a shiver of cold water. "Damn, you're good." I said.

She chuckled a little and gave my shoulder a squeeze. "Let's go see what Cookie's got going. Smells like pot roast."

After dinner, I went to engineering berthing and stretched out on my bunk. I planned to just let dinner settle for a bit before I went for a run and a steam. I hadn't run in days, which probably wasn't helping my mood. I knew from past experience not to get out on the track with a belly full of Cookie's excellent food. My bunkies were gone and I had the quad to myself. Mitch Fitzroy had the bunk below mine. He was a machinist in the Propulsion Section and a typical engine head—a great guy with oil in his veins. Mitch and I were on the same watch schedule so he was probably in the gym or maybe still tanking up on dinner. He had a pretty healthy metabolism. Specialist Three (Electrical) Rebecca Saltzman had the lower bunk on the other side. I liked her a lot. She was from one of the heavy-G worlds and had the genetic legacy to prove it. As soon as I got stretched out, though, I nodded off. I didn't even get a chance to pull my tablet out of its holster. I just crashed and slept until the duty messenger woke me for watch the next day. I wasn't even conscious enough to catch who woke me. I realized I was still in yesterday's shipsuit and sighed. I seemed to be doing that a lot lately.

Showering made me feel better and fresh clothes helped even more. I went up to the mess deck and grabbed a coffee before heading down to relieve Diane.

Specialist Three (Environmental) Diane Ardele was a cute, little thing with elfin features and a wicked sense of humor. She had red hair and green eyes and she was another of the three women who went with me to Roubaille's that day. A smile split her face as I came through the hatch. "Hey, Ish!"

"Hi, Diane," I replied with a groggy yawn. "I can't seem to wake up this morning."

"When'd you go to bed?"

"Early. I had dinner with B then went to lie down for a few minutes to let it settle. I fell asleep until the messenger woke me for watch just now."

She looked at me hard. "Are you okay, Ish? You've seemed a bit out of kilter ever since we got underway."

"Yeah, I'm fine." I considered that might have been a lie. I just couldn't be sure. Everything seemed off—gray—dull. I tried to convince myself it was just emotional whiplash from the stay in Dunsany. "Just tired. I feel like we spent a month in port last week."

We changed the watch and she stayed around for a few minutes giving me an *I'm-not-sure-I-can-leave-you-alone* look like the ones my mother used to give me.

"Brill seems to think I need to be considering my future," I said.

"What does that mean?" she asked.

"She doesn't want me to waste my time."

She shrugged. "That seems like good advice."

"Yeah, she says I need to find myself. But how do you know who you are? Or who you're not?"

She shrugged again. "You've had a hell of a week, Ish. Those sound like questions you need to let puddle in the back of your brain for a while. Eventually they'll resolve into something."

I had to think about that for a few heartbeats but finally nodded. "Thanks, Diane, that actually helps." And it did.

She stood and headed for the hatch. "See you up at breakfast?" she asked.

"Yeah, I'll be up in a few ticks. I just wanna check the logs and maintenance records."

"Okay, see you in a bit."

I settled down to check the logs and make a list of tasks. My brain slid back into a familiar script, running through the overnight logs and checking the maintenance schedule for the next twenty-four stans. It was one of my "fast-flip" days—the name I'd given to the six-on-six-off-six-on portions of the watch cycle. At the end of a fast-flip, I would get either a break of either twelve or twenty-four stans. I'd just slept through most of a twelve, and I had eighteen to go before the twenty-four. I made a note on my tablet to change the number two water intake filter on this watch and clean the number three scrubber's field plates during the evening's leg. I felt oddly detached, as if I was watching myself from someplace outside—like one of those cheesy holo-noir shots that pan to show the character huddled over some task while the point of view spins around them. The technique always made me think of watching something in a microwave. Realizing that those panning shots usually ended in something awful happening to the character, I looked over my shoulder and laughed at myself when I realized what I was doing.

Yeah, Dunsany had been a strange port.

After breakfast I settled down with my tablet to study, but Brill's words kept coming back to me.

Do I really want to be slopping sludge at fifty?

Environmental duty was interesting in a way, and certainly one of the critical functions of the ship, but I was suddenly aware that it was a job—something I did in between the things I wanted to do. Working there was not something I did because I loved doing it.

The next question dropped my head into vapor lock as I considered what exactly it was that I loved to do. A long time passed while I sat there flipping ideas across my brain. At least two Automated System Integrity Checks—we call them ASICs—came up while I was thinking. They were nominal and I cleared them with as much automaticity as they exhibited. My problem was I had no clue as to what I wanted to do.

I had been four years old when my mom took a job at the University of Neris and spent almost my entire life there. Neris was a company planet. I lived in the university enclave with her. She was an ancient literature professor in the English department until she died in a flitter crash. I escaped deportation by signing on to the *Lois McKendrick* only a few weeks after my eighteenth birthday and a month before I was supposed to start at the university as a student.

Even back then, I didn't really know what I wanted to do. I had only agreed to go to college to humor my mother. I knew I had to find something to make a living—we were far from wealthy. It's just that I hadn't found anything remotely appealing until I came aboard the *Lois*.

My first assignment had been on the mess deck working with

Pip and Cookie. There was a sense of satisfaction in working there. Cookie always said, "We run a restaurant, gentlemen, and even though the crew can't go anywhere else, they still deserve our best efforts."

Back then, I studied all four of the divisional materials and qualified as half share in each one. I laughed at myself when I remembered my plans to collect a complete set of full share ratings because I had been so worried about being put ashore. A lot had changed in just a bit more than seven months.

When the chance came to move to Environmental, I took the offered position. The ship needed me there and I was happy to oblige. I still had a sense that the ship needed me, but that was where I stalled—stymied.

On a whim, I pulled up the Able Spacer test. Sandy Belterson, who is now a spec two in astrogation—but had been a spec three at the time—had helped me study for my ordinary spacer exam. Back then, she'd tested me at the higher level and I was shocked to see I passed that practice test. It took me just a half stan to finish another practice test and I blinked numbly at the score: ninety-two, which was well above the passing score of eighty.

Brill came in just then and found me staring into the void. "You in there, Ish?" she asked with concern.

I grinned. "Yup," I said, and began to think that perhaps I was.

"Well, it's good to see you smiling again. What'd you do last night? You disappeared after mess."

"I slept."

"Well, you musta needed it and it looks like it helped." She changed into Boss Mode and asked, "Did you happen to run the maintenance schedule? What've we got on for today?"

"Yeah, I did. I've got a water filter this morning and a scrubber field plate tonight. Diane's slated for the number two scrubber matrix. If you want, I'll come down after lunch and help with that."

"You don't mind? You've got the evening watch too."

"It's no problem. Besides, you know how I love seeing her get all mucky and wet," I said with a grin.

"Am I gonna need to chaperone you two?" she asked with a laugh.

"I'll be okay, but after Dunsany, you may wanna put a leash on Diane."

We both laughed at that and I began to think it was going to be okay after all. Although I must admit that I got a quick visual image of a wet and slimy Diane wearing a collar and leash. When I noticed Brill blush, I wondered if she'd gotten the same image, but I didn't go there. I was learning that there were some things I really didn't want to know.

"I think I'll go change that filter now, then I need to study."

"You ready?" she asked.

"I think so. I got a ninety-six on the practice test yesterday."

She put a hand on my shoulder. "I'm so proud of you. That's not the easiest stuff in the world."

"Thanks." I paused before asking, "Say, um, would you be upset if I went back to working on full share in the other ratings as well?"

"Not at all, but is everything okay?"

I shrugged. "Well, your comment yesterday about slopping sludge at fifty kinda got to me."

"I didn't mean that the way it sounded, Ish. Look at me. I'm going to be thirty next month and I'm probably going to be here till I'm a hundred and ten and they put me out to pasture."

I laughed at the image. "Yeah, maybe so, but this is what you love. You're really into the closed ecology stuff and where else are you going to be able to do that?"

"Well, there's station work."

"What? And give up all the glamour of being a spacer?" I motioned toward our sterile, utilitarian surroundings.

"You'll be up to your armpits in the glamour when you start working on that scrubber. But you're right. For me the work is still fascinating. So have you come to any conclusions overnight? About who you are, and what you wanna be unless you grow up?"

I appreciated her phrasing. "Nothing definite, other than to conclude that it's one thing to choose to slop sludge and another thing entirely to do so by default."

"Yup, that was my point exactly."

"So, when I first came on board I started out to collect all four full share ratings. Looks like I'll have one of them in a week or so, but just because I get my spec two here doesn't mean I can't go for Able Spacer, Cargoman, or Messman. Theoretically, if I pass next week, I'll be qualified already as a machinist—although the gods will need to help any division that puts me on power or propulsion watch."

"You'd be surprised how well you'd do, I think. But by all means, if you want to go for the other ratings as well, it's no problem with me. What are you thinking?"

"I don't know. I haven't gotten that far, but it just seems like one of those things I ought to do. I can probably get Able Spacer on this cycle along with the spec two. I just took a practice exam and got a score in the nineties. If I spend a couple of watches reviewing it, I could probably ace it."

"That wouldn't surprise me. I've seen your focus when you study."

"So, whatever happens after that, happens—one step at a time. Having the ratings doesn't hurt, and I might find something that I like as much as you like Environmental. It sounds nebulous, but it's something."

"Not bad for just one night sleeping on it," she said with a grin. "Lemme know if you have any other brain storms. In the meantime, I'm going to go immerse myself in the glamour of the quarterly section reports."

We laughed. "I'm gonna go swap out that water filter and get that out of the way, then maybe I'll do the VSI a bit early so I can settle down for a study break before lunch."

"Sounds like a plan," she said, heading into her office.

I watched her go. Some things are just worth taking the time to appreciate. Watching Specialist One Brilliantine Smith walk away from you was one of them. As she turned the corner into her office she caught me watching and chuckled.

After a satisfied little sigh I got on the comm-link to the bridge for permission to swap out the number one water intake system for the half a stan it would take to change the filter. I collected the tool kit from the storage locker, snagged a clean filter from parts storage, and got on with the morning already in progress.

Watch standing is like riding a merry-go-round. The repetition of the activities day after day and the way the other crew members fall into their own patterns provides a structure that becomes one long blur. You regularly see the people who are in your watch section, but the full complement of the crew is only really apparent to the mess deck worker. It's here that we all gather for meals on a cycle that isn't always set by the rotation of watches but on a convention that goes much deeper.

Breaks in this routine are both welcome and disturbing. Welcome because they provide a much needed variety to the pattern, and disturbing because they force you out of the zone and strip away the mental buffers that the process of watch standing has erected over time. Quarterly ratings tests are just such a break. Ten days out of the Dunsany Roads Orbital I reported to the office to take the spec two test for the Environmental Division.

I had watch in the morning, but Mr. von Ickles set the test so I could take it between morning and evening watches. He was very accommodating and just one of the reasons why I liked him a lot. He really seemed to care about the crew just as much as Mr. Maxwell and the captain did. I didn't get to see him much except when I took exams, but he was always nice to me and pretty easy to talk to. He wasn't quite as intimidating as Mr. Maxwell nor as awe inspiring as the captain, but still there was something comforting about him. Some air that I couldn't quite put my finger on.

I reported at the appointed time and we got right down to it. Unlike the half share exams I'd taken before, this test was a lot longer and used more simulations. After two solid stans, I put my stylus down and looked up at Mr. von Ickles. When he didn't speak, I prompted him with, "I'm done, sar."

"Yes, Mr. Wang," he said, "you are. I still can't get over the way you disappear into these tests. How do you think you did?"

"I don't know. I think I passed. I was pretty confident in my answers and I didn't have to skip any. I also didn't run out of time."

He turned the display so I could see the ninety-eight. "A hundred is max. And just between you and me, that one item you missed, I thought you had the right answer. I'm going to bump that back up to Confederation headquarters because I think the scoring key is wrong," he said in a kind of disbelieving tone.

"Which one was it?" I asked.

"The calculation for the amount of time to bring that tank of water up to a viable temperature for algae growth. I thought your calculations were right, but the answer key disagreed."

"Is it really an issue since it won't make a difference on me passing?"

"No, but for someone else those two points might make the difference between passing and failing. You are now officially ranked Specialist Two in Environmental and I will note that in your jacket. And to think I knew ya when," he said with a big smile.

"Thank you, sar."

"So, Mr. Wang, does this mean you're giving up your quest for full share ratings? Are you going to specialize in Environmental?"

"No, sar, I'll be back tomorrow for the Able Spacer test."

"Tabitha Rondita is taking it too. Can you be here at 0900?"

"Sure. We're on the same watch rotation."

"Excellent, then I'll see you both tomorrow."

As I started to leave, he stopped me. "You know this only goes into your jacket. It's up to the captain, Mr. Kelley, and Ms. Smith as to whether you get the open spec three berth."

"Yes, sar, I'm aware of that."

"Okay," he told me, then lowering his voice he added, "don't be too disappointed if they wait until Betrus to make it official."

I considered that for a heartbeat or two. I really had expected that once I passed the test, I'd be able to get the promotion right away. "In the grand scheme of things, sar, all it means is a higher mass allotment—which doesn't do me any good out here in the

Deep Dark—and about a hundred creds in my pay packet that I should more than make up for with my co-op merchandise. Thanks for the heads up, though, either way will be fine."

"Very well, Mr. Wang, are you really doing that well trading?"

"Yes, sar. Pip and I have been very fortunate. Since Darbat we've made something over eight kilocreds from private trading, sar."

He blinked at me several times as he processed that. "You mean eight hundred creds, right?"

"No, sar, that's eight thousand credits between the two of us. We're splitting that of course. It's not eight each."

He barked a laugh. "You're not kidding, are you?"

His response puzzled me. "No, sar. Why would I?"

"But that's at least five times more than your salary and share for the same leg."

"More like eight, sar, yes. Why?"

He shook his head in astonishment. "You're making more money than I am!"

"Well, sar, have you considered joining the co-op?" I asked with a grin. "The co-op took in four hundred creds in fees from Dunsany alone. Of course we'll split that with the booth managers, but we've started out well."

"And you organized this thing, didn't you?" he asked.

I shrugged. "Well kinda. I came up with the idea. Pip thought it sounded good and we found others in the crew to help out. Pip really runs most of the meetings with the steering committee. I've helped where I could."

He looked at me hard for about five heartbeats. "Mr. Wang, have you ever considered the academy?"

The question took me sideways for a moment because all my life *the academy* meant something different. "You mean the officer's academy, sar?"

"Yes, Mr. Wang, the Confederation Merchant Officer Academy at Port Newmar."

"You mean have I ever considered going there?"

He chuckled. "I should know better than to ask you stuff like that right after a test, but yes, Mr. Wang, that's the gist of my question."

"No, sar. I don't know anything about it. Other than it's where you go to learn to become an officer."

"Consider it, Mr. Wang," he said with a nod. "That's an order."

By the time I finished the test it was just after 1600. I had two hours before going back on watch. I hit the gym and pounded out a couple dozen laps on the track. The usual collection of first section watch standers was there. I even spotted Tabitha on her customary rowing machine. It seemed odd that she was only an ordinary spacer. I don't know why, but when Mr. von Ickles had said she was taking the able spacer test, it was kind of a jolt. She'd been aboard much longer than I had, and I found it disconcerting that she hadn't gotten the rating before. Not holding the position I could understand. After all, you only got the rank if the ship had an opening, and I could certainly see staying with a ship you liked even at a lower rank. The *Lois* was that kind of ship. But not taking the test didn't make sense.

As I ran, I thought about what Mr. von Ickles had said, and considered what was involved in going to the academy.

Would I consider leaving the Lois? Could I?

The whole notion was coming at me too fast, so I put the idea aside and let the running trance take me.

When I stepped through the hatch into Environmental to relieve Diane at 1745 she almost screamed at me, "Well?"

"Well, what?" I asked, completely confused.

Brill stepped out of the office. "I think she'd like to know if you passed the test, Ish," she said, considering me with her hands on her hips. "I'm kinda curious myself."

"Oh, yeah, I passed."

Brill smiled and Diane did a little happy dance behind the console. "You didn't think to let us know a bit earlier?" Brill asked.

"Oh, crufty nuggets! I'm so sorry," I said coming back to reality perhaps for the first time since the test. "I'm such a ninny."

Diane teased, "We were beginning to wonder if you'd flunked and put yourself out an airlock in shame."

"I really am sorry. I get so groggy after those tests that I went straight for a run afterwards. I should have come down before I went to the gym."

"So, give us the whole scoop—we need details, man, details." Brill said.

"I missed one question but Mr. von Ickles thought my answer was right and that the grading key was wrong. He's going to file some kind of correction request with the Confederation."

Brill and Diane looked at each other and back at me. "That's amazing." Brill finally said.

"Yeah, I'd be pretty surprised if no one else noticed a problem before now."

"No, doofus. It's amazing that you got a ninety-eight." Diane just leaned on the console and shook her head with a *what-am-I-going-to-do-with-you* look on her face. "It defies belief. You went from engineman to spec two in one leap with no background, no special training, and only two months of study. Don't you realize how crazy that is?"

"Well, I did spend a month studying spec one by mistake," I reminded her.

"Yeah, and I'm beginning to think we should've kept you working on those materials so you could have taken that test instead! My gods and garters, Ish, this is amazing!"

"Thanks," I said, but I didn't really see what the big deal was. All the material had been right on my tablet, and it wasn't like watch standing didn't give me plenty of time for studying.

"I'll ask Mr. Kelley to put you up for the position right away, Ish, but he and the captain will be the ones making the decision."

I shrugged. "No worries. I already told Mr. von Ickles I'm not concerned about the timing."

Diane waved me over. "Mr. Wang, all operations normal. No maintenance scheduled or performed. You may have the watch."

"I relieve you, Ms. Ardele. I have the watch."

They headed for the lock and I settled behind the console and started the beginning of watch rituals. "Oh, by the way, B, I'd like to talk to you about the academy sometime when you have a chance."

Diane kept chuckling and headed on out to get some dinner, but Brill turned back to look at me. "Which academy?" she asked after a moment or two.

I was still running the logs and checking the maintenance schedule so I wasn't looking at her when I said, "Port Newmar."

She was still standing there when I finished my checks. "Is that what you want?" she asked, her eyebrows drawn together in a frown.

"What?" I asked because I completely mislaid the thread of our conversation while I got my watch going.

"The academy?" she asked with as much exasperation as I've ever heard from her.

"I don't even know what that means, B. How can I possibly know if it's what I want? Mr. von Ickles ordered me to consider going, so I'm looking into it. Since he hasn't ordered me to make a decision I'm covered for now," I said.

Brill, for some reason, wasn't getting the joke. "You'd have to leave the *Lois*," she said at last.

"Yeah," I said with a sigh. "That's a big minus, but let's not get ahead of ourselves. I'm still working on what I wanna be unless I grow up." I smiled but she didn't return it.

Finally she nodded. "Yeah, okay. Just keep me up to date on what you're thinking about, though, okay?"

"Of course, B. I can't see anything happening too soon and I don't think it's something I can decide between here and Betrus, do you?"

She shrugged. "I don't know. I'm gonna go get some dinner. See you on the mess deck?"

"Sure. Cookie's frying chicken tonight and I'm starved."

She turned and left then, still frowning. I thought she said something else but I only caught "...careful what I wish for" before the hatch closed behind her. Whomever she was talking to, it wasn't me.

Sometimes that woman is a puzzle I thought to myself. Then I laughed at the *sometimes* part.

It only took a few more ticks to settle into the watch and by 1815 I was ready to head up for something to eat. I was looking forward to some quiet time with my tablet afterwards, as the only thing on my schedule was the VSI and an unknown number of ASIC acknowledgments. I joined a group who had already eaten and I was right about the fried chicken. It was great. Brill seemed a little distracted but I didn't mention the academy again and neither did she. In the back of my mind, I was a little miffed that this woman who had been on my case about my future was now apparently upset because I was doing what she asked. In any event, Diane and Francis were both there ,and we had a nice time in spite of the occasional frown that creased Brill's brow.

I ate quickly and went back to work, taking a piece of granapple pie and a fresh cup of coffee with me for company. If she wanted to talk, she knew where to find me. It still freaked people out that I could eat in Environmental. Most couldn't stand breathing the thick, green-smelling air, let alone mixing it with food. The odor didn't bother me. I actually found it kinda reassuring. After spending so many weeks there, I hardly noticed it any longer.

As I ate my pie and kept an eye on the readouts, I pulled up information on the academy at Port Newmar from *The Spacer's Handbook*, a kind of encyclopedia of everything there was to know about life in the Deep Dark. The information was sparse, but one thing I hadn't foreseen was that the academy was actually a college with a pretty high tuition of ten kilocreds a year. I realized that I had surprised Mr. von Ickles with my recent trading success but I didn't understand how he expected me to come up with forty kilocreds plus the additional money for room and board.

The article went on to note that a person could graduate with a science degree in one of three specialties and there were also some minors. Having spent most of my life at the university enclave, none of this was difficult to decode. The fine print said, "Successful completion of this course of study leads to a Bachelor of Science Degree and the opportunity to sit for the Confederated Planets Joint Committee on Trade Third Mate's License Exam."

So the bottom line was, four years of school, at least sixty kilocreds, and you still had to pass the exam. I idly wondered how difficult the test was and why anybody bothered with the academy anyway.

The ASIC nagged me again and I put the academy out of my mind. I spent the rest of the watch going through the Able Spacer test materials and running practice exams, except for the half stan I took off for the VSI. Francis relieved me right on time. All told it was a quiet watch, but I'd learned a thing or two.

Tabitha looked surprised to see me come into the office for the exam. "What are you doing here? I thought Engineering was yesterday."

"I'm a glutton for punishment. I'm also going for Able Spacer," I told her.

"Just like me?"

"Tabitha, nobody could be just like you," I teased.

Mr. von Ickles interrupted, "If you two are quite ready?"

"Yes, sar," we both answered together.

He sat us on either side of the office and we began. It wasn't as rigorous as the spec three test had been, but I took my time and finished it just ahead of Mr. von Ickles announcement, "Time!"

Tabitha was still there, too, and we both looked up as we put our styluses down.

"Congratulations, you both now rate as Able Spacers and I will so note this in your individual jackets this afternoon."

Tabitha and I both grinned and I lingered afterward, dithering with my tablet while she left the office. When she was gone, I turned to Mr. von Ickles. "I considered it, sar," I told him.

"That didn't take long," he said.

"Well, sar, I looked it up in *The Handbook*. I didn't realized that the academy is a real college. To be honest, I didn't know what to expect."

"And your problem with college is...?" he asked. "Wasn't your mother a professor?"

"Yes, sar. I'm very familiar with the institution, and I know that the costs go way beyond tuition. There are books, room and board, lab fees. All in all it can get very expensive really fast."

"All true," he admitted. "And at the academy you have expenses for uniforms and other required gear, along with the expense of maintenance to keep it all cleaned and in good shape. Is that the only problem?"

"Well, no, sar. *The Handbook* said that you don't get a license but just the degree and you have to sit for the license afterward. That means that even after spending four years and about sixty kilocreds you'll still have nothing."

"You'd have a degree," he pointed out.

"What good is a degree in being an officer? What if you don't pass the test?"

He laughed out loud at that. "Mr. Wang, you are a test taking machine. Do you seriously mean to sit there and tell me that, having completed four years of intensive, specialized training specifically established to teach you what you need to know in order to pass that test, you think you might actually fail it?"

"Well, sar, when you put that way..."

"Mr. Wang, I came through the academy myself, graduated just three stanyers ago. I'm going to sit for second in a few months. I went because I wanted to sail in the Deep Dark. I could have been a deck hand, and we need deck hands, but somebody encouraged me to look beyond that. I'm not going to tell you it's not hard. It's damned hard. I'm not going to tell you it's cheap. It's not cheap. The question is whether or not it's worth it, and you're the only one who can decide that. I think you'd be a good officer. What you believe is totally up to you."

"Thanks, sar, I appreciate the candor."

Chapter Four
Dunsany Roads System: 2352-May-15

We were twenty-one days out of Dunsany Roads and just securing for transition at about 1030 when Brill broke the news that the captain was going to wait until Betrus to give me the promotion to spec three.

"I'm sorry, Ish," she said when she came back from the captain's pre-jump briefing. "It's the time-in-grade thing. You're just so junior that they don't want to move you up too fast."

"It's all right. I told you before, it doesn't matter to me. Thanks for pushing it forward, but don't waste any more time on it."

"But it's not fair," Diane said. "There's no minimum time-in-grade for that slot."

"It's okay, Diane."

I wasn't sure why she was so upset, but something had her all in a twist and Brill was still being weird about the whole academy thing. For the previous two weeks, I couldn't get her to talk about it, even during the day when we were the only two in Environmental. All she'd say was, "You have to make up your own mind."

"I have made up my mind. I'm not going." I kept trying to tell her. But she wouldn't pursue the subject further.

We jumped into Betrus at 1035 and secured to normal operations at 1045, so I went on my VSI and tried to clear my head. It was a nice day for a walk and it got me out of the section for a little while. There would only be a few ticks left before Diane relieved me and I could go run a few laps and maybe take a nap. I'd already started on the Messman and Cargoman exams. By the next cycle in July, I'd be ready to take them and—with a bit of luck—have the whole set of full share ratings.

The ongoing problem was that I was no closer to figuring out who I was. I wasn't even sure what that meant. Diane was right, though, this was one of those questions best left to puddle in the back of my mind. It didn't make any difference if I decided today or even this week. We were twenty days out of Betrus and nothing was likely to change before that.

The VSI was almost as good as a run, though. I had to concentrate on punching the test sequence buttons in order for more than a hundred of the sensor packages stretched across the length and breadth of the ship in the correct sequence. By this time I thought I could do a VSI in my sleep, but I kept getting distracted and had to back track. I made it back by 1130 and had a few ticks to spare before Diane relieved me.

That was a fast-flip day and I had to be back on watch at 1800 so I grabbed a quick lunch. Cookie had made a delicious lamb with garlic dish which he served with egg noodles and sweet peapods. Going through the line, I noticed that Sarah Krugg looked much better. She'd been pretty banged up when she signed the Articles at St. Cloud three months before. She'd come aboard with visible bruises on her face and arm and some not so obvious ones as well. Pip found her a bit disconcerting because she claimed to be the daughter of a South Coast shaman. Personally, I thought if there is such a thing as a shaman's gift or power—whatever you wanted to call it—I really believed she might have it. There was too much we really didn't understand in the universe for me to say it didn't exist or wasn't possible. She certainly had the magic touch with biscuits. Cookie's biscuits were good, but not even he could match her results. I wondered if that bothered him, or if he saw it as a challenge.

Seeing them working together, I also wondered if maybe Cookie wasn't a bit of a shaman himself. Specialist First Chef Ralf al-M'liki from the M'bele sector was the undisputed king of the galley, but also a bit strange. It was nothing you could put your finger on, and in a good way, but there was no getting around that he knew things others did not. I always chalked it up to intuition and good observational skills, but whatever it was, I saw that same mysterious quality in Sarah. Together they were amazing.

Pip stood next to Sarah at the serving line and he flashed his trademark grin at me. "Hey, Ish, we need to talk. Meet me here at 1400?"

"You bet." Whatever Pip had in mind was usually distracting and often humorous.

"Thanks. Now move along. People are trying to get fed here." He waved his serving spoon.

As I surveyed the crowded mess deck for an empty seat, I realized how much I missed him. When I had worked on the mess deck, Pip and I were joined at the hip. Now we had to make a special effort. It wasn't because he was all that busy, but because I was now on the watch stander merry-go-round. Opening that door started me thinking of other people I missed, like Alvarez, the Second Mate from the *Duchamp*. Talk about a long distance non-relationship. About a hundred billion kilometers separated the *Lois* from the *Duchamp*, which was over in the Bink system. I would occasionally bury my face in my civilian jacket she had worn just to catch her scent. Gods, but I could be such an idiot.

I settled at a table to eat my lunch, plagued by the same set of questions that was supposed to be puddled in the back of my head, ripening. Who am I? What did I want?

"You seem even more distracted than normal, Ish," Sandy Belterson said from across the table. Specialist Three (Astrogation) Sandra "Sandy" Belterson was what my mother would have called "a peach." She had been on brow watch that first day when Pip picked me up at the shuttle and as such was the first person I had met on the ship.

"Hi, Sandy. You might say that. Things have been a bit weird this trip."

She laughed. "They've always been weird, Ish. You're just starting to notice."

I had to admit there was probably more to that than I wanted to believe.

"So? Tell yer Aunt Sandy. What's on your mind?"

"Well, I've been taking stock of where I am and where I'm going. Just coming out here on the ship was a big step and I've learned so much." I sighed and ate some of the lamb and pasta. It was scrumptious.

"So, what's the problem?"

"Mr. von Ickles asked me to consider the academy."

"At Port Newmar?"

I grabbed another bite before continuing. Garlic laced the rich lamb and I was hungrier than I thought. Watch standing will do that.

"Yeah, and when I mentioned it to Brill she's been persnickety ever since."

I saw a twinkle in her eye that made me think she was enjoying my discomfort too much.

"Am I entertaining you?" I asked.

"Yes, actually. Men can be pretty dense sometimes. Let me ask you, how would you feel if Brill left the ship?"

"Devastated, of course."

"Well, you think she doesn't feel the same way?"

I had to digest that along with the lamb for a tick. "Okay, point taken. But she's the one who prompted me into this whole trying to figure out what I want to be if I grow up endeavor. She pointed out that I probably wouldn't be satisfied slopping sludge all my life, so I would think that looking into the academy would be a good thing."

"Perhaps, but maybe what she had in mind was you finding a different job on the *Lois* that would keep you happy for the next ninety to a hundred years that doesn't involves sludge. Giving out advice is pretty easy until you get slapped with the reality of it taken to a logical conclusion."

"Meaning there's a big difference between what she thought she was suggesting and what it really entails?"

"It's possible." She paused. "Would you consider leaving the *Lois* for any reason?"

I thought about it awhile while I chewed. It was a fair question. "The *Lois* is my home. She took me in when my mother died and I'm really very happy here."

"So there's no problem then. Stay and enjoy your life aboard. But let me ask you something. *Have you ever wondered why there aren't any old spacers?*"

"What do you mean? We have some old spacers aboard the *Lois*."

"Really? Who? And if you look in my direction, buddy, you're going to be plucking that plate out of your rectal region."

"Well, Francis is fifty," I said while I tried to think of anybody older.

"How long do you think he'll live, Ish?

"One thirty, one forty, maybe,"

"So fifty makes him old? He's still in the first half of his life."

She had me on that one and she knew it. "Okay, I guess you're right. But what's your point?"

"You consider him an *old spacer* because you don't have anybody to compare him to. The only people older are the captain and Mr. Maxwell. Francis is actually still a pretty young man."

I thought back to mom's colleagues at the university and realized she was right. Many of them had been over a hundred and still teaching full-time.

"There are older people working in the Deep Dark but you don't find them on ships like the *Lois*. They run their own mom-and-pop ships. You won't run across them in a spacer bar and you won't find them at the Union Hall."

"Why is that?"

"Think about it. If you worked for yourself and have your family around you, why would you go to a spacer bar and get into that whole scene? Why would you look for a new berth?"

"Oh."

"Oh, indeed. Ish, most people work commercial like this for maybe ten, twenty stanyers, then they get out. Crew is, ultimately, a dead end job. It's fun for a while as you found out in Dunsany Roads, but it gets old fast. Eventually you get tired of chasing and want to start building. Brill's coming up on her ten stanyer mark. I've only been doing this for five and I'm already thinking about getting out and settling down myself. I'm not officer material. I just don't have any interest in that."

"Yeah, what about officers? There are a lot of older people doing that."

"Officers are different. It's the difference between labor and management. We're labor. They're management. They make a lot more money and have a lot more opportunities. They work very hard for both, but if you're an officer, you can always get your master's ticket and get your own ship and run it the way you want to."

"Doesn't that hat assume a lot of money and smarts?"

"So? What doesn't? Anybody can sit for an officer exam. A lot of people who never went to the academy do just that. You just need to pay the fee, show up on time, and take the test. The problem comes later. You're right to have your own ship takes a lot of money, but if you're a mate, you need to convince somebody to hire ya."

"Okay, so what's the problem?"

"Well, say you're a skipper and you want to hire a second mate. Are you going to hire someone who studied on their own and passed the exam? Or would you prefer a person with the degree from the academy?"

"Oh." Sometimes I'm really stupid. "Of course."

Sandy shrugged. "Now aren't ya glad you talked to your Aunt Sandy?"

I sighed. "I'm no closer to figuring everything out, but you've given me a lot to think about."

"Hang in there, Ish. You're in a tough place now but it gets better." She flashed me a warm smile.

"Thanks, Sandy."

I finished my lunch, bussed the tray, and headed for berthing. I set my tablet to bip me at 1350 so I would be sure to catch up with Pip. Lucky I did, too, because it bipped me awake before I even realized I was asleep.

CHAPTER FIVE
BETRUS SYSTEM: 2352-MAY-15

Pip was just stowing the swab from afternoon cleanup when I stuck my head into the galley. It seemed so familiar, like I had just stepped out of it, but it also felt like I had not been there in a year. Three months on the watch stander merry-go-round had done odd things to my time sense.

"What's goin' on, Pip?" I asked to get his attention.

He grinned and waved. "You've been such a stranger. I wanted to touch base about Betrus."

We got coffee and settled in at one of the tables. "So, what's the latest off the beacon?" I asked.

"Prices are good. We've got a bunch of mixed cargo in the empty container, and we've laid in extra frozen chicken and beef for stores trading. We should do all right."

The empty container started as a kind of challenge from Mr. Maxwell. The basic idea was to give Pip an empty container and see how good he was at picking cargos for it. So far Pip's container had contributed about two hundred kilocreds to the ship's profit pool. The stores trading was a way that Pip and Cookie reduced overall ship expenditures and got us higher quality ingredients to boot. The ship generally carried stores for four months while underway. Typically we were only out between forty and sixty days, which meant we carried a lot of extra stores from place to place. Pip had worked out a system of rotation and procurement where he bought extra of whatever was going cheap in one port and sold it at a good price where it was scarce. We always had our one hundred and twenty days of stores, but with the way they moved it in and out— buying, selling, and trading in each port of call—Pip and Cookie managed to take a cost center and turn it into a revenue generator.

They fed the crew better than before and made creds in the process. It sounded like perpetual motion to me, but the food was great and the captain seemed pleased.

Pip used my portable to create and run some pretty elaborate simulations. He used automated routines to update his own personal trade database from beacon feeds. He usually ran the simulations for pairs of planets along our projected course. He even had what he called, *level one alternatives*, which were the ports that the *Lois* might go to if we got diverted. Mr. Maxwell was impressed and I thought that he might be grooming Pip for something, which would be great as Pip was a good guy and deserved it.

"—so I was thinking we could just barbecue the kids and sell the parents as slaves," Pip said.

"What?"

"Welcome back." He snorted a laugh in my direction.

"Sorry, I'm a bit distracted."

"So, I see." He sipped his coffee. "Wanna see the figures from Dunsany?"

"Are they good?"

"Very. We're walking out with about five thousand one hundred creds and the co-op grabbed another five hundred. There's a waiting list for booth managers for Betrus and I think we'll have something like seventy five percent of the crew selling there."

"Wow. That's up from what? Fifty percent on St. Cloud?"

"Yup. Something like that. Word is spreading and even people who weren't really interested in the past are now climbing on the cargo train."

"I wouldn't be surprised if Mr. von Ickles got in on the act. We had a little discussion about the co-op when I tested last cycle."

"What'd he say?" Pip asked.

"That we make more than he does."

Pip laughed at that. "Probably so. Third mates get a good share and a nice salary, but as good as we've been running lately, we're probably making as much as the captain."

"Well, if it hadn't been for Sarah selling all those Lucky Stones in St. Cloud, we'd have a whole lot less than we've got now," I told him. "Give credit where it's due."

Pip paused at that. "She's good. Do you suppose she cast a spell or something to get all those people to buy at ten creds?" He gave one of those little back and forth looks to see if anybody heard him asking a stupid question.

"I don't know. She is a South Coast shaman, after all. She stayed up all night stringing the stones with leather thongs and blessing them. Maybe she worked some kind of compulsion into them at the same time." I suggested with a little shrug.

He looked at me with a shocked expression, "You don't think—" he started to say until he saw my grin.

"Gotcha!" I said.

We both laughed at that. As many times as he'd gotten me in the past, it was good to have the shoe on the other foot, and I realized once more just how much I missed him. We had had such fun in those months when we worked hip-to-hip in the galley.

"How's she doing?" I asked.

"She's getting better. Works with Cookie every day on bread and they've starting changing the soup stocks too. One word: yum. They get together and it's—I hate to use the word but—magical. She cuts him no slack at all and he seems to enjoy that, too." He stopped there and gave a little shrug. "It's like a father-daughter thing almost."

"Yeah, well, I don't know much about fathers." Mine was somewhere out in the Diurnia quadrant but I didn't know where. He and my mom broke up when I was four and for all I knew he could be on the ship. Well, except that I'd see his name on the roster. All mom ever said when I asked was, "He's a good man, Ishmael. We just can't stand each other."

"Well, there's good and bad there," Pip said focusing on the coffee in his mug. Pip's father owned two ships but Pip enlisted his aunt's help to get aboard a freighter instead of working for him.

"What is the story with your family, Pip?" I asked.

"Dad casts a long shadow. I already told you that."

"Yeah, but what does that mean?" I pressed.

"It means that if I stayed on his ship—ships, now—I would have to do things his way. I want to do something else."

"That's no answer. What did he want?"

"Look, all I ever wanted to do was trading projections. Buying and selling is like—well, I suppose it must be what gamblers get addicted to. I started working on my earliest simulations when I was ten. They were terrible but they got better. My mom was the cargo picker on our ship. She knew what she wanted to move and she had a gift for finding good deals. Nobody can out haggle her," he said with a little faraway look.

"So? Wouldn't they let you pick cargo?"

"Some, but they were always second guessing my decisions. Once in a while they'd let me pick some, and my projections beat theirs by a factor of two." He scowled. "But even so they just wouldn't listen to me."

I sipped my coffee. "You need to clean this urn."

"What?"

I held up my cup and said, "Number two is beginning to pick up some scum inside. Rinse it down with vinegar and hot water when you cycle it next time." My mouth was on autopilot but I was thinking about what he'd said. It sounded like every father-son cliché in the book, but then I remembered Diane telling me that clichés only got that way because they happened enough to prove true.

"So, what broke it for you?" I got back on subject. "What pushed you over the edge?"

"About the time I was getting ready to get my secondary ed certifications, they started pressing me about going on to school."

I snorted. "Ha. You should live with a professor."

He chuckled at that. "Good point."

"So? Why didn't you go? I agreed just to get my mom off my back." There was a bitter-sweet overlay on that one. I'd agreed but she had died. Now that I couldn't afford to go, I thought I might just want to. Ironic.

"They wanted me to follow in their footsteps. Go to their school. They were getting quite adamant. Even filled out the applications and were lining up their classmates to provide recommendations. Dad was more interested in me carrying on his reputation than in what I wanted. They'd done everything but buy the tickets to Port Newmar."

"Port Newmar?" I asked with a little prickle of disbelief. "Don't tell me. They wanted to send you to the academy?"

"That's what I've been telling you," Pip said with no small amount of exasperation.

"Sorry, I'm a little slow today. Just woke up from a nap. Why didn't you want to go to the academy?" I asked in what I'd hoped was a neutral tone.

"Four years of course work?" he asked. "Just so I can take the test to be able to do what I was already doing?"

"Well, if you put it that way," I said.

"Besides, I can sit for the exam anytime. I don't need to go to the academy first."

"Really? I don't mean to bring up a bad memory, but do you remember your cargoman exam?"

"Of course, it was horrible."

Philip Carstairs, cargo genius, couldn't take tests to save his life. He knew the material backward and forward but he couldn't pass a written test. I'd arranged with the education officer to get him an oral exam and he passed not just his cargo handler exam but he jumped up to cargoman.

I just looked at him for a few heartbeats until he lost the belligerent expression and looked back down into his coffee.

"I probably couldn't pass it even with the four years of course work," he said into his mug.

"Why, Philip Carstairs, do you mean to sit there and tell me that after having completed four years of extensive, intensive, and specialized training specifically established to teach you what you need to know in order to pass that test, you think you might actually fail it?" I asked him with a grin.

From behind me I heard Mr. von Ickles chuckle. "Very good question, Mr. Wang. I couldn't have said it better myself." He took his refilled coffee cup and sauntered off the mess deck.

"Damn, this ship seems small sometimes," I said. I could feel myself turning red.

Pip looked at me with his head cocked. "Why do I get the feeling that I'm missing something?"

"Probably because it's the *Lois*," I said. "There's always something more than meets the eye."

"Don't make me come over there and hurt you," he said. "You know I can and would. What was that all about?"

"Mr. von Ickles told me the same thing. He wants me to consider going to the academy. Everybody's been on me about what I'm going to do with my life since we left Dunsany."

"Well, after that performance, they probably figure you need some direction."

I chuckled while Pip drained his coffee and said, "Come on, it's gym time. I need to get in a work out before we start dinner, and you look like you could use a run."

CHAPTER SIX
BETRUS SYSTEM: 2352-JUNE-04

Perhaps it's some kind of universal law that just when you think everything is fine, bang! You get hit in the head. We were two days out of Betrus and it had seemed like a long haul from Dunsany Roads. Part of the problem was due, in no small part, to my inability to let go of the images of that night with Alicia Alvarez. Every time I opened my locker, I caught her scent on my jacket. I should get it cleaned, but I just couldn't bring myself to do it.

The other issue, was the continued nagging about my place in the universe. This quest for identity was not foreign to me. When your mother was an ancient lit professor, you come to grips with the existential early on. Who am I? Why am I here? Nobody had any really good answers in the old books. It seemed to me that it wasn't the kind of thing you could answer except in hindsight. The problem I was up against was that, at eighteen, I didn't have a whole lot of hind to sight and I just wished people would leave me alone to deal with it.

I was just getting ready to relieve Francis for the afternoon watch when Brill stormed into Environmental by slamming the hatch open so hard it bounced off its stops. It was the first time I'd ever seen her angry and she appeared to be making up for lost time.

I looked at Francis who shrugged in return.

Brill grabbed the hatch, slammed it closed with both hands, and threw the dogging lever with a wrench that I thought might twist it out of its socket. She stood there with her back turned for a tick, and when she turned around she was under control. If I hadn't seen the performance with the hatch, I wouldn't have known she was upset. She wasn't even breathing hard.

"Mr. Wang, when you've relieved the watch, would you join me

31

in my office?" she asked. Ice had nothing on the cool in her voice.

"Of course, Chief," I said to her back as she passed us and entered her office.

Francis and I finished the formalities. He shrugged and gave me a lop-sided smile before heading for the hatch. It opened easily enough although it wouldn't have surprised me to find it stuck from all the slamming. I did a quick scan of the displays, slaved my tablet, and followed Brill into her office. We were the only ones in the section, but I think she needed the comfort of her own space. Whatever bothered her, it was not going to be fun for either of us.

When I entered, she stood in the middle of her office with her whelkie in hand. The whelkie was a small wood carving of a heron that I had given her when I joined the section. They were made by South Coast shamans and were supposed to have magical properties. She stroked it absently with her fingers, and I couldn't be sure she even knew that she was.

"You're not going to get the promotion to spec three, Ish," she said with a catch in her voice.

"Okay," I said with a shrug. "No big deal."

She looked at me then, chewing her lower lip. "You're being replaced by a spec three that's waiting for us in Betrus," she said.

I waited.

"Home office finally processed Gregor's transfer and did so with a replacement from there. We picked up the orders from the orbital beacon last night. I've just come from a meeting with the captain and Mr. Kelley." She struggled for control. "I tried to argue for you and the captain is very angry at the home office right now. She assures me that she'll do everything in her power for you, but she has no choice but to bring on this new guy as soon as we dock."

"I see," I said. "What will happen then?"

"I don't know. She had all the senior staff there when I left. They're fighting for you."

I heard the unspoken *but* in her voice. The ASIC popped up and I cleared it on my tablet without leaving the office. "Correct me if I'm wrong, but no slot, no job?"

"True. But the officers can be creative with slots," she pointed out. "Look at what they did for Pip."

"Good point," I said, and took a deep breath. "Well, I'm crew for a couple more days, so I've got a watch to stand." I started to leave.

She nodded and said, "I tried, Ish. I really did try."

I turned back to her and wrinkled my nose. "Do you slam hatches like that for everybody?" I asked with a grin.

She colored a bit at that and chuckled. "Um. Not exactly

professional decorum, huh?"

I shrugged.

She got a wicked look on her face. "You shoulda seen the captain!"

I stepped out of the office, took a deep breath, and said, "Trust Lois."

After that it was hard to focus on my duties, so I made an extra effort. It would have been too easy to overlook something and I concentrated like it was a test. In a lot of ways, I suppose it was, just not the kind I was used to. I didn't find anything in the logs and there was no maintenance scheduled. The only thing I had to look forward to was my VSI walk-through.

That wasn't the longest watch I ever stood. It's hard to find a longer watch than the twelve hour overnight port-duty watches. But it was close. My mind kept trying to tell me it would be okay, but my gut kept reminding me of what it was like on a company planet with no job, no resources, and no friends.

Brill stayed in her office all afternoon. I didn't dare get too close. Not that I was afraid of her. I was more afraid of myself. I didn't know what I'd do, and I didn't want to break down into pitiful sobs. It occurred to me that she might be feeling the same way. More than once during that afternoon I found my own whelkie—a dolphin—in my hands with my thumb stroking the smooth, oiled wood.

What worried me most was that I hadn't heard from the captain. I liked and respected her a lot. On the one hand, she knew I was on watch and would be unlikely to summon me in the middle of it. On the other, I doubted she had answers for me yet. All I could do was trust Lois and pay attention to my current duties.

My watch eventually ended. Francis showed up a few minutes early, a very unusual thing for him to do. "It's all over the ship," he said. "Raw deal, Ish."

"It's just one hand and the game isn't over yet," I told him with what I hoped was more assurance than I really felt.

"She still in there?" he asked, nodding at the office.

"Been there all afternoon. Unless she slipped out while I was on VSI."

He sighed and I think I did too.

When he took the watch I headed out to get cleaned up for dinner. I didn't even make it out of the hatch before the captain's summons hit my tablet. I stopped for a tick in berthing to splash some water on my face and wash the cruft off my hands. I straightened my shipsuit and wished that I had gotten my lucky stone back from Brill in Dunsany. I let out a small laugh and went to see what the captain had to say.

When I entered the cabin, the senior officers were with her—Mr. Maxwell, the First Mate; Mr. Cotton, the Cargo Chief; and Mr. Kelley, the Engineering First Officer. They looked calm, cool, and collected, which I didn't take as a good sign. These people were pros had dealt with crew changes for longer than I had been alive. I couldn't imagine I was the first junior crewman to get bumped off a ship. Just the thought put a lump in my gut, but I stood braced at attention as best as I could.

"Relax, Mr. Wang," the captain said. "I know you're just getting off watch but I wanted you to know what we know. You're going to be mobbed when you leave here."

"Thank you, Captain," I said.

"First, I assume you already know that you're getting bumped from the Environmental Section?" she said it like she wanted confirmation, but only as a formality.

"Yes, sar," I said. "I've been informed."

"Second, I hope you understand that I'm not pleased with this unwarranted interference with the smooth operation of my vessel, but that I have a duty to the owners."

"Yes, sar, I understand completely, sar." The hell of it was, I did. It was rock and hard place time. Nobody liked it but getting squished periodically was part of a rating's job.

"Third, I need to tell you that your contract with Federated Freight permits them to put you ashore at half pay if no alternate berth is available. If an alternate berth is located on any other Federated Freight ship, but you refuse to take that position, as is your right, you'll receive no pay."

"Thank you, Captain," I said. "I wasn't aware of that, but I appreciate the warning. Will that provision be a problem?"

"We're still looking into that," she said. "At the moment, no. There are presently only three other ships in Betrus and only one belongs to Federated Freight. She has no openings for you to turn down. If you have to go ashore, you'll get at least half pay."

We all knew that half pay wouldn't go far on the orbital in terms of paying for room and board, but nobody mentioned that.

"Last, you should be aware that you are eligible to bump any junior crewman from the ship with the proviso that you are qualified to take their position. You are rated at half share in all four divisions and full share in two more. It is your right to bump any quarter share crew aboard which includes most of the Deck and Engineering crews."

"So, is what you're saying is that I could stay, but only at the expense of a shipmate, Captain?"

"Precisely."

"Thank you, Captain."

"Will you be exercising that right, Mr. Wang?" Mr. Maxwell asked.

"No, sar," I replied. "It's my problem and I'll deal with it, sar."

In my previous dealings with the captain and senior officers, this was the point in the conversation where they did a little look around and nod thing. I found it ominous that they all just stared straight ahead.

The captain said, "Thank you, Mr. Wang. We're still working on this, but that's all for now. You are dismissed."

"Thank you, Captain," I said, and fled the cabin.

Dinner was well underway by the time I got there and when I stepped onto the mess deck, I thought it got a little quieter. Cookie had made a fish and pasta dish with a spicy cream sauce and peas. Sarah smiled at me, but I wasn't sure if she understood what was happening. Pip definitely knew and he looked angry. I shot a smile his way and, and he just gave me a little shake of his head. "Later," I said. Cookie hovered in the background and I couldn't read the expression on his face. It looked almost like pride but I couldn't imagine why that would be.

Brill and Diane sat together and there was an open seat so I settled there. "Is it a little chilly in here?" I asked.

"Perhaps a bit," Diane said.

Brill hid her mouth in her coffee mug and said, "Half of them think you're going to bump them and the other half know it could just as easily be them."

"Well that's silly," I said. "I'm not bumping anyone." I didn't intend to make it a general announcement but it just came out. I started eating. I could feel everybody on the mess deck looking at me and I let them. The sauce on the fish was hotter than it looked and it crept up on me just enough to make my nose run. While the conversation picked up around us, Brill and Diane just sat with me in silence. The meal was good, though, and I savored their company as well as the food. After I cleaned my plate, I smiled at them. "I'm going to go lie down and let this settle, I think. I know better than to hit the track with this much food in my belly."

Brill winked at me with a sad smile of her own.

Diane patted me on the back and said, "See you in the morning. Don't be late."

I bussed my dishes and headed for berthing. People seemed a bit more relaxed, even sympathetic now that they knew I wasn't a threat. Throwing somebody else off the ship was my right for having earned the ratings. It was within the letter of the rules, but was something I just couldn't do. They didn't know that, so it was easy for them to assume that I would claim the rights and privileges of my rank. I found the dolphin in my hand again and smiled. I pulled out my tablet to set an alarm for 2100. It had just turned 1900 and I could stand to sleep for a couple of hours. I felt a more than a little wrung out, truth be told.

I was halfway to my bunk when the ship hit something. It wasn't like a hard crash, with bodies flying and vacuum sucking us out through holes in the hull or anything like that. I heard a really loud hissing sound—like we were plowing through a veil of sand. A shifting in my inner ear told me we had changed vector. It reminded me of the moving-lift feeling I got at pull out. I didn't have time to think, because the ship went dark and silent. I felt myself floating from the momentum of my last solid step on the deck.

Dark and silent are two things you never want on a ship. Dark means the power is out. Silent means no air. Without power, air was going to be an issue. I was shocked into immobility. I froze right there, drifting awkwardly in the passage and trying to remember if I was supposed to do something. It was reflex to pull out the tablet, but there was no signal. A blinking, red LED on the side told me the network was gone. I flicked it on anyway and the back-lit screen gave me enough light to see up and down the passageway.

Altogether it only lasted maybe five heartbeats, but it seemed much, much longer. I had just about enough time to think *Gravity's Rainbow by Thomas Pynchon*, which would have made my mother proud.

The emergency power came online and with it the emergency lights, the klaxon alarm, and gravity. I was grateful for the light, could have passed on the klaxon, and the gravity, while useful, re-introduced me abruptly to the deck. I lay there for a few moments to gather my wits and make sure I hadn't done any damage. Then I scrambled to my feet and headed for Environmental as fast as I could. I passed several people on the way who all shared the same dazed expression. We didn't stop to talk. If we lived, we could talk later. I made it through the hatch just as the klaxon cut off.

"All hands to General Quarters. All hands to General Quarters. Section leaders report via radio to the bridge."

Brill and Diane stumbled in behind me and Francis sat in the chair running diagnostics on the console. Brill began barking. "What've we got, Francis?"

"Complete power loss for five seconds: emergency power online, operational status unknown, ShipNet offline, data feeds to all systems not available. Blowers are on, but whether they're moving anything useful. I can't tell."

"Diane, Ish, grab portable sniffers and make sure nothing nasty is in here. Then stick one into the main air intake and see what we're sucking in. Watch the O2 and CO2 levels. We can add oxygen but if the CO2 starts to build, getting rid of it will be a challenge."

She went to her office, pulled out a rack of radio communicators, and started passing them out while calling the bridge and giving her status report.

Three tics later we gathered at the largely useless console.

"Report," she said.

"Nothing in the sniffers. Air mixture is good for now," Diane said. "Scrubbers look okay. Nothing in a power fluctuation should damage them."

"Same here on the sniffer. Nothing unusual coming in the main intake stream. I left mine taped up with the audible on. If it picks up something out of range, we should hear it," I said.

"Console seems operational," Francis added. "But without Ship-Net, there's nothing it can do. I can't tell if the sensors are even alive."

"Immediate danger?" Brill asked.

We all shook our heads.

She got on the radio to talk to the bridge while we settled down to wait. Diane stuck her head in every scrubber cabinet again looking for problems. Francis and I took another inspection tour around the section but found nothing amiss.

At 1915 the overhead speakers pipped on. "This is the captain speaking. Here's what we have, people. We ran through the residue of an unreported coronal mass ejection with an associated EMP. The high speed mass took off some paint but the EMP toasted our sail generators and knocked down ShipNet. We've notified Betrus Orbital. We are in no immediate danger. We're just going to be a bit delayed getting into port. We're on a ballistic trajectory inbound, but going too fast for the tugs to snag so we're going to have to do a fly by and come back on the other side. Repeat. We are in no immediate danger. If the condition changes, I'll let you all know. That is all."

We were still in the *look-at-each-other-and-shrug* mode, just before shifting into the *now-what-do-we-do* stage when Brill's radio bipped and Mr. Maxwell's voice came over the little speaker.

"Brill, Is Engineman Wang there?" he asked.

"Yes, sar, standing right here."

"Have him collect his portable and report to the bridge at his earliest convenience, please."

"Aye, aye, sar," she said.

"Maxwell, out."

"Beats me," I said without waiting for the question. "I'll let ya know as soon as I can." I raced for the hatch, my locker, and the bridge, in that order. I climbed to the top of the ladder in less than a tick and gave a breathless "Engineman Wang reporting as ordered."

Mr. von Ickles waited at the top of the ladder. "You brought it?"

I held up my portable computer.

"Okay, Ishmael," he said. "I need you to focus, just like this is a test."

I don't know what was more disturbing, seeing him scrape a pile of toasted circuit boards off a console and onto the deck, or the fact that he used my first name.

"Set it up there and get it booted." He handed me a cube. "This is the minimum ShipNet code. Run it."

I let my brain sink into the task at hand. All the stuff going on around me faded out as I focused. I mounted the cube and recognized the language and realized my computer couldn't read it. "I'll need ten ticks, I have to make some changes," I said without looking up and without waiting for permission.

"You have eight."

I did it in five and booted ShipNet on the portable. It crashed, but I found the error and tried again. The second time it stayed up. I sat back and watched as displays across the bridge winked to life. I heard people laughing and some cheering before a short word from the captain restored quiet efficiency to the bridge. I looked up and around then, with that feeling like I was surfacing from one of my ratings exams. Mr. von Ickles looked down at me with a big grin.

"Did I pass?" I asked.

"Congratulations, Mr. Wang, you are now certified spec two in systems and, if we live, I will so note in your personnel jacket," he said with a laugh.

"If we live—" I started to say and then noticed the forward port. A planet filled the view and the captain's words, "ballistic trajectory," came back to me. I turned back to the portable and took a quick status of the system. The network pushed the portable hard, but without the big databases and other ancillary information it managed the load. With the portable serving as the central routing hub, secondary hubs across the ship came online and began distributing the processing.

Everything seemed to be going well until I noticed the battery status. "Power, sar. I need to plug this in or the battery will go within a stan."

He pointed to a receptacle inside the console. It looked like somebody had ripped the panel out. I reached down, plugged in the portable, and watched the indicator shift from drain to charge. The extra power gave the processor another jolt, kicking it out of low power mode and it started to gain ground on the backlog of queued commands.

I pulled out my tablet and brought up my Environmental watch stander display. CO_2 was up. Particulates were up. O_2 was a little low but within parameters. I brought up the sensor overlay used during VSIs and ran an all-node query, watching as they flashed in order. Three of them were out near the port bow section but all the rest were operational.

"Sar? Request permission to report to Brill?" I said to Mr. von Ickles.

He glanced at my tablet and said, "Her tablet should be live too. Bip her with it. Any problems?"

I shook my head, "No, it's just that we have some sensors off-line on the port bow. I want to get them logged so we can add them to the queue. The rest they'll see on the big console down there."

The acknowledgment came back almost instantly.

"Got it!" Mr. Kelley almost shouted from across the bridge.

Mitch Fitzroy crawled out from under a console with a sooty smear across the top of his face and a big smile across the bottom.

I noticed the captain for the first time when she said, "Bring us about, helm. Yaw ninety degrees port, flat."

The helmsman replied with a crisp, "Yaw ninety degrees port, flat, aye, sar," and the big planet outside the front port began to slide off to starboard.

"Mr. Kelley, if you could provide a small vector adjustment so we miss that planet, I'd be grateful," the captain said with a wry smile.

"Aye, aye, Captain. All ahead full and damn the red lines," he replied.

There was a slight moving-lift sensation in my inner ear. As it faded so did the tension on the bridge.

"Have we sufficient fuel, Mr. Kelley?" the captain asked.

"Yes, Captain. We'll miss it. Although you may want to straighten the ship as we go by so the stern doesn't bump," he said.

The way everybody chuckled at that, I assumed it was a joke.

Mr. von Ickles grabbed a roll of tape and ran a couple of strips across the portable so it wouldn't slide off the console, being careful not to cover any critical heat vents or data ports.

Then he patted me on the shoulder and said, "Come on, Mr.

Wang. I've got another little test for you." Over his shoulder he said, "We're headed down to Systems Main, Captain."

"Thank you, Mr. von Ickles. Carry on."

He left at a near trot and I followed right behind him. Systems Main was right under the bridge. I don't know what I was expecting, but certainly something larger than we ended up at. It was the size of a closet—a walk-in one, but still a closet.

"Follow your nose, Mr. Wang," he said. "There's at least one burned board down here. We need to find and replace it."

He started opening panels and sniffing on one side of the room, so I started on the other. It was tight but we worked side by side. The fourth door I opened, I didn't need to smell. I saw a puff of smoke get sucked out by the back draft from opening the door. "Found one. Or two," I said.

Mr. von Ickles stepped up beside me and squeezed down to look in. "Yup. Phew. I hate that smell."

He unclipped a couple of latches and the interior of the cabinet rolled out. He showed me where to release the door hinge so it would fold back against the next door and we were able to see the entire rack at once. There were about thirty-five cards mounted in the rack. At least half of them were scorched.

"Looks like it got a little hot in here," he said. "I wonder why. Okay We need to pull all this crap out and replace them. It's part of the main ShipNet communication array and probably the reason the net is down. The network routers need these controllers to stay in sync across all the peripheral systems."

"My portable is carrying all this?" I asked.

He laughed. "No, your computer is carrying just enough for the control systems to talk to the instrumentation. There's no supporting databases and half the instruments on the ship are reporting a malfunction just because the data they need for calibration isn't available. Lesson later. Parts now."

"Tell me what to do, sar."

"Move over," he said, and slid on his back under the drawer and out beside my feet. "The power bus is the blue cable in the back. Pull it and that'll take power off this cage."

I found it, released the safety catch, and unplugged it. A sizzling I hadn't been aware of stopped.

"Good. Now pull the cards. All of them and toss 'em out in the passage so they're not underfoot. Don't worry about breaking them. I'm going to get replacements and pray we have the full set." He looked again down into the cage. "We should. Most of these are standard router and comm boards." He smiled at me. "I love standardized parts. Don't just stand there. The clock's ticking. I need you to keep treating all this like a test and focus."

With that, he ran out of the closet.

I turned to the rack and took a quick look at the layout in the cage. I found the releases and started pulling cards. Some were pretty hot, but I had the cage cleared and even released it from its slides and shook out the residue as best I could. It looked pretty clean except for the scorch marks around three of the sockets and along the upper rails. I was just locking it back down when Mr. von Ickles came in with a pile of cards in static-proof envelopes stacked like firewood in his arms. He thrust them at me and slid under the case again.

"Gimme that one right on top, please," he said, and I handed him the card. He had a belt knife that made short work of the protective covers and he mounted it in the middle of the cage. "Nice work clearing away," he muttered as he seated the card and clipped the latch down. "Next card."

I handed him card, after card, after card. Each one he clipped in with precision and efficiency. Slice, position, mount, seat, clip, next. We went through the pile so fast I barely had time to get a grip on one before he called for the next. He reached back, plugged in the power cord, and locked it down. With a nod of his head we grabbed our respective sides and slid the rack back into the bulkhead.

"One down," he said. "See if there are any more."

We found four more cabinets with damaged cards but nothing as extensive as the first. It took less than half a stan to go through the whole closet and we were pretty confident nothing else was toasted. We backed out and he pointed to a big green button mounted just inside the door with the word reset on it. "You want to do the honors?" he asked.

"Do we need to take the portable down first?"

He shook his head. "The ship's system will detect it. It'll be fine."

I shrugged and pressed the green button hard.

"Not that one!" Mr. von Ickles yelled.

I jumped about a foot but the button had already lit and glowed green. I could hear the fans powering up in the closet. I looked at him and I'm sure my expression was just as bad as I felt.

"You're fine, sorry. I was just trying to lighten things up," he said with a grin and we both started laughing. "Come on, let's go see how the folks upstairs are doing."

We returned to the bridge and I could see that things had calmed down. The network displays were all up, and only a couple had blinking red highlights.

"Report, Mr. von Ickles," the captain said.

"Systems Main operational, Captain. There was some serious burning in the network bus cabinet. Best hypothesis is the EMP started a cascade and the network took it the hardest."

"I thought we were hardened against that occurrence, Mr. von Ickles," she said.

"We are but it happened anyway. Either the hardening isn't as hard as we thought, or the EMP was stronger than the rated specs."

"ShipNet status?" she asked.

"Cabinet is hot. Net should be live, but I haven't had a chance to inventory the systems. We may yet find some surprises."

"Carry on, Mr. von Ickles."

"Aye, Captain."

We stepped back to where my portable was taped to the console. I could see in the status display for the ShipNet software that a lot more nodes were up and the main system had taken the load. Almost nothing was being routed through the portable anymore.

I turned to Mr. von Ickles and asked, "Do you want to keep this up here until the repairs are completed, sar?"

He looked at it and then at me. "Actually, I'd feel safer if we shut it down and stowed it in a grounded locker. Say, one in Engineering berthing." He raised his eyebrow at me to see if I understood his message.

"In case that wasn't the only stray EMP, sar?"

"Exactly so, Mr. Wang. Exactly so."

I shut down the portable, removed the program cube, and peeled it off the counter. I tried to hand the cube to Mr. von Ickles but he said, "Why don't you store that with the portable? Just in case."

"Are you certain, sar?" I asked. "This is important code."

He laughed at that. "I think it might be safer with you than me. Just keep it locked up. It can't hurt to have a backup."

I shrugged. "Aye, sar. Anything else I can help you with, sar?"

"I think saving the ship is enough for one day, Mr. Wang. Why don't you go stow that, and see if you can give Ms. Smith a hand in Environmental. You're dismissed, Mr. Wang."

"Aye, sar. Thank you, sar."

"Thank you, Mr. Wang," he said.

I headed back to Environmental. If nothing else, I would get a few more days aboard while we made the long pass around the back side of the planet and finished our emergency repairs.

Chapter Seven
Betrus System: 2352-June-04

The ship was settling down. I could feel it as I left the bridge and headed to drop off the portable and program cube in my locker. It was nothing I could put my finger on—more of a general sense. The low glow of emergency lighting filled the passageways, which meant the main reactors and generators remained offline. Given the burning in the data cabinets, I was hoping they stayed that way until everything could be thoroughly checked. I didn't fancy having a reactor lose containment just two hundred meters away.

I felt almost chipper when I stepped back through the hatch into Environmental. The smell hit me the moment I entered.

"What's the matter?" I asked as I opened the hatch.

Brill, Diane and Francis stood gathered around the console. They looked up when I spoke and Brill said, "What do you mean? The ship's had EMP damage."

"No, what smells?" I asked.

Diane laughed. "It's Environmental. It's supposed to smell."

Brill frowned and straightened up, testing the air with her nose. "He's right. The smell is off."

Diane said, "Can't be. Most of the smell comes from the scrubbers, and I checked them when I first got here."

"Check them again," Brill ordered.

While Diane and Brill went off to check the scrubber cabinets, I looked at the diagnostics running on the console. "Something wrong with it?"

Francis shook his head. "Nothing. Just waiting for ShipNet."

"ShipNet is up. I just came from the bridge."

He looked startled and punched the reset to kill the diagnostic run. The console came up with the standard displays. Water was

good. Air was good. CO2 was climbing. Not a lot but definitely
on the rise.

"Brill?" Francis called.

I heard Diane say, "Uh, oh."

Francis and I looked at each other and bolted for the scrubber
cabinets.

When we got there, Brill was already on the radio to Mr. Kelley.
"Yes, sar," she said, "all four scrubbers are contaminated. I don't
know by what, but the matrices are already showing deterioration."

"CO2 levels okay?" His voice sounded tinny on the little radio.

Brill looked at Francis who nodded but pointed upwards. "Yes,
sar, for now, but they're climbing." She watched Francis to confirm
what she was saying and he nodded.

"Do what you can, B," he said. "Lemme know if it gets worse."

"Aye, aye, sar. Environmental, out." She turned to Diane.
"What have we got?"

"Dunno. Never seen anything like this. It's like they've been
poisoned by something." Her face pressed close to the matrix.
"Seems like the phycoerythrin is breaking down in the cells."

Phycoerythrin was the pigment tracer that identified the photosynthesis receptors in the bacteria. No phycoerythrin meant no
photosynthesis and no carbon dioxide scrubbing. Normally the algae was a reddish-brown, but presently they were turning a kind of
blue.

"Would particulates do that?" I asked.

"What kind of particulates?" Brill said.

"Smoke, burned circuits, melting plastic? I don't know. When
I was on the bridge I checked levels, we were okay on O2 and CO2
but the particulates were high. I bipped it to you, remember?"

"I do, but that shouldn't cause this. That's what the field plates
are for. They pull all that junk out of the air mixture before it hits
the matrix."

"True. If they're running," I said. I crossed to the panels for the
field plates on the number two scrubber. I opened the inspection
door and looked inside. "Brill? Shouldn't there be a plate in here?"
I asked knowing the answer myself, but not really believing my eyes.

"What are you talking about?" she asked, coming around the
scrubber and crouching down to look in beside me.

"The plate's gone," I said. "There's nothing but empty mounting brackets."

Francis and Diane came to look over our shoulders. "Pixies?"
Francis asked.

"Too heavy for a pixie," Diane said. "Those things mass a good
five kilos."

"Well if they were fast pixies maybe they stole the plate while the gravity was out."

"That's it!" I said.

They all looked at me. "Ish," Diane said, "we were kidding about the pixies."

I grinned. "I'm not." I got down and stuck my head in the door so I could look up to where the other half of the field mechanism ran across the top of the intake vent. "Yup. Pixies." My voice echoed weirdly inside the cabinet.

Brill nudged me so she could get a look. "Damn it!" she said.

When she pulled her head out, I could see she was already calculating. "How fast can we change out all four scrubbers?"

"With all of us working it would take four stans. But it'll take more than half a day before they begin working again." Diane confirmed what we already knew.

When I had first come aboard, this practice of stating and restating the obvious confused me. Now I recognized it as a kind of mutual reality check for the group to make sure everyone had an idea of what the other person was thinking.

"Francis," Brill said, "go run the numbers. How much time do we have? Diane, Ish, start on number three. Pull the frames and strip 'em out as fast as you can."

He bolted for the console and Brill called Mr. Kelley. "Environmental reporting, you'll need to see this, sar. It's serious and won't take long."

Diane and I had done this as a team for so long we had three of the matrix frames out before she finished speaking.

Mr. Kelley showed up in two ticks. "Whatcha got, Brill?" he asked.

She took him back to the scrubber and showed him where the field plate was supposed to be. "What the—?" he said as he dragged his head out of the cabinet. "How'd it get up there and what's holding it?"

"Magnetism," she said. "Francis, would you kill the power to number two scrubber please?"

"Securing power to number two now."

When he said "now" the missing scrubber plate dropped with a clank and bounced out of the inspection hatch at Mr. Kelley's feet.

"How are they normally connected to the base?" Mr. Kelley asked.

Brill answered, "They just sit in those sockets. While the power is flowing, they're locked down magnetically."

"So, when we lost power, we lost the lock, grav failed long enough for it to unseat, and when the power came back on, the field kicked in with the plate out of position."

"No field plate, dirty matrices, dead bacteria," Brill finished. "How much time, Francis? I need to know now."

"Ten hours until CO2 reaches critical," he called back.

"Oh, shit," Mr. Kelley said.

Francis came in to help me and Diane while Brill conferred with Mr. Kelley. "Can you get me somebody to fix these plates while we clear the matrices? I don't wanna put good matrix back in a dirty stream."

He pulled out his comm and started making calls.

With Brill and Francis helping, we got number three stripped down and restarted within a stan. Mr. Kelley fixed number three's field plate himself and tested it for us to make sure it worked. While he was working, his back up team including Bert Benson, Janice Ivanov, and Arvid Xia came in. He set them to work on the other field collector plates and by the time we'd finished with number three's frames and had them reloaded, the other ones were ready for us.

Francis, Diane, and I started on number one scrubber while Brill consulted with Mr. Kelley. "We're going to be desperately close, Fred," she said. I didn't like that she was calling him Fred. It meant things were really as bad as I had thought.

"I know, B. We can add more oxygen, but we have to get rid of the CO2. How much calcium hydroxide do we have?"

"About eight tons but how do we get enough air over it?"

Calcium hydroxide was a natural CO2 absorbent. We kept a supply on board but I hadn't been sure what we used it for. Now it all made sense. The problem was surface area.

I kept slopping frames as fast as I could. Diane was pulling them out and handing them to Francis and I. We were pulling dying matrix out as fast as we could split the frames and we were darn fast.

Brill was asking, "Can we rig up some kind of canister filter with it in it? Like they use on the little ships?"

Mr. Kelley had his tablet out now and was running figures. "Too much air, the canisters would calcify into limestone too quickly. We need some way to expose as much surface as we can."

I finished stripping out the latest matrix and bent to stretch my back. "Spine!" I shouted.

Diane handed me the next frame and I kept working as I talked. "The spine. It's like a big straw." I finished stripping matrix and tossed the empty frame into the *wash me* pile. Diane handed me the next one. "It's only about two meters wide, but it's two hundred meters long. Spread the calcium hydroxide on the floor, CO2 is heavier than oxygen and it'll pool between the hatch combings. If the powder calcifies, we can scrape it up, put down more powder, and drop the limestone out the lock." Diane handed me another frame.

Mr. Kelley pulled out a tablet and punched numbers.

We finished stripping down number one and broke out the hoses to wash it all down before breaking out fresh matrix. We started laying down cleaned frames. Francis and I made them up, Diane sprayed them with new bacteria, and Brill hung them before he stopped running numbers.

"It's gonna get stuffy in here, but it might work. We need to increase flow or the CO_2 will pool in the lower parts of the fore and aft sections."

Brill said, "Run a long exhaust duct from the lifeboat deck to the after section. Pull everybody you can out of there. Blow the air from the boat deck into the after section and let the pressure differentials bring the fresh air back. You can set up a little bit of circulation and keep the highest levels of CO_2 running across the surface."

He added that to his calculations as we finished with number one. The problem was not in getting them rebuilt, it was the time it would take for the algae to bloom and begin scrubbing. We were shaving off a few valuable minutes by working quickly, but we were short by too many to make much difference if we couldn't manage to control the overall CO_2 levels.

"Better," he said. "Might be enough." He pulled out his comm, headed for the hatch, and was lining up people and equipment before he left the section.

We kept building frames. Diane latched the lid back down on number one and I looked at the chrono, 2200. If I were still alive at 0900, we'd probably make it.

We started on number four and nobody talked. We just worked.

By 2330 we had all the scrubbers rebuilt, and settled down to check the numbers. CO_2 was still climbing, but the engineering crew hadn't finished rigging the duct work. Some of the Deck gang had been put to work spreading the calcium hydroxide on the deck along the spine. They were shooting for two, five-centimeter-deep strips along either side of the spine with about a half meter open area in the middle to walk on. It would take almost all the powder we had to cover that much space but it gave us a large surface area to stream the CO_2 laden air across.

By 0200 the CO_2 was almost at alarm critical levels and the crew had started up the blowers to push the heavy air all the way down the spine. As the pressure differential between the bow and stern sections built up, the air they pumped aft began working forward through the spine and across the absorbent powder.

By 0400 the CO_2 levels had stopped rising but just moving around was difficult. Everybody was yawning. Of course, that might have had something to do with everybody being exhausted, too. The air felt even heavier than normal in Environmental.

By 0500 the CO_2 levels started rising again. The engineering crew found that the powder had formed a crust preventing additional absorption where the calcium hydroxide had reached its capacity. We all went out with brooms and broke the crust to expose the powder underneath to the air. It was hard to move and the brooms grew heavy.

By 0800 the CO_2 levels began falling again. The scrubbers came online a bit faster than we had expected. It was still hard to breathe and I had a pounding headache, but I began to see smiles.

By 0900 we knew we had it beaten. Two of the four scrubbers were stripping out CO_2 at maximum capacity, the third was running at about fifty percent and the last was kicking in about twenty percent.

At 0930 the overheads piped and the captain's voice came over the speakers. "This is the captain speaking. Full power should be restored within the hour. The CO_2 and O_2 levels are getting back to normal range. The sail generators should be back online this afternoon. We'll be a couple of days late, but we'll arrive thanks to your hard work, dedication, and ingenuity. You make me proud. That is all."

After a few moments, the announcer came back on with, "All hands secure from General Quarters. Secure from General Quarters. Set normal underway operations. First section has the watch."

I clambered up off the deck where I'd been sprawled and relieved Francis who was the last person to assume the watch before General Quarters. We all chuckled when he said, "Mr. Wang, ops are finally normal. We probably had some scheduled maintenance but we didn't do it. You may relieve the watch."

"I relieve you, Mr. Gartner," I said. "I have the watch."

CHAPTER EIGHT
BETRUS SYSTEM: 2352-JUNE-05

The captain was as good as her word and power came up within a few ticks of her announcement. Brill sat with me to keep me company, and awake, for the remaining half of my watch. We even managed to replace the three toasted environmental sensors I had found up on the port bow. The *Lois* had taken a hit but she was still with us.

Diane came back after a couple of hours of sleep, a shower, and some food. Cookie set up a serving line with Pip and Sarah. They made omelets for those who wanted them and sandwiches for those who didn't. It had been a long night for everybody. Without full power, Cookie had to scramble to feed us. He did well with what he had.

Diane relieved me and tried to shoo away Brill but she protested. I didn't stay around for the thrilling conclusion of their discussion and trundled off to my bunk. It seemed as though I had just hit the pillow when the watch stander woke me to relieve the watch again. I grabbed a quick shower, fresh clothes, and coffee before heading back to Environmental.

I found Diane wide awake with a funny smile on her face and I wondered what that was all about until I saw Brill sacked out on the deck. We had a quiet discussion and decided we should wake her and send her off to bed. This time when Diane suggested she might be more comfortable in her bunk, she went. Besides, I told her, it sets a terrible example for the help. She laughed at that and patted me on the shoulder before staggering out of the section. I relieved Diane and settled down to see what maintenance had backed up on us. There wasn't much, but it kept me awake. The VSI was an interesting experience. Walking through the crusted calcium hydroxide was an eerie reminder and I wondered how we were going to get rid of it.

When Francis came to relieve me for the mid-watch, the section was almost back to normal. I gave him the full list of maintenance I had done along with the shorter list of things that needed doing that I had not had time for. He relieved me and I managed to get all the way up into my bunk before falling asleep. I didn't manage to get out of my clothes or anything like that, but I wasn't complaining.

I thought I was tired enough to sleep the twenty-four hours until I had to go back on watch, but I didn't even make it to lunch time. I might have except for a treacherous bladder that insisted on being drained or it would do something juvenile and unpleasant. As a result, I got up around 1030 and took care of business. Surprising how alive you can feel with a shower, a fresh shipsuit, and enough air to breathe.

It was too early for lunch and too late for breakfast, but I went to the galley anyway. I could at least get a cup of coffee and figured I could probably cadge something food-like from the watch cooler even if I couldn't get Cookie to feed me. The thought made me grin. I couldn't imagine Cookie not feeding anybody who showed up hungry.

When I got to the mess deck, I found a tired looking Mr. von Ickles waiting. He smiled when he saw me walk in but waited until I got coffee and snagged a pastry before calling me over. "Are you recovering?" he asked with a smile.

"Yes, sar. Thanks for asking. Been a busy couple of days, but I'm feeling almost as human as normal."

"We need to do an incident report for the insurance company to validate that we did everything possible to mitigate damages. Do you have a few ticks to answer some questions while it's fresh in your mind?"

"I don't know how fresh it is. After all the CO_2, I'm not sure I remember my name, but I'll give it a go."

He beckoned me out of the mess deck and led the way to the ship's office. Mr. Maxwell and the captain were both there as well.

The captain smiled and said, "Thanks for taking the time to talk to us, Mr. Wang. It's a pain, but we have to do this or the insurance company quibbles over every million they have to pay out."

I thought that was a joke so I chuckled politely in case it was, and briefly in case it wasn't. "No problem, Captain. I'm off till midnight." That was a joke, but nobody laughed. I sipped my coffee and waited for instructions.

The captain nodded to Mr. Maxwell who started a recorder and listed off the people in the room, the date, and the time. Then we all had to go around the room and state our own names. After that, it got a little more interesting.

The captain asked most of the questions, and I noticed that Mr. Maxwell and Mr. von Ickles did something like keeping score, but I couldn't tell what was making points.

"Mr. Wang, please tell us what happened starting at just after 1900 on June 4, 2352 . What did you observe? What did you do? Only state those things you have direct knowledge of and not anything you heard from others please."

She stopped me when I got to the part about turning on my tablet even though I knew the network was out. "Why did you do that, Mr. Wang?"

"So I could see what was going on, Captain. The screen was blank but it gave off enough light that I could see around me a bit."

"What did you see, Mr. Wang?" she asked.

"Nobody else was in the passageway at the time, Captain. When the power was restored, I fell to the deck."

"Were you injured, Mr. Wang."

"No, Captain. I was a bit stunned but that's all."

"Please go on, Mr. Wang."

When I got to the part about jamming the snout of the sniffer in the main air intake, we stopped again.

"Why did you do that, Mr. Wang?"

"Well, Brill sent Diane and me out to check for gasses in Environmental so we were sure we weren't pumping anything problematic out into the ship and then she asked one of us to see if anything was coming into the section. I stuck the nose of my sniffer into the intake manifold and it was clear, but since we didn't know what was going on in the rest of the ship, I figured we better keep an eye on it. I couldn't very well stand there with it, so I taped it down, cranked up the audio alarm and left it. Without other sensor capabilities, it was the best I could do."

"Very logical, Mr. Wang," the captain said.

"Thank you, Captain."

"Please continue, Mr. Wang," she said again and I began to hope I wasn't going to miss lunch.

We got to the part where I went onto the bridge with the portable and she made me pause to describe the machine with brand name and full specifications. I was afraid she was going to ask for the serial number, which I didn't know, but she let me jump ahead to the part where Mr. von Ickles had me boot it up.

"What did you do when he gave you the program cube," she

asked.

"I mounted it and began looking at the code. There was a problem with the scripts that needed some adjustments so they would run on my machine and I fixed them. I missed one so the initial load failed, but I saw where it croaked and I got it on the second try."

"And are you a computer expert, Mr. Wang?"

"No, Captain. I used to play around with them a lot back in school but I am particularly familiar with my mother's machine, sar."

"Why is that, Mr. Wang?" she asked.

"Whenever she would have trouble with it, I had to fix it for her. I also had performed a few upgrades. When she died I stripped her stuff off to backup cubes and reloaded it fresh." I was proud of myself for not choking there.

"Yet, in spite of not being an expert, you spotted a problem with ShipNet code and fixed it in less than ten ticks?"

"Yes, sar. But it took two tries, and there really wasn't that much to fix." I wanted to be honest.

"Please go on, Mr. Wang."

We continued in this vein for some time. We would jump ahead and stop periodically for additional details. They were particularly interested that I thought Environmental smelled bad and what the problem turned out to be. We finally got through the part of using the spine as a giant cartridge filter and using the brooms to break up the crust when the CO2 level started rising.

"Why brooms, Mr. Wang?" she asked.

"Because we had them, Captain. We needed something that was wide enough to punch a good hole without scattering the powder everywhere. The bristles on a broom worked really well, and we had plenty of them handy."

Then I had to go on about replacing the sensor packs and the scheduled maintenance and was just about up to the point where I had to wake up to pee before they finally ran out of questions. Frankly, I was getting a little annoyed because I knew Cookie was already serving lunch.

Finally, Mr. Maxwell said, "Thank you, Mr. Wang." He shut off the recorder.

The captain said, "Thank you for your time, Mr. Wang. Dismissed."

As I was leaving, Mr. von Ickles said, "Oh, Mr. Wang?"

I stopped and hoped it wasn't going to be another question. "Yes, sar?"

"We lived," he said, and then winked.

I smiled. "Yes, sar, we did."

They let me leave then and as I was heading back to the mess deck I pulled up my personnel jacket on the tablet. Sure enough there I found a Specialist Two (Systems) rating dated 2352-June-04 and, oddly, it was endorsed by the captain, Mr. Maxwell, Mr. Kelley, and Mr. von Ickles. That was the strangest addition to my ratings collection.

Seeing my ratings made me think of finding a new berth, which in turn reminded me of what waited on Betrus. I sighed at the thought, but lunch called and I was going to answer before my stomach ate my backbone. I just reminded myself to trust Lois.

Lunch was more than half over by the time I made it to the mess deck. The officers had kept me talking for over two stans. Judging from the looks of things, a lot of the crew had eaten and left. I grabbed a plate and went through the line. Sarah looked tired but all right. She had circles under her eyes but nothing like the bruised look she had when she first came aboard. She smiled and gave me an extra biscuit with a wink. Pip was a little worse for wear with a small cut and bruise on his forehead.

"What happened?" I asked as he dished up some rice and beans.

"Gravity," he said ruefully. "Found the edge of the prep table on the way down."

"Ouch! I landed on a nice flat deck myself. You okay?" I asked.

"Oh, yeah...hard head, soft heart. That's me. Just a glancing blow."

Sarah teased him by adding, "He dented the prep table. Took Engineering more than a stan to straighten it out!"

She was definitely doing better.

"You get back to work," Pip said with a grin and bumped her hip with his. He turned back to me, "Still I was luckier than some."

"Really? What happened?"

"You been under a rock? You really need to check your linkages into GossipNet."

I gave a short laugh. "I've been kinda busy the last couple of days, what with trying to stay alive and all."

"Sandy fell wrong and broke her left arm. She's only just come out of the autodoc, but she can't stand watch," he said. "Jaime Schwartz, you know, that blond cargo handler with the big blue eyes?"

"Oh, yeah, I know who you mean."

"She was here and got thrown up against the coffee urns and got a couple of burns. Half a dozen people have cracked ribs from landing sideways on stuff."

"I had no idea," I said. The grilling I had just endured in

the office made sense now. There'd be a lot of insurance people investigating with all the damage to the ship but more because of the injuries to the crew.

"Nobody seriously hurt though?" I asked.

He shook his head. "No. Sandy got the worst of it. I don't know what's going to happen there."

"We'll find out eventually," I told him and he nodded. Biddy Murphy from Cargo came up behind me in line then so I got out of the way and went to find a seat.

My old bunkie, Beverly, was there so I grabbed a seat next to her. She greeted me with a tired smile and a soft, "Hey there, boy toy."

When she first started calling me that after Gugara, I used to find it embarrassing. Now, I wished it were true. She was also one of the three women that came with me that day shopping at Henri's. Bev sported a buzz cut, piercings, tattoos, and moved with the smooth, deadly animal grace of a hunter. If it wasn't for the fact that we served on the same ship, I really wouldn't have minded being her toy. I laughed quietly. "Hey, bunkie. How you doing?"

"Tired," she said while nursing her coffee. She had a set of empty plates in front of her. "But I'm okay. Pip told you about Sandy?"

"Yeah," I said, "Do you know what happened?"

"She was on the bridge. Gravity cut out and she was reaching for the console to keep from drifting around when it came back on and threw her against the edge arm first. Clean break. She'll be all right, but it hurts a lot. She's on light duty for at least two weeks."

"How's the section coping being short-handed?" I asked.

"Ms. Avril has stepped into her watch for now. We'll be docked in a couple of days. So we'll see what happens there."

The tone in her voice told me she remembered what waited for me on Betrus. We both sighed and I tucked into lunch.

Chapter Nine
Betrus System: 2352-June-10

We docked in Betrus only four days late. Our ballistic pass around the planet had given us a pretty good sling shot ride around and off at a tangent deeper into the gravity well of the system's primary. After we got the sail generators up and running, we had to climb back out and re-negotiate our path to the orbital. Approach and docking had been routine, if subdued. Sitting there in Environmental, we all knew our team was about to be broken up. It was good to get back to dock, but it was sad too. The exact feeling was hard to put a finger on. Sad to be leaving the ship we fought so hard for. Glad to be alive to feel sad about it. There was a bit of anger too but in the grand scheme of things my situation seemed pretty anticlimactic. Being so close to dying made being put ashore feel a lot less onerous.

As we were on final approach, the *who goes first* routine of assigning watch sections got a bit awkward. Those with the most seniority had first dibs. Brill picked second watch and then looked at Francis. He took first and left third section for Diane.

"I'm sorry, Ish, but you'll be relieved shortly after docking, and I want the new guy with me tomorrow morning."

"Figured," I said, and shrugged.

We secured from navigation detail at 1745, Francis took the watch and he shook my hand as I left, no longer a watch stander. "You done good, Ish."

I headed for the hatch to pack my duffel. I didn't know when I would be going or how much time I would have to prepare. I figured it paid to be ready. Most of the crew was either on watch or at dinner. The captain had not yet declared liberty. Rumors circulated that the company reps and insurance people were dithering about when and how—and apparently, if—they wanted to interview the crew. In the meantime, everybody hung around and took advantage of the free meal. It made it a bit easier to pack with no one around. It reminded me of my move into Engineering from Deck. There had been no one in either space and I felt disoriented until Brill burst in and made me go shopping. I grinned at that. We'd traveled a long road in just a few weeks.

I finished cleaning out and stood the duffel bag in the locker and slammed the door. I had no idea when I would have to go, but I was about as ready as I could be under the circumstances. Nothing for it but to go to chow.

The mess deck was a-buzz but there was nothing unusual in that. After the last few days, we all felt a bit closer, I think. Several people smiled and nodded in my direction as I made my way to the mess line. Some of them looked sad. Some of them had hopeful expressions. I myself was holding up pretty well. We were here. It was happening. Grace under pressure and all that. "Cry in the flitter on the way home," my mother used to say. It seemed silly at the time, but now I thought I could appreciate it a bit more.

Cookie had pulled out all the stops with his spicy, sizzling beefalo. It might have been my favorite meal. I got a little pang thinking he probably had done it on purpose, but Sarah smiled at me across the line.

"Trust Lois," she said, before going back to her work.

She had spoken the words so fast, I wasn't even sure I'd heard them. I moved on to Pip who looked as chipper as he could under the circumstances. The cut on his head was almost healed, but he still looked a little the worse for wear. We just shrugged at each other. There wasn't much to say.

I settled at a table with Bev and Rhon. I didn't see either Diane or Brill and I knew Francis would have come and gone already. What with packing and all, it was near the end of the dinner hour.

"Hey, Ish," Rhon said. "Any word?"

"Nope, nothing yet, but the new guy is supposed to be reporting ASAP. I'm not detached officially yet, but it's probably only a matter of time."

Bev just looked at me. "If you get put ashore, you won't be crew anymore," she said with a kind of huskiness in her voice.

Rhon gave Bev a glance and then looked at me with an odd gleam in her eye. "That's true. You won't be crew," she said.

Bev actually growled in the back of her throat. Not a word—just a growl. Even I knew it was a warning. Rhon looked at her and kind of settled back down in her seat. I confess, I rather liked the feeling it gave me.

Then my tablet bipped and the spell broke. I looked at my dinner and then pulled the tablet out. As I feared, it was a meeting with the captain but I had a half stan before I had to be there. I had time enough to eat, and the whole while, Bev watched me with a little smile on her face. I liked it, but I think Rhon found it a bit unsettling.

At the appointed time I presented myself to the captain's cabin. The usual suspects were gathered around the conference table, and she wasted no time. "Mr. Wang, your replacement has not yet reported, but we have a little problem. It seems we're short-handed, quite literally, with Ms. Belterson's broken arm. Ms. Avril has been covering her watches, but I need my Second Mate back." She paused then, and I hated it when she did that because I never knew if she was waiting for me to say something or just catching her breath.

"How can I help, Captain?" I asked.

"We still have no open position, but we have a temporary need to cover the port-duty watch rotation. We could just double up, but if you'd be willing to stay aboard for a few more days and help us out, that would give us that much more time to see if we can work something out."

"Sure, sar. I'd be happy to."

"We're likely to be kept in Betrus longer than our planned stay in order to make repairs and ensure the ship is thoroughly checked out, Mr. Wang. Just so you're aware." She turned to Mr. Kelley and asked a question that I knew she already had the answer to. "How long do you think, Mr. Kelley?"

"At least five days, probably six. Could be as many as ten, depending on spare part availability, Captain," he said. He had a little smile forming at the corner of his mouth. I could see it, and he didn't try to hide it from me.

"Mr. Maxwell," she said, "would Mr. Wang be an acceptable temporary replacement for port-side duty?"

"I believe he will suffice, Captain," he said without even looking at me.

"Well then, Mr. Wang, will you accept a temporary promotion to Able Spacer assigned to Deck Division for the duration of our stay?"

"Yes, Captain, I will," I said without hesitation. I had no idea what was going on, but I knew something was up. When these three started looking like this, there was always something cooking. It was, after all, the *Lois*.

"Mr. Maxwell, please see that the ship's records are updated as such."

Mr. Maxwell hit the enter key on the tablet in front of him. He'd had the transaction ready to go. "Done, Captain."

"Thank you, Mr. Maxwell." She turned to Mr. Kelley. "Do you have anything you wish to add, Mr. Kelley?"

"Yes, Captain," he said, and turned to me. "Thank you, Mr. Wang. It has been a pleasure having you in my crew."

"Thank you, sar. I enjoyed it."

The captain said, "Very well then, Mr. Wang, you are dismissed. If you would report to Mr. von Ickles in his office at your earliest convenience? Please give him my compliments and notify him that you are on second watch section for the duration of our port stay."

"Aye, sar." I said. "Thank you, sar."

"Thank you, Mr. Wang. Dismissed."

I left the cabin thinking that these people were some of the sneakiest, most conniving people I had ever met. I still had no idea what they were up to but I was willing to be the audience participant in their little magic show.

I reported to Mr. von Ickles immediately, I'd learned long ago that *earliest convenience* was officer-speak for *right away.*

Mr. von Ickles smiled when I presented myself at the office and said, "Able Spacer Wang reporting with the captain's compliments, sar. I'm to tell you that I'm assigned to second watch section for the duration of our port stay, sar."

"Very good, Mr. Wang," he said. I felt like I should pay attention to his hands because I had a feeling that the magic trick was about to be sprung. "Second watch has the duty at 0600 and you will assume brow watch at that time. Do you have any questions, Mr. Wang?"

"No, sar."

"Very well, Mr. Wang. Since you are now temporarily assigned to Deck Division, please move from the Engineering berthing area and find suitable accommodations in Deck berthing. When you are done, notify the officer of the day so we can find you in the morning."

"Right away, sar. I'm already packed."

"Oh?" he said with an arched eyebrow. "Did you think you were going somewhere, Mr. Wang?"

"I had heard some rumor to that effect, yes sar," I said with a grin.

"Don't believe everything you hear, Mr. Wang. Dismissed." By the smug look on his face I knew something was in the works.

"One thing, sar?" I asked.

"Yes, Mr. Wang?" he answered.

"Is there a course in sneakiness at the academy? Like Sneaky

101 or something?" I asked him.

"No, Mr. Wang," he said. "Sneaky 101 would be a freshman level course and that wouldn't be something you could teach at that level."

"Thank you, sar. It was just an idle thought."

"I quite understand, Mr. Wang," he said.

On my way out the door he added, "It's Sneaky 450—an upper level course." He winked when I turned around to face him. I turned once more, closed the door behind me, and went to move back to Deck Division's berthing area.

When I got to Deck berthing, there was a bunch of excited people milling about. A lot of the crew were betting that the captain would declare liberty before 2100 and I suspected they were right. We would be in port a long time, though, if what the captain had just said was true. I wondered how many people knew. I got cat calls when I walked in with my duffel bag and a lot of good-natured jibing about not being able to get rid of me, but I got a sense they were glad to see me—even if it was for just a few days.

I looked around and had my choice of four lowers and one upper. Uppers were popular in Deck for some reason. The upper was above Rhon Scham and across from Fong Xi Pa, one of the astrogators. There was a lower across from Sean Grishan, but I knew the co-ed crochet team used that as a kind of informal work space. There was a lower under Tabitha and Beverly was on the other side of the partition. That might work. There was a lower under Pip and across from Beverly. I didn't trust myself there. I had a bad case of Bev and I wasn't sure I could handle being that close, even for a few days in port. The other was on the end and against the bulkhead and I claimed that. Arthur James, a spacer apprentice had the upper above me. Sally Green, a cargo loader, had the lower across the way, and David ben Dour, an ordinary spacer, claimed the bunk above her. I knew them all, of course, from my mess deck days. They were hanging out in their bunks, waiting for liberty, and welcomed me when I moved in. I cursed myself for being a coward and not taking the lower next to Beverly.

I tried to remind myself that it would only be a few days, but then I remembered that the cast of the Little Theatre of the McKendrick had put on an excellent one-act play not that long ago and began to hope that Lois could work another miracle.

Chapter Ten
Betrus System: 2352-June-11

Sean Grishan woke me at 0515 with a friendly smile. "You're still here?" he whispered.

"For the moment," I replied groggily.

"I'm glad," he said, and left to wake the next person on his list.

I crawled out of the bunk, stubbing my knee on the deck. After almost a stanyer in an upper, getting used to the lower was going to take some time. Shower, shipsuit, coffee, pastry—the only difference on this watch was I headed to the main lock instead of down to the Environmental Section.

Fong was on duty when I got there and it was good to see him. He was one of those people on the other side of the watch stander merry-go-round so I only knew him from the mess line. What always astonished me was his red hair, freckles, and green eyes were in such contrast to his name. You would have expected him to be named Patrick O'Reilly not Fong Xi Pa. Parents can be funny like that.

He smiled when I came to relieve him. "Hey!" he said, "I heard you were joining second section."

"Yup, musical chairs, nobody wants to keep me. Can you give me the quick tour? What do I need to know that's not in the standing orders?"

"It's easy," he said. "These are the camera controls so you can see what's outside before opening the lock. These controls over here operate the lock itself. The inner door override gets set automatically when we dock, but you can manually enable it if you need to." He pointed out the very simple controls, all neatly labeled. "All the crew, of course, have their own access, but visitors show up occasionally. Officers from other ships usually."

"So, I'm basically the doorman?" I asked.

"Yup, that's it. If there's a more boring post on the ship, I don't know what it is."

"Don't say that," I warned him. "Next week you'll be on it and wish you were back here."

He chuckled at that. "More truth than fiction there. The only other thing you need to know about brow watch is, if you need to leave for any reason, call the messenger to relieve you. If all you want is coffee or something from the mess deck, the messenger is supposed to get it for you. About the only thing you really need to do yourself is pee. Everything else, ask the messenger."

"What about mass adjustments?"

"You've been through the drill enough on that side of the desk. Stand 'em on the scale, grab their id, book 'em out or book 'em in. The system handles the reconciliations. Only odd stuff is when you have to book mass to the ship or somebody not there on the scale." He pointed to an icon on the console. "That's the mass adjustment. Use your judgment. Only hard rule is everything gets booked to somebody. Anybody that goes over their allotment is not your problem. The system will flag them and command will deal with it."

That was all familiar from my Able Spacer exam, but it was good to have it confirmed.

"Ms. Avril is Officer of the Day and Art James is your messenger. Anything you don't know just ask one of them. Art probably won't know, but Ms. Avril is nice. She knows you're stepping in to help out and if it weren't for you, she'd be out here. Expect her to come down in half a stan or so to see how you're doing."

"Thanks, Fong. It sounds too easy, but I'm not going to complain."

"Boredom is never easy and you're here for the next twelve hours, so I hope you've got a lot to do on your tablet and you find that chair comfy."

We both laughed at that, but I eyed the chair before he was out of sight. It didn't look that comfy. I sighed. "Only a few days, anyway," I told myself.

One thing I had not anticipated was the traffic in and out. Fong talked about it being boring, but I really enjoyed watching the comings and goings. It wasn't long before I saw the second mate, Jillian Avril, coming down the passage toward me.

I stood as she approached. "Good morning, sar."

"Hello, Mr. Wang. Welcome to second section. I understand you'll only be here while we're in port?"

"That's what I've been told, sar. Happy to help out while Sandy's recuperating."

"What will you do after that, Mr. Wang?"

"I don't know, sar. Maybe set up permanent residency in the flea market."

She recognized a joke and I was sorry I had not had a chance to get to know her better. Speaking of people on the other side of the merry-go-round, she was on the other side of the planet from where I had spent my time aboard. "Well, message the ship's office if you have any questions or if anything seems out of the ordinary. You can also bip me on my tablet. Your messenger is Art James and you can call him by bipping him too. I know you've never stood this watch before, but if you can work environmental, I'm pretty sure you can handle the lock. I'd rather you bother me over nothing—"

I broke in with, "Than not bother you over something." We laughed. "Standard watch stander rule everywhere, isn't it, sar?"

"True, Mr. Wang, very true. I was on the bridge the other day. You did an amazing job getting that network back up."

"Thank you, sar. I just did what needed doing."

"Well, you did it when it needed to be done, so thanks." She gave me a little wave and headed back down the corridor. She looked almost as good going away as Alvarez. I wondered idly if it was a trait of second mates.

I shook that idea out of my head as soon as it hit and settled back down to the watch.

Around 0900 the hatch call alarm sounded and I looked on the camera to see who was ringing our bell. An average looking blond guy wearing the green and gold of Federated Freight had a duffel over his shoulder and was smiling into the pickup like he expected me to be looking. I half expected him to wave. Visitor protocol required me to go out to him so I slipped open the small lock and exited.

He smiled as I walked out and he stuck out his hand. "Hi, I'm Spec Three Environmental Charles Colby. I think I'm expected."

"Hello," I said and shook his hand. "I'm Ishmael Wang. Welcome to the *Lois McKendrick*. Hang on just a sec while I check with the OD?"

"You betcha." He handed me his data chip and I slotted it into my tablet. It contained instructions to report to the *Lois* on Federated Freight letterhead, so I bipped it to Ms. Avril's tablet with an inquiry on instructions.

It came back instantly: Identity confirmed, messenger on his way.

I nodded at the lock. "Come on aboard."

We went back inside and it was just a few ticks before Art showed up and took him in tow. "Good luck," I told him. Art looked at me kinda funny but it wasn't Charles Colby's fault the company assigned him to the *Lois*. I hoped people were not going to take my problems out on him.

I settled down again and pulled up the station net ship's status report to see who was in port. I found no names I recognized nor any open berths I was qualified for. I shrugged and pulled up the Messman instructional materials. If I was going to have to sit there, I might as well work on finishing out my collection. I was kind of afraid I might have to make use of them. The few people in and out of the lock didn't really bother my studies. Everybody knew the drill and everything moved along smoothly.

Art came back just before lunch. "Hey, Ish, you want to eat first or second?"

"What's that mean?"

"When Cookie starts serving, do you want first dibs? Or do you want me to eat quick and then come relieve you?"

I shrugged. "Which is better?"

"You've been sitting there for the last six stans, man. Let me eat quick and I'll come out and sit here for a while. Take your time. You can stop by berthing and wash your face or something if you want. It's about the only break you'll get."

"Is that okay?"

"Oh, yeah. Most people just can't stand this job and they drive the messengers crazy. You've been great! This has been the easiest port-side watch I've pulled in a stanyer. Lemme eat first and you can take your time coming back. It'll be fine."

"Okay, you're on. Thanks, I could use a change of scenery."

"See ya in a bit," he said before pattering back down the passage.

He was back in what seemed like just a few heartbeats. Art was still chewing when we did a *temporary relief* entry in the log according to SOP, and I headed for the mess deck. It did feel good to get up and stretch. I relished not being in the lock. It gave me a whole new perspective on the watch standers that I'd been walking past all those weeks.

While I was sitting there, Brill brought Colby in for lunch. She smiled when she saw me and gave a little shrug to my raised eyebrow.

After they loaded a couple of trays, I nodded at the empty chairs at my table as invitation. We were the only ones on the mess deck and it was the natural course of action. Brill looked a bit uncomfortable, which I thought was a little odd. If anybody should be uncomfortable, it should be me.

Colby still wore his affable smile and sat down with an odd flourish—he plunked his food down, leaned on the table, and swung a leg over the back of the chair like he was mounting a horse or something. I thought if he did that with the full crew at mess, he might kick somebody in the head.

Brill said, "CC, I believe you've met Ishmael Wang?"

He smiled in my direction with a nod. "Oh, yeah. He brought me aboard."

Brill turned to me and asked, "How's life on second section?"

"Well, it's a little soon to say. It hasn't been a whole day yet, but I think twelve hour watches on the lock are going to be challenging."

She nodded at that, a knowing smile curving her lips. "Well, perhaps it'll be more entertaining watching people straggle back in the early hours."

I turned to Colby and asked, "So, how are you adjusting, Charles?"

"Please, call me CC," he said. "It's been interesting so far. Nothing I haven't seen before, of course. It doesn't look too much different than the *Nora*."

"The *Nora*?" I asked. I carried the conversation and wondered what Brill was thinking. She didn't look happy, but neither did she look as upset as her silence indicated.

"Yeah, the *Nora Owen*. She's a sister ship to the *Lois*. They were built together, actually in adjoining docks."

"That must make it easy to find your way around," I said.

"Mostly, but there are enough differences in deck plans that I have to be a little bit careful. That part is disconcerting. When you come around a corner expecting to find the water intake valve and it's a scrubber manifold, your brain does a little hiccup," he added.

"CC will probably be standing watch solo next shift. He knows the drill as well as you do."

I don't think she meant to say that because she gave a little wince.

"As well as you do?" he asked curiously. "You're familiar with Environmental?"

"Yeah, I held your slot since Gregor left the ship in St. Cloud."

"And you're on gangway watch now?" he asked. "I thought that was a Deck job."

"It is. The normal watch stander broke her arm. I'm filling in while the ship is here in port and Sandy heals up."

"Then what?" he pressed. I wondered if he understood what he was asking.

"Then I get put ashore and have to find a new berth," I told him calmly.

I saw the recognition on his face. "You mean I'm bumping you?" he asked.

Brill answered, "Yes, CC, you're bumping him. We got word when we picked up the beacon on our first approach, just before we ran through the CME residue."

He looked genuinely sorry. "That's a raw deal for you, but I thought I was replacing an engineman."

"That's what I was when I took the slot," I told him.

"What are you rated now?"

"Which division?" Brill asked with a proud little grin.

"Which division what?" CC said, looking a little confused.

"He's rated in all the divisions," Brill told him.

"Cargo handler, food handler, spec two environmental, spec two systems," I said.

Brill looked at me when I said that last one. "When did you get systems?" she asked.

"Last week. Mr. von Ickles gave me a field test on the bridge."

I got a very serious *you've-been-holding-out-on-me* look from her then.

CC recovered enough to say, "So I'm confused. You've earned two spec two ratings since St. Cloud?"

"He should have been spec one in environmental," Brill said before I could reply. "Miscalculation."

"Wow, and you went from engineman to spec two?"

I shrugged. "I worked hard and had a lot of support."

"It took me a year and that was just spec three to spec two. Do you have a lot of background in environmental?"

"No, I'm just good with sludge," I said with a straight face.

"But you just said you're being put ashore. The *Lois* has no open slots?" he asked.

I shook my head. "We don't get much turn over."

I became conscious of the time and that I needed to get back on watch, but I hated to be rude.

"Well, with your ratings, why don't you just bump somebody else?" he asked at last.

"It's my problem. I'm not going to foist it off on a shipmate just because the regs say I can."

He grinned and said, "Wuss!" I think he meant it as a joke but Brill slapped the table hard.

"Uncalled for, Mr. Colby!"

CC looked like he'd been hit with a brick. He rocked back in his seat at the vehemence of Brill's response and held up his hands, palms out. "I'm sorry!" he said instantly and maybe even sincerely. "I didn't mean anything by it."

"It's okay, B. I've been called worse."

"Not in front of me, you haven't," she replied, still angry.

"Sludge monkey?" I suggested.

I blindsided her with that and she laughed. "Okay, you win." She sat back into her chair. "I'm sorry, CC," she said after a moment or two. "This has been a stressful week or so."

"No, I'm sorry. You're right, it was uncalled for. I spoke without thinking."

"We've had a rough time of it. We're all still strung a little tight," she said.

He considered us for a moment before replying, "I can see that."

I glanced at the chrono and realized I needed to get back on watch. I ate the last bite and excused myself. "Nice talking with you, CC. See ya round the mess deck, B."

Cookie had put out a big plate of cookies and I snagged a few, along with a fresh mug of coffee, to take back to watch with me. Sarah stood in the galley reading something on her tablet but smiled and waved. I returned the gestures.

Brill and CC didn't say anything to each other before I left the mess deck. I just gave them a little salute with my coffee mug on the way out the hatch.

I sighed and went back to resume my watch.

About 1430 Sandy Belterson came back aboard. The medics had come to take her off as soon as we docked and she'd spent the night at the orbital's clinic. The four days aboard with a broken arm weren't too bad. We had an autodoc for emergencies and she had taken the quick-knit treatments long before we clawed our way back to the orbital.

"Hi, Ish, fancy meeting you here! How'd this all happen?"

"The captain offered me the temporary duty on second section until you're well enough to stand watch."

"Until I'm well enough to stand watch?" she asked.

"Yeah, with your broken arm, you're on a no-duty status."

"I am?" she asked.

"That's what I've been told. They said you wouldn't be able to stand the gang way watch with your broken arm and offered me the job so I could stay aboard while the ship's getting repaired."

"Seriously?"

"Yup."

"Well, tell me, Ish, does that seem odd?"

"In what way?"

"Well, you've been sitting there since—what? 0600?"

"Yeah. Why?"

"Have you had to do anything you couldn't have done one handed?"

I thought about that for a long moment. "They wouldn't.

Would they?" I asked.

Sandy just shook her head. "This group? It's hard to tell. But if I'm on no-duty status, I'm certainly gonna milk it for all it's worth."

Just out of interest, I pulled up her record and saw the *no-duty/injured* flag as big as life. I showed her the record. "Enjoy it, I guess."

She pursed her lips a little as she considered. "Ms. Avril's got the watch?"

"Yeah, said she'd be in the office."

"Well," she said with an elaborate show of straightening her sling, "I'd better go make sure she knows I'm back."

"I have it on good authority that they teach sneakiness at the academy," I told her.

She laughed at that. "Well, if they do, I know who wrote the book for it. If anybody asks, I'm back and still injured."

"Okay, Sandy. Get well soon," I said.

"I think I'll be well when they tell me I'm better." She headed down the passageway into the ship and gave me a little wave with her broken arm.

Chapter Eleven
Betrus System: 2352-June-11

I could tell that the low-key afternoon drew to a close around 1630, as traffic picked up. People who had been off for the day scrambled back to get ready for the night watch. Rhon Scham relieved me at 1745. I had twenty-four hours to myself before I needed to return to watch and I wondered what I would do with all that time. I felt a little out of it again.

It was chow time, though, so I headed for the galley. The mess deck was almost deserted when I arrived. I saw Sarah bustling about while I loaded up at the buffet. She hummed a cheerful ditty and seemed like she belonged there. It hit me funny, seeing her there like that. She had the same kind of *I-am-in-the-right-place* look that Cookie did, but I never thought that way about Pip.

Brill came in and I went to snag a table for us. "So? How's the new guy?" I asked as she settled.

She grinned. "Well, he's no Ishmael Wang in the brains department."

"You got a smart one for a change?" I asked with a wink.

"You know I can hurt you if I have to," she said.

We ate for a while. Cookie's lamb and potatoes deserved attention and we both paid them proper homage for a few ticks.

"He'll be okay, I think," Brill said. "He knows the drill pretty well. He says our section is set up with about a ninety degree twist compared to what he's used to on the *Nora*, but he knows his stuff well enough."

"But?"

"But why is he here? We're not the military. Home Office doesn't move people around. Or at least not crew. They may move an officer or two occasionally, but not crew. Why is he here on

Betrus?"

My mind was still on Sarah and my mouth started running by itself. "Maybe Lois wanted him aboard," I said.

Brill twisted her mouth into a lopsided grin. "You're talking about the ship that way again."

I blinked a couple of times trying to remember what I'd said. "Oh, sorry. That was weird even for me."

"Actually," she said with a sigh, "it's pretty typical for you. You think the ship is manipulating us?"

"It wouldn't surprise me," I told her. "But not really. Something's going on but it has nothing to do with magic ship juju."

"Like what?" she asked, chasing the last of the lamb around on her plate with the tines of her fork.

"Well, like why is Sandy on no-duty/injured status?"

Brill just blinked at me for a tick. "Is that a trick question? She broke her arm on the bridge the other day."

I gave the faintest of nods to the table where Sandy sat with Dick Graves, the spec one astrogator. They were having a quiet discussion about a mathematical inversion sequence while they ate.

Brill glanced that way and looked back at me with a thoughtful look on her face. "Hmm...I would have thought that somebody on no-duty/injured with a broken arm would actually be using that sling."

"Yeah, I was thinking the same thing myself. And when Sandy came back from medical today she made the really interesting observation that gangway watch really didn't need two hands."

Brill frowned at that. "I wonder if anybody else has asked that question?" she said as much to herself as to me. "How long did they say you were going to be on second watch?"

"Until we finish repairs to the ship and get underway."

"What repairs?"

"Mr. Kelley seemed to think we might need as many as ten days to get the ship back in shape. He specified parts availability as a limiting factor."

"Parts?" she asked. "What kind of parts?"

"Dunno. But I can tell you we went through a ton of communications boards. ShipNet was a smoldering pile of rubble. Literally. I burned my fingers on them."

"That's not supposed to happen," Brill commented.

"Funny, that's almost exactly what the captain said too."

"You had quite an adventure up there, didn't you? Speaking of which...when did you get the spec two in systems, and why didn't you tell me, you rat?"

"Oh, well, we were kinda busy and I wasn't sure Mr. von Ickles meant it when he said I'd passed a test and that he'd update my jacket if we lived."

"If we lived? Wasn't that before we found out about the scrubbers?"

"Yeah, but it was also before we got the ship's vector changed enough so we wouldn't slam into Betrus."

"Slam into Betrus? What are you talking about?" she asked but I could see she put the pieces together by the way her eyes flashed. "Ballistic trajectory...we had no steerage," she said softly.

"Yeah, it seemed that way."

"But the captain said we were in no immediate danger. She repeated it!" Brill said.

"True, maybe she just didn't want to start a panic."

"What the hell was going on up there?"

"I suppose quite a bit, but all I was doing was getting the ShipNet code to run on my portable. Once it came up they adjusted course so everything turned out just fine. Between that, and replacing a bunch of fried circuit boards, I guess it was enough to qualify for a non-written exam."

"And you didn't think to mention that we nearly slammed into a planet when you came back? Or that you were responsible for saving us?"

I snorted. "I hardly think I saved the ship. There were a lot of people working to keep our behinds behind us. I didn't even find out about the new rating until after my debriefing interview."

"Your what?" she asked with that *tell-me-more-tone* she had.

"Yeah, I guess it was the day after? Mr. von Ickles took me back to the office and the captain and Mr. Maxwell recorded the interview for the insurance people. As I was leaving he mentioned 'we lived' so I checked my jacket and saw the spec two systems and the captain, Mr. Maxwell, and Mr. Kelley all endorsed it."

She pulled out her tablet and looked up my record. "Interesting. I wonder what they're up to."

"Dunno, but they put on a good performance offering me this post, so I'm just trying to play my role."

"You any good at improv?"

"I hope so, because nobody's giving me any lines."

"Well, I guess you're in no immediate danger."

We both laughed so loud that Sandy and Dick looked over to see what was so funny.

As we were bussing our dishes I asked, "So, are we going out tonight? Is there a group?"

She shook her head. "I don't know, but I'm played out. Babysitting golden boy was exhausting. He'll be okay, but after the week we've had, I just want to sleep. I don't know who else is around."

"Not many. I saw Bev go out earlier and she hasn't come back. Where's the favored watering hole here?"

"Got me. I didn't go out when we were here before." We pointedly did not mention her last night in Dunsany or the dreamy looking expression she wore for the whole next day.

We separated at the passage and I headed for Deck berthing. Pip wasn't in his bunk, but Art was just changing into his civvies.

"So, where's the place to be on Betrus?" I asked him.

"Hey! Ish. Down on the oh-two, turn to port off the lift. Look for a lazy eight. That's it."

"Lazy eight? A cowboy bar?"

"Cowboy bar?" he looked at me strangely. "What's a lazy eight got to do with cowboys?"

I sighed and started again. "It's a joke, nothing. You mean an eight lying down horizontally?"

"You got it. I don't know why they have that as the sign. It's not the name of the bar."

"Lemme guess. It's called Infinity?"

"How'd you know?"

"Lucky guess."

"Good guessing. I'm going out to get something for dinner. Maybe I'll see you there later," he said.

I was flabbergasted that he didn't know the symbol then I remembered Fong saying, "Art probably won't know," but I didn't really think the comment was supposed to be that literal. The odd thought crossed my mind that Lois was taking care of another one. And probably me too.

Go out or stay in. After twelve mind numbing hours on brow watch I only had to think about it for about three heartbeats before I headed for my locker and started strapping on my civvies. Before I left, I made one pass through the head, cleaned my teeth and swiped some Depil across my face. I trimmed the hairs in my nose and clipped my nails for luck. I remembered Dunsany and began to wonder if I wanted to go out after all. When I slipped into my jacket, I could still smell Alvarez on it. I almost took it off and went back to my bunk.

"You're being stupid," I said to the face in the mirror. He agreed with me.

I stood there for a tick, then pulled the dolphin from my shipsuit and stuck it in one pocket and put my tablet in the other. The dolphin clicked against something and I found Henri Roubaille's data chip where I'd left it. I wondered if my next ship would be headed back to Dunsany so I'd be able to buy a few fresh shirts. I stowed the chip in my locker and slammed it shut.

In two ticks I was off the ship and heading across the docks. I had a feeling that Rhon was watching me walk away in the camera pickup so I casually slipped the jacket off for a moment so she could get a good look. It gave me a giggle to think of her watching. As soon as I got out of pickup range, I put the jacket back on and laughed at myself.

What I was about to do, I didn't really consider until the lift doors opened on to the raucous and humid oh-two level. One thing about living with a single woman all your life, you get sensitized to context and the lift opened on to a potentially hazardous environment. I kicked myself for not realizing it sooner. Two levels down from the docks was into the industrial section of the orbital and the rough side of town as it were. While everything above the docks—levels one and up—was the nicer sections. If Betrus Orbital was anything like Dunsany, I was definitely about to step into *naughty* country.

It was early yet, according to station time, so it wasn't as crowded as it might have been. I wasn't terribly worried that something would happen on the way to the bar, but I remembered the sense of security in walking with Bev. She could walk through the densest crowds and they would part for her like silk on a razor. Of course, she had that black-leather, she-bitch thing working for her. I was not going to be able to do similarly in my corduroy pea green coat and blue jeans. I tried to remember the cat-like way she walked and just thought, *panther* as I stepped off the lift. I turned to port and headed down the corridor.

I didn't have to go far before I realized that panther might work for Bev, but it was not going to work for me. It only took being bumped twice to push me off my stride. I recovered and figured I'd try dolphin instead and concentrated on swimming through the sea of people, between the shoals of spacers, and around the various obstacles. I was amused to find that it worked and the sea of humanity parted around me much the same way they parted around Bev.

I laughed out loud at my own idiot mind as I remembered that panther was the wrong word for Bev anyway. Bev was a wolf. I remembered that growl she'd given Rhon on the mess deck and almost ran into a bulkhead. Chuckling at my own lunacy, I swam on and found myself outside a door with a big elongated eight horizontally across the top of the door. Welcome to Infinity I thought, and slipped between two shoals of spacers and darted into the bar.

Inside was so much like *Jump!* on Dunsany that I had a moment of *déjà vu*. The decor was a bit more beat up. Drink straws and the odd toothpick littered the floor, but the little area out of the sound path was there as well as the ranks of tables around a tiny dance floor. Even the bar looked almost the same. The lights shining on the bottles behind it were different colors, but I wondered if perhaps the layout was part of some Confederated Planets Joint Committee on Spacer Bars specification. I looked to where I thought Al would be if she were there, but I knew the *Hedley* was not in port. Last I heard, they were headed for Ablemarle. And the *Marcel Duchamp* with the delightful Second Mate Alicia Alvarez was probably docked at Bink. Standing there, thinking of them, made me hope that they were having a good time. They were good people and deserved whatever happiness they could find. In the meantime, I ordered a gin and tonic from a waitress in a cut down shipsuit—hers was pink and black where the waitresses at *Jump!* wore a solid white. Then I proceeded to get a feel for the room.

In the booth a DJ was just setting up to start making a lot of noise and I gathered from the instruments on the adjacent stage that a live band would entertain later in the evening. A group of about fifteen assorted spacers draped themselves around three tables in one corner and appeared to be well lubricated, but not yet at the screaming-laugh stage. Several smaller groups camped out around the periphery and a small shoal of men and women stood at or near the bar in full contact cocktail party mode. They were not yet drunk, still maneuvering and posing. One dark-haired woman with olive skin and flashing eyes jolted me into thinking she was Alvarez for a half a heartbeat, but I blinked and chuckled at myself.

I walked further into the bar looking for a fascinating woman. I knew she was there. That was another lesson I had learned from my mother. I couldn't count the number of times she had come home complaining about the pigs at the pub who only looked at the big breasts and short skirts when the place was filled with really interesting people. Usually those were the nights she came home alone. Being a teenage boy and listening to your mother cry herself to sleep like that makes a certain impression.

As I made the turn around the back side of the bar, I found her. To be perfectly honest, I didn't believe I would—at least not so early in the evening. The DJ still tinkered with his set up and, while drinking was an all-hours event on the station, there was something about the clock that pushed us into the 2200 to 0200 time slot. We weren't even close to it yet, but there she sat.

In the reduced lighting it was difficult to get a read, but she looked a bit older than the average spacer and she was dressed— not just dressed up, but dressed. She had on an impeccably tailored blouse in what might have been white or pale blue. The lights made it difficult to tell, but it was a very light color. She wore a dark-gray, wool jacket over it. I couldn't really tell because of the way she sat, but I thought she was wearing matching slacks. In the one word description category, she defined class.

I found it very interesting given the locale. If she were with a group, it would have made more sense, but she sat alone at a table where she had the only chair.

I faded into the woodwork for a time and watched. She sat alone but apparently relaxed, which was unusual even for a woman alone in a restaurant, let alone a spacer bar.

I crossed to where she sat, deliberately moving into her line of sight before coming toward her. "I hate to drink alone. May I join you?"

Her eyes flicked to my face then went back to looking at nothing out in the distance. "That line was old even when I was your age, kid," she said but had a bit of a smile. I took note that she didn't say no.

"All the good ones have been old for much longer than that, I suspect." I smiled back. "I still don't like to drink alone."

"Sorry, kid. Only one chair and I'm not getting up," she said, not even looking this time.

"Chairs are not the problem. If you tell me to leave, I'll be gone."

She looked at me then, in a quick up and down motion, before staring back at nothing. "I'm old enough to be your mother. Do you have some kind of Oedipal complex?"

"Actually, and not to be rude, but I think you're old enough to be my grandmother. That's a comment on my age, not yours. Besides which, I have no desire to kill my father and you don't seem to be the Jocasta type."

She looked at me directly for the first time. "Jocasta?"

"Oedipus's mother. Her name was Jocasta. You don't seem much like her."

"Did you know her well?" she asked, half-a-smile flickering at the corner of her mouth.

"No, but you don't seem the type to hang yourself," I told her.

"Don't be too sure."

I smiled at her then and stuck out a hand. "Call me Ishmael," I said.

"Is that some kind of comment about me being a whale?" she blurted.

I shook my head. "No, Ahab was obsessed with whales. Ishmael was just swept up in his wake, as it were. And I'm not that

Ishmael." I kept my hand out. "Are we going to play stump the chump in the literature category all night or are you going to introduce yourself?"

She looked me in the eye for the first time. She had beautiful eyes but they were so sad. They were also calculating. Finally her lips curled up on one side in a charmingly crooked grin, and she slipped a cool, smooth hand into mine. "Cassandra."

"You're kidding, right?" I asked.

She was still looking me in the eyes and she hadn't let go of my hand. "What do you think, Ishmael?"

"I think I need to find a chair," I told her but made no move to reclaim my hand.

She nodded one tiny nod, slipped her hand from mine, and used one of those well manicured fingers to indicate which chair she thought I should fetch. I knew right then that I was in for an interesting evening. I pulled up the chair and settled across from her where I could watch her face. She drank without speaking. Delicate sips, looking into the glass each time as if to verify the location of the loose pieces of ice. I nursed my gin and tonic. It was my first and I suspected it would be my last of the evening. I was not much of a drinker, although I appreciated the social lubrication that such rituals provided. We didn't speak again for quite a while.

Finally she asked, "Are you always like this?"

I considered the question with a great show of pondering. "No, sometimes I'm much worse." There was something familiar about her. I couldn't place it. It wasn't the perfectly coifed, cropped, gray hair. It wasn't her face. She didn't look like anybody I recognized, just somehow familiar. Despite my earlier comments, she looked Roman or Greek with a strong nose, direct eyes, firm chin, and lips I needed to stop thinking about before things got out of hand.

"Okay, Ishmael," she said. "What's the game?"

"No game. I walked in, got a drink, and sought the most interesting looking woman I could find. That would be you, and so far you're living up to my expectations."

"I'm an interesting looking woman?" she asked with a disbelieving chuckle. "What does a buck like you find interesting in a woman old enough to be his grandmother?"

"Well first, I never knew my grandmothers, so I don't have any preconceived notions on that front. Second, you're sitting alone in a spacer bar. That's interesting. My sense is that people come here to drink and to socialize. You're doing the drinking, although not very much and not very fast. I'm curious as to why you're alone. Last, you're wearing one of the most exquisite suits I've ever seen and I'd bet it was tailored for you. Spacers don't come here in suits like that. So, you're an enigma." I smiled and took a drink without taking my eyes off her. "And I like a woman with a little mystery."

By then we both finished our drinks and the waitress came over. "Whatever the lady is having and I'll take a ginger ale," I told her.

Cassandra snickered as the waitress was leaving. "Ginger ale?"

"Why not?"

"Don't you want to get drunk first?" There was a shadow of bitterness in that question.

"First?" I asked.

"Before you make a pass at me?"

"Oh, I already did that."

"What? You're drunk?"

I shook my head, "Made the pass. I'm just waiting to see how it gets received."

"You're serious," she said with a strange smile.

"What are you doing here, Cassandra? You're not where you need to be."

"Oh? And you know where I need to be?"

I shook my head. "No, I don't know you well enough to know that, but here doesn't seem like a good place for you. If I had to guess, I'd say you know that too. But here you are anyway."

"Why not? Can't a woman go out on her own?" she asked, challenge in her tone.

"That's not what I'm saying, but something's wrong here and I can't put my finger on it." I shook my head. "This is a meat market, but you didn't come here to get laid. I don't think you know why you came here."

"You don't know anything, kid," she said, sliding her empty glass away from her with a flip of her fingers.

The waitress brought our drinks. I paid and gave her a nice tip. When I looked back, Cassandra was closed off again. That eerily familiar feeling was beginning to bother me.

"Why did you come here, Cassandra?" I asked.

"I can go where ever I like," she snapped.

The DJ finished his setup and started making a lot of noise at that precise moment. Cassandra seemed almost startled by it in spite of the fact that she'd been sitting there not ten meters from him for the last half stan. We were way too close to the speakers.

I stood up, downed my drink like it mattered, and skittered the empty across the table. I held my hand out to her and nodded toward the door. She looked at her drink, looked at my hand, and back at the drink. The music went into a particularly painful riff and she stood, leaving the drink but taking my hand. I led her out of there and we made our way to the lift.

She walked beside me. I held on to her hand and she did not try to reclaim it. It reminded me of Alvarez in a way. She stayed closed off. I wondered what she was thinking but it was still turning out to be an interesting evening. We got on the lift and I punched six.

"Do you know where you're going?" she asked, pulling her hand from mine and crossing her arms in front of her.

I shook my head. "Somewhere up there. Six should have restaurants and shops. Not too many people around so we can walk without getting bumped into. But not so few people that I need to worry about you trying anything funny with me."

She had a dazzling laugh.

In the light of the lift she was absolutely striking. Yes, she was probably sixty, but as Sandy had pointed out, that was barely middle aged. She had a classically gorgeous face and the gray in her hair wasn't solid like I had thought when in the bar. It was more of a silvery highlight in her pale blonde hair. She stole my breath. The suit emphasized the lushness of her body, and while she was only a little taller than I was, still statuesque.

"What?" she asked.

I blinked and looked away, not even aware I had been staring. "I'm sorry. Seeing you in the full light took me by surprise. Please don't take this the wrong way, but the light in that bar was rather faint and while I knew you were something, I had no idea you were this beautiful."

"Please. Spare me." It wasn't just a bitter edge in her voice; it was bitter to the core. Bitter enough to drip on the lift's deck and sizzle on the metal.

I looked at her out of the corner of my eye. "Spare you?"

The lift opened and we walked out. She was as stiff as a titanium cross-brace. "Spare me, pup. You think I don't know what you're doing?" Her voice was raised and a couple on the other side of the corridor looked over to see what the commotion was about.

I looked at her for a long moment. "Perhaps you'd care to enlighten me, Cassandra," I said at last.

Noticing the curious stares of the people around us, she turned away from the lift and started walking. There's something about station corridors. You can't just stand in them. I don't know if it's the curved horizon that drags you forward, but she was no more immune to whatever force it was than anybody else I knew. I fell into step and waited. "I have a mirror," she said bitterly.

"Perhaps you should let somebody check it out. It seems to be reflecting badly."

"Do you take me for an idiot?" she spat.

"Well, I didn't up to now, but you may convince me yet." I was afraid I knew what this was about. I had seen it before and I didn't know how to deal with it any better now.

"Oh, give me a break!" She turned on me and got right in my face. She was actually about three centimeters taller than me. Not a lot but enough that she could look down. "I'm an old woman! I've had more men try to get into my pants than you can imagine. That 'oh, you're so beautiful' line might work on young chickies but you can't expect it to work on an old bat like me. What do you take me for?"

Gods, she was incredible. I just looked at her and felt a smile steal across my face. I noticed a closed shop behind her with a glass window in the door. I caught her arm and whirled her about so she could see her face in that mirrored glass. I never would have been able to move her if I hadn't caught her by surprise. I pointed to the window. "You're magnificent. Look at that face!" I grabbed her chin and tilted it to the side. "Yes, you're older than me, but if the problem is that I'm too young then I can accept that. Truthfully, I probably don't have much to offer someone like you. But if this is what it means to be an *old woman* then I can't wait to get old enough to take you on because you're worth any ten of those *young chickies* that seem to have you so bothered." I caressed the side of her face and watched the way my hand moved across her cheek and skin, tracing the cheekbone. "Look at that structure. There's a woman there—somebody who's worth spending time with." I slipped my fingers through her hair, still watching her in the mirror and slowly getting a hand full of the softly cropped hair at the back of her head. I gave it a little tug and felt the resistance but also the quickening in her breath. "Look at that gorgeous creature. So alive I can barely stand to look at her for fear of her fire." I released her hair and let my hand slide down her neck as I slipped an arm around her from behind. I hugged her to me so I could reach my mouth up to her ear. "Look at that shape," I whispered. "That's the shape of a woman—a fully grown woman, not some half developed child." I pulled the tail of her coat back and let my left hand trail down her side, cupping her hip bone before moving down the outside of her thigh, smoothing the luxurious fabric. I looked at her eyes in the mirrored glass and said, "That's what your mirror should be showing you." I gave her a tick or two to look. "If it's not what you're seeing, maybe you need to get your eyes checked."

We stood like that for several heartbeats and finally she let out a quivery breath, and smiled at me in the glass. "Damn, you're good," she said, a little laugh in the back of her throat.

I knew at that instant who she reminded me of. I shrugged and said, "Classical training. Don't underestimate the value of a liberal arts education." I had no idea what the phrase meant, but it was something I heard around the house a lot as a kid.

She straightened away from me and I let her go, letting my hands slide across her body in a farewell caress. She turned to me and started to say something, but I stepped in close and kissed her mouth very, very gently. She kissed me back. It was wonderful but in two heartbeats, it was over.

I stepped back to give her room. "You were about to say goodnight, weren't you," I said.

She looked at my face for a long moment. "Yes, I was. But thank you for the use of the mirror." She reached out with one of those long-fingered, cool hands and cupped my cheek in her palm. "It's the circumstances, Ishmael."

"I understand," I said and added, "Captain."

Surprise splashed across her face. "Captain?" she asked.

"You are a captain of one of the ships docked here, aren't you?"

"Yes, but I'm not in uniform. Guessing an officer, okay I can get that, but how did you know I was a captain? It wasn't a guess, was it?"

"No, not a guess." I turned my mouth into the palm of her hand and kissed it. "You could be naked and I'd still know."

She caressed my cheek before withdrawing her hand. "Now that's a line I haven't heard," she said, the edge of a grin curling her lips once more. "I'm half tempted to test it out."

"Goodnight, Captain. Safe voyage," I said, then I turned and left her there while I went back to the ship alone.

Chapter Twelve
Betrus System: 2352-June-12

Breakfast woke me. Rather the need for breakfast did. I had gotten back to the ship early and took the opportunity to go for a long run and relax in a much needed sauna. I didn't know which ship Cassandra was from and it was just as well. It pained me to see her hurting so much. I hoped I'd helped her, but I'd probably never find out.

Pip was on the mess deck and grinned when he saw me coming. "There you are! I saw you more when you were an engineer." He started throwing together an omelet for me.

I grinned. It was true. "Well, if you weren't sneaking off the ship through the cargo lock all the time," I teased him. "How'd the co-op do yesterday? And don't be so stingy with the mushrooms!"

"It went well. I think they've cleared a hundred creds anyway. I missed the final tally for the day, but it was well up there by afternoon. How are you holding up?"

"It's nerve-wracking," I told him. "I keep hoping against hope that something will break, but I have no idea what. There are a couple of open berths with other companies out there now, but I can't see anybody on the crew going for any of them. Unless somebody leaves, we're full, and I'm surplus."

"Well, you're still here now. What is it you always say? Trust Lois?"

"Oh, I do. There's stuff flying around behind the scenery. I have no idea what, but there's stuff flying."

"What are you up to today?" he asked.

"I need to get some sleep. I've got the night watch and the last twelve hours on the gangway was hard enough during the day. I can't imagine what it's going to be like at 0300 tomorrow."

"I'll make sure the urn's full for ya. You remember where we keep the coffee if you need to make a pot, right?" he teased.

"Funny man. I think I can figure it out."

He slipped the omelet on a plate and I went to find a seat. I was the only one there which made choosing easy. I just took the first one. Pip came out to sit with me while I ate.

"Where were you last night?" I asked. "I was looking for you to go out around 2030."

"Oh, I ran into that pair from the *Alistair* at the flea. Jeanette and Katie?"

"The tag team with the bet from back on Dunsany?"

"Yeah, that's them. They wanted me to prove it wasn't a fluke."

"Tsk! Tough break for you—all that performance pressure."

"Well, I took it as a complement on my warm and sensitive nature," he said self-righteously. "And I keep my fingernails clipped. So what do you have planned for today?"

"I'm gonna go up to the flea this afternoon and see if I can find anything to buy."

"Well," he said, "don't get too carried away. My mass allotment is only fifty kilos."

"Oh," I suddenly realized a further implication of my leaving. Pip and I had pooled our mass allotments and traded jointly. "How's the batik going?"

"Very well—we sold about half of it already. Nothing to write home about in terms of profit, but we've broken even on the prints already and only sold half so we're on track to double that. It's all we can do at this point," he said.

"Well, that and be ready to jump on any opportunities that come our way."

"Did you jump on any last night?" he asked with a leer.

"I met someone interesting and we went for a walk. Beyond that, a gentleman doesn't tell," I informed him primly.

"I know that. That's why I asked you."

We shared a laugh but I refused to tell him any more.

After breakfast, there wasn't much to do. It was too early for shopping, and I'd had my run the night before. I didn't really feel like studying because I planned on using that to keep me awake during my next shift. So I did what any self-respecting spacer would do. I stripped down to boxers and ship-tee and crawled back into my bunk. It felt horribly decadent and I wondered if I could really go back to sleep. I squirmed a little, nestling down into the mattress and settling my face against the pillow that was still not quite cool from when I had gotten out to get breakfast. The silky stroke of the linen from the pillow reminded me of that smooth, cool, immaculately manicured hand against my face as I dropped back out of reality and into sleep.

Maybe it was the accumulated stress, or perhaps just sleep debt, but I drifted in and out—mostly out—until 1600. I had vague recollections of quiet conversations in the berthing area. I remembered when I decided not to get up for lunch. The bunk was just too comfortable and I had some very interesting dreams going. It felt delicious, asleep but aware that I was asleep. The one image I carried back to consciousness was of a dolphin swimming in a dark sea, cresting and diving, up into a star-spackled night and down into the velvet deep, the water stroking sensuously across my skin. I woke myself trying to remember some phrase that my mother used to say. "You don't need to be Ferlingetti to figure that one out." No, that wasn't right, but it was close.

"Nice nap?" Sally asked from her bunk across the way. "You certainly look like you enjoyed it."

There was a teasing lilt in her voice that made me notice where she was looking. "Pervert!" I told her with a laugh, and adjusted the tented covers so my waking condition was not waving in the air.

"Hey," she said with a grin, "you put something that interesting out there you can't blame a girl for admiring. Another few ticks and I was going to start selling tickets. I know a few people who would pay real credits for that floor show."

I chuckled and threw my pillow at her. There was something both intimate and innocent about the whole experience—a sense of a big sister teasing a little brother—something very Lois-like. I wondered if other ships had that, which was like a bucket of cold water down my back, as the realization that I might soon find out sluiced over me. I was able to clamber up out of my bunk without further embarrassment. The chronometer said I had time for a run and a sauna to get pumped up for the night watch, so I took advantage of it.

I presented myself at 1745 and Fong was waiting. "You have no idea how glad I am to see you!"

"After the other day, I think I have an idea. That chair isn't all that comfortable."

"They make 'em that way on purpose to help keep you awake."

"No doubt," I replied. "No doubt."

We performed the requisite incantations to change the watch. "Anything else I need to know?" I asked as we traded places.

"Ms. Avril has the OD. Mr. Maxwell is still aboard. Mr. von Ickles and the captain are both ashore. The captain will probably be back."

"How bad is the overnight?" I asked and he knew what I meant.

"I actually prefer it. The entertainment value is high and the blackmail opportunities are limitless," he said with a grin. "Especially for anybody coming back after 0200."

He caught me with that and surprised a short laugh out of me. He just waved and headed back into the ship.

When Art came to arrange dinner, I took first because, having missed lunch, I felt famished. Cookie had done a lamb and rice dish with banapods and a chilled salad of canned legumes. It was delicious, and I ate quickly. Pip was in the galley and waved but didn't come over. I could see he was busily cleaning up and remembered too well the opportunity that in-port mess afforded for getting off work a little early, even if you did have to stay aboard.

Art was surprised to see me so soon. "You're going to regret this," he said. "It's a long shift."

I grinned. "Well, I'll just have to pester my messenger all night."

"You wouldn't be the first one. Seriously though, just bip me when you want coffee and I'll bring it out."

He disappeared into the ship and I settled down with the Cargoman training materials. I was scoring ninety-five percent on the Messman practice exam. If I managed to stay with the ship, I'd be testing again in just a few days. If not, well, I could always test at the Union Hall. I sighed and dug into the work.

Traffic in and out of the lock was pretty steady until about 2100 when it tapered off. At 2130, the captain came back aboard followed by somebody I couldn't see. I stood as she came into the lock and walked up to the watch station. "Good evening, Mr. Wang," the captain said. "Would you log my guest aboard, please?"

"My pleasure, Captain," I said, and Cassandra stepped up to the station.

"Captain Cassandra Harrison," she announced with a light dancing in her eyes, "commanding the *Samuel Slater*."

"Thank you, Captain," I said and hoped my smile wasn't displaying anything more than proper respect from an able spacer to a captain.

Captain Giggone took her by the elbow and they headed into the ship. "Wait till you try this, Cass, I got it on Neris and it's just ambrosia."

Around midnight, just as I was considering bipping Art to bring me another coffee, I heard them coming back. The soft laughter was charming and I wondered just what the ambrosia had been. It certainly sounded like they had enjoyed it.

"Mr. Wang," Captain Giggone said, "please log Captain Harrison out."

"Of course, Captain," I said with a smile.

"Thank you, Ishmael," Captain Harrison said with a wink.

They headed to the lock and I keyed it open for them. It was a small space and I wasn't trying to eavesdrop but even over the noise of the opening lock I heard the captain say softly, "You seem so much better, Cass. I've been so worried about you."

Cass smiled broadly at that, patting the captain's arm. "Thanks for being there for me all this time, Alys. I got a new mirror recently and I think I'm finally ready to move on."

They gave that woman-to-woman hug with a cheek-kiss thing—the real one that only very good friends do, not the fake one that colleagues trade—before Captain Harrison headed off the ship. "Next time you buy dinner!" Captain Giggone called after her.

Cassandra waved and called over her shoulder, "Deal!" Captain Giggone punched the close button and crossed her arms against the cold as she watched her guest leave. She looked thoughtful as she walked up to the station and I remained standing as she approached.

I expected her to walk right by, but she stopped and looked at me out of the corner of her eyes without speaking for as much as two ticks. Finally she said, "Cass Harrison was my roommate at the academy. I've been very worried about her for the last couple of stanyers. Her husband left her for some orbital chippie and she was devastated." She wasn't looking at me then, but more inwards as if telling herself a story. "I talked to her when we first docked and she was, if anything, worse than ever. That was two days ago." She looked at me then. "Did she seem like a woman on the edge of a breakdown to you, Mr. Wang?" she asked.

"I'm sure it's not my place to say, Captain, but no. She seemed, if you'll pardon my saying so, magnificent."

"An excellent word, Mr. Wang," she said with a considering smile. "Magnificent, yes."

She gave me an odd look and I was afraid of what she was about to say next, but she only asked, "You wouldn't care to explain how she knew your first name would you, Mr. Wang?"

"I couldn't say, Captain."

"Thank you, Mr. Wang," she said with a small smile and headed back into the ship.

I settled back down to my studies, but I kept seeing that image in the mirror when, for that briefest of instants, I'd held that magnificent woman in my arms. My mother had written a paper on the metaphor of mirror in literature through the ages. She published it in one of the university journals. The thrust of the article had been how the mirror symbolized magic. I couldn't help but think maybe she had missed the mark slightly with her emphasis on symbolism.

Watch was pretty quiet from that point forward, for which I

was grateful. One close brush with the high and powerful per day was my limit. I did find out what Fong meant though about the blackmail possibilities inherent in opening the lock for returning crew who celebrated a bit too vigorously. For example, I learned that Rhon Scham had a delightful little honey bee tattoo that I'd never seen before. Given the number of saunas we'd shared, it made me see her in a whole new light.

When she came to relieve me in the morning, looking a bit worn around the edges but cheerful enough, she just said, "Souvenir of Siren." We chuckled and she took the watch while I went to breakfast.

When I went into the mess deck, I found CC settling in with his omelet.

Pip looked a little tired, and as he fixed my breakfast I asked, "Tag team from the *Alistair* again?"

"Yeah, they can be quite a handful."

"We better get underway soon, before they kill you!"

He considered that for a moment, bouncing his spatula in his hand. "Maybe, but can you think of a better way to go?"

"Maybe old age?" I suggested.

"Okay, death by tag team at one hundred and forty! Beat that."

I just laughed and shook my head.

I took my omelet over and sat with CC. "How's the solo watch standing going?"

"You've stood that watch before so I don't need to tell you." He laid his head on his shoulder, closed his eyes, and made snoring sounds.

"Yeah, now you know my secret for studying."

"You really passed the spec two exam? I'm not doubting you. Thats just a lot to grasp all at once."

"Yeah, well I started by studying spec one by accident. I got stuck and thrashed there for a month. By the time I discovered the mistake, I had almost worked through the entire spec one curriculum. Dropping back to spec two wasn't so hard after that."

"Why didn't you just finish and go to spec one. Brill seems to think you should have."

"Nah, there was too much math in one of the science components. I didn't have that background and the curriculum assumes you know it. I need to find a way to learn that." As soon as I said it, I remembered the advanced math curriculum on my portable and made a mental note to kick myself later for not thinking of that sooner.

"You learn pretty well on your own, then?"

"I seem to do okay. If I can read it, and it's clear enough, I can usually get my head wrapped around it. I've always been that way and it's paid off here."

"Yeah, the *Handbook* is good that way—at least at the lower levels."

Sean Grishan came in for breakfast just then and shot CC a dirty look before he noticed me sitting with him. He looked and seemed a bit confused by that. He collected some coffee and a pastry then disappeared again.

"How are you adjusting to life on the *Lois*?"

He sighed. "Oh, peachy. It's so pleasant starting a new berth being hated."

I ate in silence for a bit. "I know it's not your fault, but not everybody here sees the big picture."

He shrugged and sighed again. "Well, you have a lot of friends who seem to blame me because you didn't get that spec three berth."

"Sorry."

"I don't see why you just don't bump somebody," he said, resting his fork on the side of his plate and staring at me across the table.

I shook my head. "No, I'd rather go ashore than hurt one of the crew by making them take my place."

"Doesn't that make you a bit of a martyr? I don't mean to sound cruel, but you have the rank and have earned the privilege. Everybody here has the same opportunity."

"That's true but I have to look at myself in the mirror. I don't see the value added to the universe if I just take my problem and pass it on to someone else."

"Well that's the way the universe works, isn't it?"

"It might seem like that some days, but I'm hoping that it's just a short-term karmic debt."

He blinked at me. "Do you always talk like that?"

"Sometimes it's worse," I told him with a grin. "Early childhood training."

He had no idea what I was talking about. I didn't want to explain, so I tried to distract him. "What were you doing on Betrus that the company had you available?"

"What?" he asked, apparently having a bit of difficulty following the left turn in the conversation.

"You were on Betrus? The Company didn't fly you in special to take this job, right?"

"Oh, right. I was working environmental on the *Matthew Boulton* on a loop from Dunsany out to Barsi and back around through Ablemarle. One of her scrubbers had a water leak that was constantly dribbling. The day before we were to pull out for Niol, I slipped in a puddle. My relief found me knocked out cold and they took me to medical. Apparently I cracked my skull on the deck and had a concussion so the skipper had to ground me."

"Yuck. How long you been here?"

"Four months," he said with a grin.

"You don't seem too upset about being grounded for that long."

"Well, it was job related, so they had to give me full pay and expenses."

"So, you've been sitting here milking it for four months?"

"Yup. It's been pretty cushy, but I'm ready to get back to work. Hard as it is to believe I started to get bored."

"Why didn't you ship out before?"

"Why would I? Pay's the same either way and here I didn't have to work. Besides, there hasn't been any other Federated Freight ships come through with an environmental berth open. About two months ago I got a bip from home office that I'd be assigned to the *Lois* if I didn't find a berth before then."

"They got tired of paying you for sitting here, huh?"

"Yeah." He grinned again. "They got tired of it after about the third week and bugged me once a week ever since, but there's nothing they can do about it. The regs say I don't have to take a job that's lower than the one I left. On their books, you were an engineman so they could force me into your slot.

"End of your gravy train, huh?"

He shrugged. "Yeah, but I'm ready. Betrus is not the cultural hub of the galaxy. Like I said, I was getting bored—finally."

We had finished eating so I made some excuse so I could head out. Whatever I felt about the new guy, he was here and we had to deal with that fact.

It was 0700 so I grabbed a few of Cookie's pastries, two fresh mugs of coffee, and headed down to Environmental.

"Hey!" I called when I stuck my head through the hatch. "You missed breakfast."

Diane was sitting behind the watch stander's console and she didn't look happy.

"I brought you fresh coffee and a pastry," I said as I crossed over to her.

"Thanks for the coffee, but I'm not real hungry this morning. I grabbed a pastry before I came down."

"So what's wrong?" I said as I ate the pastry myself.

"The new guy," she answered with a frown.

"Already? What up?"

"When was the last time you handed off a watch with pending

scheduled maintenance, Ish?"

"Not counting last week?"

"No, not counting that. We had so much crap flying we all passed it on until we got out from under, but even then we were clear within two days. There are no extenuating circumstances now."

"He didn't do his overnight maintenance?"

She shook her head. "Number two input trap was scheduled for cleaning."

"Messy, but not difficult."

"Agreed," she said.

"Maybe he didn't see it in the log?"

"He relieved me with it."

"What?"

"When I relieved him he said, 'Number two input trap maintenance scheduled but not performed. You may relieve me.' And that was it."

"Did you ask why?"

"Oh, you bet I did. He said he didn't think it was that important and that I could pass it on if I wanted."

"Was that his first solo watch?"

"I think so. Brill has been sitting with him, but you know how that can be—sporadic. This might have been the first one he actually saw."

"But you don't think so?"

"Oh, I think it was the first one he saw here, but what kind of ship lets environmental maintenance slip like that?"

"The kind that lets a scrubber leak on the deck, maybe," I said.

"What?"

I just shrugged. "Just something he mentioned. In any case, he's here now and I think we should keep in mind not to blame him for something the company did."

"But you're gonna get grounded here because of him!"

"Maybe, maybe not. There's stuff happening in officer country that we don't know about, and perhaps something will turn up." I smiled at her. "I'm not grounded yet, and even if I am it's not because of him."

"True," she said, then she slapped me on the arm. "You ate all the pastry, you sludge monkey!"

Chapter Thirteen
Betrus System: 2352-June-15

We'd been docked for five days and still had no estimated time of departure. Usually four days was our limit and it looked like we still had some time left to go. The captain wasn't saying what, but it seemed obvious that we were waiting for something beyond repairs. The crew was getting worn out from the long watches and late nights ashore. I suspected that more than one person's cred balance was beginning to feel the pinch. It was odd—as much as we looked forward to getting into port when underway—we all felt a kind of frustration about being nailed down. I almost wished the waiting were over, even if it meant leaving me behind, just so the ship could get back underway.

As for me, I stayed close to the ship. I had no motivation for private trading and the co-op had sold everything that anybody had brought with them. The results had been pretty spectacular, and Pip and I had close to seven kilocreds in our joint account. Every once in a while he asked me to go to the flea market, if only to pick something he could take to Niol. Neither of us really wanted to think about the consequences of the next port, so he didn't push and I hadn't gone shopping.

Waiting was aggravating. I knew something was happening, but nobody would say what. I had a sense that I wouldn't be staying on Betrus, but I couldn't operate under any other assumption without information to the contrary. It was all well and good to say, "Trust Lois," but it got harder with each day we spent docked.

I had the day watch on the fourteenth but didn't have the heart to go out after, so I was up early for breakfast. The mess deck was pretty busy in spite of being in port because the free meal saved credits for cash strapped spacers. Almost all the crew showed up for breakfast every day. Pip, Sarah, and Cookie worked hard to keep up and still maintain a rough kind of in-port watch schedule. I noticed all three of them were often working, even when I knew one of them should have been off-duty. Mr. von Ickles was having his breakfast at the officers' table when I entered and he waved me over before I could even get my coffee.

"Mr. Wang, I know you're off-duty today, but I wonder if I could ask a favor of you?"

I shrugged. "As long as I'm clear by 1800 so I can go on watch, sure. I've got no plans."

"Excellent, I need your advice on a procurement issue. Can you meet me at the main lock at, say, 0900?"

It was an odd request, but he was the officer so I just said, "Yes, sar."

As I walked away, he added, "Civvies, Mr. Wang."

"Civvies, aye, aye, sar!"

I met him at the appointed time and had to work to suppress a certain level of curiosity. We checked out with Fong and headed across the dock. We walked in silence until we were well away from the ship.

"What do you know of EMP hardening, Mr. Wang?" he asked.

"Not a lot, sar. Usual method for small devices is a grounded shell that intercepts and bleeds off the charged particles, but I have no idea how we shield a whole ship."

"The ship is the shell. We keep a slight charge on the skin while underway. It's actually an artifact of the fields that we use for the grav keel and sails."

"Then how did the EMP fry the network, sar?"

"The very question, Mr. Wang, the very question!" he said. "How indeed?"

"May I ask what we're procuring, sar?"

"A portable computer. I want your input. The spec should exceed the capacity of the one you brought aboard by at least a factor of two. You know the most about that machine so you're the best one to advise me."

"I see, sar." And I did. With me leaving the ship, the backup provided by my portable would be going as well. "I can see why you would like a new portable before I leave the ship."

"Don't be so sure of that," he said, but the look on his face kept me from following up.

There were three vendors on the orbital and we visited each of them. Mr. von Ickles asked me to interact with each sales guys while he stayed in the background and listened. It took the rest of the morning to visit all of them and determine the precise configurations each could offer within the time frames we had. Of course, our time frames were nebulous—in the next couple of days—so it wasn't that easy for them to specify something that was too complicated or would require equipment to be shipped in.

After we finished, he took me to a coffee shop where we ordered a light lunch and got down to comparing.

"So, what do you think, Mr. Wang?"

I pulled up the notes from my tablet and consulted them.

"The first place had some excellent equipment but with the differential in price, I'm not sure the extra cost is worth it. His integrated systems just didn't have the kind of oomph I'd expect for that kind of money.

"The second place had consumer grade equipment. Not junk but just not up to spec. If I'm gonna put my neck on the line, I wouldn't trust that stuff. Most of it wasn't even as good as the one I have.

"The third one had good gear but nothing in the configuration we would want to run a backup ShipNet on in the event of another occurrence."

"So, none of them have what we need?"

"Not off the shelf, no, sar." I concluded.

"I hear a but," he said with a grin. "Give."

"The cases from that first guy were expensive but also really good. We're interested in armored equipment and he had three full machines he was trying to sell. If we skipped the bells and whistles, his case and bare system would be a good starting point," I said as I munched my sandwich. "The case he had on that second system was actually excellent for what we're going to need—hardened to mil-spec with shock mounting and grounding."

"We need some of those bells and whistles that you're dismissing," he said.

"Yes, sar, but that last place had them and they were good brands at fair prices. If we start with the base from that first shop, and the guts from the last, we can integrate it ourselves on the ship and have a better machine than either one of them could provide individually."

"I don't wanna risk our lives on the cheap, Mr. Wang," he said.

"Me either, and it won't be cheap, but it's not just the price, sar. It's the quality of the components. The first place was betting on the cases and charging as if the guts were the same quality, but they weren't. The last place had great quality components but he was skimping on the cases to make up for it."

"And you can do this integration?"

I looked at him for a moment and then decided he was testing me. "Sar, you're the licensed systems guy. You know what I'm talking about is nowhere near rocket science. All that stuff is load-and-go. With the right operating system support, this isn't any more complicated than making coffee."

"So, how do you know this, Mr. Wang?" he asked, a smile tugging the corner of his mouth.

"I dunno. Just something I grew up with, I guess. I upgraded my mom's machine enough times. Why? Doesn't everybody know this stuff?"

He looked at me but didn't answer. "Well, let's eat up and go back. I'll do the buying, but if you see me doing something you think is wrong, stop me, okay?"

"That's not terribly likely, is it, sar?"

"No," he admitted, "but with our lives on the line, don't you think it would be a good idea to have a second pair of eyes?"

"If you put it that way, sar, I'll be watching like a hawk."

We finished eating and visited the two shops again. Mr. von Ickles even added some things I wouldn't have thought of, but they were obvious when he picked them off the shelves. Extra communication ports and more storage would make our *uh-oh* box that much more effective at integrating ShipNet and instrumentation.

We were both fairly well laden down by the time we got back to the docks. I felt like a kid with a new toy and Mr. von Ickles had a grin so wide, I was not sure he could get it through the lock without turning sideways. It was going to be an awesome machine. I just hoped I was going to get to play with it a bit before they set out.

We got back to the ship at about 1430 and by the time we had all the gear stowed in the office, it was almost 1500.

"All right, Mr. Wang, this stuff is secured and I appreciate your assistance today. You should probably go get a nap before watch."

"We're not going to put the machine together?"

"No, *we* are not," he said with particular emphasis on the *we* part.

"Yes, sar," I said feeling a pang of disappointment. After all the discussion over lunch about whether or not I could do the integration, I hoped that I would get a crack at it. I understood his desire to do it himself. He was going to be sailing with it, after all. "Thanks for an interesting day, sar."

He gave me an odd smile that looked a lot like *cat-and-canary* time, but I couldn't imagine what it was about so I headed back to berthing and got out of my civvies. I had just enough time for a short nap, followed by a run and a sauna before I had to get out to the gangway.

Watch was uneventful. With so much time in port, most people had exhausted themselves, or their resources, or both. A couple of the hard-core partiers went out, but were back before 2400 and the ship might as well have been underway. I finished the cargoman study and I was pretty sure I could pass both messman and cargoman exams without any problem. What had seemed so complicated just a few months before seemed almost trivial. I wondered what I was going to do on watch for the remaining time I had aboard and I wished—not for the first time—that they would just get on with it and announce a departure. The blank above the ship's telltale on the lock was disconcerting, and we had to be burning through docking fees at a horrendous rate. That was going to make a mess of the share pool for the next leg.

Rhon came to relieve me in the morning and I crawled into my bunk without breakfast. It had been a long, frustrating, and miserable night. I woke just before lunch and hadn't had any dreams, and Sally pretended to be disappointed that I wasn't providing any entertainment.

"Why do you think I took the lower bunk with two young guys across from mine?" she asked me with a salacious wink. "Scenery!"

She was a sketch. I was pretty sure she was joking. There was no penalty for looking, if you didn't count the frustration from not being able to touch. That particular thought started with a big pile of computer parts in the ship's office but cycled rapidly through Diane, Bev, and Brill, which made me think of Cassandra so I pulled out my tablet and checked ship status.

There it was, SSlater: ENR Dunsany. I thought, *Safe voyage, Captain*, and brushed my fingers across the screen.

That's when I noticed that the AMoore had docked. That was the tanker that Gregor Avery had left us for in St. Cloud. She was another Federated Freight ship and she posted an opening for ENV3. Looked like life was about to get really interesting.

Crap, I thought.

"Well, I better at least look," I said to myself and followed the icon trail to the full listing. The system matched my jacket against the berth and a green *Qualified* showed up on my screen. Before I could click the icon to apply for the job, my tablet, and every tablet in the berthing area, bipped. People were already buzzing before I could get the screen changed.

The captain had posted a departure date and time. We had two days left.

Double crap and *be careful what you wish for*, ran through my head, remembering my idle wish from the early morning hours.

Thinking ahead, I realized I had one more day watch and then

I would probably have to leave the ship and everyone I knew. It didn't feel as bad as the night they told me mom had died, but it was close. I wanted to just curl up there and have a good cry, but I would have felt silly. So I heaved myself out of the bunk and headed for the showers. I cried there. The water was good camouflage and the door gave me some privacy. The spasm passed quickly, though, and I got dried off and zipped up in time for lunch. It was going to be hard, but a free meal was a free meal. I tried valiantly not to feel sorry for myself—and failed.

I ate lunch. I think I sat with Rhon Scham and Biddy Murphy. The mess deck was a-buzz with excitement but I felt very much alone and out of it. I ate quickly and bussed my dishes. As I left the mess deck I remembered the *Audrey Moore* and the open berth. Ironic that it was the same level that Gregor took. I sighed and reached for my tablet thinking something darkly Shakespearian along the lines of, "If it were done when 'tis done, then 'twere well it were done quickly," but I couldn't be sure which play, or even if I was remembering it correctly.

I pulled my tablet out of the holster and almost dropped it as it bipped in my hand. The captain wanted to see me at my earliest possible convenience.

Crap again, I thought. Well, at least I knew there was a berth I was qualified for and I might not be stuck on Betrus for long.

Chapter Fourteen
Betrus System: 2352-June-16

When I got to the cabin, I was surprised to find the captain alone. Under the circumstances, I had expected to find all the senior officers present. I gave a little mental shrug. She hired me alone, she could fire me similarly—except she didn't appear to be getting ready to do that.

"Come in, Mr. Wang. Please have a seat." She indicated the conversational grouping around a low table.

"Thank you, Captain," I said and sat.

"Did you see that the *Audrey* had docked?"

"Yes, Captain. I was just about to put my jacket out when your call came."

"Do you want to go there, Mr. Wang?"

"Not particularly, Captain, but even a poor berth is better than no berth."

"I talked to Captain Peters about you when I saw that the *Audrey* had the opening. The berth is Gregor Avery's. He got himself arrested in Dunsany for fighting and the authorities wouldn't let him leave. So the *Audrey* is short. They've got a machinist working the watches now, but they're not happy with his performance, so they've posted the berth."

She gave one of those exasperating pauses then and I didn't know if I was supposed to speak or if she were just catching her breath.

"Thank you for looking into it, Captain," I said.

"I asked Ernest not to hire you. I wanted you to hear that from me."

"Thank you, Captain," I said, but I had trouble getting my brain untangled from that.

She looked at me with an odd expression like she was not sure why I was thanking her. She waited for several heartbeats, but I could not imagine what she was waiting for.

"That's all you have to say, Mr. Wang?" she asked. "Thank you, Captain?"

"Yes, Captain. I'm a bit confused, but thank you for telling me directly." The roaring in my ears made it difficult to concentrate.

"You're welcome, Mr. Wang," she said with an amused little smile.

We sat there and she looked at me as if expecting me to do something. I began to panic a little. "Is there anything else, Captain?" I asked.

She laughed. "You're not going to ask, are you?"

"If the captain wants me to know, I'm certain I'll be informed." The words sounded stiff.

"You have so much faith in me?" she asked, cocking her head to one side.

"Yes, Captain, of course."

"Thank you, Mr. Wang," she said after a few moments.

"You're welcome, Captain."

After another long pause she asked, "Tell me, Mr. Wang, have you ever considered the academy?"

I laughed. Her question was so unexpected and on top of everything else it just burst out. "I'm sorry, Captain, it's just that I've been asked that a lot lately."

She didn't seem offended that I had laughed. She seemed amused. "Really? Who else has asked?"

"Mr. von Ickles brought up the subject during the last testing period, Captain. He's been quite insistent that I think beyond the immediate difficulties of attendance."

"Has he?" she asked. I could see her making the mental note and I hoped I had not gotten him into trouble.

"Yes, Captain. He really seems to think I should go."

"What do you think, Mr. Wang?"

"Seriously, Captain?"

"Please, I'd like to know what you think."

"First I thought he was crazy—meaning no disrespect to him, of course," I added.

"None taken," she said with a little laugh. "Please continue."

"I don't know what I expected but I didn't realize the academy is a college."

"Yes, and a good one."

"I was expecting something more like boot camp," I said. "College is...well...a college. I grew up with the university as my neighbor, so I'm pretty familiar with how they work."

"Well, there's a certain boot camp aspect as well, so if you're disappointed about that I can assure you from personal experience that you're wrong."

I had to laugh again at that. "No, Captain, I'm not disappointed but colleges are expensive. This one is not any more expensive than most, but I had a hard time thinking I could justify spending that kind of creds on a college."

"Had a hard time? Have you changed your mind?"

"Well, not exactly, Captain. I just realized I wasn't looking at it from a long term perspective. One thing I know is that having an education, and the credentials that back it up, is pretty important. I'm young and stupid, but my mother-the-professor taught me that lesson."

"So where does that bring you to?"

"Well, money aside, I've had the most fun of my life since you came aboard at Neris. I've learned a lot and made friends like I've never had—ever. The *Lois* has become like a family to me." I knew I had crossed the line at some point, but she did not frown, so I plowed on. "These last few days, starting with the news that I was being bumped, and through that whole mess with the EMP and the scrubbers and all, I really began to think I belong out here in the Deep Dark."

"But you have some reservations?" she asked.

"Yes, Captain. I've been aboard less than a stanyer. Will I still feel this way at the end of my contract? Will I want to renew? I don't know," I said with a small shrug. "Sitting here today, I can't imagine that I wouldn't want to continue, but what if I'm wrong and it's just the novelty of it that I'm enjoying."

"That's a fair question. How does that apply to the academy?'

"The academy is a huge commitment in both time and money. I'm never going to be a hundred percent certain, but right at the moment, I really don't know, and I don't have sixty thousand credits to gamble on it."

She smiled. "Let me just see if I understand this. You're not worried about whether or not you can be successful at the academy, you're just worried that you'll get through it and decide you won't like being an officer?"

"Well, nothing against officers, Captain, but I'm more concerned that I'll get tired of being out here and I'll have spent the time and money to get qualified for a job I might not like in the long run."

She sat back in her chair and looked at me hard. "I think I see, Mr. Wang. So, how will you address this uncertainty? How certain will you need to be?"

"Well, Captain, I have a contract that expires in something over a stanyer. If I'm still having as much fun then as I am now, then I'll feel a lot better about trying to scrape up the necessary creds to attend."

"I think you would qualify for financial aid, Mr. Wang," she said with a grin. "If you have any further thoughts on the academy, would you share them with me?"

"Of course, Captain, but I hardly think I'm going to come to any world-shaking decisions in the next couple of days," I said with probably more bitterness than I intended.

She smiled at me and said, "Thank you, Mr. Wang. Dismissed."

I stood to leave and she said quietly, "Have faith for just a couple more days, Ishmael."

"Of course, Captain. I know I'm in no immediate danger."

She threw back her head and laughed loudly as I closed the door behind me.

She was definitely up to something. I wasn't sure what, but I did trust her. I just hoped she could pull off whatever it was. We had to be close now or she wouldn't have posted the pull out schedule. That reminded me of another problem and I headed down to Environmental to check on Diane.

When I got there, she had her head in the back of number four scrubber. I tried to shuffle my feet and make noise so I wouldn't startle her but it wasn't enough.

"Having problems?" I asked.

She jumped and banged her head. "Sludge monkey!" she said with her head still in the scrubber.

"I'm sorry! I tried to make enough noise that you'd hear me."

She pulled her head out of the scrubber and rubbed the front where she'd bumped it. "Are you, lost little boy?" she asked with a wicked grin.

"Yeah, I think so." I grinned back. "You going to take me to your house and feed me candy?"

"Honey," she said with a wink, "if I ever get the chance to take you to my house, it ain't gonna be to feed ya candy!" She laughed. "What's up?" she asked more seriously, reaching back into the scrubber.

"*Audrey Moore* docked this morning. They have an EV3 slot open."

"Another one?"

"Same one. Gregor got arrested for fighting in Dunsany."

"Figures. You gonna apply?" Her voice echoed from inside the scrubber case.

"I'm trying to give the captain a chance to keep me aboard."

"Time's running out, Ish," she said, backing out of the scrubber. "Bastard," she spit.

"Who? Me?"

"No, CC. Look at this." She held up the swab she had used on the field collection plate.

"Ick, looks like it needs cleaning."

"Colby claims he took care of it."

"What?"

"This was scheduled for his watch last night. He said it was done, but this is what I found on the collector plate."

"Back up. Last I heard he wasn't doing the maintenance at all."

"Yes, but I wouldn't let him get away with that and told Brill. She had a little talk with him and the upshot is that he hasn't passed off any maintenance for me to do, but he said he performed scheduled maintenance on the field collection plate on the number four scrubber and when I checked this is what I found."

"Maybe he got the numbers wrong?"

"I hadn't thought of that," she said, and bolted off to look.

I followed along behind and peered in as we checked them out, one-by-one. None of them looked like they'd been cleaned as recently as the previous watch, even if it was late in the day.

"Bastard," Diane repeated. "Now what?"

"You find Brill and tell her. I need to see a man about a bag of sneaky, I think."

"A what?"

"Nothing," I said. "I need a little more information and I think I know who to ask." I pulled out my tablet and bipped Mr. von Ickles.

The reply came almost instantly. "Ship's office."

David ben Dour had the messenger duty and was sitting in the office with Mr. von Ickles when I got there. "Excuse me, sar, but could I have a little talk with you about a personal matter?"

David was a good guy and took the cue. "I'll just go grab some coffee. Maybe see how Rhon's doing."

When he'd gone, Mr. von Ickles asked, "What is it, Mr. Wang? How can I help?"

"Well, sar, it's the new guy. He's causing some problems down in Environmental and I need some advice. Maybe I need somebody with some specialized training in sneakiness to help me."

He grinned at that and said, "Pull up a chair."

I gave him the two tick recap of the situation that I'd observed in Environmental and concluded with, "and I don't think this is the first time he's had a problem."

"You're not just trying to discredit him so we dump him, are you?"

"No, sar. Lois wants him aboard."

He blinked at me. "Lois wants him aboard," he repeated.

"Yes, sar. We have to keep him from killing anybody or getting killed himself."

He paused and looked hard at me for about half a tick. "Finish your story," he said at last.

I told him what CC had told me about his last ship and how he had been injured and left behind.

Mr. von Ickles eyes narrowed about half way through and I could see he was tracking the same rabbit I was. When I got done, he sat for two heart beats and said, "You don't think he slipped."

I shook my head. "No, sar, I don't. Head trauma, concussion, he probably doesn't remember much. If they were careful, he might not have seen it coming. So when he came to and found he was lying in a pool of water from the drippy scrubber with a head ache, he might have just assumed he slipped." I shrugged. "Solicitous shipmates take you to the hospital and leave you there."

He chewed on that mentally for a bit before focusing back on me. "So? Why isn't this Brill's discipline problem? And what kind of sneaky were you thinking about?"

"How desperate would they have had to be to clock him in the head with a spanner?"

"Assuming it was a spanner, but I take your meaning. You're thinking that they'd tried all the normal kinds of things and he was still putting them at risk to the point where they were willing to physically harm him?"

"Before he killed them, yes, sar."

"Why not just fire him?"

"I don't know, sar. That's one of two things we need to find out."

"What's the other?"

"Whether or not we're right about it being the crew."

He looked startled at that, but nodded. "Okay, but why bring this to me. Why not Mr. Kelley?"

"We will need to eventually, and the captain, too, but I need help getting the ducks lined up here, so that I'm not accused of trying to discredit him so I can keep my job."

"Ah, that's the kind of sneaky you need."

"I think so, sar. Have I missed anything?"

"I don't think so, Mr. Wang. Why do you ask?"

"Well, with our lives on the line, I think I'd like to have a second set of eyes," I told him with a grin.

"Why, Mr. Wang," he said with mock surprise, "you were listening."

We settled down to strategies and tactics then. I was gratified to notice the pile of unopened computer parts still tucked away in the office, but I focused on the task at hand. In less than half a stan, we had ironed out the list of questions we needed answered and I left him to start tracking them down.

As I was leaving the office, he said, "You know the *Audrey* has a berth?"

"Yes, sar, but I don't believe I'll be applying for it any time soon."

"No? Why not?"

"I never developed a taste for bunk-bunny."

He was chuckling into his tablet when I closed the door.

The afternoon was gone by that time and I had duty in the morning, but the ship was leaving the day after so I had to hurry. I headed back to Environmental to see if Brill and Diane wanted to go out to eat. It would be one of our last opportunities on Betrus. I was pretty sure I would be leaving with them, but I was not above playing the pity card to get two good-looking women to dine with me. I would have asked Beverly too, but I hadn't seen her in days. When I checked she wasn't aboard.

As I stepped into Environmental, I found Brill and Diane still discussing CC. Brill said, "But if he says he did it and he didn't that's falsifying logs."

"True, but what are we going to do about it?" Diane asked.

"Document, document, document," Brill replied. "And in the mean time, we need to figure out what's his story."

"Well, I heard one version from him," I told them. "I'm trying to confirm it."

"The slipped on the leaky scrubber tale?" Brill asked.

"Yeah, that's the one."

"You don't think it's true?"

"I think he may well think it's true, but I'm not sure he knows."

"How could he not know?" Diane asked.

"If somebody hits you from behind with a big wrench, and you wake up having people telling you that you slipped and fell, what would you think?"

"What?" Brill asked.

I shrugged. "It's possible that they were at the end of their collective ropes with him. Either afraid that he was putting the ship in danger or just tired of cleaning up his messes."

They both gaped at me. "Do you think somebody would try to hurt him?" Brill asked.

"Would you, if you thought he was putting the ship in danger?"

I asked.

"Why not just fire him?" Diane asked.

"I don't know, but that's an interesting question, isn't it? Are there any big-wigs named Colby in Federated Freight?"

They both shrugged.

"Well, the ship is getting under way in less than two days and this may be the last chance we can go out to dinner together for a long time. You guys in?"

"Oh my," Diane said. "It is."

Brill took a deep breath and blew it out before answering. "Yes, let's do it."

"Okay, main lock at 1830? Is that enough time to get yourself together, Diane?"

"Yup, should be, but..."

"I know," I said. "But we are going to go have some fun and as for the rest, we just need to trust Lois."

"Trust Lois? To do what?" Diane asked.

I just smiled. "Whatever needs doing and to let us know if there's something we need to do for her." I waved as I headed for berthing to wash up and change.

Chapter Fifteen
Betrus System: 2352-June-17

When Sean woke me for watch, I managed not to scrape my knee getting out of the bunk. I had a hard time believing that it would be my last full day aboard the *Lois*. It just didn't seem possible— even as I showered and cleaned my teeth. I even told the face in the mirror, "I can't leave. I'm not done here, yet." He didn't look like he believed me and I had a sudden pang over the *yet* part. It was the first time that I really thought that I might be put ashore. The realization that I had not been aboard a year just compounded the off balance feeling.

I contemplated the idea that we may have had just one too many glasses of wine over dinner. I made a mental note to ask Fong if he had any incriminating evidence of our return when I relieved him. In the mean time, I finished zipping into my shipsuit and fetched some sustenance from the galley. I didn't eat much as I wasn't hungry, but the coffee tasted good. Pip had taken my advice on the number two urn, and the pastry had a different texture. I suspected that Sarah had been busy.

Fong just shook his head and laughed. "You looked perfectly sober and relaxed coming back in."

"How much do you want for the digitals?" I asked him with a grin.

"Seriously, I didn't take any digitals," he insisted.

"Okay, video?"

He shook his head. "Sorry, if I had any salacious evidence of misconduct between you and any member of the crew, I could get big creds, but I'm doomed to remain a poverty-stricken spacer of uncertain provenance."

"Who would be bidding?"

"Almost any of the women aboard. Rhon's been capturing the lock pickups just on the odd chance," he said with a laugh.

"You are kidding, right?"

"Yes," he said with a smug grin, "but I had you going, didn't I?"

"Yeah, you got me."

We shared a laugh and he headed into the ship. He was a nice guy. I hoped I wasn't going to be put in the position of having to miss him.

About half a stan later, Mr. von Ickles ambled out to the watch stander station. "Good morning, Mr. Wang. Are you enjoying your last gangway watch?"

"Oh, yes, sar. A regular laugh riot, sar."

"The *Boulton* is en route to Umber, but I've got a query at the orbital there. It'll hold until she makes contact. We should have a reply by the time we hit Niol. I talked to Mr. Maxwell and he's contacted the station medical for an update on Mr. Colby's medical records for our files. Those we should have any minute now. No word yet on why he might have high level protection, but if what you suspect is right, we'll have enough documentation by the time we get to Niol to take action and find out for ourselves."

"You keep saying *we*, Mr. von Ickles."

"Do I?" he said with a smirk. "I mean the ship, of course."

"Of course, sar, easily misunderstood, sar."

"Your instincts are right, though," he said. "Something's not right there. We just need to find out what."

"I appreciate the information, sar. Thank you."

He winked and headed back into the ship.

The shift continued with the usual comings and goings. I even saw Beverly crawling back aboard—mid morning. She looked terrible.

"Are you all right?" I asked.

"No!" she snapped. "You can't leave the ship. I'm not done with you." Without further explanation, she stumbled down the passageway toward the berthing area.

I sighed. I hoped all this was moot. Even with all the reassurance from the various indicators, I still had no job and, according to the existing scenario, I would be leaving the ship in the morning. I sighed again and bipped Art for another coffee.

When Rhon relieved me that night she looked subdued. She thought I was leaving. She did all but throw her arms around me and sob. I told her I would see her in the morning.

Mr. Maxwell met me at the head of the passage and said, "Expect a summons to the captain's cabin around 0900, Mr. Wang.

You're at liberty, but please be aboard no later than 0830."

"Aye, aye, sar," I said.

He nodded then and ambled back up the passage and climbed the ladder to officer country.

Whatever they were planning, I would know in a few stans. In the meantime, dinner sang its siren song as the aroma of spiced beefalo wafted all the way out from the galley and I followed the call.

For a last night in port, it was pretty busy on the mess deck. I heard several people making plans for going out later so it was not turning into one of those hunker down and wait it out nights. I contemplated the possibility of heading to Infinity myself. If the hints were real, then I could expect something odd to happen in the morning and I would be leaving on the *Lois*. One more night out before heading into the Deep Dark sounded good. As I filled my plate, I looked around for somebody to go with.

"Hey, Ish!" Pip said. "Fancy a bit of a boy's night out? Last night in port, you know."

"Just what I was thinking," I told him. "You have any ideas?"

"Several, but they'll have to keep until later." He clapped me on the shoulder and scurried back to the kitchen.

I found a seat with Brill, Francis, and Diane. "Are you saving this for CC?" I asked with a grin.

"Short-timers can sit here, I guess," Francis said with a smile. I plunked myself down.

"Where is he, anyway?" I asked.

"Getting changed for liberty. He has some goodbyes to say, apparently," Brill said, her face deadpan.

"Thanks for dinner last night, guys," I said to Diane and Brill. "It meant a lot."

Francis turned to me and lowered his voice. "Are you really leaving?" he asked.

"Honestly, I don't know. I don't think so, but I have no job at the moment. I'm on liberty until 0830 and I have to be ready to meet with the captain at 0900."

"Cutting it a little close, aren't they?" he asked.

"Not if they're planning on leaving me here."

He frowned in thought. "True."

I turned to Brill and Diane then. "How'd golden boy do on watch today?"

"No maintenance scheduled for today," Diane said. "So no new evidence."

"Well, I guess all you can do is keep an eye on him."

They nodded and we all dug into dinner. The beefalo was delicious and Cookie even came out of the galley to say hi.

"So, have you any news for us, Ishmael?" he asked.

"Sorry, Cookie. I think I'll be finding out in the morning just before pull out."

"Sarah thinks that Lois isn't done with you, and I believe she is right. So, what would you like for dinner tomorrow night?" he asked.

"Tomorrow night you'll be underway, Cookie," I pointed out.

"Exactly, so what would you like?" His grin lit up the table.

"You know that chicken with cream sauce you make with the pasta and vegetables?"

"Indeed," he said, "that's what we'll have for dinner tomorrow night, then." He clapped me on the shoulder, "Have fun with Pip tonight, but stay out of trouble!" He shook a warning finger at me and headed back to the galley.

"Lois isn't done with you?" Francis asked.

"If that's what Sarah thinks, who am I to argue?"

"Well, at least we know what we're having for dinner tomorrow," he said.

Diane and Brill just looked sad. I turned to Brill and asked, "Are you going out tonight, too?"

She just shook her head. "After Dunsany, I'm still a little raw."

Diane and I both burst out laughing. Francis looked confused. When Brill's brain finally caught up with what her mouth had said she just groaned and hung her head, but she was smiling.

I looked at Francis, "And you? Big plans?"

He shook his head, "I used up all my big plans days ago. I just want a good night's sleep and to shake this system off my shoes. I wanna be moving again."

We all finished our dinners. The spicy beefalo was spectacular and I savored every morsel. As certain as I was that the ship would not leave without me, I could not ignore the reality that I might be sitting on the orbital watching them go. There was a lesson for me there. As sure as I was, it was all out of my control. I chuckled at the idea that I had ever thought anything else.

When we broke up, Diane headed back to Environmental, Brill headed for her bunk, and Francis headed for the sauna. Brill looked over her shoulder at me as she left. "See you at breakfast," she said, and stepped out into the passage. I sighed, wishing it could be breakfast in bed. I caught Pip's eye in the galley and pointed down mouthing the word "berthing" and he nodded.

It was time to get ready. I wondered if the *Alistair* tag team would be around.

By 2030, Pip and I checked out with Rhon at the gangway.

"You are coming back, aren't you?" she asked uncertainly.

"You bet your bee," I told her.

She grinned. "I'll hold you to that."

As we crossed the dock and headed for the lift, Pip asked, "Bee?"

"Yeah, she has a little honey bee tattoo."

"Really?" he said. "I've never seen it."

"You've never had gangway watch," I commented dryly.

"Was seeing the tattoo worth the watch standing?" he asked.

"No," I admitted, "but it did liven up the night a bit."

"Where is it?"

"About six inches down from her navel."

"But that's—"

"You see some interesting things struggling back aboard at 0300," I observed. "Now where are we going?"

"Head for the oh-two deck."

We didn't go to Infinity as I expected. Pip took me to a little bar to starboard. It was about a quarter of the way around the station almost as far from Infinity as you could go without approaching it from the other side. Compared to the club's big, raucous cavern, the pub was a cozy place. Padded booths lined the walls and several tables filled in the floor. The bar stood as an island in the middle and you could walk all the way around it. In the far corner a trio of musicians fiddled with instruments but the sound checks were subdued and there was no dance floor. Small groups were scattered about, mostly in the booths but some gathered around tables.

We walked in and Pip picked a table to the side where we could watch the people coming and going. When the waitress came over, I almost didn't recognize that she was the same one from Infinity but without the cutdown ship suit. She greeted Pip by name and offered to get him "the usual" so I figured he'd been here a few times.

Pip turned to me. "They brew their own beer here. The chocolate stout is good and they have a very nice ice beer that'll kick your ass."

I asked the waitress, "What's your favorite?"

"I like the amber bock," she said.

"I'll take that, then, please."

We settled in and I turned to Pip. "This doesn't seem like the kind of place I'd expect to find the tag team."

"They introduced me," he said. "Just because they're hedonistic perverts doesn't mean they don't appreciate a nice pub."

"They introduced you?" I asked.

"Sure. What do you think they do in the booths?"

That startled me so much I twisted my head. I didn't notice any kind of lewd behavior going on when we came in, but I certainly didn't want to miss out.

"Made ya look," Pip said.

We were still chuckling when the waitress brought the beers. I paid and told Pip he'd need to get the next round.

The bock was good and Pip was admiring his beer when the tag team showed up. Pip rose and kissed each soundly before holding their chairs.

"Katie, Janette, this is my friend, Ishmael Wang," Pip did the introductions.

"I recognize you," Janette said. "You were at the table that night on Dunsany."

"That's me."

"You were the perfect straight man. Thanks."

I raised my glass in toast and we ordered them beers when the waitress came back. The jazz trio started playing but the music served as a pleasant accompaniment and not a wall of sound. The tag team really were delightful women. Katie had a warm smile and an innocent face that belied the wickedly sexual sense of humor beneath. Janette was the devil-may-care one. She was completely not self-conscious. I could see why Pip found them so fascinating— other than the obvious attraction of being called upon to sacrifice himself upon the altar of their bodies.

We had a couple of rounds and it was obvious that they wanted to take Pip back for one last night of fun before they headed out. The *Alistair* was getting underway before the *Lois*, so they were short on time. It was equally obvious that they didn't know what to do with me. Pip seemed to think I would be going along for the ride, as it were, but the tag team kept looking at each other and casting quick glances in my direction.

After almost half a stan of dithering, I turned to Katie. "You girls better take him and get what good you can out of him. He's not going to be worth squat tomorrow if you don't." I winked at her and gave her a little head nod.

Pip turned to me, a frown of concern on his face. "I thought we were going to have a boy's night out."

"Pip, you moron, I got burned out by the Maguire twins when I was sixteen. Don't worry about it. I'll see you on the ship in the morning."

Katie gave me a kiss on the cheek and said, "We won't hurt him too much." They led him out of the pub and turned toward the lift.

I still had half my beer left and it was good beer. The trio was in the middle of a set and I had no place I needed to be, so I settled down to enjoy both of them.

About the time the trio wrapped their last number and my glass held nothing but a little foam, the waitress brought me another beer and pointed to a lady at the bar. I raised the glass in a toast and she raised hers in return. I smiled when I realized that the other woman on the far side of her was egging her on, and I suspected she was being dared. I sat back to see how it would turn out. After a few ticks she stood and came over to my table.

She wasn't gorgeous, but she was quite cute, perhaps in her mid twenties. I couldn't get a read on the group she was with, but she was definitely a spacer. I stood and held a chair for her, positioning it so she couldn't see her friends back at the bar giggling at her discomfort without looking over her shoulder.

"Thanks for the beer," I said. "My name is Ishmael." I stuck out my hand.

"Wendy," she said. She shook the hand with just the tips of her fingers.

I twisted in my seat so I could look over her shoulder and keep an eye on her friends but still see her face. "So, they're giving you a hard time, eh?" I said, hiding my mouth in the top of the glass.

She giggled. "A bit—they think I'm the shy one."

"And are you?"

She shrugged one-shoulder and said, "Yeah, a little I guess." She looked into her glass.

"What ship?"

"*Anson Phelps*. You?"

"*Lois McKendrick*. What do they think you should do?"

"They were hassling me earlier about being too picky. So when we came in, and you were sitting here with your friends, I said something like, 'he's cute, too bad he's already with somebody.' I figured having shown an interest they would leave me alone."

I laughed. "Then Pip and his friends took off and I'm here alone so they think you should make a pass at me?"

"Something like that."

"I'm flattered," I told her with a grin.

"Flattered?"

"That you thought I was cute enough to make a pass at," I paused and gave her a little flirty look that I knew her friends could see because they were doing that hand to the face, peek through the fingers, *I'm-not-really-looking* thing in our direction. "You do think so? It wasn't just something you said to shut them up?" I leaned forward a little.

"Oh, yes," she said, her eyes flitting up from her drink to look at me in small glances. "I spotted you when we walked through the door."

"Tell me, Wendy," I said, leaning in a little more. "Do you get more points if I kiss you, or if you kiss me?"

"What?"

"Somebody here is gonna get kissed and I just wanna make sure you get the credit for it with the peanut gallery at the bar."

She looked at me straight on for the first time since she'd come over and I smiled.

"Would you mind terribly," she asked, "if I kissed you first?"

"Be gentle with me, Wendy," I told her and tilted my head so the audience would get a good look when she closed in.

She paused about half way to me.

I looked her dead in the eyes and said, "Please be thorough. I hate being just half-kissed."

She leaned into me then and did a very thorough job of it indeed.

After quite a long time, she pulled back a bit and asked, "Was that thorough enough?"

"Well, your friends got quite a charge out of it, but not half as much as I did," I told her after I caught my breath again. "Do you suppose you might do that one more time, just to see if you like it?"

"Hmm," she said, finally relaxing, "Yes, I suppose I might. In the interests of research."

It was actually quite a long time before I caught my breath. "Damn, you're good," I told her.

"You're just saying that," she said.

"No, I wouldn't do that to you," I told her.

"Not even if you thought it would get you anywhere?"

"Where would I need it to get me?" I asked.

"Oh, I don't know," she teased. "Maybe into my bed?"

"Well," I said, leaning in and whispering, "do you want me in your bed?"

She just brushed her lips across mine and said, "Bed, hell, if you don't take me out of here right now, that table will have to do." As soon as the words left her mouth, the *did-I-say-that-out-loud* look flashed across her face.

So I kissed her firmly and said, "Your place or mine?"

"Do you have a place?" she asked.

"No, but I can get one."

"Mine," she said, "I'm not waiting that long for yours."

"My gracious, I do believe I may not be safe with you."

"I won't hurt you," she paused, "unless you ask very, very nicely." She giggled and added, "I'm sorry, but I've always wanted to say that."

"Well hold that thought and let's go say it where your friends can hear."

She laughed and started to balk, but I stood and helped her to her feet. I held out my arm so she could hang on to it. She led me to her friends, who were now giggling almost non-stop among themselves. At last one noticed our approach and said, "She's not going to bring him over here, is she?" The girl who spoke had pure panic on her face and I don't believe she knew I could hear her.

As we approached, Wendy said, "Girls, this is Ishmael. Ishmael, my shipmates. I won't bother with their names because when I'm done with you, you won't remember your own."

They gasped and tittered as she kissed me solidly again.

"Am I going to be safe with you?" I asked.

"No," she said, "but I won't hurt you unless you ask very, very nicely." Then she took my lower lip in her teeth and just let them scrape gently across.

I swallowed hard and said, "That sounds fair enough."

We turned as a pair and she led me out of the bar. "Don't wait up, girls. I'm going to be a while," she called over her shoulder.

She strutted proudly until we got around the corner and out of sight and then collapsed against the bulkhead as her legs gave way from the uncontrollable laughter.

"You know you left them gaping after us? I'll bet they're still sitting there with their mouths hanging open."

We were both laughing now. As we got closer to the lift, she said, "Thank you, Ishmael."

"For what?"

"For putting on such a good act. You made my reputation in there."

I stopped in the middle of the corridor and turned to her. "What act?" I asked with my lips just a centimeter from hers. "Do you want to go back and use the table?" I waited to see what she would do.

She kissed me very nicely. "After due consideration, I think the bed might be more comfortable for you."

"Have I mentioned how much I admire a woman who knows what she wants and isn't afraid to demand it?" I asked with a grin.

"Well, right now, mister, I want you to get on that lift. When I get you to my room, I'll see what else can I think of."

Several hours and at least three different instances of "I've always wanted to try that" later, we both collapsed in a pile of sweaty sheets, giggling like kids. When we stopped laughing, she looked up at me and asked, "When do you have to be back?"

"I have to be aboard by 0830. You?"

"Not till noon," she said.

We both looked at the chrono, 0315.

"Do you want me to leave so you can sleep?" I asked.

"Actually, I was kinda hoping you'd stay and sleep a little with me."

I rolled over and pulled my tablet out of my jacket, set the alarm, and put it down where I could grab it easily, before punching the light controller and pulling the blankets around us.

"What time did you set it for?" she asked, already beginning to drift away as she snuggled into me.

"0600. That should give us enough time to go around again before I leave—if you're interested that is."

She giggled sleepily and said, "Good." Then she nodded off.

Chapter Sixteen
Betrus System: 2352-June-18

Wendy kicked me out of the room at 0745. "With you around, I'm impossible. I'm not going to stop grinning for a week," she said, wearing only a smile and a sheen of sweat as she kissed me good-bye at the door. "Git," she said, and slammed the panel in my face. I could hear her giggling behind it. I had time for a quick shower and fresh shipsuit before I met with the captain to find out what was happening so I headed for the ship.

Fong was on watch when I went through the lock. He blinked when I came in. "You musta had quite a party if you're just coming in now," he said with a smirk.

"Yes I did. Now I get to find out what the captain has cooked up."

"Good luck, Ishmael. I think everybody on the ship is rooting for you."

"Thanks, Fong, I expect I'll be around awhile longer. I just don't know in what capacity." I waved as I headed into the ship and, in spite of my brave words, hoped it wasn't the last time I would be coming aboard.

Sally Green was in her bunk and saw me come into the berthing area. "Woo hoo, look at you. Just dragging yer tomcatty butt back in now?"

"Dragging is the operative word there, I think," I told her with a wink.

I got cleaned up and zipped into a fresh shipsuit just in time. My tablet bipped at 0845 with my summons to the captain's cabin.

"Good luck, Ish," Sally called.

"Thanks, Sal." I gave her a little salute on the way out.

The captain had all the usual participants with her at the table, along with Mr. von Ickles who sat to the left of Mr. Maxwell.

"Thank you, Mr. Wang," the captain began as soon as I braced to attention. "I know this has been a difficult time for you, but in spite of that, you have performed your duties with your customary professionalism and grace."

"Thank you, Captain," I said after the pause.

"We've been waiting for a message from home office that authorizes us to create a new position. In light of the critical failures we encountered coming into Betrus, the senior officers submitted a petition to create an assistant position in Systems to aid Mr. von Ickles in his duties. That authorization arrived at 0830. In light of your contributions to the resolution of our system failures, we are prepared to offer you that job. The position is a spec two systems slot, reporting to Mr. von Ickles. It pays scale for spec two, and carries the customary full share and mass allotment. What say you, Mr. Wang?"

"I say, yes, Captain. I would consider it an honor."

"Mr. von Ickles?" she said.

"Yes, Captain?"

"Find us that flaw before somebody loses a ship."

"Aye, aye, Captain."

Mr. von Ickles ushered me out of the cabin and we headed for the bridge. "Rather anticlimactic, wasn't it?" he asked.

"Not from where I was standing, sar."

He grinned at me. "Were you worried?"

"I knew you were all working hard on something. I knew that if anybody could pull it off, the officers of the *Lois* would. But, yeah, I was worried that it just might not have been possible at all. There had to be some doubt as to whether or not it would fly because we've been waiting all this time."

"Good analysis," he said. "Just between you and me? I was sweating bullets."

"It's behind us now and I am very pleased to be working with you, sar."

"Sucking up already, Mr. Wang?"

"I believe in getting off to a good start, sar."

"Oh, we are gonna have such fun, aren't we?"

"I believe so, sar," I said. "What do we do first?"

"Well, we need to get you set up on the bridge and find you a duty station. There's a spare systems console there and you'll be with me there during navigation evolutions—pull out, docking, transitions. That'll be your duty station. There's not a lot to do if everything goes well. If it goes bad, then it'll get furry fast."

"I can understand that."

We stepped onto the bridge with a lot less formality than I had in the past. Remembering that, I asked quietly, "Do I need to ask permission or anything when I come up here by myself?"

He just shook his head. "You're part of the bridge crew now. You're required to be here." We crossed to a row of stations, not unlike my old post down in Environmental. "When you need to be here to work, just come up and work. If there's something going on, stay out of the way. If it's really interesting, pay close attention. Best still, if there's something happening, watch the ship's network and see how it works. You've got a little bit of a grace period here. Everybody's gonna be adjusting to the fact that you're here and not expecting too much from you—yet."

"Yet?"

"Adding a new slot has an effect on the finances of the ship. You're an expensive insurance policy, and we need to get you contributing an added value or the company will take the slot away once we solve the EMP problem."

That put a different complexion on the situation. "I understand, sar, and thanks for telling me. We'd best get at this then, huh?"

"I wouldn't sweat it, Ish. Compared to what we've pulled off already, the rest is going to go just fine." He laughed and started running me through the console diagnostics.

Being on the bridge reminded me a bit of the library at the university on Neris. When I was too small to leave at home, Mom would take me with her when she did her research. I remember the quiet purposefulness of the big halls. There were low conversations all around and occasionally heated arguments in some of the graduate study rooms, but generally there was a kind of low hum of background activity. Everybody had something to do there and, for the most part, they got on with it.

Information displays around the bridge were the main source of illumination. Consoles had red glow patches so you didn't bump into them in the dimness, and the screens all showed data on a black background to keep the ambient light levels down. It was all rather moot while docked, because the orbital, which was only a few meters outside the forward port, glowed like some monstrous full-moon peeking in the window. It was bright enough to cast shadows in the otherwise dim bridge.

We finished running diagnostics and brought the console up. "Normally you won't need to run the diagnostics. We haven't used this station for a while, so it's just as well. Does it look familiar?"

"Yes, sar, it's the same basic station as in Environmental."

"Correct. The hardware is standardized throughout the ship. All the consoles in all the divisions are the same. Cheaper that way. The only real difference is the software behind each. Down in Environmental you didn't need the reactor controls, and down in Power they don't need the scrubbers. About ninety percent of the code base is shared in common and, while that cuts down on code error, it also means that if the code that turns on the lights in berthing is wrong, then the code that turns on the sail generators is equally wrong."

"Isn't that a little risky?" I asked.

"Like getting into this tin can and sailing out into a vacuum isn't?"

"Well, if you put it that way..."

"We won't be playing with that stuff. It's in; it's tested; it's good. What we have to concentrate on, and ninety-nine point nine-nine percent of the time it's as boring as Environmental, is to keep the systems alive and kicking. We spend most of our time managing the data archives, running system backups, and optimizing data. Occasionally we may need to replace a bit of hardware. Until we came into Betrus and blew out the data cabinet, the most serious problem I had to deal with in the two stanyers I've been aboard was a burned out comm repeater down in the spine that kept sending all the engine control commands back to the bridge with the data equivalent of: occupant unknown."

"Understood, sar," I said. Privately I wondered if the magic show was not over, but slipping into a more subtle second act. If the ship was as reliable as he said, it made no sense for me to be sitting on the bridge.

Mr. von Ickles slipped into the seat at the next console—obviously his normal post—and began bringing up displays of his own. "I'll slave your console to mine for now. You'll be able to watch when we get underway and when we get secured from navigation stations. Then we can begin putting together all those lovely pieces of equipment down in the office."

I felt a little shiver of anticipation. "Yes, sar."

He ran through a quick systems tour on the console and showed me how to configure the bridge consoles to act like any other console on the ship. The elegance felt right to me. He brought up a schematic of the ship that was the same one I used for VSI and overlaid the fiber data runs, wireless access points, data storage closets and consoles. It included my environmental sensor packages along with every other sensor, feedback, and control package in the ship from locks, to cargo container latches, and to engine mount gimbal positions.

"Impressive, sar."

"That's just the static picture," he said. He hit a function key on his console and they all started to blink. "That's the data flow view. The speed of the blink represents the amount of data flowing. Some just spit out a packet every once in a while, others are constantly being updated and sending data back."

It was like looking at a viewer showing how all the nerve cells in the ship fired in real time. He shut it off and we went back to the static picture.

"No need to leave that running if we're not going to be here," he said. "Let's get some lunch before the show begins."

I looked at the chrono—1200. The morning sublimated into the afternoon as the reality hit me. The ship would pull out and I would be going with her. I had a new job. I had a new boss. Lois was not done with me yet.

As we headed down to the mess deck, Mr. von Ickles said, "Consider yourself on third section and grafted to my hip. We haven't had a chance to figure out what to do with watches in port yet, but underway, you'll be on third section rotation for the time being. We may shift you to second eventually to cover systems support on a wider span on the clock. It's all new to us, Ish, so have patience with the jerking around you're probably going to experience."

"Sar, I'm just glad to still be here to be jerked around. Believe me."

"Your first task underway is going to be putting the *uh-oh* box together and getting ShipNet to run on it. I hope we never have to use it, but if we do, I want it up immediately. We'll need to figure out some protocol for it, so be thinking about where to store it, how to bring it up quickly, and anything you can think of that restores some minimum level of control in the event of another data cabinet crash."

"Makes sense. Then what, sar?"

"Then we find out how an EMP got through the shielding and burned out that data cabinet." He paused for a moment, his eyes focused somewhere in the distance. "Then we figure how to stop it from ever happening again."

When we stepped onto the mess deck the number of smiles focused in my direction shocked me. Things had been moving so fast all morning, that I hadn't had a chance to tell anybody. Brill, Bev, and Diane all sat at the same table, along with Francis and CC. I grabbed some grub and settled with them.

Francis grinned at me. "We just can't get rid of you, can we?"

"Not yet anyway." I grinned back.

Brill smiled and Diane had a big grin of her own. Beverly looked almost teary and I wondered if she felt okay. The last time I had seen her she'd been crawling back aboard snarling. I made a note to get her aside and find out what was going on.

CC asked, "So, how'd you manage this?" It came out a bit colder than I think he meant it to.

I could see Diane start to tense up so I jumped in. "After the accident coming in, the officers re-evaluated their systems support needs and convinced home office to add a new slot. At least long enough to figure out what happened and how to deal with it." I shrugged. "I got first dibs."

"Nice," Brill said. "What'll you be doing?"

"First task is to recreate the emergency network controller. They don't want to rely on my portable."

"Good plan," Francis said. "Then what?"

"Well, then we try to find out how the EMP did all that damage to begin with."

"How are you going to do that?" Brill asked.

"No idea, but I can't imagine that's the first CME this ship has been through in nineteen stanyers, not even the first with an EMP." I turned to Francis, "You're the expert in astrophysics. What are the odds?"

Francis grimaced. "Well, first, I'm not sure we're talking about the same things. These CMEs happen all the time on every star we've visited. They all have some things in common including a leading wave of high-energy charged particles."

CC turned to me and asked, "Who is this guy, Mr. Science?"

"That's Doctor Science to you," I said with a grin. "Go on, Francis."

Francis snickered at the look on CC's face but continued. "So, a surface event on the star splashes some of the corona out into space. It's not like a ripple on a pond but more like a sneeze. Star snot."

"Francis, we're trying to eat here," Bev said. "Not all of us have the same strong stomachs that you environmental people do."

"Oh, sorry," Francis said. "Anyway, this stuff goes sailing out into space and it goes a long, long way. Depending on the nature of the original event it might be tightly focused or it may be really loosely dispursed, but it can happen as often as ten or twenty times a day, every day during the stellar maxima, maybe only once a day during minima. It's not predictable."

"So, the EMP?" I prompted.

"Oh, yeah," he got back on focus. "These events are layered. The front layers are highly energized particles really similar to a classic EMP. They can toast electronics and disrupt electrical systems. They hardly ever interact at planetary levels because the atmosphere intercepts them. They could in theory threaten the orbitals, but they happen so often that the orbitals are designed to deal with them. So are ships, for that matter."

I think everybody had glazed over by then. So Francis said, "Okay, think flash-boom."

Diane said, "What?"

"Flash-boom," he repeated. "You ever see lightning on a planet?"

"Yeah," she said, "of course."

"Well, the flash of the lightning is like the high energy particles from our stellar sneeze. The boom is like the actual mass that's being ejected. It trails it."

I jumped in with, "But we went through the mass, I heard it hit the hull, and then the EMP took out the generators."

"Well, maybe yes, maybe no," Francis said. "Remember that normally, the energized particles are moving out a lot faster and ahead of the CME residue. Whatever we ran into was not the standard particle front."

"Okay," I said, "but then what was it?"

"Once in a while a CME front gets a charged particle front behind it, either from a second event in the same area or from a kind of secondary splash. We don't really know why, but the effect is that the outer shell of particles forms a kind of magnetic cup that holds those highly charged particles."

Diane said, "Can you translate that?"

"A regular highly charged particle front is like a lawn sprinkler, this other thing is more like a water balloon."

"That doesn't sound like EMP," I said.

"It's not—EMP is just a kind of pop-physics shorthand to tell people what happened to their satellites without having to get into the actual messiness of what really happened."

"And you said these are rare?"

"Yeah, that's why we know so little about them. We can see them on stellar coronagraphs as they occur but getting in front of them is a matter of luck."

"Bad luck, in our case," Brill said.

"How rare? One in a thousand?" I asked.

"We're not really sure. Could be like one in a hundred or maybe one in ten thousand. We would need to put a shell of detectors around a star to find out and so far there aren't enough creds in the galaxy to justify that kind of effort."

"Wait," I said, "What did I hear hit the hull? Sounded like a veil of sand."

"Probably was," Francis said. "Little bits of grit that got swept ahead of the wave. Not the particles that came from the CME itself, which are usually hydrogen molecules and such, but space is filled with actual dust."

My brain did a kind of two-step as I looked around the table. Francis was more alive and animated than I had ever seen him. It was as if he had worn some kind of disguise, for all those months I had known him and this was his real face. Everybody around the table, except CC, were—if not mesmerized—at least paying very close attention. I got one of those weird flashes and thought, *Francis is in the wrong place.*

My fork clicked on the empty plate and I looked down, wondering what had happened to my lunch. I looked around to see if somebody had taken it, when I noticed Mr. von Ickles was bussing his dishes. He looked in my direction and I gave him a nod. "Well, shippies, duty calls and I must answer."

As I was walking away from the table, I heard CC ask, "Does he always talk like that?"

I think it was Diane who answered, "No. Sometimes he gets really weird."

We got to the bridge just ahead of the captain and the other officers. Captain Giggone took her seat and waited. It made me think of what it must be like backstage at the ballet. The cast was gathering. I could almost hear the orchestra tuning up in the pit. Mr. von Ickles pulled up the overlay and flashed a snap of the data map. On the right panel on my console he put a status chart showing communications packets in various modes—voice, email, synchronous text, video, control, command, and about eight others I didn't recognize. On the left was a scrolling log of traffic identified as system main status messages. It scrolled too fast to read unless you were completely focused on it. The middle screen refreshed every few seconds, but it wasn't showing real-time.

Mr. von Ickles said, "I leave it on refresh so that we see it if something changes slowly. The pattern changes show up better in a delayed display. In a live feed your eyes adjust to the flows as they change. This way, changes flash into a new configuration and you can spot them."

As I watched the display, first one and then a second smaller blob appeared on the schematic. We had a golden line running from us to each of them.

"The tugs," Mr. von Ickles murmured. "We're getting close."

"Make the announcement, Mr. Pa," the captain said. "Set navigation detail."

"Setting navigation detail, aye, aye, sar," Fong said from his station at the back of the bridge. I heard the announcement from this side of the speakers for the first time.

The director had just stepped to the podium and tapped her baton. A kind of hush settled as the last few members of the team settled into position. While other members of the crew might be reporting to duty stations around the ship, the bridge crew was in place already. The only obvious activity was a trading of places as a few people stepped forward and others stepped back.

I heard Salina Matteo talking into her headset, but I couldn't make out the words. The captain stood and walked to the back of the bridge, looking out at the stern of the ship. I couldn't see from my angle but I suspected the tugs were out there somewhere.

"Prepare for pull out, Mr. Pa," she said. Her voice wasn't loud, but it carried all over the bridge.

"Prepare for pull out, aye, aye, Captain."

He spoke into his headset and looked at a ship status screen hanging down from the overhead. "Secure forward locks. Make ready for pull out. Disable docking clamp interlocks," he said.

The status display went red and then green at the bow as the locks were secured. I watched the command and control channel traffic on my display as it scrolled down. A message flashed back from the forward locks and Fong said, "Locks are secured. Docking clamp interlocks are offline, Captain. Ship's board is green once."

"Thank you, Mr. Pa," the captain said, and looked to Salina Matteo who nodded once at some unspoken question.

"Astrogation ready?" the captain asked.

"Astrogation online and running, Captain. Ship's board is green twice," Ms. Avril reported.

"Systems ready?"

"Systems are online and running, Captain. Ship's board is green thrice," Mr. von Ickles said.

"Mr. Maxwell, are we ready?"

"All ship's boards are green. We are ready for departure, Captain," he said.

"Log departure at 2352-June-18, 1332."

Somebody said, "Departure logged, aye."

"Make the announcement, Mr. Pa. Stand by for pull out in ten. Mark."

I had listened to the announcement from the galley and from the Environmental Section but hearing it on the bridge, watching everything as it happened, was like the first time. As he counted down, his eyes fixed on a digital read out of the time, people all around me executed their assigned tasks in an amazing choreographed performance. When Fong got down to one, I saw the docking clamps release in a flash of yellow and red on the screen in front of me and when he said, "Mark," the communication channels to the tugs turned white as they engaged their fields to gently pull us away from the orbital. I felt the normal *moving lift* sensation in my ear but the feeling was amplified by the surface of the orbital moving away from us. My brain needed some time to convince my eyes that we were moving and the orbital was not.

We eased back slowly at first but gained momentum. The tugs towed us backwards for half a stan then cast us loose. The representations on my screen disappeared as first one, then the other cut out of our network data stream. We drifted backwards on our momentum as the tugs peeled off and went wherever tugs go. Perhaps to help the next ship dock in the now empty berth. Slowly, majestically even, the ship turned away from the orbital and began maneuvering to begin the long climb out of the Betrus gravity well.

The whole process of coming about, firing up the kickers to move us out of the immediate vicinity of the orbital, and eventually extending the gravity keel and solar sail fields took three solid stans but it flashed by in a heartbeat. I didn't have time to think of all the people waiting it out in the galley or in Environmental or anywhere else. Here, we sailed the ship. I could sense from the pace on the bridge when we were about to shift to normal operations and secure the navigation detail. It was as obvious and inevitable as the arc of a tossed ball. All the pieces came together, more and more of them locking down, until there was only one and then that, too, merged, when the captain said, "Make the announcement, Mr. Pa. Secure from navigation detail, set normal operations, first section has the watch."

"Secure from navigation detail, set normal operations, first section has the watch. Aye, aye, Captain."

"Log it at 2353-June-18, 1635, Mr. Maxwell."

"So logged, Captain."

"Good work, people," she said. She stood and left the bridge.

I looked over to where Mr. von Ickles watched me, a little smile on his face.

"So? Was it good for you?" he asked.

It was all I could do to not burst out laughing. "Yes, sar. That was something."

"They say you always remember your first time."

"I can see why, sar." I chuckled. "Whew."

"Well, you've got time to shower and get a run in before dinner. We're off until mid-watch. Come up here then and I'll work with you on the console and show you some things. We've got the afternoon tomorrow and you can work on the *uh-oh* box then."

"Sounds good, sar."

The next few days flew by in a blur as I attempted to find my way in the new environment. Putting together the portable was easy enough, right up to the point where we had to power it up. Mr. von Ickles found where I reversed a jumper clip on the main board. After fixing that, we were up and running. We used the basic ShipNet code that I had modified before and loaded it on the portable's drive so that it fired up as soon as the machine booted. We were as close as we could be to being ready, without actually taking down the ship's network to test it.

"I think we should wait until we're docked for that, okay?" Mr. von Ickles said with a laugh.

"Good idea." I rubbed my chin thoughtfully. "Sar? I have another idea, but I don't know how practical it is."

"What's that, Mr. Wang?" he asked.

"Could we build a spare main cage? Keep it powered down in a grounded locker. That way if we need it, we can just pull the old cage and load the new one up without playing poker with the damaged cards."

"Spare cage?"

"Yes, sar. The cage is on sliders. If we have a spare one built, we just lift the burnt one out, plug the new one in, and we're up and running. That's the majority of the repairs that we had to do last time. We'd still have to track down the odd board here and there on the other racks, but that wouldn't take much time compared to rebuilding the cage like we did."

He looked at me, blinking mechanically as he processed what I was saying. "So elegantly simple," he said. "We take the initial load with the *uh-oh* box, swap the cage, and replace the burnt boards. Voila!"

"Yes, sar."

He thought about it for about a tick, before saying, "We have a spare cage, but only one. Let's hold that idea for when we get to Niol. I think I can convince the captain to buy a second one."

"Sounds like a plan, sar."

"In the meantime, let's rig up a grounded locker in Systems Main to store the *uh-oh* box in, and then get to work on solving the EMP problem."

It didn't take too long and soon we had settled in at a console.

"The first step is understanding what happened," Mr. von Ickles told me. "I want you to pull the system logs and give me a breakdown of everything that happened starting five ticks before the event." He sat beside me and demonstrated how to extract the logs for the time period in question. There was a lot of data and I knew it would keep me busy for a long time. He patted me on the shoulder as he headed out. I melted into the task and started digging in.

Fifteen days out of Betrus, I finally had a list of major events and took them to Mr. von Ickles.

"This makes no sense," he said.

"True, sar, but those are the facts as near as I can reconstruct from the systems logs."

"According to this, all that stuff burnt out after we were through the CME. Some of it as much as a full tick later."

"Yes, sar."

"Let's go see what Mr. Kelley has to say about this."

We headed on down to Mr. Kelley's office. I could see Mr. von Ickles running what I had showed him through his head. He was deep in thought and I didn't want to disturb him while we passed through the various passageways. When we presented it to Mr. Kelley he got that same confused expression.

"Are you sure?" he asked.

"That's what the logs say. These devices were recording data up to that point, sar," I told him. "They may have been recording longer but when the main hub went off line, a lot of the data collection packets would have been dropped."

"But, Mr. Wang, this says the hub was online half a tick after the main generators were blown down. At the velocity we were traveling, the whole event should have been over in less than half a second."

"Yes, sar. And I recovered the logs from local data storage aft. Some of those controllers didn't toast out until a full tick after the event."

He held the list and looked at it for a long time, then looked at Mr. von Ickles. "Can you give me a simulation showing the locations by time for when these died?"

"Sure thing, Fred. You think it's significant?"

"Maybe. What I'm seeing here is that we failed from stern to bow and back to stern." He pointed to a reading. "This unit is in the stern, it's one of the first ones that fried. I would have expected to lose one of these up in the bow first. Like this environmental sensor package here." He pointed again. "This time stamp says we lost it almost fifteen seconds later. The main data hub blew after that, and then we really started losing things in a cascade all the way back to the engine room."

"Does that mean what I think, Fred?" Mr. von Ickles asked.

"If you're thinking that the damage wasn't caused by the EMP, then yes."

"Mr. Wang, can you put together a graphic display of this data? I think Mr. Kelley and I need to talk to the captain."

It took a couple more watches, but I finally got a display I was happy with. When played back at one-tenth speed every second of real time was on the display for ten seconds. The pattern was unmistakable. Just as Mr. Kelley had picked out from the raw data, the failures started in the stern, worked forward, and then aft again.

Something about the pattern bothered me, but I couldn't put my finger on what that was. I turned the simulation over to Mr. von Ickles and Mr. Kelley and let them worry about it awhile. In the meantime I set about learning my way around the ship's systems.

Twenty-six days out of Betrus, we jumped into Niol. Any idea I had had that the transition would look differently from the bridge than it felt in the galley was quickly eradicated. Unlike getting underway, transition was as simple as if someone had changed the channel on the holo. One instant we were looking into one corner of the Deep Dark, and the next moment all the stars had moved and where it had been dark before, a brilliant dot of light marked the system's primary. Welcome to Niol.

While on morning watch three days after transition, I sat back in my seat on the bridge and took a deep breath. It felt like the first one I'd had since leaving Betrus Orbital. My calendar indicated I had nine days until the next exam period but the opportunity to study had been limited to my off-duty hours. Between building the *uh-oh* box, wading hip deep in data logs, and working through the timed display, the first three weeks of the voyage had disappeared as if they had been sucked into the Deep Dark. For ten days I had been crawling through the virtual ship on my hands and knees—in some cases it required a literal trip as well. Mr. von Ickles had me tracking data runs to see how the physical components formed the web of information that kept the *Lois* safe, moving, and on course. He also had me doing the routine data management tasks, like backing up the systems and rotating log files.

The systems were amazing. I never really thought I knew all that much about computers, networks, and the like, but when I tried to talk to people—like Pip or even Brill—their faces would glaze over faster than when Francis started talking about charged particles. Speaking of Francis, he was spending a lot of time lately with Mr. Kelley, Mr. Maxwell, and the captain as I'm sure they were tapping his knowledge of astrophysics to try to explain what had happened to the ship. Trying to make sense of the data model had proved to be quite the puzzle. All of the officers and most of the people in the Engineering Division were trying to figure it out.

Looking around the bridge, I saw Mr. von Ickles had just finished his last log entry in preparation to turn over the watch to Mr. Maxwell. Noon approached quickly and my stomach grumbled at the delay. I stood up, stretched, shook out my legs, and arched my back to get some of the kinks out. I had been so absorbed in the systems work that I had hardly moved, and yet I was soaked in sweat as if I'd run five kilometers. Mr. von Ickles teased me about my ability to get so absorbed. "In the zone," he called it.

While waiting for the watch change, I walked to the front of the bridge and looked out the forward port. The bright spot that had been dead ahead when we jumped in had shifted a bit as we lined up for the spot where Niol would be when we got there in about four weeks. Some of the spots out there were planets and some were stars, but I wasn't a good enough astronomer to tell them apart. Behind me I heard Mr. Maxwell say, "I relieve you, Mr. von Ickles. I have the watch." All around the bridge the rest of first section relayed the same message to their respective counterparts at helm, astrogation, and engineering.

I nodded toward Bev, who looked much better than she had at Betrus. She flashed me a warm smile in return as she settled into her routine at the helm. Mr. von Ickles waited for me at the ladder and I hurried to join him as my stomach gave another growl, reminding me how long it had been since I had eaten. The sounded like "January."

Even Mr. von Ickles heard it and laughed. "Not eating enough, Mr. Wang?"

"Doesn't seem possible that I'd be so hungry from just sitting there, but I seem to be burning calories somewhere."

"I'll see about getting you a water-cooled helmet," he said. "To keep your brain from melting."

He peeled off at officer country to go wash up in his stateroom while I continued down to deck berthing. Hungry as I was, I really wanted to at least sluice the sweat off my face and hands before eating, and I got to the mess deck later than the crowd as a result. That worked in my favor because the line was short, and I could load up my plate without feeling guilty about not leaving enough for the people behind me. The menu included steamed fish with a spicy red sauce, rice, and some banapods. Sarah and Pip always had a smile for me as I went through the line but I couldn't remember the last time I had a good sit-down chat with Pip. We hadn't even had a chance to pick a trade cargo while in Betrus, despite having been there for almost nine full days. Sarah still looked like she fit well in the galley, but Pip looked more out of place every time I saw him.

The down side of being late to lunch was finding a place to sit. I lucked out and spotted an empty spot beside Brill, who sat with Diane and Francis. I made a beeline for it. CC wasn't there, so I figured he must have the watch.

"Hi!" I said as I plopped down, after getting no response and seeing their faces, I added, "What's wrong?"

Diane said, "Guess."

"One letter, repeated?" I asked.

They nodded in unison.

Brill said, "Give us some good news? Do you know if we can fire him?"

I shrugged. "I haven't heard anything. There should be some information waiting for us in Niol when we pick up the beacon."

Francis asked, "What's the word on the electrical failures?"

"Well, it wasn't the EMP—the charged particle field part—that blew out the systems like we thought. Nobody has any more ideas now than when we were at Betrus. Less really, because then we thought we knew why and how. Now we have tons of data that disputes our original theory, but none of it makes any sense."

Brill said, "It's been driving Fred Kelley crazy. The Power team is tearing the ship apart trying to solve the mystery."

Diane asked, "So, you're adjusting to life on the bridge?"

I snorted. "As much as can be expected, I suppose. I'm not sure why I'm up there, to tell you the truth. I could work anywhere there's a console."

Francis said, "Mr. von Ickles is too smart to let you float around loose. He wants to keep you where he can see you."

We all laughed. "I'm actually glad to be there. It's not like I have a lot of interaction with the gang on watch up there, but Mr. von Ickles keeps me on my toes. I suspect watch might be pretty nasty if I were back in the auxiliary bridge all the time."

"A lot like being down in Environmental, huh?" Diane teased.

"Well, not quite that bad," I said.

"Sludge monkey," she said, and grinned.

We all fell quiet then. I ate while they picked at the remains of their lunches. Nobody seemed in any hurry to get up.

"So, what's up with CC?" I asked at last.

Brill said, "Same old tricks. We got on him for not doing maintenance but logging it was done, so now he's back to not doing it. I've written him up, docked his pay, everything short of taking him by the hand—"

"Or ear!" Diane broke in.

Brill chuckled. "Or ear and dragging him to do the work. I'm at my wit's end. I can't punish him any more than I have, other than putting him ashore. He seems totally impervious to any threat or disciplinary action. We can't flog him." She shrugged. "Even Mr. Kelley doesn't know what to do."

"Do we need to find a spanner?" I asked.

Brill snorted. "You know, when you said that back on Betrus I thought you were way off base, but having tried to deal with this chuckle-head for the last month, I'm a lot closer to dropping him out a airlock that I ever thought I could be."

"Well, let me go see what I can uncover," I said.

We drifted our separate ways after lunch. Brill wanted to check in on CC and Diane tagged along. Francis and I headed toward berthing. I was pretty sure I'd see him later in the afternoon in the gym. I headed for my bunk and started reviewing the cargoman and messman practice exams again. I hadn't been giving them a lot of attention but after a couple of stans I fell back in the groove again. I dropped a calendar note to Mr. von Ickles to reserve a seat for my last two full share exams for the next cycle.

The chrono said 1500 so I had three stans before I needed to get back on watch. I set my tablet to wake me at 1630 and lay on my bunk to grab some sleep while I could. I left enough time to get in a run and a sauna before watch.

When I headed up the ladder to the bridge at 1745, it was the first time since Betrus that I didn't have a list of tasks waiting for me. I felt loose and alert from my run and sauna—almost relaxed. I sat down at the console and started running through the system inventories. Status was good, no backups were scheduled, and the log file rollover would happen automatically after midnight. I just needed to snag them in the morning and burn them to a cube for archiving.

I found myself looking at the time delayed graphic showing the cascade of sparks starting in the stern, running in a stream to the bow and then cascading back again. I could not shake the feeling that there was something there, but I just couldn't see it.

Mr. von Ickles saw the display and came to look over my shoulder. "Maddening, isn't it?" he asked.

"Yes, sar, it is. I'm missing something. I just don't know what that something is."

"Well, if you knew, then it wouldn't be missing would it?" he asked with a grin.

"Speaking of maddening," I said without turning my head. "Our friend in Environmental is being resistant to efforts to modify his behavior to something approaching adequate."

"I've heard that as well. There's a lot of discussion in various places, but so far nobody has got any ideas. We're still weeks from getting the orbital beacon so all we can do is keep an eye on him."

"There wasn't anything in the medical records?" I asked.

"Nothing damning. Blunt trauma to the back of the head."

"He's not responding to any of the normal disciplinary actions. Are there any abnormal techniques you can think of?" I asked.

"Nothing that won't get us fired. He may be immune, although we haven't established that yet," Mr. von Ickles observed. "On the other hand, we are not."

"Well, I know one crewman who can't be fired."

"Besides our friend?" he asked. "Who?"

"Lois," I said.

He stood there silently mulling that over for a couple of ticks while we watched the looping graphic. "How does that help us?"

"I don't know, but if normal methods don't work, maybe we need to try magic."

"Mr. Wang, you may be more devious than even Mr. Maxwell," he said.

"Thank you, Mr. von Ickles. I'll take that as a compliment."

"It is, Mr. Wang. It is." He sighed. "Now if you can use your magic to figure out what caused that," he said, pointing to the cycling display. "I'll believe you're more devious than the captain."

"Why would that be devious, sar?"

"Because every attempt at logical explanations has failed. The answer has to be something either heinously devious or pathetically simple."

"Well, when it comes to simple, I'm your man, sar," I assured him.

He snorted. "You are many things, Mr. Wang, but simple is hardly one of them." He clapped me on the shoulder and went back to astrogation to check our position.

Lois? I thought. *What are you playing at?*

CHAPTER NINETEEN
NIOL SYSTEM: 2352-JULY-30

We were still over two weeks out of Niol when the next round of exams came up. Mr. von Ickles teased me unmercifully for the whole week prior, but on the mid-watch before my steward exam he offered to let me have some time off to study. I didn't need it, so I went back to working through the systems inventories and thinking about the system failure.

Trying to unravel the mystery made me think about some detective guy mom had always talked about, Hemlock somebody. He had used a phrase that went something like, "When you've ruled out the probable, then the improbable, no matter how impossible, is the only solution left." I remembered reading his stories, but I preferred Shakespeare, who had more sex. Hemlock just had a violin, a sidekick named Watson, and his disguises. One story he even passed as a woman. Well, Shakespeare did that a lot, too, and suddenly it came to me. I knew how we could make an impression on Mr. Charles Colby. I spent the rest of the watch making notes on my tablet.

As we headed down the ladder from the bridge, Mr. von Ickles asked, "Last minute studying?"

"I had a breakthrough on one of two problems," I said.

"Do I want to know?"

"If you don't mind, sar, I think you'd prefer to have the ability to deny any knowledge."

"I appreciate that, Mr. Wang," he said with a smile. "And now that we've established that you've refused to tell me your plans, perhaps you might fill me in on some of the details I'm not supposed to know?"

I went over the basic concept and he offered some enhancements that I wouldn't have considered. In the end he said, "You may be the most deviously disturbed individual I have ever met, Mr. Wang. It's an honor to know you."

"Thank you, Mr. von Ickles. I do try. And may I say, sar, you're no slouch yourself."

"You're very welcome. And may I add how pleased I am to have you on my watch?"

"Because of my skill and native wit, sar?"

"No, Mr. Wang, because I feel the sudden need to keep you under close observation."

"Thank you again, sar."

"You're quite welcome, Mr. Wang. Carry on."

"Yes, sar. Thank you, sar. I'll see you in the office after break-fast, sar."

I hurried off to the mess deck and managed to pull Brill aside.

"I'm ready to kill him myself," she said without preamble.

"If you do that, you'll have to stand his watch," I said.

She laughed. "It would be worth it! At least I'd know he's not going to poison the ship."

"You willing to try magic?"

"I'm willing to try anything!" she said, then gave me a funny look. "Wait. Magic?"

"In a way. I'll explain more later. We have a lot of setup work to do. We'll only get one shot, so it has to be good."

"You have that look in your eye, Ishmael," she said with a grin. "I think I'm going to like this."

"Okay, the hard part is going to be backing off on him," I said.

"You can't expect me to ignore him!" she objected.

"Oh, I didn't say ignore him. Just give him enough rope." I outlined the plan quickly and her face went from frown, to disbelief, to amusement.

"All right, I'm in," she said. "But if this doesn't work, can I kill him?"

"If this doesn't work we may need to, but let's save that as a last resort, shall we? Death is so final."

I gobbled my way through two plates of scrambled eggs and sausage, four biscuits, and three cups of coffee. The meal was delicious, and I began to feel like maybe things were beginning to come together.

Trust Lois, I thought, then laughed out loud. Biddy Murphy and Rhon Scham were at my table and looked at me with a bit of concern. "Mid-watch," I said. "Just a little punchy this morning. Sorry."

They nodded and I excused myself to go take the messman exam.

I was the only person taking any steward exams that day—no surprise there—so Mr. von Ickles met me in the office at 0715. I finished by 0830 and he shook his head in amazement. "You're slipping, Mr. Wang. Only a ninety-two on that one."

"I'm distracted this morning, sar, and tired after a long night of plotting."

"I can understand that perfectly well, Mr. Wang. I'll see you on the bridge this afternoon. Try to get some sleep."

"You, too, sar. And thanks."

"You're welcome, Mr. Wang. See you in a bit."

My brain boiled over with ideas. I was afraid I might not be able to sleep—for about forty-five seconds. I was glad I had set my tablet to wake me in time for a run and a sauna before watch. As I ran, I looked around for the right accomplice. It had to be somebody with just the right tone. Somebody who could make CC believe.

I knew exactly who it should be.

The afternoon watch went quickly. I spent it laying the groundwork for my little magic show. The systems console gave me access to all the pieces I needed and Mr. von Ickles even showed me some tricks that I wouldn't have thought of. He had his own brand of sneaky that I grew to admire. CC would have the evening watch and then he'd be off for twenty-four. When he came back on duty, life was going to become very interesting for Mr. Charles Colby.

When watch ended I headed for supper. Going through the mess line, I saw Pip and Sarah.

"Hey, guys, you're just the people I wanted to see. I've got a little favor to ask."

"Anything, Ish," Pip said.

Sarah just nodded.

"I'll be back after mess. I need some help with a project."

They shrugged and looked puzzled, but I had to move along to keep from blocking the mess line.

Brill had Diane and Francis sitting off to one side and I went to join them.

"Okay," I said. "I got the systems work done today, and I think we have our voice talent lined up. We can test it tomorrow while he's off. All I'm missing is the guest of honor, but we have a few days to find her. We've got almost two weeks before we pull into Niol. If we can't do it in that amount of time, it won't happen at all."

Francis said, "I made sure he knows about the pooka. He was already familiar with the concept, but I made a joke about seeing her walking the passages in the middle of the night."

I grinned. "Excellent. We just have to play it loose. His warped brain will do the rest."

"Diane," I said to her, "you're going to be playing the receptive ear on the back side of the watch. It's up to you to keep him off balance. It's going to be hard because he's going to be suspicious that it's a set up. We have to convince him that we think she doesn't exist."

Brill touched my arm to get my attention and leaned in close to my ear. "Ish, Lois doesn't exist."

"Perfect!" I said with a grin. "You could almost convince me."

They each wore a similar little worried expression as they stared back at me. I just laughed and finished my dinner. "If you'll excuse me, I need to go write some scripts for tonight's recording."

By 2030 I had all I needed and I headed to meet Pip and Sarah. I found them sweeping and swabbing down the galley. I checked the mess deck to make sure we wouldn't be overheard.

"Okay, guys, we have a little problem and I need some help," I said. I grabbed a broom and helped them sweep while I explained the situation with CC. "So, we've tried everything and nothing is working. I think Lois wants us to help him understand the danger he's putting the ship in by not doing his job."

Pip says, "Okay, Ish, you know you're—"

"Yes, yes, I know. The point is we need to give Lois a voice to tell him how much he's hurting her."

We finished sweeping and Sarah stood with her arms folded tightly under her breasts. "You want me to be Lois's voice?"

"Yes. Lois has helped you already, and it's time for you to help the next person in line. You're a shaman. Healing is your specialty and we need to heal Charles."

Pip looked at me like I had lost what few marbles he credited me with, but I didn't care. Sarah had the voice and believed she was a shaman. I knew she thought that the ship had helped her. She'd be able to sell it like nobody else aboard, but I needed her to believe.

Sarah on the other hand examined my face. I didn't know what she was looking for, but I made myself as open to her as I could. "You want to scare him," she said.

"I want him to understand that he's hurting Lois. We've tried other ways to make him understand, and now I want Lois to tell him directly."

"Why not ask Lois to tell him, then?" she asked me. "Why have me *pretend* to be Lois?"

"Because I don't think he can hear her like you and I do. I can't do it because he wouldn't believe a man's voice."

"You want me to speak for Lois?"

"Yes, I want you to be Lois's voice. Tell him how he hurts her so he can hear it for himself."

"What do you want me to do?" Pip asked.

"Keep watch. I don't wanna be caught making the recordings."

He grinned. "You're serious."

I nodded. "I've already rigged the speakers in Environmental, and tomorrow Francis and I are going to mount a few more with some special controllers on them. By the time he comes back on the mid-watch tomorrow night, Environmental will be wired for sound."

"Where do you want to record?" he asked.

"Here in the galley, where I can get a little echo."

"Are you up for this, Sarah?"

"Yes."

Pip headed out to the passage and kept an eye open, while I settled down with Sarah and my tablet. We recorded Lois's pain for about half a stan before Pip gave us a sign and we stopped recording. Sean Grishan came into the galley, got a cup of coffee and a cookie, and left.

Sarah said, "That's enough for now."

"Are you okay with this?" I asked her. "I'll delete it right now if you're not."

She smiled. "It will be fine. Thank you."

She turned then and walked out of the mess deck.

Pip stood there shaking his head. "She's still a little odd."

"Pip?" I said.

"What?"

"We all are."

He considered that for a moment, before nodding in agreement. His face broke into a grin. "I wish I could be a fly on that wall."

We both chuckled. "Come on, I heard there's a gym on this ship. Let's go check it out."

He slugged me on the arm. "You are never going to let me forget that, are you?"

"Never!" I said, and slugged him back.

The watch stander didn't have to do much to get me moving in the morning. I was anxious to get up to the bridge and start cutting up the audio. I had the normal daily stuff to deal with first—backups, securing the logs, checking for systems problems. I had all that finished by 0800 and pulled Sarah's audio off my tablet.

Mr. von Ickles showed me how to mount the headset so I could listen and edit without disturbing the bridge crew. By the time I got done clipping, cutting, splicing, and arranging, the watch was almost over and I had expanded the half a stan of recording into almost two stans of Lois in pain. About half way through Mr. von Ickles came to listen to some of it.

"Who's the voice?" he asked.

"Sarah Krugg."

"She's good," he said. "You think she sounds a little too real?"

"Too much like Lois?"

"No, too much like a person." He took my tablet over to the air vent and recorded almost a full tick of blower sounds. "Here, load that."

When I finished, he showed me how to mix the voice and ventilation noise together so it sounded like the blower was speaking. Even though I knew how it was put together, it still made the hair on my arms stand up. I tried to imagine what it would sound like down in the Environmental Section late in the watch with nobody else around.

"Sar?" I said.

"Yes, Mr. Wang."

"You think I'm disturbed, then you come up with that? Well, sar, you bested me."

"Thank you, Mr. Wang. I like you too."

The watch changed just as I finished the audio editing. I had just enough time to load it to the storage space I had prepared in Brill's system account before heading down to the galley for lunch before I needed to report to the office for my last full share exam.

When I got to the mess deck, I found CC there with the rest of the environmental team so I just gave Brill a nod and a wink and sat with my bunkies, Art James and David ben Dour—good guys, both of them. Art wasn't the brightest bulb in the overhead, but he had more heart than any three professors I had known back on Neris—Mom excluded, of course. David was good natured and moved from moment to moment without letting any problems he ran into bother him too much as they passed.

Lunch was my favorite chicken and pasta dish, and I enjoyed it so much I went back for seconds. When Cookie saw me he beamed from the back of the galley, and I gave him a nod and a thumbs up for the meal. He took such good care of us.

At 1330 I presented myself at the office and found Mr. von Ickles waiting with a funny grin. He offered no explanation for his expression, and set me right to work on the cargoman exam, which would round out my complete collection of full share ratings. Knowing it was the last one I'd be doing for a while, I sank into it and just let the experience unfold. When I surfaced at around 1500, I looked up at him with a grin. "How'd I do?"

"You missed two," he said, and turned the screen around so I could see the score.

Behind me, the room erupted in applause, which startled me so much I almost fell off my chair. I turned around and found the captain, Ms. Avril, Mr. Kelley, Mr. Cotton, and Brill standing just inside the door. From the sounds of things the passageway outside was full as well. There was clapping and cheering. It was crazy.

When the ruckus finally died down, the captain said, "Mr. Maxwell is on watch, but sends his regards as well. It's not every spacer who sets himself on the path of becoming full share rated in every division. Those that do usually live to regret it." She smiled and looked very proud. I knew, of course, that she and Mr. Maxwell were the only other people on the ship to have a full set of ratings. I felt like I was in pretty good company. "Congratulations, Mr. Wang, and happy birthday."

Everybody had to shake my hand and wish me well. It got to be quite a scene. When they finally cleared out, it was just Mr. von Ickles and me.

"You set that up, didn't you, sar." I said.

"Yes, Mr. Wang. I did."

"Thank you, sar. Now, if you'll excuse me, sar? I need to see a woman about a pooka."

"Dismissed, Mr. Wang," he said, then he smiled and held out his hand. "Congratulations, Ishmael. Happy birthday."

"Thanks," I said, and shook his hand.

Rigging the extra speakers didn't take long with Francis and I working together. I showed Brill where and how to trigger the audio. I had created three programs for her to use. The first was a few seconds of Sarah's quiet sobbing in various permutations. The crying faded in and out over the course of a full stan and I rigged the playback so that it would run on a random cycle. The second was a collection of *please-stop-you-are-hurting-mes* again, in various permutations from very faint to a bit louder, but none were very loud. The last was a mix of the sobs with the *please-stops* interspersed. The volume range on this third one was medium to loud. I had her play a few snippets of each to test them out and both Diane and Francis looked a little shaken by the experience.

"My gods, Ishmael," Diane said. "That's positively frightful. Are you trying to scare him to death?"

I shook my head. "Just trying to put the fear of Lois in him. I was going to add some threats, but I thought the pitiful sobbing would work just as well, especially as it gets louder."

By then it was time for me to hit the track and get my sauna in before the evening watch. Mr. Colby would be meeting the pooka at the best possible time to make a lasting impression: mid-watch in the Deep Dark.

The plan had been to let the sobbing run for about a week, just to soften him up. Then start the second tier with the *please-stops*. We hadn't counted on the effectiveness of Sarah's voice. After a couple of days with the sobbing fading in and out during his watch standing hours, CC started to look a little less sure of himself when he showed up on the mess deck. I don't know exactly when it started, but after about four days, I noticed Sarah would lean over to CC and say something to him whenever he was in the mess line. Pip, who stood beside her, grinned. Whatever it was, it spooked CC even more. I made a mental note to ask Pip what Sarah had said.

While the Environmental haunting went on, I went back to trying to find the problem that had crashed ShipNet and almost killed us.

What I needed was more information because what I had from the logs wasn't much help. A week and a half out of Niol, I went to find Rebecca Saltzman in Engineering berthing.

Mitch grinned and Rebecca smiled when I stuck my head into

my old quad. "You lost?" Mitch asked.

"Well yeah, in a way," I told them. "I'm working on the system failure. Can you two look at something and tell me what I'm missing?"

They both shrugged. "I'll look at anything you wanna show me, big fella," Rebecca said in that heavy-G growl of hers. She had a big grin on her face because she knew what that voice did to me.

"Behave!" I told her with a laugh. "I'm trying to work here."

"Sorry," she said, but she didn't look that way.

Mitch just sighed and shook his head.

I played them the delayed graphic on my tablet a couple of times.

Rebecca watched intently and said, "I've seen this. Mr. Kelley watches it over and over."

"Him and every other officer on the ship. We're missing something obvious."

"Why obvious?" she asked.

"Because as devious as the officers of the *Lois* are, they'd have spotted something tricky by now."

"What is it supposed to be showing?" Mitch asked.

"Those are all the component failures from five ticks before we went through the EMP," I said. "I plotted them by location and time. I expanded the time scale so every tenth of a second real time is one second on the display."

"That's why it seems so slow," he said, nodding to himself.

Rebecca and I looked at each other. Rebecca shrugged.

"Yes, Mitch, that's right," I said. "That's why it seems so slow."

"Play it again?" he asked.

I shrugged and keyed it.

"So this is what broke?" he asked after it had run its cycle again.

"Yup. Do you see anything?"

He shook his head. "Nope." He laid back down on his bunk.

Rebecca shook her head helplessly. "I don't know what to tell you, Ish. I didn't spot anything either."

"Thanks, guys. I appreciate your time."

Mitch grinned at me. "No problem, Ish. You sure you won't move back?" He nodded at Rebecca. "She's been moping around since you left and asking me if I have any blue jeans. What's that about?"

Rebecca threw her pillow at him, blushing and giggling. For his part, Mitch had a mischievous look and tucked her pillow behind his head.

We all had a good chuckle, even Rebecca. "Any time you want

to move back, Ish. You can sleep *on top of me!*" she said and stuck her tongue out at Mitch.

"Rebecca!" Mitch snorted.

"What?" She pointed to the unclaimed upper bunk above her. "Up there! You've got a dirty mind, Fitzroy."

Jennifer Agotto, one of the machinists from the Power section, spoke from the other side of the partition, "Well, he didn't have one when he moved in here, ya hussy. You're the one that got it all dirty!"

We all had another laugh. I think Rebecca laughed hardest of all.

I was about to leave when Mitch said, "That's only the stuff that failed, right?"

"Yeah," I said, "why?"

"Well what about the stuff that didn't fail? If you add that in somehow, maybe it'll tell you something."

Rebecca looked at him like he had sprouted a second head. "How can you tag something that didn't happen?" she asked him.

He shrugged. "I don't know, but when we started getting Ship-Net back online, lots of systems were just waiting to be powered up. They weren't damaged at all."

I thought about that for a full tick. "Thanks, Mitch. You're on to something there."

Rebecca looked startled. "He is?"

"Yeah. I just don't know what, or how, but it's something to try besides just running the same clip over and over."

I took that idea with me to the bridge for that afternoon's watch and started going back through the logs.

We were about a week out of Niol when I went to lunch and saw Brill, Diane, and Francis all grinning. Smiling in anticipation, I got my lunch and joined them.

"What's the cause of this joyous gathering?" I asked.

Brill said quietly, "Mr. Colby did his maintenance last night."

Diane added just as quietly, "And did a first rate job of it too."

"Excellent. You should probably kill the sob-track for tonight," I said.

Brill nodded. "Already done."

"Think it'll stick?" Francis asked.

"Hard to say, but you can always turn it on again."

Just then CC came through the mess line. He looked horrible, like he hadn't slept in a week. His shipsuit had a big smear of something on it that could have been almost anything. I wasn't sure I wanted to know. He seemed almost afraid of Sarah as he approached the line and, sure enough, Sarah leaned forward and said something to him. Pip's expression changed from a big smile to confusion when CC smiled and thanked her before moving on down the line.

"What was that?" I wondered aloud.

Brill had seen it too. "I don't know but it looked strange."

I got up and went for coffee, swinging by to have a quiet word with Pip. Then I came back to the table and sat down. "Well, I think perhaps it might stick."

"What'd she say?" Francis asked.

"Pip said that for the past few days she's been saying things like, 'Remember Matthew.'"

"Remember Matthew?" Diane asked, then comprehension dawned. "Wasn't he on the *Matthew Boulton*?"

Brill and I both said, "Yup," at the same time.

"How did she know he was on the *Matthew Boulton*." Diane asked.

"I don't know. Maybe she overheard it. It's not a secret."

Brill asked, "So, what did she say today?"

"According to Pip she said, 'Lois thanks you.'"

We all just sat there and ate our meals in silence for a long while.

At one point, Brill said to me, "That girl is spookier than you are."

Diane looked at me for a long time before turning back to Brill. "I think it's a draw," she said.

Chapter Twenty-one
Niol System: 2352-August-15

Those last few days on approach to Niol were both spectacular and frustrating. It seemed like we zoomed in on the planet in a matter of stans and then just hung out there, inching in for days on end. It really wasn't that long, but it seemed it. It had been a long trip from Betrus—eight weeks—and we were all ready to get ashore again. The image of Wendy wearing nothing but a satisfied grin and a sheen of sweat kept popping into my brain at odd, and often unfortunate, moments.

Third section had the mid-watch before docking. I had been wrestling with what Mitch had suggested for a week without making any progress. About halfway through the watch, I stood and walked to the bow to look at the orbital creeping in. We would dock before the day was out and after eight weeks of analysis, I was no closer to understanding *what* had happened, let alone *how*. Sure, we knew the outcome. We had plenty of burned boards and some crisped out electrical runs, too, but those were just the symptoms. We needed to know what caused that burning and for that we had no idea.

"Problems, Mr. Wang?" Mr. von Ickles said from behind me.

I turned and rested my elbows on the port combing behind me. "How do you mark that something didn't happen, sar?"

He blinked. "You can't," he said after a moment's consideration. "Absence of evidence is not evidence of absence. Logical rule from the dark ages. What are you trying to do?"

"This systems problem, sar. We've been gnawing on it for weeks."

"Yup," he agreed. "Any insight?"

"I've been thinking that the answer has to be something obvious, sar."

"Why?" he asked.

"The four most devious minds in this end of the galaxy haven't spotted anything tricky, sar."

"You make a good point," he said with a considering tone. "But don't underestimate yourself. I hear the maintenance schedule is back on track in Environmental."

"Remind me to tell you more about that because I don't think I can take the credit, sar."

"Okay," he said, and startled me by taking out his tablet and actually making a note. "Back to the problem at hand. Why does it have to be something obvious?"

"Well, if it's not something tricky? What's left, sar?"

"Well, that's obvious."

"You see my point, then, sar." I smiled and continued. "Well, the first thing that occurred to me was that, if the data weren't telling us what we needed to know then we either had too much, too little, or the wrong data."

"Obviously," he said warming to the discussion.

"So I took the graphic down to Engineering berthing to ask Rebecca Saltzman if she saw anything missing, sar."

"Did she?"

"No, sar, but Mitch Fitzroy was there and he made an interesting observation."

"Mitch?" he asked with a raised eyebrow.

"Yeah, don't sell him short. He may have the answer, if we can just figure out how to look at it, sar."

"Are you going to keep stringing me along, Mr. Wang? The watch will be over in a couple of stans and I was kinda hoping to find out how this story ends before then."

"Mitch pointed out that the graphic only shows what failed, sar."

He nodded for me to continue.

"He suggested we should look at what didn't fail."

Mr. von Ickles went absolutely still—like a freeze framed holo. I don't think he even blinked or breathed for almost a tick. "Obviously," he said at last.

I shrugged. "You see my dilemma, sar."

"How to track what didn't fail."

"Yes, sar."

"What an interesting observation. What was his rationale for that? Did he say?"

"Mitch, sar? He said something like, 'When we started bringing up ShipNet, lots of stuff was just waiting for us to power it back up. Maybe you should look at what didn't fail.' I can't be sure of his exact words, but that's the gist of it."

"He's right," Mr. von Ickles said. "And it is obvious," he added with a grin.

I saw it then, or rather heard it as I played back in my brain what I had just said, *waiting for us to power it back up.*

Mr. von Ickles must have seen the revelation spread across my face. "Exactly, Mr. Wang."

"Obviously, Mr. von Ickles."

I started digging through the logs again—just as before, there was a lot of data.

First section relieved us on time and we grabbed breakfast before setting navigation detail. I saw Mr. von Ickles having a conversation with Mr. Maxwell, Mr. Kelley, and the captain. At one point, Mr. Kelley said "Mitch?" in disbelief so I knew what they were talking about. While they chatted, I brought up the systems schematic and started monitoring the communications traffic the way Mr. von Ickles had shown me on the way out of Betrus. Eight weeks of watches with my head in the console—sometimes literally—had been an education in its own right. I knew I had a knack for dealing with what my mother had called, "the damn devil box" but working with Mr. von Ickles had shown me new levels that I had not known existed. I sucked it up like a sponge. It was hard work, but it was fun as well. I rather enjoyed the idea of being paid to play.

There was the same kind of performance on the bridge on docking as there had been when we set out. This time it played out in reverse as we furled the sails, retracted the grav keel, and shut down systems. The kickers came online and nudged us to where the tugs could guide us in. Eventually, the nose of the *Lois* just kissed the docking ring and the locking clamps snapped down to make us part of the structure of the station itself. It seemed like such a delicate grasp to hold the mass of the ship and cargo but it did the job. Finally, we secured the final systems and switched to station power. The ship came to rest.

"Make the announcement, Mr. Pa," the captain said. "Secure from navigation detail. First section has the watch."

She waited for Fong to finish before turning to her first mate. "You may declare liberty at your discretion, Mr. Maxwell."

"Thank you, Captain. Make the announcement, Mr. Pa."

Mr. von Ickles surprised me by stepping up to my station and saying, "I wonder if you would be able to meet me at the lock in about a stan, Mr. Wang? I have a little procurement problem I'd like your help with."

"Of course, sar." Frankly, I was a little disappointed. I'd been hoping to grab some bunk time before heading up to the flea market to see what Niol had to offer, but Mr. von Ickles was always good for a surprise.

Bev had the watch and checked us out with a sly grin. "You watch out for him, Mr. von Ickles."

"Oh?" he said. "Why is that, Ms. Arith?"

"You've been working with him for the last eight weeks and you have to ask, sar?"

"I see your point, Ms. Arith, and I'll take your warning under advisement."

I grabbed a shower, changed into civvies, and met him at the lock. As we reflected on Bev's comments we both were chuckling as we stepped out into the stinging cold of the docks. We headed for the lifts and I still had no idea what was up. "Excuse me, sar, but can I ask where we're going?"

"Lee," he said.

"Excuse me, sar?"

"Try, 'Excuse me, Lee,' Ishmael," he said. "We're off the ship and off-duty, so I think we can leave all that *sar* stuff at the lock, don't you?"

"I think we can, yes." For some reason I was inordinately pleased with this."

"After all, you didn't call Alicia Alvarez 'sar' when you were on station, did you?"

"Well, not in the bar," I replied.

"Not in the bar—" he began, and then stopped and looked at me. "You never cease to amaze me, Ishmael."

We'd reached the lift and got in. Mr. von Ickles—Lee—punched the oh-two button.

"We're going to purchase something down on the oh-two level?" I asked.

"Yep," he said with a grin.

After a moment, he turned to me and asked, "You called her sar?"

"Well, not in the bar."

The lift stopped on oh-two and we got off. It was mid afternoon station time, and my internal clock reeled in confusion, having been up all night for the mid-watch, and all morning with navigation detail. I was thinking that lunch sounded good, but station time would indicate something more like dinner.

I followed Lee around to port and he ducked into a quiet bar not terribly far from the lift. The sign over the door said: *Shaunessey's.* The interior was wrapped in dark wood—along with not-quite-leather. It looked good and I began to understand what Lee wanted help procuring.

We settled at a table and he ordered a small pitcher of a medium ale. "You don't mind helping me with this beer, do you?" he asked.

"It's kinda early in the day, isn't it?"

"Well, we've been working for the last ten stans, we're off-duty, and it's coming up on evening here. I think we've earned it," he said. "Your objection is based on what?"

"Since you put it that way, I guess it's based on nothing more than the artificial constraints of an arbitrary time frame."

"Exactly my point, Ishmael." The waitress brought the pitcher and Lee did the honors with a certain amount of flair and obvious expertise.

"You called her sar?" he asked again as he was pouring.

"Well, only when she gave me an order," I told him.

"When she gave you an order?" he shook his head and pushed a glass in my direction.

I shrugged. "She was quite demanding. I did my very best to comply."

"I bet you did, Ishmael." He raised his glass and toasted, "To satisfying demanding women!"

I tapped my glass to his and drank deeply. That was a toast I could get behind.

We settled back for what looked like would be a rather extensive session of procurement. "So, tell me what happened in Environmental?" he asked.

I filled him in while we finished the pitcher and ordered a second. He laughed at the part where Sarah reminded him about the *Matthew*.

"Did we ever get that packet from them, by the way?" I asked.

"You mean an answer from the *Boulton*?"

"Yeah, did they respond?"

Lee shrugged. "It was rather non-committal actually. They were having disciplinary problems with him and there had been a couple of close calls in Environmental. Basically what we ran into."

"But?" I prompted.

"But there was nothing in his personnel jacket—which we already knew—and their chief engineer just said that there was no evidence of foul play."

"Absence of evidence—" I began.

"Exactly."

"Did they try to fire him?" I asked.

"They were going to give him one more leg to shape up or ship out. Then he was injured, and he's been sponging off the company ever since."

"So much for my conspiracy theories."

"Maybe yes, maybe no," he said over the rim of his beer.

"Oh?" I asked and I really liked the *tell-me-more* quality of my reply. The practice was beginning to pay off.

"Well, there are no Colby's on the board or anything," he started.

"But?"

"His mother is Charlotte Colby of the New Farnouk Colby's?"

"Beyond Federated Freight's home office being on New Farnouk, that doesn't mean anything to me." I shrugged. "I'm a bumpkin, remember?"

"High society, VIP on the New Farnouk circuit," he said.

"I think I see where you're going."

"Ex-mistress of Alvin T. Merrick," he said.

"The Chairman of the Board of New Farnouk Development Corp, Alvin T. Merrick?" I asked.

"Small galaxy, huh?"

"Would he have interfered?"

Lee shrugged. "Dunno, but if he did get involved, it wouldn't be pretty."

"Merrick might not be his father," I pointed out.

"True," he agreed and sipped his beer, "but I'm still glad we don't have to find out."

"Amen!" I toasted. We clinked, drained, and put the glasses down.

He nodded and we stood up and headed back to the ship.

As we approached the lock he turned to me, "Thanks, Ish. I hate to drink alone."

"You're welcome, Lee. Any time I can help out with these little procurement issues of yours, please let me know. Next time, I'll buy."

He keyed the lock and said, almost admiringly, "You called her sar."

"It seemed only polite under the circumstances."

Chapter Twenty-two
Niol System: 2352-August-16

Third section had the day watch our second day in Niol. I used the time to finish the data extractions for the log entries on systems that had shut down cleanly. I had the new data plugged into the time-delay model by the end of the watch.

It was odd working on the bridge with the ship docked. I had gotten used to the dimness of the lighting while underway. When in port, the light reflecting off the orbital's bathed the area in a glaring illumination. It was rather thrilling to see the ships docked on either side of us. The dock to port had been empty when we had arrived but the *Josiah Wedgwood* occupied the next berth beyond. The *John C. Calhoun* rested to starboard and I smiled, remembering our last night in Dunsany Roads.

I wasn't alone on the bridge. Salina Matteo was on third section and her station was there as well. A short woman, she wore her hair longer than any spacer I ever met. Not that it was long, by any means, but when almost everybody else wore their hair in one close-trimmed configuration or another, her page-boy cut seemed very long by comparison. She had one of those smiles that peaked out and disappeared again, never lasting for long, but was thoroughly enchanting when displayed. She was also one of the older spacers in the crew. I thought she was nearly as old as Francis—probably in her middle forties—which put her, I realized with a shock, at the same age as my mother.

Salina had relieved second section by the time I got up there, since I stopped at the office to check in with Mr. von Ickles. She already had her ship status updates running for the next few legs of the trip and smiled a greeting. It was pleasant having the place to ourselves, each engaged in our own routines.

By noon I finally had all log transactions that recorded systems shutdown events extracted and loaded into my delayed time display. I flashed a copy of it down to Mr. von Ickles in the office before Salina and I went down to get some lunch.

Stepping onto the mess deck was more like the in-port mealtimes I had remembered than those we experienced the last few days at Betrus. Sarah had the duty in the galley and she was decorating an elaborate cake that I assumed would be dessert for dinner, since the lunch buffet already had one of Cookie's granapple cobblers on it. The crew had money and most were out spending it, leaving the mess deck practically deserted. It was comforting in a way, but also a bit troubling. An extra couple of days in-port made a big difference to so many of them. It seemed odd to me. Even ignoring the creds that Pip and I made trading I was never in danger of running out during our port stays. Most people must burn through a lot of creds.

I felt a little awkward eating with Salina since I really didn't know her very well. We had spent the morning together working in silence on the bridge, though, and we were the only ones on the mess deck, so it would have been rude to sit someplace else. She was easy to be with, even if we didn't talk much. Every once in a while she had one those little, flashing smiles.

"How are you coming on figuring out what went wrong?" she asked.

I shrugged. "We looked at the failed components for a couple of weeks. I finished adding the systems that shut down without failing just before we came down here. I'm not sure what that will tell us, but it's worth looking into."

"You'll find the answer—between you and Mr. von Ickles," she said with one of her little smiles.

"Don't forget Mr. Kelley, Mr. Maxwell, and the captain. They're all trying too."

"Oh, I wasn't discounting them, but they'll only be able to see what you and Mr. von Ickles show them. Then they'll need to interpret it."

"I wish I could think of what else we might need to know." I sighed.

Just then Mr. von Ickles popped into the mess deck, grabbed some food, and settled with us. "You guys mind if an officer sits with you?"

Salina considered him for a long moment. "It'll be okay, I think, sar," she said with a grin.

"Thank you, Ms Matteo," he replied with a little bow. "You are both generous and understanding."

"We were just talking about the latest iteration of the failure display," I told him. "Did you get a chance to see it?"

"Yup, and it's interesting. We were green, all green within a half second of the event," he said.

"What?" Salina asked. "How can that be?"

"The ship did exactly what it was supposed to do and protected itself when we hit the charged particle field. It was a huge charge, but the ship shut down everything the way it was supposed to."

"Well, then how did those components fail if they were shut down?" she asked.

"Excellent question," he said. "Ish?"

I could see where he was going with this. "I'll get right on it after lunch," I told him. "Silly not to have thought of it before. I could have grabbed all that data at once."

"I don't know," he said. "If you build this last bit into its own overlay, we'll have complete and separate graphics for proper shut down, the restarting, and the failures. If that doesn't show us something, then we're missing a lot more than I think. When we solve it, we should write it up and publish an article. This has been such a struggle."

"Wouldn't Mr. Kelley do that?" Salina asked.

"Oh, I'm sure he'll write up an engineering article, but I'm talking about the data visualization aspects," he said. "Maybe submit to *The Journal of Visual Data*."

"You're kidding, right?" I asked.

He shook his head. "Classic problem, innovative solutions. Timed displays have been around for as long as there have been moving pictures, but this is an interesting application of time-delay visualization of a complex system interaction. Somebody else might benefit from it."

"You sound like my mother," I said.

Salina chuckled. "I think your mother probably had a higher voice than that."

We all laughed at that, but I knew what I would be doing for the next couple of watches. "What did you do before you had me to slice and dice data for you, sar?"

"We didn't. Which is why, Mr. Wang, we made the case to home office to create this slot. We live and die by data analysis and if it's all the same to you, I'd rather skip the dying part."

We all raised our coffee mugs and toasted that.

"This afternoon, though, we have another little task. I got permission from the captain to test the *uh-oh* box at 1500."

"Excellent, sar!"

He turned to Salina and said, "So, Ms. Matteo? Wanna help

crash ShipNet?"

"How are we going to do that without destroying the ship?" she asked.

He grinned. "Very carefully, Ms. Matteo. Very carefully, indeed."

We finished lunch and all headed up to the bridge.

Mr. von Ickles brought up the main systems display on his console and we looked it over carefully.

He pointed out the key factors. "Main reactor/generators are off line while we're on shore power. All the heavy field generators are secured and the docking clamps are on interlock so even if we lose power, they'll hold us." He smiled at me. "Go get the *uh-oh* box, and lets boot it in parallel and see if it still works."

I fetched it from the locker while he and Salina brought up a couple more ship's displays. It booted right up and brought the ShipNet code online. Theoretically we could have shut off the primary routers in Systems Main and kept a minimum control of the ship with the laptop serving as a central core. It wouldn't be pretty, but it might make the difference between living and dying.

The three of us went through a checklist that Mr. von Ickles had prepared. Salina had a couple of ideas and I suggested some things too. When 1500 rolled around we were as ready as we could be.

I went down to the systems closet to wait out the last tick while Salina and Mr. von Ickles readied themselves on the bridge. The first test was to see if the computer would take the load if it was already booted when the main router cage went off line. Salina did the honors on the announcement and at the appointed signal, I pulled the power coupling from the back of the main router cage. My tablet lost its link for a moment, then locked back in. I got the "power up" message from Mr. von Ickles and plugged the cage back in. If I hadn't linked back up, I would have powered up after a tick.

The next test was to check to see if the box would assume the load if the net was down when it booted. It took a couple of ticks to prepare, but I finally got the "standby" message from Mr. von Ickles and pulled the plug on his mark. The delay was almost nonexistent as my tablet lost its link and re-acquired. That did not look right. It should have taken longer. Mr. von Ickles sent the "power up" message and I restarted the cage again.

The last test was a test of the catastrophic failure of the Systems Main. I got the "standby" message, but this time, on his mark, I pulled the main breaker to the whole closet. My tablet lost its link for quite a while, but within three ticks it was back. There was not much there, but it was connected to the network and there was basic communication. Mr. von Ickles sent the "reboot and secure" message over the tablet.

When I got the Systems Main closet restarted, I went up to the bridge to find Mr. Kelley, Mr. von Ickles, and Salina all smiling. "Well, that wasn't what I expected," Mr. von Ickles was saying, "but it worked when we needed it, so I guess I'm not going to complain."

Mr. Kelley agreed, "Yeah. I thought the system redundancies would pick up with that single cage failure. The net shouldn't crash if we lose just one. But when the whole closet went down, the box gave us enough to keep basic power and steerage way."

"It's definitely a last resort option," Mr. von Ickles said. "But if we need it, I'm glad to know it's here."

We secured from testing and told the rest of the ship over the speakers.

"Since you're here anyway, Fred," Mr. von Ickles said, "take a look at this."

He brought up the revised data display showing all the systems shutting down, then the pause, and the cascade of failures.

"What the—" Mr. Kelley said.

Mr. von Ickles nodded. "Thanks. I thought I might be crazy, but that's definitely not what you expected to see, is it?"

"Can you play that again and pause it one second past the event?" he asked.

Mr. von Ickles did so and Mr. Kelley leaned into the monitor as if being close to it would make him see it better.

"This says the ship was green one second after the event. By this time the EMP is well beyond us."

Mr. von Ickles nodded his agreement. "Not only that! Look how long it takes for things to start failing."

He keyed it to start again and we watched nearly six seconds elapse before the first failure—an atmospheric pressure sensor on the aft boat deck. After that the cascade of failing sensors, fuses, and boards all the way to the bow and back took another half tick while sporadic flashes in peripheral areas indicated an almost random pattern of systems and subsystems failures throughout the ship.

Mr. Kelley just stood there looking at it for a long time. "I had always assumed that the system didn't respond properly," he said at last.

"Yup, me, too," Mr. von Ickles confirmed. "I've got Mr. Wang stripping down the logs one more time to look for the systems as they come back online. There's something we're still not seeing."

After the day watch, I was ready for some off-ship entertainment and I found Pip waiting for me in deck berthing. "Are we going someplace?" I asked.

"I hope so. I want a meal that I don't have to clean up after for a change."

I remembered that feeling very well and we hustled into our civvies. By 1830 we were at the lift and I punched level eight.

"You don't want to go down to the oh-two deck?" he asked.

"I'm with you on the meal. It's been a long time since I've eaten off ship and I'm ready for something a little different. Nothing against the oh-two level, but I want something a little more—upscale, shall we say."

He grinned. "Well, ain't we gettin' all hoity-toity! You sure you wanna be seen with such a ruffian and low-class individual as myself?"

"You can hold my coat while I eat," I told him.

"Yeah," he said. "Right."

The lift opened on eight and we headed out to starboard.

"You have any insight as to what might be up here?" he asked. "Why did you picked eight instead of nine?"

"In my starved and weakened condition, that was as high as I could raise my arm."

"As long as you had a good reason."

We found a friendly looking place with a menu heavy on chicken and fish. It was rather late station time, going on midnight, but a small line of people stood in the passage. We didn't have to wait too long and we got a nice table overlooking the corridor where we could sit, enjoy a meal, and watch people.

We settled in, got our orders placed relatively quickly, and had that kind of *well-we-are-here-so-what-will-we-talk-about* pause before Pip said, "What the hell have you been up to, Ishmael? I don't think I've seen you for more than a stan total in the eight weeks since we left Betrus."

I laughed. "I missed you, too," I said, and proceeded to give him the run down on the *uh-oh* box and my work trying to unravel the mystery of the systems crash. He already knew about Lois and CC.

"What happened after I left you in Betrus? In that bar?"

"Oh, a very cute girl picked me up and took me home with her for the night."

"A cute girl picked you up?" He said, and laughed. "And I've been feeling guilty about leaving you there for the last two months?"

"Thanks, Pip, but never feel guilty about something like that. Especially after I told you to leave. Kate and Janette weren't really into having two guys. Whatever mystical hold you have over them, they weren't interested in me. You were just wasting time."

"You're a strange man, you know that?"

"So, I've been told."

The waiter brought our food then and we tucked in. I had ordered a nice grilled munta and Pip had a chicken dish. We enjoyed our food without talking for a while.

"We need to restock," Pip said at last. "We've got tomorrow and the next day to find some trade goods. How much mass do we have now? We're both full share, but you're spec two, so that's fifty for me and eighty for you?"

"Yeah, bump up to fifty for full share, then ten for spec three and twenty for spec two. I'm still only using about ten with my clothes and stuff so I've got seventy available."

"Holy handmaidens, that's one hundred and ten kilos. What can we get?"

"I don't know, Pip. Are we going to Umber or Barsi?" I asked. "And what should we buy differently for either."

"We're scheduled for Umber. Ocean planet with only a couple of small islands for land mass. Pirano Fisheries owns the planet, same group that has the fisheries in St. Cloud actually. All the people live on floating cities. They're apparently huge."

"So anything wooden has to be imported?"

"Yeah, wood, stone, and most textiles. They export fish including a lot of shellfish. Also various seaweeds and seaweed products."

"Well, I'm off tomorrow. I can try to scope out the flea. Maybe convince Beverly or Brill to talk to me again."

"Oh, man, Beverly," Pip said. "I thought she was going to lose it when it looked like you were gonna get stuck on Betrus."

"What?" I asked.

"It's true! She was a mess for that whole stay."

"I saw her dragging back late one night. She didn't look too good."

"You have that effect on women, Ish. Once they've had a taste of the Ishmael charm, they're ruined for mere mortals."

We chuckled, but I filed that bit of information away. "She's on mid-watch tonight, but maybe I can convince her to go shopping with me after lunch."

Pip held up his drink and I touched my glass to his as we chanted, "Better deals in the afternoon."

The conversation lagged a bit as we tucked back into the food.

"How're you doing on the stores trading?" I asked. "Is it still pulling your chain?"

He looked up at me and finished chewing a mouthful of chicken before answering. "It's gotten pretty much automated. I'm not really doing much anymore. A little tweak here, a little tweak there, but Cookie has it down pretty good now. I just make the data changes."

"How about the empty container?"

"That's going really well. I've got a base budget of fifty kilocreds to fill it each time. We've pulled anything from one hundred fifty to two hundred fifty back out."

"Nice ratios," I said, and sighed.

"What's the matter, Ish?"

"What the hell am I going to do?" I asked him. "And for that matter, what are you going to do? Isn't your two year contract just about up?"

"Oh, well, I extended for another year. It'll expire in August 2353," he admitted.

"Why?" I asked him.

He looked startled by the question. "What? I'm going to leave just when we're starting to get established? If we buckle down and do some serious trading—with the co-op and our mass allotments, we'll be sitting on fifty or sixty kilocreds in a year."

I looked at him. "You're serious?"

He shrugged. "We've already split four and there's seven in there again. That's from a standing start with almost no mass allotment."

"Well, we had a lot of luck," I pointed out.

"Luck only has a little bit to do with it. We picked cargoes that turned really good profits. Yeah, Sarah made the most of the stones, but she's thrilled with her commission, and we were just doing business."

"But we've been six months making eleven thousand," I said. "What makes you think we can turn that into fifty or sixty by this time next year?"

"Two things, mass and money. We started with almost none of the first and darn little of the second. We now have enough to take just about anything we want."

He made sense. "But that doesn't answer the question for the long term. What are you going to do next year when your contract is up?"

"I don't know. What are you planning to do?"

I pushed the last bit of carrot around on my plate and said, "I told the captain I'd make up my mind about the academy."

"Make up your mind about it?"

"Yeah. Mr. von Ickles brought it up. Then the captain took me aside while we were dithering around in Betrus." I looked up at him then to see how he was taking my news. "They think I should go."

"What do you think about that?"

I couldn't read his expression. "I don't know. I think I need to get some kind of credential. A degree is good. If I'm going to go ashore, I'll need a trade or something. That's what pushed me out here to begin with."

"Well, you've got credentials to spare at the moment," he said.

"Very true. But—I don't know. If I stop thinking about the creds. If I assume, that somehow the ability to pay will be there. Then most of my objections to going are silly."

"So the only thing stopping you is the cost?" he asked.

"No, not the only thing. I'm coming up on a year on the *Lois* in a couple weeks. It's been a blast." I shrugged. "If I still think it's fun at the end of two, then maybe I need to go invest some time and money and get a third mate's certificate and see where that leads me."

"What? And leave the *Lois*?"

"Maybe Lois will be done with me by then," I pointed out. "Yes, I know," I said forestalling his comment on talking about Lois as if she was real.

We finished dinner and the waiter took our plates while offering dessert, but neither of us was in the mood, so we settled up and headed out to walk off the meal.

Finally Pip said, "How much will it take?"

"How much will what take?"

"How much will it take to go to the academy?"

"Conservatively? Sixty kilocreds for the four years."

"Fifteen a year?"

"Yeah, something like that. Ten for tuition and half again more for room and board, books, and equipment."

"So if we make sixty kilocreds over the next year, you'll have half of what you need?"

"Yeah. Assuming I want to go next year."

"Well, even if you decide not to go, that would be a nice little nest egg to do anything you like, eh?"

"True."

"Okay, well, hell. What are we worrying about this now for?" he asked with a grin. "We're two stud muffins out on the town. Why aren't we down on the oh-two looking for lust?"

Behind us a woman's voice said, "Philip? Philip Carstairs, is that you?"

Pip stopped in his tracks, blanched as white as a ship-tee, and turned. "Oh, hi, Aunt P. What are you doing on Niol?"

Aunt P turned out to be a distinguished looking woman with spacer-cropped salt-and-pepper hair, a lithe build, and a burly guy in tow.

"Hi, Uncle Q," Pip said.

"Phil, you rascal," Uncle Q said with a grin. "What in the name of the seven sisters are you doing here? I thought you were at the academy?"

I arched an eyebrow at Pip, noting the similarity in build between Pip and his uncle.

"Uncle Quentin, Aunt Penelope, this is my shipmate, Ishmael Wang," he made the introductions like they were barbed wire. "Ish, this is my aunt and uncle, Captain Penelope and First Mate Quentin Carstairs." He looked like he wanted the deck to swallow him. "On my father's side."

"How nice to meet you." I stuck out my hand in their general direction. I didn't know who I was supposed to shake first, so I let them decide. The captain took priority and she gave me a firm and warm hand shake. The first mate's grip threatened, but never actually attempted, to crush my hand.

"You're his shipmate?" Aunt P asked with a little head twitch like some tall bird.

"Yes, Captain," I said. "We're on the *Lois McKendrick*."

Aunt P looked up at Uncle Q for a flashing instant before turning back. "We thought you were in Port Newmar, dear."

"Yes, Aunt P, well, that didn't exactly happen."

"So I see," she replied primly. She looked over to her first mate again.

He spoke this time. "Well, this is hardly the place for a family reunion. Why don't you boys come back to the *Penny* and have a beer and we'll catch up?"

I started to beg off and Pip gave me the *if-you-leave-me-here-I-will-hunt-you-down-and-kill-you* look so I merely shrugged, leaving the actual negotiation to him.

"I think we have time for one. Thank you, Uncle Q. We'll have to leave soon because we have duty in the morning, of course." Pip was talking quickly and I saw Aunt P's eyes narrow, but she didn't say anything.

They started walking and we fell into step. Pip walked beside Aunt P who took him by the arm. Not so much as to walk arm-in-arm with her nephew, but perhaps to prevent his escape. I walked on the other side of Uncle Q. He looked down at me curiously from time to time, a kind of bemused half-smile stamped on his face.

Before it got too awkward I said, "So? What brings you to Niol?"

"Triangle trade, Ishmael," he said. "Boat parts for the fishing fleet from here to Umber. Bulk fertilizer to Barsi, frozen food from Barsi to here."

"Not very exciting," Aunt P added, "but it has put our three boys through the academy and paid off the *Penny.*"

I leaned forward and looked at Pip, walking along on the other side of her. He looked like he was marching to the gallows. I had no idea families could be so entertaining.

Uncle Q and I had become fast friends by the time we got off the lift at the docks. Pip wasn't faring so well with Aunt P, but they were catching up. We headed to starboard where the orbital docked the smaller freighters. We walked up to a standard lock and Aunt P keyed it open. The telltale said: *Bad Penny* with a departure date of 2352-August-20.

Aunt P marched aboard as soon as the lock was open enough. Uncle Q stood back to let Pip and me go in first. Aunt P spoke into an intercom just inside the lock saying, "Roger? We're home, honey."

A disembodied voice from the overhead said, "Okay, Mom."

What struck me was how tiny it felt. I thought the *Lois* was small, but this was like walking into a tram. We had to enter single file even through the lock. The passage wasn't more than five meters long before it opened into what looked like a living room. It was probably larger than the living room Mom and I had in our flat back on Neris. It had a rug on the deck, a coffee table, even a pair of sofas arranged in a classic conversational grouping. I felt like I had stepped into something out of Lewis Carroll.

First Mate Uncle Q crossed to the small wet bar and said,

"Drinks? Anybody for drinks?"

"Gin and tonic?" I asked hopefully.

"Of course," he said. "Philip?"

"A beer would be good, Uncle Q, thank you."

He handed Aunt P what looked like a whiskey neat without her asking, and she sucked about half of it down in the first go. He handed me a very nice gin and tonic, complete with citrus wedge. "Thank you," I said. "Just like mother used to make."

He grinned, but Aunt P looked at me a little funny. "You drank gin and tonics with your mother?" she asked.

I shrugged. "Yes, sar, she didn't like to drink alone."

"Just Penny, dear. I'm Penny when I'm at home."

"Philip!" a new voice boomed out of the passage followed by a junior version of Uncle Q. "What the hell are you doing here? I thought you were at the academy?"

Pip looked a little embarrassed by all the attention. "Yeah, well, things didn't work out the way everybody expected."

"When you left home, you were heading for Port Newmar," Aunt P said. "Did you get shanghaied along the way?"

"Not exactly. I didn't actually get on the liner for Port Newmar," he said, sucking on his beer. "I signed the Articles and shipped out as a quarter share in the environmental section on the *Marcel Duchamp*."

"How'd you get on to the *Lois*?" Aunt P asked. "They didn't let you transfer?"

"No, they traded me."

The overhead took a dent when Aunt P's eyebrows bounced off of it.

"The *Lois* had a crewman who wanted to transfer into Environmental. Pip—er Philip—was willing to help them out. It was a good move for everybody," I said.

Roger in the meantime helped himself to a beer, threw himself down on the sofa, and put his feet on the coffee table.

I looked around and except for the obvious things, like the hatch combings and the lock that I could see from where I sat on the couch, I could have been in somebody's house. I supposed, in a very real way, I was.

The conversation flagged for a moment and Roger grinned and offered, "Uncle Thomas is going to throw a rod, when he finds out."

I looked at Pip and gave him the *oh-we-do-have-to-chat-later* look.

Aunt P sighed and asked, "What in hell were you thinking, Philip Carstairs? Your father and mother are expecting you back with your third mate's ticket ready to go! How have you managed to fool them into thinking you're actually at the academy?"

"Semester in space," he said miserably.

"Semester in space? For two stanyers?!"

He shrugged. "Well, you know how they are with things like that. They probably don't even notice that it's been that long."

Uncle Q said, "Well, they were proud of you for winning that scholarship so they didn't have to pay tuition and fees." He winked. "That was ingenious."

Aunt P slapped him on the leg. "Don't encourage the boy, Quentin," she snapped. She turned back to Pip. "You know we're going to have to tell them, Philip."

Pip nodded, a miserable expression on his face, but he didn't say anything.

Aunt P threw herself back in her easy chair and took another pull of whiskey from the glass before heaving a sigh. "So, what are you planning, Philip?"

He looked up. "Well, I just wanted to get a feel for what it's like on the other side before I got tied down at the academy, Aunt P. Take a year—or two—"

"Or three?" she interrupted.

He shrugged. "Or three. See whether I could make it out here trading on my own for a bit."

She stared at him. "You always were the hellion of the group," she said. "Are you going to hide out for the rest of your life?"

"Actually, Ishmael and I were just discussing going to the academy over dinner, weren't we?"

All three seemed to remember I was there and focused on me. "Are you interested in going to the academy, Ishmael?" Aunt P asked.

"I don't know," I told her honestly. "It's something that Captain Giggone has suggested. I don't know how I can manage it, but I'm thinking about it."

"Alys Giggone has talked to you about going to the academy?" Uncle Q asked.

"Yeah, I told her I wanted to work out my contract and see if I still liked it out here before I committed that kind of time and money."

Aunt P smiled. "Well, if I know Alys, you'll make up your mind the way she wants, and you'll like the decision too."

I smiled at that. "No doubt, sar—er—Penny. No doubt."

Uncle Q asked me, "So what's your rating, Ishmael?"

Pip started laughing, but he got it under control quickly. "You're gonna love this answer. Go for it, Ish."

"Well, I'm rated cargoman, messman, able spacer, spec two systems, and spec two environmental."

The statement lay there on the coffee table feeling lonely for a time before Roger said, "Gawd!"

"You're rated full share in all four divisions?" Aunt P confirmed.

"Yup, he is," Pip said with a small grin in my direction.

"You look so young," she said. "How long have you been a spacer?"

Pip choked back another laugh.

"Well, I'll be finishing my first year in a couple of weeks," I said, uncomfortable with the way this was going.

"And do you come from a spacer family?" Aunt P persisted.

"Um, no. My mother was an ancient lit professor at the University at Neris."

Aunt P and Uncle Q looked at me, then each other, and then back at me. "No wonder Alys wants him to go to the academy," Uncle Q said.

Aunt P just nodded with a speculative look in her eye. "You looking for a berth, Ishmael?" she asked.

"No, Penny, thank you. I quite enjoy my work on the *Lois* for now."

"Well, if you change your mind, let me know," she said. "Somebody with your skill set is highly marketable."

Pip said, "Oh my, look at the time! We've both got duty in the morning, we better head back."

It surprised me when Aunt P didn't argue. She just stood and walked us to the lock. While Uncle Q was saying goodnight to Pip, she managed to get between Pip and me. "He's an idiot, but he's our idiot. Watch out for him, Ishmael. It's been a pleasure to meet you. Please give my regards to Captain Giggone."

"Thank you, Penny, I will." I shook her hand and then Uncle Q's on the way out of the lock. Pip and I walked back down the docks toward the *Lois*.

I laughed all the way. Pip just looked miserable.

Chapter Twenty-four
Niol Orbital: 2352-August-17

I had the day off and I wanted to shop, but I also needed to take Bev with me. I hadn't spoken to her at any length in weeks, and I missed her. I set my tablet for 0545, knowing she would be getting off watch and heading for breakfast or bed around then. I intended to catch her at one or the other. As it was I caught her in the passage outside deck berthing and we arranged to meet at 1300.

Pip was at the omelet station on the mess deck and still looked upset. I grabbed some coffee and a plate.

"Good morning, Philip," I said with a grin.

"Please," he said, throwing some onion and mushroom into the pan.

"Then talk to me. As much as I'm enjoying this, what in the universe were you thinking?"

He did a little left shoulder shrug but didn't look up from the pan. "I just didn't want to be shunted off to the academy without any say is all," he said after a few heartbeats.

"What? They were holding a gun to your head?"

"You've met Aunt P and Uncle Q. Mom and Dad are at least as bad. Dad's the bulldozer in the group and Mom is good at making you like being bulldozed."

"When you said you came from a trader family, you weren't kidding. Aunt Annie, now Aunt Q and an uncle. Are there any more?"

"Well, not counting the various cousins, there's another aunt on my mother's side and my father has two sisters. I have an older sister and a younger brother."

"They all trade?"

"One way or another. My father's older sister is a broker on

Sargass Orbital. She handles the import-export end of the trades there. She's not a spacer as such, although she's rated spec three in ship handling. My big sister is third mate on Dad's new ship and baby brother is still living at home and standing helm watches."

"Do all of them have little flying living rooms?"

"What?" He looked confused. "Oh, the *Penny*? Yeah, actually, that's pretty typical on the smaller ships. The *Penny*'s rated at eight metric kilotons. She carries palletized freight and bulk cargo, not like the *Lois* with the containers. The *Penny* has four big holds amidships instead of the spine."

"How can she turn a profit carrying that little?" This whole conversation had taken an odd turn in my brain and I had no idea where it was going.

Pip slipped the omelet out of the pan and into my plate. He added a couple of biscuits to keep it company. "Well, to begin with, the salaries are low, and they're fast as hell. The *Penny* probably only needs seven days to get out of the well here, maybe less depending how heavy she's running. She can jump to Barsi and be back on station here before we could make it out to the Burleson limit. She's under ten metric kilotons so she only needs a captain and a certified small ship engineer. Aunt P has both of those. Uncle Q has first mate and system/comm papers. Cousin Roger passed some level of engineering papers—I'm not sure what he's rated these days—but he likes living at home so they let him stay aboard and help out."

"They're all academy?" I asked as what he said sunk in.

"Oh, yeah," he said, and followed me out to sit at a table while I ate.

"The living room?" I asked. "I don't know what I expected, but it wasn't a Berkman-Neuman conversational grouping with optional bar just inside the lock."

"How did you know it was Berkman-Neuman?" he asked.

I sighed. "I didn't. It's the only brand I know. Focus, Pip."

"I told you, that's home. They have a living room and a big eat-in galley. The whole thing isn't as big as the galley here, but they only have to feed a half dozen people most of the time, if that. Aunt P and Uncle Q share the captain's cabin of course, and that's almost as big as the one here, the kids shared the staterooms. There's no berthing area at all to speak of."

"It was so—homey."

"Ish? It is home! What did you expect it to be?"

I shrugged. "I don't know. A little *Lois*, I guess. Is that the kind of ship you grew up on?"

"Oh, yeah. The *Bad Penny* and the *Epiphany* are sister ships, almost identical. We even sailed the same routes sometimes. It was a big treat to trade rooms with a cousin. I flew on the *Penny* a lot as a kid actually."

"What? You'd swap kids?"

"Basically. It was great fun to run a leg with Aunt P and Uncle Q. I don't know why. Just different, I guess."

Salina Matteo came in for breakfast and Pip got up to fix her an omelet. They both came to sit with me after he was done. "Morning, Ish," she said. "You're up early, too, I see."

"Pip and I went out to dinner. Ran into his aunt and uncle for a drink and came back early." I hoped to get a response out of Salina to add to Pip's embarrassment.

"How nice!" She turned to Pip. "Did you expect to find them here or was it just coincidence?"

"Coincidence. They're running an indie on the triangle trade around the Umber-Barsi-Niol loop."

"How pleasant that must be for them."

"They like it. Put my cousins through the academy."

The surrealism of the conversation was making me feel very off-balance. It didn't match the image of the lonely spacer that I had formed since coming aboard.

Salina nodded. "I kinda wish I'd gone when I had the chance, but with Roberto and the kids, it made more sense to specialize in astrogation."

"Roberto and the kids?" I asked, feeling my universe slip just a bit further off axis.

"Yeah," she said, smiling and tucking into her omelet. "Roberto, my husband. We have two kids."

"You have a husband and two kids?" I repeated.

"Yup. Married into the family business. His father thought I was after his money, but I really only wanted his tight little buns." She winked.

I almost choked on my coffee.

"What business?" Pip asked.

"Oh, the family runs the *Barca Roja*—it's a thirty kilotonner over in the New Caledonia quadrant."

"Family co-op?" Pip asked.

"Yup," she said, beaming with pride.

"Isn't that hard?" I asked.

"What? Running the *Barca Roja*?"

"No, being away from your family."

"Oh, 'Berto and I see each other a couple times a year. We've been married a long time, but the reunions are something special, let me tell you!" She winked again.

Jennifer Agotto sauntered onto the mess deck and Pip went to fix her some breakfast.

"I'm sorry if I seem particularly stupid this morning, Salina. Meeting Pip's aunt and uncle and visiting their ship—I don't know. It was so different from what I expected."

"You're a land rat, aren't you? You don't come from a spacer family?" she asked, chasing a bit of egg around her plate with her fork.

"Right. Mom was a university professor. We lived on Neris almost my entire life."

She chuckled. "So you expected their ship to be like this?" She flourished her biscuit to indicate the mess deck.

"Well, I had nothing else to go on."

"The *Lois* is pretty typical for a big corporate carrier, but there's ten indies for every ship like this."

"So, why are you here when you could be with your husband and kids on the *Barca Roja*?"

"I needed some space. Working for the family can be a little claustrophobic at times. Besides, my daughter wanted to see what it was like working on a corporate carrier." She shrugged. "It just worked out. We'll probably head back when our contracts are up."

"Your daughter?" I asked.

"Yeah, my daughter."

Pip had finished fixing Jennifer's breakfast by then and they both sat down with us.

"Morning, Mom," Jennifer said, and gave Salina a little peck on the cheek.

Pip must have seen the look on my face. "What? You didn't know?"

Jennifer looked around and asked, "What's going on?"

Salina smiled. "I think our young Mr. Wang here is getting an education in spacer life."

Jennifer turned to me. "You're not a spacer?"

"My mom was a lit professor. The *Lois* is my first ship."

"You've got to be kidding?"

Pip shook his head. "Nope, he's serious."

Salina looked up from her plate. "He thought all ships were like the *Lois* until he saw Pip's aunt and uncle's ship last night."

"You have family in-port, Pip?" Jennifer asked. "How nice!"

Her comment wasn't any kind of *oh-my-god-that-is-so-amazing nice*. It was more like *nice haircut* nice.

Pip grumbled, "Yeah, well." But he didn't offer anything more.

"What ship?" Jennifer asked.

Pip sighed. "*Bad Penny*, eight tonner out of Deeb."

"Oh cool, one of the Unwin-eight hulls?" Jennifer asked.

"No, Manchester-built Damien."

"Ooh, fast ship! Is there any more darberry jam?"

Pip got up to fetch a jar of jam while Salina continued to be amused over her coffee cup and Jennifer dug into her sausage and eggs.

"You've done pretty well for a land-rat," Jennifer commented, looking up from her plate. "You always wanted to run away to space?"

"Actually, I had to get off planet or be deported when my mother died," I said.

"Oh, I'm sorry. I didn't know." She looked to her mother—my gooey gray matter was still trying to absorb that one, her mother—for support.

"Thanks, but it's okay. It's been almost a stanyer now. It was a shock, and I've had to adapt fast."

Salina smiled. "You've done very well for yourself, Ishmael. I'm sure she would have been proud of you." She reached over and patted the back of my hand. I almost teared up right there at the table.

I kept my head down and said, "Thanks," into my coffee cup.

Luckily Pip came back with the jam and we got distracted.

"Is everybody aboard a spacer?" I asked, trying to get back on even footing.

"I think you and Sarah are the only two people aboard who don't come from some kind of spacer family," Salina said.

"Francis," Pip added. "He was a scientist."

"Okay, and Francis. There's probably a few more."

"You're kidding!" I said.

She shrugged. "Who do you think isn't spacer born? Besides you three?"

I had never considered the question before. "Bev?" I asked.

"Her parents are members of a merchanter co-op running the Siren to St. Cloud loop. Her mother is first mate and her father works systems, I think."

"Brill?"

"Her father runs an orbital somewhere. I forget which system, but she'll tell you if you ask. Her mother is third mate on one of the system shuttles there."

"Rebecca Saltzman?"

"Are you kidding?" Pip asked.

"What?"

"The Saltzman's are one of the oldest trading families in the business. I think they have a fleet almost as big as Federated

Freight's now and every single crewman is family."

"Why is she here then?"

"You never worked for family, have you?" he asked with a bitter little smile.

"The whole crew?"

Salina shrugged. "Well, except for you, Sarah, and Francis. There's probably a few more that I don't know about. It's not like I pay that much attention. It's just not that big a deal. Most of us just have some connection in the business. It's how it works."

Jennifer asked, "If you'd never wanted to be a spacer, how'd you get here?"

"Jennifer?" Salina said in that rising-tone-warning.

"What?" She said. "I'm just asking."

"It's okay. My mother was killed in a flitter crash. The company was going to deport me because I didn't have enough creds to buy passage off planet and I couldn't stay without being an employee. I didn't want to be a marine, so I went to the Union Hall on Neris and waited for a quarter-share berth."

"Somebody musta liked you."

I shrugged. "The manager said I reminded her of her nephew." I shot a quick glance at Pip, who was studying the inside of his coffee mug. "She helped me pack a duffel and when the *Lois* came in and unloaded what's his name last year, I got his slot."

"And the rest is history," Pip said. I think he was trying to break it up before any more of his family tree got dragged into the story. Or that his parents thought he was starting his third year at the academy.

Chapter Twenty-five
Niol Orbital: 2352-August-17

Bev had introduced me to the flea market. I still carried a mental image of her in black leather pants and matching jacket with what looked like an aluminum pullover under it. When I met her at the lock, she wore the leathers—she always wore the leathers—but that day she had a pale yellow blouse under it. With her military buzz cut hairstyle and four kilos of surgical steel piercings, the touch of yellow made her seem as feminine as I had ever seen her. Not that she could ever be mistaken for a man. There was never any doubt that she was female to the core, but this was nice too.

She was still an intimidating figure. She moved with a dangerous grace and fluidity that wasn't just for show. She didn't carry any weapons, but I had watched her sparring with some of the other crew. I was pretty sure she didn't need any.

She smiled after I looked her over. "Are you almost done drooling?"

"No, but let's go shopping. I've got a lot of mass to fill!"

She laughed and we headed up to level nine and the flea market. "What are we looking for?"

"Wood, textiles, maybe even some stone. Umber is a water planet and I want either something land-based or reminiscent of land, I think. Whatever it is, it needs to be high quality."

"Good point. No sense dragging crap from one system to another."

I couldn't believe how good it felt to be walking with her again—just being with her. I liked moving along in her bubble as people in our path slipped by to either side. Some stopped to look back at her. Of course, walking a step behind gave me an excellent view as well.

She looked over her shoulder and said, "If you don't stop watching my butt and start looking for goods, this is going to be a waste of time."

"Speak for yourself!" I teased, but I stepped up beside her. It pleased me when people looked back and forth between us and smiled.

The flea market didn't inspire me. We saw lots of kitschy handicrafts—stencil work on plain canvas, studs and stones in fabric goods, the usual collection of mediocre artwork. Niol was a manufacturing hub specializing in machine parts for the secondary spares market. There was not a lot of ancillary contribution to the flea market trade from the fabrication shops on planet. Bev and I must have browsed for over a stan, and I began to get discouraged.

"You'd think with the forests down below, we'd see some kind of wooden toys or something, wouldn't you?" I asked.

"Not necessarily."

A demon stepped in our path suddenly, and I saw a blur of black leather that stopped a centimeter from the nose of a mask. The woman wearing the mask froze and gave a little squeak. I didn't blame her. I felt like squeaking myself.

"I'm so sorry," Bev said, stepping back and dropping her hands to her sides. "Your mask startled me and it was just a reflex."

The woman pulled off the mask and said, "Oh no, I'm sorry. I should know better than to startle people like that."

She had a whole booth full of marvelous masks—everything from elegant dominoes, to faces of animals, as well as abstracts. Some were merely decorative and others were fully functional. I snapped digitals and flashed them to Pip while we talked to her. She was more than happy to discuss wholesale pricing so long as we were taking them out of the system. Beverly and I both bought several as samples and just to have. We confirmed that she would be around for a few days so we could come back later and arrange for a bulk purchase.

"I have bundles of them down in my storage cube," she said. "I'd love to unload some of them. Everybody here's seen them and, in this business, it always has to be something new." She had a most delightful giggle and she used it to good effect.

Three booths later we came upon a silk carp. The vendor was a tall, slender woman. and she had the carps hung all around her booth. As we walked up to them, I laughed because Bev had no idea what they were.

"They're like wind socks," I said. "You hang them out to catch the wind and on a really windy day, they look like they're swimming."

"Not a lot of wind on a ship," she pointed out. "Or orbital for that matter."

"But there is on the ocean."

The woman's name was Estelle and she created the carp from remnants of cloth that she bought by the bundle. The stitching was lovely and the colors ranged from monochromatic reds and blues to explosions of orange, black, and gold. They ran in varying lengths from about a meter to three giant ones that were over four meters long. Each came with a sewn in harness in the mouth and had a short lead with a swivel clip for attaching it to the main flying line.

"We used to have one of these when I was a kid," I told Bev.

"I never lived on a planet long enough to really get used to it," she said. It was the first personal piece of information I could remember her sharing. We lived so much in the "right now" for the stanyer I had been aboard that neither the past nor our future had come into the discussion.

Again I took digitals for Pip but Estelle had no interest in any kind of bulk trade deal. Her entire stock was in the booth. Still she had a lot of them, even after Bev and I bought a few. I actually considered sticking one to the wall above my bunk just to dress up the space a bit, they were that nice. We found out that she, too, would be around for a couple of days but needed to leave the orbital and get back down to the surface soon.

We wandered about looking at things for a couple more stans but, of all the stuff we saw, the masks and carps were the only two that had the kind of unique quality that I looked for in trade goods.

As we left the sales floor, Bev surprised me by stepping close enough to take my arm and walk hip-to-hip. "I wish I could bottle your nose for trade goods, Ish. I'd love to can it or something. You sure can pick 'em."

"Naw," I said, too flustered from hot leather against my outer thigh to be very cogent. "I just look for things that are different."

"So do I, but the difference is you find it," she said. "I'd have walked right past these carp."

"Well, I knew what they were and they're perfect for sale on Umber. I wonder if I can get Sarah to bless them," I added.

Bev laughed. "Only if you let her sell them. I swear that woman is a selling machine!"

I laughed with her and we walked in silence for a while.

"Are you okay now?" I asked her without looking down.

"Yeah," she murmured. "I think so. It was hard there for a while."

"Betrus was a very hard place to be," I admitted. "You wanna tell me about it?"

"I thought I was going to lose you," she said without looking at me.

"Lose me?" I asked. Sometimes I could be so stupid.

"Yeah. Lose you. You may remember that you were about *that close*,"—she held up her thumb and forefinger about a millimeter apart—"to being put on the beach?"

"Well, yeah, but—"

"I know," she said almost bitterly. "It was stupid but I couldn't help myself." She acted like she might want to say more, but she didn't.

"What'll you do if I go to the academy?" I asked out of thin air.

She stopped and jerked me around by the arm. "What? You're going to the academy?"

I was a little afraid she was going to hit me—and not the playful slug in the arm but full on in the face. "I don't know. But I'm thinking about it at the end of my contract next year."

She looked into my face. "If you apply, you better tell me that very day! I don't want any surprises like that."

I thought she was being a little demanding. "Why? What'll you do?" I asked in challenge.

She grinned a naughty grin and said, "Book a hotel room. You're not getting away without a proper send off." She took my arm again and hugged it even a little closer than might have been, strictly speaking, proper. I found I did not mind at all.

Remembering my conversation over breakfast I asked, "Did you know Salina Matteo is Jennifer Agotto's mother?"

"Yeah, why do you ask?"

"I had my view of the universe shifted radically at breakfast this morning."

"Damn, that musta been some omelet. Was it the mushrooms?" she asked with a devilish glint in her eye.

"No, I found out that almost everybody on the ship is from a spacer family of some kind."

"Oh? You didn't know?"

"I didn't think there were such things as spacer families. All I have to go on is the *Lois* for personal experience."

We walked in silence for a few more meters. "But you knew Pip came from a trader family," she said.

"True, but it was an abstract idea until I met his aunt and uncle and saw their ship."

"That musta been something to see." She laughed. "You on an indie."

"What's that supposed to mean?"

"Just that I'd have liked to see your face when you walked into the living room."

It was my turn to stop and turn her to face me. "Do they all have living rooms?"

"No." She laughed. "Some of them are more like the *Lois*, but if you changed your mind about your picture of trader families, you musta felt like you were stepping into a dreamscape. Off the dock and into the living room, right?"

"How'd you know?"

"Most common small ship configuration. If you're docked, you don't wanna have to go far to answer the front door should anybody come to call. Did you see the bridge?" she asked.

"Didn't get past the living room."

"It's usually outfitted like a kind of den. It's where the family spends most of its time underway. Of course, the smaller ships have less time underway too." She looked up at me, then and asked, "So is that why you're thinking of going to the academy? Gonna start your own spacer family?"

The way she said it made me chuckle. "I didn't even know what that meant until last night. The captain and Mr. von Ickles have been trying to convince me to go for the last three months."

"Really? How'd the captain get involved?"

"I'm not sure. We were talking about the possibility of my having to leave the *Lois*, and she asked if I'd considered going to the academy and it just kinda went from there."

"So? You're thinking about it or not?"

"I told the captain that I wanted to stay with the *Lois* and at least work my contract out. It'll be up this time next August and if I still like being in space and I think I'd like to continue, I'll consider going."

"What's the hang-up? You not sure you want to continue being a spacer?"

"No. Actually, at this point I can't imagine being anything else, but I've got about sixty thousand good reasons why I can't go."

"Sixty thousand? Gah!" she said. "I had no idea it was that expensive."

"Tuition alone is forty, but I need room and board too."

She nodded and hugged my arm again. I felt no need to talk a lot more after that. She held on until we got on the lift.

"So, you come from a spacer family, too?" I asked.

"Yup. Grew up in a merchie co-op. I left to get some seasoning and haven't gone back yet. Someday, maybe,"

I just sighed and shook my head.

"What?"

"It's just—I never realized how closed the community is. You almost have to be born into it."

"Or luck into it like you and Sarah. Yeah. But it's not that much different from any specialized trade. Doctors tend to breed doctors. Teachers tend to breed teachers. You probably would have been a professor if you'd had a chance."

I appreciated that she didn't say, "If your mother hadn't died."

The lift opened and we went across the docks heading for the ship. "Thanks for going with me, Bev. I really needed to touch base with you."

"Any time, boy toy." She looked absolutely serious as she keyed the lock open. "And I needed to touch base too, thanks."

Chapter Twenty-six
Niol Orbital: 2352-August-17

On watch, I couldn't concentrate on the logs. I really needed to extract the data for the systems that had restarted normally and add a new layer to my graphic but my whole image of the lonely spacer, tragically bereft of hearth and home, had been ripped from me in just one day.

Salina asked, "Are you okay, Ish?"

I turned my chair so I could face her where she sat at the console. "It's just been such a weird day—meeting Pip's aunt and uncle last night and seeing how they lived shipboard, finding out that you were married and have your daughter with you here, discovering that I'm much more of an outsider than I ever thought, it's a bit much to process." I sighed. "I guess I'm having trouble adjusting to the idea that spacers have real lives like anybody else. I had this whole notion of 'spacer bar, love em and leave em, and don't screw with the crew' so ingrained in my head that, now, I'm feeling like I don't really understand anything."

"Well, that's a start. You can't possibly understand what it means to somebody like Pip to be a spacer when his father, mother, grandparents, and their parents all have been spacers. But you also need to figure out a way to realize that not knowing is okay."

I had to process that for a few ticks. "I think that helped actually."

"Okay... in what way?"

"You made me realize something that I knew but never really grasped before. For all of you, it's a connection to your past, to a heritage."

"Yes. Exactly."

"One of the problems I'm having is that I don't have that kind of connection—any heritage—even before I came out here. It was always just me and my mother. She was a teacher. I have a vague recollection of my father, but I haven't seen him or heard from him in fifteen stanyers. I never even knew who my grandparents were, let alone what they might have done. I'm an only child so I don't know any of this sibling stuff and how it works. Hell, I never had a best friend until I came aboard the *Lois*."

"Well, you poor thing. No wonder you're so lost! Is there anything I can do to help?"

"I think you just did."

I turned back to my console then and found that I was able to concentrate. By the time the watch was over, I had all the data extracted and a first cut on the reconstruction to show Mr. von Ickles. I sent a copy to Mr. Kelley as well before Salina and I headed for the mess deck. It still caught me a little bit sideways to think that she was hurrying down to have breakfast with her daughter, but the longer I thought about it, the more I liked it.

I remembered one of my mom's old stories about a sailor who wound up in a foreign land and slowly came to love and respect the people of this new home even more than those of his birth. He had to learn a new language and new ways of thinking, but eventually he figured out how to get along, and he really started to enjoy that life. Unfortunately, somebody killed him in the end because he was too happy or successful or something. Except for that last bit about being killed, I had an idea of what he must have felt like when he realized the full depth and scope of his adopted culture. I was not sure what word to put on it. Hope, maybe.

All through breakfast I watched Salina and Jennifer. Once you knew, it was obvious. Or perhaps it had always been obvious and I had just been too wrapped up in other things to notice. Or, more likely, they had been on the other side of the watch stander merry-go-round and I'd never had the opportunity to notice them at all.

One thing was for sure, after slogging through data for twelve hours, I needed a little quality time with my bunk and a blanket. As soon as I finished my breakfast, I headed that way.

Something woke me suddenly and I almost sat up. I was that startled, and it's not a good thing to do from a lower bunk so I was glad I had suppressed the urge. I never found out what it was— sound, dream, or maybe an odd vibration in the hull. *Maybe Lois just thinks I should get up*, I told myself with a little grin. The chrono read 1520 and I wondered how Pip was making out at the flea market.

I didn't have anywhere I needed to be, so I just lay back down and stared at the over head there in the quiet of the afternoon. I thought I could hear the low murmuring of Sean, Sarah, and Tabitha down at the other end of the berthing area. They were the main members of the co-ed crochet team and had some project going on that excited them. I lay there and thought about Aunt P and Uncle Q. I had never thought of life on the *Lois* as particularly regimented, but compared to the *Penny*, we were practically military. I wondered what it would be like to sail your living room. I must have fallen back to sleep at some point because I woke from a dream of sitting in an easy chair on the bridge of some ship with an old-fashioned spoked ship's wheel. Bev was there in her leathers but she didn't have a blouse on under the jacket, which I enjoyed a great deal. She was saying, "You gonna sleep away your last night in port, Ish?"

But of course, that was wrong because Bev was actually there in berthing standing over my bunk saying, "You gonna sleep away your last night in port, Ish?" She was already in her leathers and I was disappointed that she had a blouse on under the jacket. It took me a bit to get my eyes blinked open.

"No. What time is it?"

"Just coming up on 1900. What do ya think? You wanna go out hunting?"

"Sure, just lemme grab a quick shower and I'll put on my civvies."

"Quarter stan, main lock," she said, and left.

Pip was just coming out of the san, as I went in. Apparently we were going out as a group and I wondered who else was coming along. "Did ya buy anything?" I asked in passing.

"Yup. Close to fifty kilos of stuff. Shower now, talk later." He started pulling clothes out of his locker while I headed for the shower stall with my jeans and briefs in hand.

Ten ticks later, Pip and I headed for the lock and our last night in Niol.

Diane, Brill, Bev, and Francis were waiting and they were having one of those *I-don't-know-what-do-you-wanna-do* discussions.

We checked out with Rhon and headed out to the docks. In spite of what Bev had said, nobody looked like they were on the hunt. Maybe they had gotten it out of their systems earlier in the stay, or maybe, like me, they just were not in the mood.

We hit the lift and punched oh-two by default, but as we headed down, I asked, "Okay? Meat market or something else?"

Pip looked at me sideways, but he sighed and raised his right hand. "Something else."

One by one, they all raised their hands. "Something else." Brill looked relieved. Francis just looked tired, and I wondered what he had been up to in port.

When we got to the oh-two, I took them to *Shaunessey's*. While it was still early according to ship time, station time here was a bit ahead so *Shaunessey's* was in full swing. Or as full as the quiet pub got. There was some music coming from somewhere but all I could tell was that it was music. It was busy but far from full and we had no problem putting a couple of tables together so we could sit in a group.

I ordered some finger foods to go with the beer because I'd missed lunch and dinner and didn't want to drink on an empty stomach. We settled down and began a quiet evening of talk. Francis turned out to be quite amusing in his own way. Having known more than my share of Ph.D.'s he was probably funnier to me than the rest of the group, but he acted as a kind of bridge for me between my old life and my new one.

We had been there about a stan and were working on our second round when Pip stiffened and I heard a woman's voice say, "Hello! Can we join you?"

Pip was a little tangled at the back of the table so I stood and introduced Aunt P and Uncle Q to everyone. I enjoyed Pip's discomfort much more than I should have, but if we had seemed like family before, having real family at the table just enhanced the notion. They started telling stories of spacer life and kids. Penny and Quentin didn't embarrass Pip by talking about his childhood. They stuck to stories about Roger and Pip's siblings. Diane mentioned how kids on their co-op ship used to sneak into the lifeboats to neck, until their captain played the holo-tapes of their make out sessions during the evening meal. Even Brill, normally a bit of a wall flower had some funny stories about the conflicts in lifestyle between her station manager father and spacer mom. I just absorbed it, thinking about what their stories might mean to them and to me.

Eventually the table talk fragmented and we had quiet conversations in smaller groups on different corners of the table. I found myself talking about the academy to Francis and suggested that they should probably have a Ph.D. astrophysicist on the faculty. Of course, by then we had been through a lot of beer. I was probably a tad less responsible than I should have been.

Through it all, Beverly sat beside me, Brill beside her. Diane had collected Pip, Quentin, and Penny on the other end of the table and I could see Pip was beginning to appreciate Diane for more than just her cleavage. She saw me looking and winked. It was a good group. Only five beers and I loved them all. I laughed at myself and checked the time on my tablet. It had just passed midnight.

I stood and everybody looked at me. "You guys stay if you want, but I have morning watch and I need a little sleep before I have to go to work. I bid you all goodnight."

They all came with me, a few drained glasses and others just let them sit half empty. We all sauntered back to the lift, through the throngs of spacers on the prowl and a few who had already connected. The lift took us up to the docks. We bid Penny and Quentin goodnight and safe voyage before splitting up and heading for the *Lois*. Penny gave me a small hug and a motherly peck on the cheek before she left—lovely woman, Penny Carstairs.

We walked along, semi huddled against the cold and I found myself holding one of Brill's arms while Beverly held the other. Francis was leading the way, waving his arms like a drum major, while Diane cuddled up to Pip behind us. I didn't know who was more surprised, Diane or Pip, but Brill smiled when she saw it and I did too.

CHAPTER TWENTY-SEVEN
NIOL ORBITAL: 2352-AUGUST-19

When I got to the bridge for morning watch, the pre-departure tension had already started to build. Mr. von Ickles took his place at the console beside me and we talked about the new simulation.

The data showed that the ship had shutdown systems and components just as the designers intended, and it had restored the systems according to specification. After that point, things started going wrong and the problems started in the aft boat deck. I hoped the data would mean something to Mr. Kelley.

We only had the watch for a short time before the captain came onto the bridge and the party started in earnest. I had enough experience in the systems console to run my own displays and Mr. von Ickles made no comment as I scanned first through the data integrity checks, then the high level diagnostics. I pulled the morning logs and got the virtual ship as ready for getting underway as the real one.

The tugs arrived, linking into our communications network and tying on their towing fields. The captain choreographed the whole extravaganza and, once more, it went off without a hitch. As we dropped back, I thought I saw the *Penny* docked but I couldn't be sure. At the designated distance, the tugs dropped their links and we came about, setting sail for the Deep Dark and Umber beyond.

As we secured from navigation detail and assumed normal watches, I turned to Mr. von Ickles. "I see what you mean about the first time, sar," I said with a grin. "But it's still quite a show."

He smiled back at me. "Yes, it is, Mr. Wang. Yes, it is."

I pulled up the failure display one last time to watch it run through. I let it loop, replaying the incident in my mind as the graphic ticked by. The other officers on the bridge came to look at it, even the captain. Mr. Kelley stood behind Mr. von Ickles, pulling on his lower lip with thumb and forefinger while staring at the looping display. There was something there, but we weren't seeing it.

The simulation was on the third loop and I was staring dreamily at the place on the schematic that represented where I had been walking when the power went out. The gravity failed, sending me adrift, and when it came back on I slammed onto the deck.

"Gravity," I said, and added, "sar." when I realized I had spoken aloud.

They all looked at me. Mr. Kelley squinted his eyes in thought. "Keep going, Mr. Wang."

"Gravity went out and the ship slewed a little, sar. It was enough that the field collector plates on all four scrubbers unseated and got sucked out of position before the power came back up."

Mr. Kelley nodded, "I remember. Damnedest thing."

I pointed to the boat deck where the first sensor went dead. "We're assuming that the EMP killed this, sar, Right?"

"Yes, Mr. Wang. What else could it be?"

"What if something fell on it, broke it, and shorted it out? Would that have taken out all those systems, sar?" I asked Mr. Kelley.

"If something fell on it?" he asked. "But—" He leaned into the display.

Mr. von Ickles, Mr. Maxwell, and the captain all stared at the screen as well.

The captain ordered, "Freeze that, if you would, Mr. Wang, just before the point where the boat dock sensor fails."

"Aye, Captain," I said, and inched the display forward. until the frame directly before the component failure.

"Oh, for crying out loud," Mr. Kelley said in disgust.

The captain was shaking her head. "That can't be right."

"Right or not, that's what happened unless Mr. Wang made a data error, Captain," Mr. Kelley put in.

The captain said, "Mr. Wang, can you please double-check the status of the Systems Continuity Breakers at this point in time?"

"Yes, Captain." I scrolled through the list of systems data. "The sensor grid for the SCB shut down normally when the power overrides took everything off-line, sar."

"When did they come back online, Mr. Wang?"

"They didn't, Captain. At least not within the window of this log data."

Mr. Maxwell shook his head. "So all the fault breakers were offline?"

"Yup," Mr. Kelley said. "The ship was wide open. When the systems cabinet failed, that's probably all that kept us from having that spike rip right through the sail generators."

"It's so obvious!" Mr. Kelley said in disgust.

Mr. von Ickles looked startled at that and glanced at me with a grin.

"We were looking for some kind of EMP interference wave or a flaw in EMP shielding," Mr. Kelley just shook his head. "I'm gonna be kicking myself for the next stanyer over this."

The captain asked, "What fell on it to short it out? Was it from physical damage? Do we know?"

"Not at the moment, Captain," Mr. Kelley said, "but I'll know as much as we can find out in a couple of tics. Mr. Wang? Can you pull up the maintenance records for the period beginning at this point and going forward until you find anybody doing anything in the boat deck?"

I popped another list up on my starboard screen. It took a tick or two but I found the record identifying the replaced sensor. "Sensor broken. Heat damage. Scorching on casing." It was initialed AX.

"Hardly conclusive," Mr. Kelley was muttering, "but that's as solid an explanation as we've had in weeks."

"When you get a chance, Mr. Kelley," the captain said, "would you ask Mr. Xia about that sensor head?"

Mr. Kelley was still gazing at the display and nodding slowly to himself. "Aye, aye, Captain. And I think I'm going to go take another look at the boat deck myself. All this time I've thought the EMP caused these failures."

"We all were, Fred," Mr. Maxwell said. "Mind if I tag along?"

"Nope," Mr. Kelley shook himself from his contemplation of the display. "Let's go see what we can find."

The captain clapped me on the shoulder. "Nicely done, Mr. Wang," she said, and the officers, except Mr. von Ickles headed off the bridge.

Mr. von Ickles smiled at me from his console. "You said it had to be something obvious. I almost laughed out loud when Mr. Kelley said it."

"Well, you see what you expect to see, sar," I said with a shrug. "I've certainly done my share of that lately."

"Still, what made you think of the gravity?" he asked.

"When it came back on, I dropped hard. It made something of an impression, sar."

"Was the deck damaged?"

"No, sar. I checked."

We sat there grinning at each other for a tick and he said, "Nice work, Mr. Wang."

"Thank you, sar."

We both secured our stations then and I headed for the mess deck. Cookie had spiced beefalo on the menu and I was hungry enough to eat one raw. It felt good to be underway.

While I ate lunch, Mr. Kelley and Mr. Maxwell came onto the mess deck. Mr. Kelly had a portable fire extinguisher with him and brought it over to me. It was metal, heavy, and about half a meter long. It also had a scorch-mark along the base.

"Let me guess, sar," I said to him. "It hangs above the burned out sensor?"

"Yup," Mr. Kelley said. "I thought you might like to see it."

Mr. Maxwell continued, "This seems to support your hypothesis, Mr. Wang. The boat deck uses magnetic latches."

"The cleanup crews found these down all over the ship, but nobody thought to do more than just pick them up and re-rack them," Mr. Kelley said. "We'll want to take that little item up with the designers."

"But, sar, why don't they fall off the bulkhead every time there's a power fluctuation," I asked.

"I don't know, Mr. Wang, but we might have taken enough of a yaw when the sail generator went down that they just slipped off the latch in zero-g."

Mr. Maxwell added, "We seem to have excellent evidence that the ship worked exactly as designed, but we do need to look into adjusting the continuity breakers. If those had been on, this wouldn't have been able to do so much damage. Thank you for your work, Mr. Wang. Well done."

Three days out of Niol, I began to get worried.

We had just taken over the evening watch and I finished my routine maintenance and systems scans. There was nothing left to do. For weeks I had had the data and systems problems stemming from the near catastrophe in Betrus. Now, the statement Mr. von Ickles had made about needing to find a way to make the position permanent came back to me. What possible value could I add on a regular basis to make it worth keeping my slot open?

Mr. von Ickles must have seen me sitting and staring at my console because he came over and asked, "Are you all right, Mr. Wang?"

"Troubled, sar. What am I going to do to contribute now that we've got the EMP problem solved?"

"Ah, you're worried they're going to take the slot away?"

"No, sar. Well, yes, sar, a little." I had to correct myself. "But the bigger problem is why am I here?"

"Well, that's a question men have been asking themselves as long as we've been capable of asking," he said with a grin.

I had to chuckle. "I meant what am I contributing to the trip, sar."

He smiled an odd, almost gentle smile. "So did I, Mr. Wang. Isn't that really the question we all ask ourselves? What am I contributing to the trip?"

It clicked into place then. All of it. The whole swirling mass of angst and uncertainty snapped into focus. I took a deep breath and let it out. Not a sigh, but something like it.

"When you put it like that, sar," I said with a smile, "it's so obvious."

"So, what do we need to be more effective as a ship?" he asked.

"Well, sar, the mechanics of the ships operations seem pretty well optimized."

"You might be surprised about that," he said, "but go on."

"Well, sar, Pip and Cookie built some software to help with market analysis and trading. Would it be appropriate for me to work on that? Maybe take some of what I've learned in building these displays to help them visualize trades maybe?"

"Perfect, Mr. Wang. Why don't you look that over and see what we can do to help out? You might also check with Sandy Belterson on her astrogation updates."

"Really, sar?"

"The ship is designed by people who know how to build ships, but they don't necessarily know what it takes to make their living flying them. What makes sense for them is sometimes less than intuitive for those of us out here in the Deep Dark."

"You think I could help, sar? I don't know the first thing about this stuff, really."

"I think that gives you a leg up on the people who designed it, Mr. Wang," he said with a grin.

"How's that, sar?"

"Well, they thought they knew what we needed done. You're laboring under no such false belief."

I spent the rest of that mid-watch running Pip's cargo simulations. I got a feel for what it was doing, very loosely, but I was going to need to talk with him about what he needed before I could mess with it. I thought I saw some things I could do with the way he plotted price trends against cargo and port. While I was at it, I took a look at the cargo manifest reporting. Compared to the systems display we had for communications status, cargo manifests seemed rather—for lack of a better word—primitive. Of course, if that was all they needed, then perhaps I was trying to fix something that wasn't broken.

Still, it was something to do and by the time the watch was over I had lined up about eight different projects. I didn't know if any of them had merit, but until I looked into them, I wouldn't know. The next day was my twenty-four off so I took a run and a long sauna before heading to my bunk. As I settled down to sleep, I thought about Bev, the flying living room, and the academy. I wondered where Brill might work in there, or even Pip.

Chapter Twenty-eight
Umber System: 2352-October-05

We were two days out of Umber and Pip was ecstatic. All the way from Niol we worked to improve his cargo trading software. We spent the first few weeks just bringing me up to speed on what it did and how it did it. I developed some new code for him that let him siphon off more of the beacon data on cargo pricing. In addition, I had discovered that we could get access to Confederation economic indexes as we passed the jump beacons so we were able to begin adjusting our trade expectations based on baseline economic data. I did not understand it myself, but I was happy to set up the data handling and visualization routines.

"This is fantastic," Pip gushed as we pulled in the orbital beacon data. We were sitting on the mess deck at mid-morning as he studied the new displays of the current commodities data.

"But is this going to help you make more profitable trades?" I asked.

"Are you kidding? I'll be able to find cargo opportunities that I never would have seen before. With this level of detail two or three days out... wow."

"It just doesn't seem like that big a deal. Are you sure?"

"Look, Ish, in trading you need two things: information and time. You need the information to know what's possible, and the time to decide what to do with it. With these new displays and the extra economic data we're going to start making better trades right away. Look," he said, pointing out one of the new pricing trend lines. "That line is dropping like a rock. If we wait two days to sell those igniter plugs when we get to port, and if that trend continues, we'll have lost three percent on the value of the trade. If we can lock in the price now, that's money we'll be making that we didn't even know about before."

I saw his point. "But why isn't everybody doing this?"

"They're probably trying to. We're succeeding because you've given me a set of economic tools that are custom-built for exactly what we're doing. We really need to show this to Mr. Cotton. He'll be impressed."

"Okay, what do we need to do next with this?"

"I really think we need to get Mr. Cotton and Mr. Maxwell in on the brainstorming."

"Sounds reasonable. Mr. Maxwell's on watch now. Why don't you talk to him this afternoon, maybe get Mr. Cotton, too? I've got the afternoon watch, and maybe we can sit down after cleanup tonight and go over it?"

Pip agreed and I headed to the gym for a pre-watch run and sauna. I had about a stan before I had to report to the bridge. After thirteen months of running almost every day, I could now run for most of that time without any problems. I had been working on picking up my pace, since I was doing reasonably well with endurance. It felt good.

When I got to the bridge I marveled over the big blue ball that was Umber. I never found out why they named a blue planet for a shade of brown, but there were stranger things than that. The system we'd just left, for example, Niol, was an acronym for "Not In Our Lifetimes." The original settlers had thought that about the prospect of making the planet profitable. They had been wrong, of course, but the name stuck.

Dick Graves sat on the bridge, working with Sandy Belterson to start the astrogation updates. It was a lengthy process that often ran from two to three days depending on the volume of pending updates. It required gathering data before docking, through the port-visit, and a day or more past departure. I watched awhile as they laboriously took data from one screen and pasted it bit by bit into another screen.

"There isn't a process for loading those records?" I asked.

Sandy gave me one of her *you-really-don't-understand-this* looks and said, "Yes, Ishmael, there is. You're looking at it."

I grinned at her. "I was thinking of a more automated process. Like a command that would grab all the updates and put them in the database, but I see your point."

Both of them shook their heads, and Dick said, "Nope. This is just one of the banes of the astrogator's existence. The problem is that we have to find the ones that apply. We can't just take all of them so we have to do it manually."

"Why can't you take them all? And how do you know if you

missed one?"

Sandy pointed out the contents of an update. "Some of these are for areas of the galaxy we'll never go, like this one is for the Harnden quadrant. There's no sense to grab that, it just wastes time. And we don't know for sure if we missed one. That's why there's two of us doing it."

"So, you're culling the updates because it would just take too long to do them all?"

Dick grinned at me and said, "Exactly. This stuff takes forever."

"If we got the system to do it, so we could grab them all in a tick or ten, is there any reason why that would be a problem?"

"If you could figure out how to do that, you'd be a hero to astrogators across the galaxy," Sandy said.

Dick shot me a squint-eyed look. "Why? Do you think you can?"

"I'm still trying to figure out why it hasn't been done already. It looks like it would be pathetically easy to do, so what I can't see is why hasn't somebody else done it by now?"

"I don't understand," Sandy said. "How could it be pathetically easy? We have to grab the updates of the beacons and manually go through them."

"True, but this information comes from the same source that Pip's cargo data is coming from—the jump and orbital beacons—right?"

"Well, I don't know about Pip's cargo data," Dick said, "but yeah, these are coming from there. We get a few from the jump beacons, but most of it comes from the orbital loads."

I took them over to my station and showed them the cargo and price loads that we captured for Pip and what we did with the data to match it against our flight plans and projected alternatives. It didn't take long to give them the tour and when I was done they both stared into my screen like—well, I don't know like what. Their expressions were something between disbelief and lust.

"Sandy," Dick said, "would you mind carrying on with those updates, while I have a long chat with our savior here?"

Sandy shook herself away from peering into the screen. "Well, the shorter that long chat, the better," she said with a little grin. "But if you could move it along, I'd be grateful." She headed back to her station. Mr. von Ickles smiled at me from the other side of the bridge.

The rest of the watch went by in nothing flat and by the time it was over, Dick had given me a little tour of the astrogation system. The basic structure was not that much different from the cargo data. The actual content was different, but they had very similar underlying principles. When first section came to relieve us, Dick and Sandy had their heads together, talking excitedly as they headed down the ladder.

Mr. von Ickles followed me off the bridge. At the foot of the ladder he said, "You seem to have gotten over your concern about being a burden on Lois."

"Yes, sar, in a way. I still want to feel like I'm contributing but between Pip's cargo stuff and this new project in astrogation, I think I can."

"I think so, too, Mr. Wang. Mr. Maxwell was just telling me that the cargo work is excellent and I think you can expect a few little tasks from him on our next leg. He and Mr. Cotton both would like some enhancements to the manifest system to get a better representation of the load we're carrying."

"Well, sar, I'll stop worrying about job security so long as I'm doing some good."

He clapped me on the shoulder. "You're helping Lois. You may not feel like it, but think of this like working on the mess deck. We all work better and more effectively because we don't have to worry about fixing a meal every time we're hungry. You're finding rough places in the systems that have fallen through the cracks. Systems officers like me know about them, but we're tied up with routine office work. System specs, who might be able to address them, typically need to be justified eighteen ways to Sunday before a slot is opened up. Your position is unique because we got it approved based on a threat to the ship, not on a demonstrated work load."

My stomach growled loudly enough for him to hear it.

"I guess I shouldn't have mentioned the mess deck," he said with a laugh.

"Well, perhaps we could head down there, sar? I think Cookie's got lamb chops for dinner." My stomach growled in agreement and Mr. von Ickles led the way.

During the approach and docking at Umber, my mind started wandering back along the voyage. The cargo systems were shaping up and I looked forward to working with Dick Graves on the long in-port watches. We had a prototype astrogation update system in place but Dick wanted to get Ms. Avril's input on it. We would have time to sit down and really go through it while in port. I thought it felt good to have things finally getting under control.

Thinking that was one of those fate tempting thoughts that I regretted as soon as it flashed across my mind. Something of that regret must have shown on my face because Mr. von Ickles leaned over and asked, "Are you all right, Mr. Wang?"

"Yes, sar. Just had an uneasy thought for a second."

"Looked like you'd been stabbed!" he commented with a quiet chuckle.

I smiled back at him, but I just knew I was going to live to regret my previous thought, so I tried to counteract it by thinking about all the miserable things I could. I knew it wouldn't work, but I hoped for some damage control.

We were soon docked and first section relieved us. It was the first time we had docked before breakfast so everybody was a little thrown off. It made little difference to me. Third section had had the mid-watch so it was just a little livelier for us. It worked out well for first section. It didn't matter all that much in the long haul. It all evened out in the end.

I stood up, stretched, and looked out on either side to see who we were near. There was another container ship docked to starboard with the double F's of Federated Freight emblazoned on the side of the bow section. The configuration didn't look quite like the *Lois*. I thought she had more cargo sections and looked longer. It was hard to tell looking back in the dark like that. On the port side was a bulk hauler in blue and gray. It had a C superimposed on an L all in a eight pointed star. I knew the logo, but could not dredge up who it belonged to. It would come to me.

I leaned down to secure my console. We had been relieved and the captain and Mr. Maxwell were negotiating liberty. I was not in any hurry to leave the ship, myself. Mid-watch was still mid-watch and I'd need a little nap before I did anything. The co-op would spend the day on preparation for a movement in force. Mr. von Ickles had let me reserve their booth. I got a kick out of handling the communications traffic for them.

As I headed for the ladder, Mr. Maxwell and the captain finished with their negotiations. I stepped aside to let the captain have the right of way on the ladder.

"Thank you, Mr. Wang," she said leading the way down, "And if you have a few moments, perhaps you'd accompany me to the cabin?"

I knew I shouldn't have thought things were under control. "Of course, Captain," I said. I tried to sound relaxed and unconcerned.

I must not have succeeded, because she glanced up at me—one quick flick of the eyes—and I thought she smiled.

I sighed to myself. If there was one person whose smile bothered me more than Mr. Maxwell's, it was the captain's. The captain's cabin was only a few steps from the bridge so I didn't have a lot of time to think about it before we were there.

"This will only take a few moments, Mr. Wang," she said,

closing the door behind us. "Please, have a seat." She indicated the sofa.

I am always a little put off-balance by that. If it was not going to take very long, why sit? Still, she was the captain. I sat.

She settled across from me and opened without preliminary. "What have you thought about the academy?"

"Well, Captain, I thought we'd agreed that I'd work out my contract before I decided."

"And the academy is, first and foremost, a college, Mr. Wang. If you wait until next September to make up your mind, don't you foresee a bit of a problem?"

"What problem, Captain?" I asked before thinking it through. "Classes start in—" and, of course there was a problem.

She waited me out.

"You're right, Captain. I would need to apply."

"Exactly." She let me stew for a heartbeat or two before adding, "You can always choose not to go, but if you don't apply. You won't have that choice."

"Well, Captain, I'd have to be accepted, too," I pointed out.

"Of course, but that's not likely to be a problem." The corners of her mouth curled into the smallest of smiles.

"They must get thousands of applicants, Captain. I'd have to beat out a lot of people."

"Approximately fifteen thousand for each fall's class. They take the top five hundred."

"Not as many as I thought, sar. My mother occasionally served on the admissions committee at the University at Neris and I know they got about five thousand, but they could only accept Neris Company employees and their families."

"It's a bit of a specialized degree, Mr. Wang," she said, half-smile on her lips and a twinkle in her eye. "As I believe you pointed out yourself."

She had me on that one. "Good point, Captain," I said with a sigh. Part of me thought, *you've got ratings. You don't need to be an officer.* Another part of me screamed, *Go, you damned fool. At least apply so you can make up your mind later!*

She waited me out.

The screaming side won. It usually did. "Well, I guess I better find out when they start accepting applications and see what I need to do, then, eh, Captain?"

"Admissions begin October first for the next fall's term. You need to fill out an application, and submit it with at least three references. Those with experience or ratings need to include a copy of their personnel jackets as well."

"You just happened to know that off the top of your head, Captain?"

"Mr. Wang, I've sent more than my share of candidates to Port Newmar. I don't intend to stop any time soon."

"Do you earn a bounty or something, Captain?" I asked, thinking they might get a referral fee.

"Indeed, Mr. Wang, I get the satisfaction of helping good people become officers and do good work. It's part of the McKendrick legacy." She paused for a few heartbeats. "I like the feeling I get from knowing that coming generations are well represented by the kind of people my great-grandmother would have approved of. Even if I'm not quite ready to fade off into the rim myself yet," she added with a smile.

"Can I ask how long you've been planning this, Captain?"

"Do you remember O'Rourke?" she asked.

"Of course, Captain. She said I reminded her of her nephew."

"Well, I've been planning since O'Rourke told me that you were good people."

"But you hadn't even met me, sar!"

"Mr. Wang, I've known Annie O'Rourke for almost thirty-five stanyers. We served together on three ships. If Annie O'Rourke says you're good people, I believe her."

"I had no idea, Captain."

"Annie said you were curious and you took responsibility. You'd have never even found out about the opening if she hadn't decided you'd work out. It was just luck that we were due in Neris and were opening up that slot when you needed it."

I didn't think it was luck, but I felt a little funny thinking it was Lois. "What happened to him, Captain? Do you know?"

"Annie said he got a job working for Neris Company as a fry cook in one of the company commissaries. He's still there as far as I know."

I thought about that for a tick. "Well, I better get going on that application then. Do you happen to know where I can find one, Captain?"

She grinned, pulled out her own tablet, and pressed a few functions. "In your inbox," she said. "Look it over now, please. I'll answer any questions you may have about it."

Somehow that didn't surprise me, although what I found in my inbox did.

"Captain, this application appears to be filled out."

"Yes, Mr. Wang. You only need to endorse it as being a true and accurate representation."

I scrolled through the pages. It had my school records from

Neris, my ratings, everything. I got to the end of the forms and kept scrolling through the letters of recommendation. The first was from the captain, followed by Mr. Maxwell, and Mr. von Ickles, completing the required three. I kept scrolling and found one from Mr. Kelley, and another from Mr. Cotton, and even one from Ms. Avril. "Every officer aboard?" I asked.

"Yes, Mr. Wang," the captain said, "and a few others."

I looked back and kept scrolling. Captain Cassandra Harrison of the *Samuel Slater*. Second Mate Alicia Alvarez of the *Marcel Duchamp*. Third Mate Alberta Ross of the *William Hedley*. Captain Penelope Carstairs of the *Bad Penny*. I'm sure I blushed over the first two names, but I couldn't place the third. I didn't know any officers from the *Hedley*.

"What's the matter, Mr. Wang?" the captain asked. "You don't recognize Al?"

"Al?" I exclaimed. "She said she was in astrogation!"

"She is. She's their astrogation officer, and a damned fine one at that. A bit eccentric, but she can plot a course to the gates of hell and have you back in time for dinner."

I was dumbfounded. "About Captain Harrison, sar—"

"I'm asking no questions, Mr. Wang. Tell me no lies. Cass sent that letter without my asking. She popped it into my inbox just before the *Slater* pulled-out. The cover note said, 'Please add my recommendation to the file.'"

"But how?" I didn't know even what I was trying to ask. Luckily the captain did.

"How did she know there was a file to add it to?" she prompted.

"Yes, Captain. I think."

"We were roommates at the academy. You learn a lot there. Some of it has to do with ships."

I didn't know what else to say.

"She also knows I have a habit of recommending likely people to the academy. Maybe she saw something in your manner on the gangway watch that she liked," she added with a grin that might have been just a touch over the line toward mischievous.

I tried not to blush, but I don't think I was successful. Hoping to distract her, I asked, "How many have you recommended, Captain?"

"You're number thirty-four, Mr. Wang."

I was expecting something like ten. "Wow, that's a lot! How many have been accepted, sar?"

"Thirty-three of them. And all have graduated near the top of their classes," she said proudly. "Not all at the top, of course. One year there were five of my people graduating at the same time. They were all in the top ten—a memorable year. Alicia Alvarez was in that group, actually," she added with another of those impish grins. She was enjoying herself immensely. Oddly enough, so was I.

"What happened with the last one?" I asked before I did the math.

"Well, if he ever endorses his application, we'll find out!" she said with a laugh.

"Where do I sign?" I asked.

Chapter Twenty-nine
Umber Orbital: 2352-October-08

When I left the captain's cabin, I felt dazed. I had just applied to the academy. I wondered if they would accept me. The captain seemed pretty confident and with her track record, she had reason to be, but it was breakfast time so I headed for the mess deck.

When I got there I found it crowded so I assumed that Mr. Maxwell had not yet declared liberty. I got some eggs, sausages, and two biscuits from the mess line—Sarah and Pip were serving. I looked around for a seat and found one beside Diane, who sat across from Francis and Brill.

Francis said, "You okay, Ish? You look a little—distracted."

Brill and Diane looked at me strangely too. "Yeah, even for you, Ish. You seem a little out of it. Has something happened?" Diane asked.

I took a deep breath and let it out. "I just applied to the academy."

Brill asked, "Port Newmar?"

"Yup. The captain pointed out that if I was really thinking about going next year, I needed to apply now."

"Oh," Diane said. "I thought from the way you said it that you'd filed your application."

"Yeah, I did."

Even Francis leaned in to hear me because I was talking so quietly.

Brill said, "But the application is huge and you need recommendations from at least three officers."

"Yeah," I agreed.

"Well, how could you apply?" Francis finally chimed in.

"She had it all."

"Who she? What all?" Diane asked.

"The captain. She sent it to me on my tablet—all filled out—transcripts from Neris, recommendations from ten different officers, all of it."

"Ten?" Brill exclaimed. "There are only six on the ship!"

"Yeah, she had a few extras."

"Like who?" Diane pressed. Then she guessed, "Alvarez!"

"Yeah," I admitted. "And Pip's Aunt Penny. How she got involved in this, I have no idea."

"Well, that's a helluva thing, isn't it?" Francis said, sitting back and shaking his head.

"I still have to get accepted and figure out a way to pay for it. But I had to apply now, or very soon." I sighed. My fork scraped plate and I realized I had no breakfast left. I didn't even have the taste of breakfast left. I must have been hungrier, and more distracted, than I thought. "I'm not even sure when the cut off is. It might be before we hit Ablemarle."

Brill looked startled at that. "I hadn't thought about that."

The overhead speakers finally announced, "Attention all hands! Now, liberty, liberty, liberty. Hands not on duty may leave the ship according to standing orders and established procedures. Now liberty."

The chrono read 0700 and we bussed our dishes to make it easier on Sarah, Pip, and Cookie. It was such a family thing to do. It rankled that, if this application were accepted, I would not be part of that family any more. I needed to hit the rack and sleep a little before I got all slobbery, but I had one more thing I needed to do first.

I found Bev on gangway watch.

"I applied to the academy," I told her.

"Just like that? No, 'Hi, Bev, how's watch?' just, 'I applied to the academy'?"

I was really tired, and she looked really angry. I didn't know what to say so I just added, "Sorry, I didn't know how else to tell you."

"Well, that was one way, but a girl likes a little warm up first."

I looked up at her and she was grinning at me. It caught me off guard and I laughed a little.

"If you're really thinking about deciding next fall, then you have to apply now, don't you, doofus?" she asked with a lopsided grin.

"That's what the captain said too," I told her.

"Ah ha! The truth comes out. It's okay, Ish. I was kidding about the 'Hi, Bev' stuff. You look like you could use a little rack time."

"I could, but I promised to let you know."

"You coulda waited until you woke up. Now, scoot!" she said, stamping her foot on the deck in my direction like I was a little dog. "I'll see you after watch."

I met Mr. Maxwell coming the other way in the passage and stood aside for him to go by. "Nice work on those cargo tools, Mr. Wang," he said.

"Thank you, sar!"

He went on past me and I kept going. I heard him talking to Beverly as I headed for my bunk. I must have made it—or they found me and put me in it—because I awoke there at 1230. I splashed water on my face, promised myself a nice shower after lunch, and headed for the mess deck. Pip had helped Sarah clean up the galley and it looked like they had things well in hand. I filled a plate with lamb, rice, and banapods and found a seat. That was not hard—I was the only one there.

Pip came out of the galley, his tasks completed for the moment. "So, what's with you?"

"What do you mean?"

"Well, you came through the mess line this morning looking like—I don't know what—and when I asked what was going on you said, 'Yes, thank you,' and wandered off."

"Oh, the captain took me down to her cabin after we secured from nav detail."

"She didn't! The nerve of that woman. Was it good for you, too?"

The image touched my giggle nerve and I started laughing.

"That's better. Now, you wanna tell me about it?"

"I applied to the academy this morning."

"And you're just telling me now? Why didn't you mention it when you started the application?"

"I did...I am...I mean...the time between starting and finishing was about a tick."

"Huh? What are you talking about?"

"I'm saying when the captain sent it to me, it was complete."

"Complete?"

"Yup," I said.

"Your personal information was on it?"

"Yup," I said again.

"Your transcripts?"

"Those too."

"Personnel jacket?"

"Attached."

"Three recommendations?"

"No."

"Well, you need three," he said.

"There were ten. And your Aunt P was one of them."

"How did Aunt P get involved?" he asked.

"You obviously have mistaken me for somebody with a clue. Unfortunately, I don't even know where to buy a clue, and if I had one, I'm sure it would be to a different puzzle."

"Our captain is something, isn't she? Now you're getting a little taste of what I was up against at home."

"Wasn't so bad. I still have to get accepted, and then I have to find a way to pay for it."

"Well, that's true enough," he said, and then changed the subject. "Fancy a run ashore this afternoon? Sarah has the duty here today because she wants to go up to the co-op first thing tomorrow and take her shawls."

"Sure, you thinking of scoping out the flea market for cargo?"

"It's the perfect time, head up this afternoon, do a little looking about, maybe make some contacts. See where we are after that. We have plenty of cash left after the masks and the carp, and a lot of mass as well. I think it's gonna work out."

"Sounds like a plan, how soon can you go?"

"1330? Meet you in deck berthing."

He was as good as his word and we were on our way at 1335.

As we stepped out of the lock, he asked, "So? Are you going to go?"

"I don't know. How much do you think we can make between now and next August?"

"Depends on where we go and what we find. The new cargo software will help the ship, but that's not going to be much use with private cargo."

As we approached the lift, a burly man who looked vaguely familiar straightened up from where he lounged by the door. Pip was contemplating cargo and had not noticed him, but it was obvious to me that he had seen us. He said, "Hello, Philip. How's the semester in space."

I realized who he looked like then—Uncle Q, but he wasn't Uncle Q.

"Hi, Dad. Fancy meeting you here," Pip replied.

Captain Thomas Carstairs didn't seem like the kind of man you would cross lightly or more than once for that matter. He didn't look mean or anything—just efficient. He reminded me a bit of Mr. Maxwell in that way. He smiled warmly enough at me, though, and held out a hand. "You're Ishmael?"

"Yes, sar. Ishmael Wang," I said, and shook his hand.

"You can call me Tom, Ishmael. You're not on my crew and we're not on my ship. Tom will do nicely." He continued to talk with me and ignore Pip. "Penny and Quent couldn't say enough good things about you. You really impressed them, and they're not easily impressed. Quent's a little soft in the head, but P's a hard-case from the old school."

"They explained a few things to me," I told him. "It was nice to see something outside of the corporate world."

"I think I'm ready for a beer. Anybody else?" he said. "I'll buy." He turned to the lift without waiting for a reply and pressed the button. It must have been on our level because the doors opened immediately. I followed him into the lift.

When I turned, Tom had his finger on the open door control and looked at Pip who hadn't said a word beyond his first. Tom just waited, holding the door open. He didn't say anything like, "Are you coming?" or "At your earliest convenience." or "Stop being an idiot and get on the elevator."

Finally Pip sighed and stepped aboard. Tom released the door control and pressed the oh-two button. When we got there, he led us to a place. It wasn't *Shaunessey's* but it might as well have been. The tablet beside the door read, *Floyd's Place*. A few quiet spacers shared an afternoon beer and a gab at the bar. We joined the flotilla and took up station at an empty table.

Tom ordered a pitcher of a medium pilsner and three glasses. We settled down with our beers before we got into the heavy chat.

"So? How long did you think you could pull this off?" Tom asked Pip after we each had about half a glass inside us.

Pip didn't answer right away and Tom didn't press him. "I don't know," Pip said finally. "I hadn't really thought that far ahead."

Tom sipped his beer a little. "Penny said she talked to Alys and you've just extended for a year?"

"Yeah, things have been picking up here and Ishmael gets done next fall, too."

"Zat right?" he said smiling at me. "What're you going to do then, Ishmael?" he asked it like he was interested.

"I don't know. I just applied to the academy but I don't know if I'll get in."

"You'll get in," he said matter-of-factly.

"Well, then there's the problem of paying for it. I'm hoping I can make enough trading over the next year to make a dent." I was talking to give Pip a chance to—I don't know what—get a handle on the situation, maybe.

"You making any creds?"

"We've been pretty lucky."

"Don't worry about the money, Ishmael. Once you're accepted, it will be taken care of one way or another."

"It's the 'another' I'm worried about," I said with a grin.

He chuckled then. "I guess I can appreciate that." We sat and finished the first glass of beer and Tom emptied the pitcher on the second round. "So? You want to go?"

"I don't know. I'm still not sure."

He turned back to Pip. "So, if Ishmael goes, you'd go, too?"

Pip looked startled. "What?" he asked. He seemed almost like he was waking up from a nap, he had that same level of disorientation.

"I asked if you'd go to the academy if Ishmael goes," his father repeated.

Pip still wasn't tracking. "How can I go? I burned that bridge when I didn't show up two stanyers ago."

"Not exactly. When Annie told me you'd shipped on the *Duchamp*, I contacted Commandant Giggone. Told him you were taking a tour as a deck hand to get some experience under you before reporting. He put your file on hold."

"You've known all this time?"

"Of course," he said with a patient smile. "Annie checked with me before she let you sign the Articles."

"But—" he started to say.

"But what? Why did she check with me? Because she's family, ya great daft thing."

"No, why didn't you say no?"

"Well, because you're family," he said as if it were the most obvious thing in the world. "You weren't ready for Port Newmar. I knew that."

"Then why did you push me?" he asked, his voice raw.

"I didn't. That was just how you saw it. I can't tell you how pleased I was when I got the deep-space from Annie."

"But you've gone along with the whole thing all this time?"

"The scholarship idea was genius. But don't you think two years is a little long for a semester in space?" he asked with a grin.

"All this time and you knew?" Pip sounded amazed. "And you didn't come after me?"

"I knew before you signed. Why would I come after you when it was too late?" he asked. "You'd tell me eventually. You'd have to—we're family."

"So what are you doing here now then?" Pip asked, half defensive and half defiant.

"Delivered a load of ship parts. What'd ya think? I dropped everything and flew out here for the hell of it?"

"Aunt P didn't message you?"

"Well, of course she messaged me!" he said with a chuckle.

"And you just happen to show up here? Our next port of call?"

Tom shrugged. "Well, I was in the neighborhood."

"I'm not going back," Pip said suddenly.

"Going back where?" Tom asked.

"Back on the *Epiphany*."

"Damn straight you're not! You're under Articles until next August."

Pip fell back into his chair. "You didn't come to take me to the academy?"

Tom screwed up his face in mock confusion. "How could I do that? You're under contract."

We sipped beer for a little, then he leaned forward and put his glass on the table.

"Okay, here's the deal, Philip. Yes, Penny messaged and I grabbed the first cargo coming to Umber. I humped it over here as fast as the *Epy* could haul. We made good time from Sargass and got here about three weeks ago. We've been running some small cargoes in and out while we waited."

The waitress brought us another pitcher and Tom did the honors around the table once more.

"But I didn't come to drag you away. Penny's message said she thought you were ready and that I should let you know it was okay." He turned to me then and said, "She gives you a lot of the credit, Ishmael."

I shrugged. "I don't know what I might have done to give her that impression, but thank you, sar—er—Tom."

"The point is—and you still haven't answered my question— your academy acceptance is on hold. I just need to let the commandant know as soon as possible so he can slot you into the new class. So? If Ishmael goes, will you go with him?"

Pip looked at me then. His expression started out as a kind of whipped dog look, but it transformed into a funny, devilish grin. He turned back to his father and said, "Well, somebody needs to look out for him."

"I still have to get accepted," I pointed out.

"You'll get in." Tom said in a tone like you might say, "The sun's out."

"Everybody seems sure of that."

Tom shrugged. "If Alys Giggone puts up a candidate, I suspect Commandant Giggone will listen."

"You said that before—Commandant Giggone?"

"Her father. And Penny sent a letter, too, didn't she?"

"Yeah, it was quite a packet of recommendations."

"No kidding? Anything over eight is pretty much automatic. How many did you have?"

Pip said, "Ten. Three of them captains."

Tom held up his glass, "Congratulations on your pending acceptance. Start thinking of how you'll say yes."

"But how can you be so sure?"

"Because Alys Giggone is one of the best judges of potential candidates in the galaxy and her father knows that. That's the only reason she's not teaching there now. You have two sure tickets on your application. One is a recommendation from Alys Giggone. The other is that you've convinced two other captains that she's right and they've put their reputations on the line in support of you. Bob Giggone may have a soft spot in his heart for his little girl, but ten letters including three from captains just proves that Alys is right."

"But I didn't convince anybody! I didn't even know I was applying until the captain gave me the application packet to endorse. The recommendations were already in it."

"And in spite of the evidence of your own eyes, you continue to persist in the delusion that you won't make the cut?" he said with a grin. "Penny said you weren't born to a spacer family so this probably seems crazy." He turned back to Pip. "So, was that a yes? Can I tell Bob that you'll be there for the next class?"

Pip looked at his father and smiled. "Yes, please. That would be very helpful. Thanks, Dad."

Tom made a theatrical grasp at his chest, "Oh my gods and garters, he said thank you!" He had a proud smile on his face and he didn't mug it up for long. Instead he filled the glasses one last time and raised his in a toast, "To Port Newmar!" and we drank.

Chapter Thirty
Dunsany Roads Orbital: 2353-July-18

After all the angst and anxiety of my first year in space, the next ten months seemed idyllic—if you think of idyllic as working twelve hours a day for weeks on end locked in a big tin can surrounded by metric mega-butt loads of nothing.

Nothing broke. The ship didn't crash. I managed not to make any more a fool of myself than was necessary to maintain my reputation as a member in good standing with the Order of Young, Stupid Males. That is not to say we didn't have a modicum of excitement now and again.

It started while we were still on Umber, the orders came down for a change in destination. We were scheduled to close the loop by running from Ablemarle back to Dunsany Roads, but the company diverted us to Barsi. We took about half the ship loaded in fertilizer and frozen fish. Pip and I did very well with the masks and silk carp in the flea market, leaving Umber with twelve kilocreds in cash and a bundle of necklaces made of shells, bones, and teeth from one of the large aquatic predators. I thought they were a bit tacky, but Diane liked them and I trusted her judgment.

By the time we got to Barsi in December, Pip and I had the new cargo systems smoothed out and we managed to bring the profit pool up by something like eight percent over projections by locking in some cargoes as early as we could and holding others until the last possible moment. That added a nice little bit to our shares. It was a good thing, too. The academy accepted me into the class of 2358 just as Tom Carstairs had predicted. The acceptance notification from the academy came aboard when we pulled the beacon data from the Barsi Orbital. The administration had appended a financial aid application packet to it. That form wasn't filled out for me, but it wasn't difficult. I had some awkward moments trying to figure out how to explain my parents' financial status. Mom's was easy, of course. "Deceased" covered it. Finally, Mr. von Ickles suggested, "Whereabouts unknown," for my father. After that I just attached my tax receipts for the previous year.

Francis surprised us in Barsi when he left the ship to take a teaching position.

He announced it to Brill, Diane, CC, and me on the mess deck just before we docked. "It's your fault," he told me with a grin.

"What did I do?"

"You were drunk on your butt in Niol that night with Penny and Quent, remember?"

"I remember very well," I told him, "thereby putting the lie to your scurrilous commentary on my state of inebriation!"

CC turned to Diane at that point and asked, "What did he say?"

She leaned over. "He said he wasn't drunk."

CC nodded and thanked Diane for the translation.

"You told me that I should teach at the academy because the officers needed to know about astrophysics. I kinda liked that idea so I threw off an inquiry to the commandant. Did you know he's named Giggone, too?"

"Yeah, he's the captain's father. What'd he say?"

Brill and Diane both looked at me as if to say "How do you know that?" but didn't interrupt for a change.

"Well, they happened to have a search open and had no luck finding anybody who wanted to teach. They offered me a contract on the basis of my credentials and sent a ticket out of Barsi on the weekly packet ship. I should be there in time to start spring term if I leave on the next transport."

He grinned at me then. "I'll be ready for you when you get there. Expect to work very hard but I'm a fair grader!"

I laughed, remembering every teacher I had ever known saying that. He probably believed it as much as they all did.

The captain posted the opening as soon as we docked and we got a spec three from the *Ozymandias* as replacement within a couple of days. He was a nice enough guy named Emile Laslo. He had cropped black hair and a grin that never seemed to go away—even in his sleep. He knew his stuff pretty well and, after getting lost only twice on the VSI, didn't have any problems. Diane liked his shoulders.

While we were on Barsi, I got to meet Pip's mother, Tammy Carstairs. A lovely woman with a wiry sense of humor that found funny in the strangest of places. I suppose, living with Tom and raising Pip, you'd have to have some kind of defense mechanism. I took to her right away. Not so much as surrogate mother figure but more like supplemental mom. She was a hell of an astrogator, too, as I was coming to understand just what that meant. She asked what I was doing in systems and after describing the cargo tools—which Pip gushed about at some length—we talked about other astrogation problems. She had some interesting ideas including considerations of planetary positioning in orbital sequence to identify the true center of gravity for a system. Theoretically, it was possible to shave as much as two days off a long run out to the Burleson limit by taking planetary positioning into account. Taking two days off a twenty day run was a ten percent reduction in overhead and was certainly worth looking into. It wouldn't work all the time, of course, because it required a specific alignment scenario with at least the major system bodies. Still, an awareness of it could certainly give us some options in laying out courses.

Pip and I didn't have much success with our trades on Barsi. The shell necklaces didn't sell that well and I didn't find the kind of quality goods that I was hoping for on the return leg. We only made another kilocred in private trading, but we picked up a big pile of entertainment cubes to take back to Umber. Those we expected to do well with, although we were already sweating what we were going to take out of Umber when we left for Niol.

Dick Graves was familiar with the planetary alignment work, but lacked the necessary computational ability to actually calculate the course based on it. We worked on the problem all the way back to Umber—Ms. Avril, Mr. von Ickles, Dick, Sandy, and I. At least part of the issue was related to having the correctly updated astrogation ephemera. Those we had automatically updating by the time we picked up the Umber Orbital feeds again.

We docked at Umber near the end of January. As expected the entertainment cubes sold well, and we were left with a few of the shell necklaces, and about twenty kilocreds at the end of our second day in port. Personally, I began to get a bit worried. Unless we earned a lot more and quickly, I wouldn't have enough creds for the ticket to Port Newmar, let alone the cost of my first year at the academy.

Pip and I had our heads together over beers at *Floyds*. Lee von Ickles was with us. He had adopted me when I joined the section, but we had been hanging around together off the ship ever since my acceptance came in. I appreciated it because we usually wound up talking about the academy. He had me convinced to start studying the advanced math course I had on my portable and when I got stuck on something, he was good about helping me with it. He had an ulterior motive, but at the time he just said, "It'll help you when you get to Port Newmar if you have this down."

"Well, how much risk are you willing to take on?" Lee asked us over the second round.

I shrugged. "I don't know, but at this rate, I'm not going to be able to go."

"Fertilizer," Lee said.

Pip looked up at that. "What?"

"We're going to Niol next. Check the prices on fertilizer. A container costs basically ten creds a ton to ship—about six thousand credits per container."

"We can rent a container?" Pip asked.

He shrugged. "Anybody can rent a container. Long as you pay the freight on it. The challenge—and the risk—is in finding something that you can afford to buy a container full of that's going to earn you more than the cost of the freight on the other end."

"That first exercise we did for Mr. Maxwell was only ten kilo-creds, wasn't it?" I asked Pip.

He nodded slowly. "Yeah, but the ship doesn't have to pay the freight, so the margins were much higher."

"True, but if you've got twenty kilocreds to invest, six goes to pay the freight and that leaves you fourteen to fill the container with. The only problem is you need to fill it with something that'll earn you more than the original investment. Fertilizer is the only thing I can think of that's cheap enough per unit for you to buy a container load of here."

"We can afford to pay thirty creds per ton. Ten goes to shipping so we can buy anything that's under twenty." He turned to Lee and asked, "What if we don't fill a container? Can we ship a partial?"

"Yeah, but check with Mr. Cotton. The price break isn't that much. You're better off filling it."

Pip turned to me then, "You willing?"

I shrugged. "The worst case is we're down some cred at the end of the day. So long as we keep from incurring any debt on the transaction, I'm okay with it."

In the end we rented the container and Pip loaded it with five hundred ninety tons of fertilizer and ten tons of frozen fish. It cost almost every last credit we had and I tried not to fret about it all the way to Niol.

The Umber to Niol run was the first real check of the new astro-gation tools. Ms. Avril and Dick Graves were pretty excited about it. Because the two gas giants were lined up on the back side of Umber's primary, we had a good chance to check the theoretical calculations against the actual threshold measurements. We might have shaved three days, but the captain approved just a small adjustment in our standard course for safety reasons. Still, we got two. We weren't able to jump any closer on the other end because we didn't dare shave the safety margins that much, but it still proved the concept. Ms. Avril and the captain were very excited. Sandy Belterson and Dick Graves were more excited by the automated database updates.

The gamble with the container paid off on Niol. When everything was settled out, we were sitting on twenty-six thousand one hundred creds, a nice profit, but we were lucky. The price of fertilizer was falling when we jumped in and Pip spotted it on the new trading software. He was able to lock in a price that saved almost a kilocred. We decided to push our luck a little more on the run back to Betrus and booked a container with a mixed cargo of glass ingots and engine parts. The fishing boats on Umber and the tractors on Betrus used the same basic diesel engines and Pip found a ten ton pallet of parts for ten kilocreds. The glass had a high margin on it and, with luck, it would cover the transportation cost. We needed a very big margin on the engine parts to turn a good profit.

Pip got a message from his Aunt P when we docked that they would meet us in Dunsany Roads. She offered to give us a ride to Port Newmar. It wouldn't be as luxurious as a stateroom on the *Benjamin Franklin* and we'd have to work passage, but it would also be five kilocreds cheaper for each of us. I still didn't know how I was going to pay for school, but at least I began to think I might get there.

I asked, "How can they afford to do that? Just drop everything and fly off to the ends of the universe?"

He snickered. "Aunt P probably has a line on some high priority cargo in Dunsany Roads that needs to be either at Port Newmar or someplace close. You wait and see. They'll turn a profit on the trip. In both directions."

I shook my head. "How can they do that?"

He shrugged. "We're moving six hundred metric tons in the container and it's costing us six thousand creds per trip. That's profit to the company. They're moving eight kilotons at a time—that's about thirteen containers worth—and it costs them maybe five kilocreds for the lot."

"That's a lot less than we were paying per ton."

"Yeah, and they're also moving cargoes like delicate electronic instruments and small, high value integrated circuits. We're paying ten creds a ton in shipping costs and they're paying less than one. They can do that because they own the ship, their expenses are really low, and they have a lot of creds and a good credit line so they can afford to take a cargo on spec that costs ten kilocreds a ton and the hauling capacity to grab a lot of it. If we could afford a container full of integrated circuits we wouldn't need to go to the academy. We could retire on it. They can also make port a little more than twice as often so where we're lucky to make port six times a stanyer, they may make twelve or fourteen."

I laughed. "You make it sound so simple."

"Yeah, but it's not. They've worked for a long time to get where they are, but believe me when I say that they are not doing this out of the goodness of their hearts. Aunt P will have profit on the ledger by the time we dock," he said proudly.

"So, you don't think it's to make sure you make it this time?" I asked with a grin.

"Oh, that, too." He laughed. "But we are gonna have fun on the trip out."

We didn't do anything too risky on Niol. Pip and I were saving our money and I found that a quiet walk around the orbital with Bev or Brill, and occasionally both of them, was very pleasant. We would slip into a café and grab a pastry or a beer and talk and laugh. We laughed a lot, we three. I tried not to think too far ahead. I wanted to enjoy what time I could get with them before I had to leave.

The pull out at Niol was the first rough one I had been through. I was watching the display and saw the field strength flicker on the starboard side tug for just a fraction of a heartbeat as they took the strain of the ship. It was enough to jolt us and while it knocked people around a little, it did no real damage. Just a friendly reminder of why we do everything so carefully. The tug skipper apologized the whole way out. The captain shrugged it off. "We've been through worse," she said.

I finished up the advanced math course within a couple days of getting underway for Betrus and Mr. von Ickles sent me the spec one systems curriculum. "With the math behind you, I bet you can pass it on the next cycle," he said.

He was right.

I took the quarterly tests three weeks later, right after transition into Betrus. I only got an eighty-nine, but I passed.

When the test was over, I asked, "Why did we do this, sar? I'll be at the academy before I ever find a spec one berth."

"Because, Mr. Wang, having passed spec one, you can now get your Confederated Planets Joint Committee on Communications license to operate mobile systems and communications."

"My what, sar?"

He grinned. "It's basically the same test. Grab the study guide from the academy library when you get there. You'll get the additional material easily enough. Take your license test as soon as you can. It's good for five stanyers and, by the time it's due to expire, you'll have been a third mate for a year. You can renew it by paying a fee."

"Sneaky, sar," I told him.

"Thank you for noticing, Mr. Wang."

The approach to Betrus was a lot less exciting than the previous one had been. I was beginning to appreciate the value in *less exciting*. Pip had handled the trading on the way in, but we hadn't picked up as much as we'd hoped we might. We made less than we had with a load of fertilizer and fish. Still it took us over thirty kilocreds which was what each of us needed to cover the first year at the academy.

The other shoe dropped when the financial aid package came back. It was for four years and contained grants, loans, and work-study, but it was capped at eight kilocreds a year. I was going to have to make up the rest, somehow. While it would cover almost all of the tuition, it wouldn't be enough to cover room, board, books, and fees. With my half of the profits with Pip, I had about enough to cover two years and a bit.

I talked with Mr. von Ickles about the problem. "You'll find a way. Believe in yourself, Ishmael. You've got two stanyers covered and only need to cover the other two." He sounded confident, but I wasn't so sure. I had visions of getting to my junior year and having to drop out because I couldn't pay the bills. Where other students would have parents to co-sign loans, I was on my own.

Well, not quite on my own. I made an appointment to see the captain on the day before we got underway for Dunsany Roads.

In the meantime Pip lined up a full container of malted barley to take to Dunsany. We hadn't had much luck with the diversified cargo strategy, in large part because we didn't have enough creds to make it worthwhile. The malted barley took practically every cred we had. Frankly, I was leery about doing it. I assumed we could at least get back to break even after paying for the container, but we really needed more. Unfortunately, with all our credits tied up in the container, we didn't even have enough left over to do much with the flea market.

Bev, Brill and I continued our walks in Betrus. It got harder for me to face the idea that I would say goodbye to them in a few weeks. Part of me looked forward to the going away party, but it still ate at me. They didn't seem too concerned and rebuffed every attempt I made to talk about what was ahead. I thought not being able to share it made it that much harder.

The day before pull out, the captain met with me.

"How can I help, Mr. Wang?" she asked as we settled at the table in the cabin.

"Well, Captain, I got the results for financial aid back from the academy. It's a full four-year package, but it only covers about half the cost. With what Pip and I have made trading—assuming we don't lose much of it between here and Dunsany, I've got enough for about two years."

"Sounds like you've made good progress."

"I'm troubled about the other two years, though, Captain. How likely is it that I could get a loan from a bank on Port Newmar?"

Well, you'll be twenty-two with good prospects and working on your education. I suspect you'd have no problem. The bankers on Port Newmar are used to dealing with broke, soon-to-be officers."

"I see. Thank you, Captain. That's really all I wanted to know. With as many people as you've sent there, I figured you'd know the ins and outs of it as well as anybody."

She smiled at that. "Probably true." She paused for a few heartbeats before continuing. "There is one other option, but I'm not sure it's right for you. Federated Freight has a plan where they'll pay up to half your tuition, books, and provide a housing allotment while you're at the academy."

"What's the catch, Captain?"

"You have to agree to work for Federated Freight for five stanyers after graduation."

I thought about that for a time before asking, "And why don't you think that's right for me, Captain?"

"Because, Mr. Wang, you're going to have a lot more, and better, offers when you graduate than being locked into a Federated Freight third mate slot. Granted it's only for five years and would probably be an easy way for you to get the funding you need, but I just have the feeling that if you can manage to scrape through without that burden on the back-end, you'll be better off."

"Thank you for telling me, Captain."

"You can always sign on to Federated Freight after you graduate, but you've made some excellent contacts outside the corporate world already and my professional opinion is that you're going to want to keep those options open after graduation."

"I hadn't thought of it that way, Captain. I appreciate your perspective and I think you're right. I'll do what I can to make sure number thirty-four doesn't break your streak," I said with a smile.

"I'm not worried, Mr. Wang."

The trip from Betrus to Dunsany Roads was bittersweet. I had read that phrase in the old stories that Mom had made me read. I never had a real appreciation for it before that last trip on the *Lois McKendrick*. In some ways the last trip seemed interminable, and in others it passed in an instant.

The cargo tracking code that we developed was now part of the main systems package of the ship and Mr. von Ickles had submitted it to Federated Freight for consideration on all their vessels. Pip had saved a copy of it and we set it up so it would run on my portable. Mr. von Ickles helped. It probably wasn't legal, but we did it anyway.

The astrogation updates flowed smoothly as well. We were able to carve a couple of days off both ends of the jump and that would result in a nice little addition to the share pool. Ms. Avril worked on refining the course display monitors to reflect the new rich data that we were able to use because of the automated updates, and was very excited about the potential applications.

We jumped into Dunsany Roads at the end of June and the beacon carried a directive from home office to remove my spec two berth on docking. It freed me to leave the ship, of course, but also robbed Mr. von Ickles of the opportunity to bring in a replacement. Personally, I was of two minds. There was no question that I had been able to help the ship become more effective and profitable. But I had to agree with home office that it perhaps might not be the most efficient application of resources.

One small surprise happened when CC took, and passed the spec one environmental test. He'd been keeping such a low profile down there that I'd lost track of him. Diane and Brill both said he had turned around dramatically since those first days and had nothing but good things to say about him. Perhaps it was just the added awareness but I suddenly noticed that he and Sarah seemed to have become something of an item. She smiled a special grin when he came into the mess deck and, for his part, he seemed a little less brash and a little gentler when she was around. Apparently Lois approved of the new CC.

Pip's trading in the malted barley was spectacular. We locked in the selling price well in advance of docking and our account stood at just over forty kilocreds. Looking back over the time frame, I thought we'd done pretty well to double our money in just a few months. Mr. Cotton and Mr. Maxwell both congratulated us. I wondered how much we would have amassed with another stanyer, but shook that idea out of my head.

When they called navigation detail for my last run into Dunsany on the *Lois*, I reported to the bridge and felt like I wanted to cry. The careful choreography of tug, ship, and orbital seemed just a bit more special. I knew it would be a long time before I got a chance to sit on the bridge of a ship like the *Lois McKendrick* again. We eased in and latched on without incident. There was a moment of quiet in me, if not in the bridge itself. It was done. A few weeks shy of two years, I could almost feel that Lois had finished with me.

I stood and secured the console, powering it down all the way for the first time since Mr. von Ickles had brought it up for me to use. I looked out at the ships on either side, not wanting to look at the people on the bridge just yet. Dick Graves at astrogation, Salina and Fong on ship handling, Sandy Belterson standing by to take the watch. Mr. von Ickles, Mr. Kelley, Mr. Maxwell, and the captain. I knew they were all there, but I struggled to get control before I tried to say anything.

"If you'd do the honors, Mr. Pa?" The captain said. "Secure from navigation detail. First section has the watch."

She waited for Fong to finish, then turned to Mr. Maxwell. "You may declare liberty at your discretion, Mr. Maxwell."

"Thank you, Captain. Make the announcement, Mr. Pa."

While Fong announced liberty, Mr. von Ickles held out his hand to shake mine. "Best wishes, Mr. Wang. It's been an honor sailing with you."

One after another they all came and if they noticed I didn't speak, they didn't mention it. The captain came last, of course, and said, "If you'd come to the cabin, Mr. Wang, we have some paperwork to finish up." She didn't wait for me, just turned and led the way off the bridge. Around us the bridge crew secured the consoles. The business of the ship continued and, even though I was no longer part of it, the rightness of it made me feel a little better.

When we got to the cabin, the captain apologized. "I'm sorry to have to boot you off, Ishmael, but it's actually going to work out in your favor."

"It's okay, Captain, I understand."

"You'll continue to collect half-pay until your contract expires, because the company dismissed the berth. You're not obligated to take anything less than a spec one systems berth and you're not going to be here long enough for that to matter."

"Thank you, Captain."

"The standard procedure is to extend the courtesy of the ship until the end of the watch, so you'll have until 1800 to pack up and say your goodbyes. It's only 1030 now so you should have plenty of time. Most of the crew will be on liberty, but you may find a few of them at some disreputable spacer bar down on the oh-two level at about 2000 tomorrow evening. *Jump!* I believe it's called," she said, a small grin pulling up the corners of her mouth.

"I think I know the place, Captain." I felt touched that the captain herself would tell me.

"You'll need to initial your logout at the gangway when you leave and surrender your ship's tablet at that time. You're not obligated to check out until 1800, of course, so if you have any shopping or anything you want to do before final check out, that's not a problem. Any questions so far?"

"No, Captain," I think I've got it.

"The last bit of business is to let you know that I got a message at the beacon from Captain Carstairs and they'll be a couple days late meeting up with you and Pip. They're expected to dock early on the twenty-first, so you'll have a couple of days real liberty on the station."

"I'm not sure I remember how to act without a watch schedule to guide me, Captain."

"My advice is sleep while you can. It's the one thing you'll never have enough of at the academy," she said with a straight face and a twinkle in her eye.

"Thank you, Captain. Good advice."

"Now, that the ship's business is complete, let me tell you how proud I am of you. You've come a long way since the scared boy that came aboard in Neris, and I'm sure your mother would be proud as well."

She caught me with that one, and I started to tear up. I could feel my control crumbling even as I tried to grab a hold of it.

"Well, silly me," she said. "I seem to have left my tablet on the bridge. If you'd be so good as to excuse me, Mr. Wang. I'll just leave you here for a few ticks."

She crossed to the door. Before opening it, she said very gently without turning, "Tissues are by the sofa. Use as many as you need." She slipped out and latched the door behind her.

I cried then. I cried for my mother, dead two years and not properly mourned until that moment. I cried for Lois because I was going to miss her so much. I cried because I was going to have to say goodbye to Diane, Brill, Beverly, Cookie, and even Mr. Maxwell. I cried because I had come to love this place and these people who had welcomed me into their home and let me make it mine for a time when I needed the shelter. I cried for me because I hurt, even though I knew that hurt would pass. And I cried because while I knew the boy I had been was still inside, I also knew he would never be the same.

In a surprisingly short time, I cried myself out. I had an astonishing pile of tissues to deal with, and the feeling that my throat might be raw for a while. I cleaned myself up as best I could and dropped the soggy wad down the disposal chute, smiling with the silly thought that part of me would be staying with the ship.

By the time the captain returned with her tablet, I was more or less under control. If she noticed anything untoward about my appearance, she didn't mention it.

"Right then," she said. "I think that's about it. There's a packet of information you might find useful waiting for you at the gangway, including storage cubes of your personnel jacket and your personal records from the ship's system. There's also information about where you might stay on the orbital until Captain Carstairs arrives."

"Thank you, Captain. It's been an honor serving on the *Lois*. I'll never forget all you've done for me."

"I know you'll do us proud, Mr. Wang," she said, and shook my hand.

"I'll do my best, Captain."

As I left the cabin, the urge to leave immediately seized me. I headed for berthing and put everything but the clothes I would wear ashore into a duffel. I wondered if they used shipsuits on the *Bad Penny* but I'd have a couple of days to sort that out. I pulled out my civilian model peeda and wondered if I could get a new tablet at the academy. In the meantime, I made sure the bank balances and other information I needed from the tablet reflected properly on smaller device. The split from our trading and my accumulated pay and shares amounted to just over twenty-four kilocreds. It seemed like an insane amount but I knew it was going to have to last for a long time.

By then it was time for lunch. I thought the mess deck would be the best place to catch any members of the crew that might be around. When I got there, it was a typical first day in port. I was the only one there. The buffet was spiced beefalo and I inhaled a lungful of the aroma so I would never forget it.

Cookie was there, of course, and he came out and shook my hand. "You have done well, Ishmael," he said with a smile. "Take care of Pip," he added with a sly wink. He didn't linger but instead went back to his work.

I got my food and settled on the mess deck just as Diane came in. "Oh good!" she said, and crossed to where I was sitting. "You're released, right?"

"Yeah, just taking advantage of a free meal. I need to be off the ship by 1800."

"Good," she said, and grabbed my head and kissed me very soundly. She came up for air after a long and very pleasant smooch, looking as dazed as I felt. "Whew! I've wanted to do that for a long time. You take care of yourself, Ishmael Wang," she added and, with another little peck on my nose, headed off the mess deck.

Cookie, Pip, and Sarah were all looking out at me—Cookie with a smile, Pip with a grin, and Sarah with a considering look. After Diane, I was a little worried about what Sarah might be considering.

Cookie and Sarah turned back to working on something in the kitchen that I couldn't see and Pip came out to sit with me for a bit. "I'm not sure it's safe to sit this close to you. I don't wanna cramp your style."

"I hope she enjoyed that as much as I did."

"Heckfire! I hope she enjoyed it as much as *I* did!"

"So, I've gotta be off the ship by 1800. There's a packet at the gangway with housing information so I better go check that out this afternoon and see what we've got to work with. How about you?"

"I'll be joining you tomorrow. We'll have to try to find something fun to do."

"Is the *Alistair* in?"

He laughed. "I'll have to look it up." He turned serious then and said, "It's gonna be okay, I think."

Sitting there on the mess deck, I could almost believe it. I got up to bus my dishes for the last time. When I turned, Sarah stood behind me. She smiled, not a big smile, but still with a kind glow to it. "Blessings upon you, Ishmael Wang," she said. She reached up to pull my head down and kissed my forehead. She released me and I smiled back at her.

"Thank you, Sarah. Fare you well, wherever you go."

Pip looked at me with raised eyebrows, but it felt right somehow. Silly, perhaps, but right and I knew it was time to go. "You're leaving now?" he asked

"Yes," I said. "Lois is done with me and it's time to move on."

"I'll tell them," Pip said without my having to ask which them he was talking about.

I thanked him with a nod.

I headed down to berthing to change into civvies. After that, it was a matter of a tick to collect my duffel, reset the locker, and run the linens into the recycler. In two ticks, I was at the lock and checking out.

Fong had the duty and handed me a thick envelope with a couple of data cubes, and several folders of information. The one marked housing indicated a hotel on level seven and listed a reservation number.

"All in order, Ish?" Fong asked.

"I don't know yet," I told him with a smile. "It seems I've already got a reservation. I was hoping to say goodbye to a few people, but I suppose they'll be at *Jump!* huh?"

"I think everybody but those with the duty will be there," he said with a grin. "You going?"

I laughed. "I think I have to, don't I?" The envelope went into my duffel along with all my other worldly possessions and the folder with the reservation information slipped into a jacket pocket. Fong zeroed out my mass allotment, accepted my tablet, and opened the lock for me.

"Thanks. See you tomorrow night."

"Safe voyage, Ishmael. In case I miss you."

"Safe voyage, Fong."

I walked out of the lock and turned to watch it close. "Safe voyage, Lois," I said, and headed for the lift.

Chapter Thirty-two
Dunsany Roads Orbital: 2353-July-18

Walking away across the icy cold docks toward the lift, I felt numb—
not outside from the cold but inside. In part I still felt wrung out
from my encounter with the captain, but mostly because I knew I
was walking away from the *Lois* for the last time. Walking away
from Beverly, Brill, Diane, and all the others. I gave a little snort
of amusement then, remembering that before coming aboard I was
the guy with no friends. On the one hand, that had made it easy
to leave Neris, and on the other, almost impossibly difficult to walk
across that dock, leaving them all behind. My brain turned numb
so I could do what needed doing.

The lift stood open and waiting when I got to it. I punched
level seven. As I got off, I realized with a start that it was the same
hotel that Alvarez had taken me to over a stanyer before. I wished
I had my tablet so I could see if the *Duchamp* was docked. Without
it for less than ten ticks and I already missed it.

"It's just a good spacer hotel, that's all," I said to myself.

Still, even after a year, the memory of that little escapade gave
me a kick in the chest and I wondered if I would ever see her again.
For that matter, would I see anybody again? Well, other than at
the going away party, anyway.

Thinking of the party made me feel a little better. They weren't
all gone—yet.

At the front desk, I gave the reservation number from my packet.

The clerk pulled up the record. "Yes, sir. Mr. Wang, is it?" He
held out a thumb pad.

"I didn't make this reservation. Can you tell me what the terms
are?"

"The suite is reserved through the twenty-first, sir." Something in my face or stance must have alerted him to the problem because he added. "The suite has been paid in advance."

"Let me guess. Lois McKendrick?"

He consulted his screen. "Yes, sir. Is there a problem?"

"No, not at all. Thank you, everything is fine." I pressed my thumb to the pad and he gave me a key. Lois still looked out for me, it seemed. The first time I had run across Lois, I remembered thinking that it was a little weird, but over time, I thought I could almost hear her. I smiled to myself thinking about how Pip teased me when I talked about Lois as if she were real.

I found the room down a side passage. I keyed the lock and stepped into a hotel suite that seemed huge after two stanyers living in the cramped berthing area. There was a living room with a wet bar and small chiller. A large holo unit hung on one wall across from a comfy looking couch with coffee tables on either side. There was also a love seat and some overstuffed chairs. It was big enough to have a good-sized party in. I laughed softly to myself and wondered if that was Lois's intention. The room had a small head—bathroom, I corrected myself—just to the left of the entry door and to the right, a door to the next room was ajar. I pushed through into the bedroom. It was not as large as the main room, but still substantial with two full-sized beds.

As I stowed my duffel in the closet, I wondered what I'd need for clothes on the trip to Port Newmar. I knew I had to buy uniforms and fill a new duffel bag when I got to the school, so I was less concerned about that. When I visited the *Bad Penny* in Niol, Pip's cousin Roger had been aboard but not wearing a shipsuit. I needed information and I reached for my tablet before I remembered it was gone. The civilian model peeda just didn't have the same communications options, and I wondered if I could find a spacer grade tablet of my own.

I really needed to talk to Pip.

I remembered my portable. If it could tie into ShipNet, maybe it would find the station net the same way the tablets did. In two ticks, I had it set up on the coffee table and logged in. The computer found the hotel connection without difficulty, and I pulled up the standard station access including messages and the Union Hall display. It listed *Bad Penny* as *inbound*.

I dropped Pip a message so he'd have my civilian address. "Should I buy more civvies for the trip or does the Penny have shipsuits?" While I was at it, I dropped Mr. von Ickles a similar query about the availability and advisability of tablets. My portable was nice, but I really missed the tablet.

I sat back and took a deep breath. The connection via the station net made me feel a bit better. I wasn't really cut off completely. I could contact people when I needed to. Of course, the only people I knew to contact were on the ship, but that would change as Pip and I started out on our new adventure to Port Newmar, or when the ship left—whichever came first.

I stood up just as the response from Pip came back. "I'll be there right after lunch tomorrow. Relax. We'll go shopping."

Mr. von Ickles' response came in right behind it. "Don't buy anything. I'll explain at the party."

I settled back on the sofa. The cushions were soft and comfy in ways that I hadn't known I had missed for two stanyers aboard ship. I snorted a soft laugh at myself. Funny the things you never notice.

The suite was almost silent. I could hear the faint environmental noises from the air ducts, and people out in the passageway as if they were a long way off. The fan in my laptop sounded loud in the hush. I sat there for as much as two ticks, listening to the quiet and marveling that I didn't have anything to do for the next few stans. Nothing at all. After two stanyers aboard the *Lois*—and during my entire life before that, if I were honest about it—I finally had nothing I needed to do, and nobody I needed to answer to.

The heady notion collapsed under the weight of not knowing what to do next.

I chuckled to myself and stood to hang my coat up in the closet beside my duffel when I remembered the chip. My fingers slid into the inner pocket of the jacket and pulled out Henri Roubaille's data chip with the flourished R on the case. I checked my impulse to hang up the coat and, instead, changed course for the door. A short visit to Chez Henri was just what the doctor ordered.

Chez Henri was still in the same place and looked the exactly as I remembered. Entering through the front doors, I noticed that even the woman at the podium hadn't changed. I was surprised when her eyes widened in recognition.

"M. Wang," she said with a smile, "how nice to see you again."

I didn't know if she really remembered me or just picked up a biosensor relay somewhere, but being greeted by name after only one visit over a stanyer before certainly perked up my ego.

"Hello, and thank you. It's good to be back," I replied, holding out the chip to her. "I'd like to see about getting a few fresh shirts? And perhaps a pair of dress slacks?"

She slotted the chip but gave the readout only a perfunctory glance before replying, "Of course, monsieur. If you'd come this way?" She led me through one of the side doors to a waiting room and pointed out a comfy chair. "Please make yourself comfortable. M. Roubaille will be along in just one moment. May I get you some refreshment?"

"No, thank you, mademoiselle. I'll be quite comfortable."

She gave a small wink and a smile as she left to return to her post.

No sooner had she exited when M. Roubaille bustled in from the other door with a beaming smile and an outstretched hand. "M. Wang! A pleasure to see you again. Without your entourage this time?"

"Yes, monsieur." I stood to shake his hand and we settled into opposing chairs. "I've left the *Lois McKendrick* en route to the academy at Port Newmar. They couldn't be with me this afternoon."

"*Dommage*, but you are moving up and moving on and you have come to me for assistance with your wardrobe. Congratulations on being accepted to the academy. An excellent establishment," he said before turning to the business at hand. "How may we help you today?"

"I need some fresh shirts and underthings. I'll be in transit for the next few weeks and I suspect my supply of civilian attire is inadequate to the journey."

He pursed his lips in a small moue of consideration and squinted his eyes slightly as he observed me. "Perhaps," he said with a small question in his voice. "Maybe we need to see what we see."

He stood suddenly and beckoned me to follow as he bustled out the same door he had entered. "Come, Ishmael. We have work."

It was a simple matter to select a few shirts and some fresh underwear, but M. Roubaille refused to stop there. "Come, come, Ishmael. You've worn that jacket and jeans for too long. It's time for you to move up. You're going to the academy and you must be properly attired," he chided me and held out a dark coat. "Just try this on."

I sighed and laughed. "Very well, monsieur." I relented and let him slip the coat on over my arms and settle it across my shoulders before turning to the mirror. I almost didn't recognize the man looking back at me. He smiled tentatively at first and then with more assurance. I recognized some of him from those many months ago when I first signed the Articles on Neris and saw him for the first time in his shipsuit in the locker room before heading up to the *Lois McKendrick*. He had grown since. Not just in frame, but there was something about the eyes and the set of his mouth in a kind of half smile. I recognized the jacket with a shock as well. It was not the same one that I had tried on at Bresheu's booth back on St. Cloud, but it was very similar. The fit was exquisite and I now recognized it as being cut in a classically elegant style. A bit dramatic, perhaps, but where I had considered it too theatrical at Bresheu's, I now realized it to be merely stylish. The dark charcoal color with small flecks of a darker gray was so tastefully done as to almost melt in my mouth.

I must have stared for a long time because M. Roubaille prompted me. "Is everything all right, Ishmael?"

My focus shifted to look at him in the mirror and I smiled. "Oh, yes, monsieur. Very good. I was just reminded of something and became lost in my thoughts."

He smiled knowingly. "It happens. This jacket looks very good on you. A bit more formal than your peacoat, but less formal than the dress uniforms you'll be required to wear at the academy functions. Perhaps a good transitional piece for your wardrobe?"

"Do you have a pair of slacks that would go with this, perhaps?" I asked with a smile. I had no idea how I was going to pay for this and still afford the academy, but I was determined to at least look.

M. Roubaille smiled and produced a pair of slacks in a slightly lighter shade of charcoal. In no time at all I wore the most exquisite outfit I'd ever seen. After the obligatory stretching, straightening, and adjusting, he pronounced the fit *parfait* and I knew that I had found what I had come for.

The moment of truth collapsed upon me then and I asked to see the accounting.

"Of course, M. Wang," M. Roubaille said with a smile, as I finished re-dressing in my original clothing. He handed me a tablet with the purchases itemized. I avoided looking at the total as I scanned down the list of smaller items at the top and reached the bottom without gasping. The prices were very reasonable and even the total with the jacket and slacks was only slightly more than I had paid a year before. I knew I had more than enough cash to cover it, but the thought of going to the academy knowing I didn't have enough to finish gave me pause.

M. Roubaille was arranging to get the slacks hemmed to the correct length with one of the assistants, and I caught sight of the lush fabric once more. Before I could talk myself out of it, I thumbed the contract. There would be plenty of opportunity for regret, and for once, I was willing to take a chance that I might regret buying the suit over the certainty that I would regret leaving it.

I handed the tablet back to him. "Thank you, M. Roubaille. That is quite satisfactory."

He smiled when he took the tablet back. "Thank you, Ishmael. We'll have these delivered to your suite within two hours. I trust that will be adequate?" he said as we walked back through the lobby and beyond.

"Very, M. Roubaille, and I thank you once more for a wonderful time." I smiled and we shook hands.

Grasping both my hands in his, he looked me straight in the eye and said with a little twinkle, "May you become the man you wish to be, Ishmael." He grinned, waved, and disappeared back into the shop, leaving me standing in the passageway with an amused smile on my face.

I headed toward the lift with no real destination in mind and soon found myself wandering through the flea market. My first trip seemed so far away and so long ago. I watched for things I might take with me to Port Newmar, thinking that perhaps a few small items could go in my duffel for sale before I left the orbital there.

"Ishmael!" The voice caught me by surprise and I looked around to find that I had practically walked into the co-op booth without noticing. Tabitha stood there with a big grin on her face and Sean was behind her selling one of his afghans to what appeared to be a local. "You lost?"

I grinned in reply as I saw more of the co-op members busily engaged in trade of various kinds. Most of them smiled and nodded toward me, but didn't break off their dealing. "No," I laughed. "Just stopped by to see if there was something I could tuck in my duffel to sell when I get to Port Newmar."

"Find anything yet?" she asked.

I shook my head. "No, I've only just arrived. Last time we were here, I found some nice batik fabric and some prints."

"Ooh," she said. "I remember that batik. It was gorgeous. That was right when we started the co-ed crochet team!"

"You guys doing okay with that?"

Sean finished his sale and came over to answer, "It's been great." He looked shyly at Tabitha who winked and grinned back. "We're making enough goods to really make some serious money. Sarah is taking to it like a duck to water, and she's getting top creds for her work too."

Something in the way Tabitha looked at Sean made me think that there was more going on than just crocheting, but I didn't get into it. I just smiled and said, "That's wonderful." After a few more ticks of small talk, I wished them continued success and wandered on down the aisles.

Seeing them reminded me that the reason we had done so well in the various flea markets was because of the co-op and it occurred to me that I wouldn't have a co-op to sell in at Port Newmar. While I could certainly rent a booth there, the idea of carrying cargo from here to there seemed, less attractive. In spite of that I wandered in the flea market until the chimes sounded the closing and I drifted out with the human tide.

With nowhere else to go, I headed back to the room. The clerk smiled and winked as I entered. I was not sure what the wink was for until I got to the room. I found my packages from Roubaille's and Beverly both waiting for me.

She sat on the sofa, clicking through something on her tablet and looked up as I entered. "There you are. Busy afternoon?" she smiled as she nodded at the tastefully bundled parcels.

I smiled back. "Passable. I needed a few things for the trip. Went up to the flea to see what I could see." I made it a little sing-songy and trying to keep my heart from pounding out of my chest.

She grinned and stood, crossing to me, and giving me a hug. "I'm glad you're back. I'm starved. Let's go get something to eat."

She led me out of the hotel and headed to starboard. She stopped at the entrance of a tastefully decorated restaurant and kissed me in full view of anybody who happened to be watching a wanton and shameless public display of affection. I did so hope somebody was watching, because I think it was worth the look. "There's more where that came from," she whispered. We went in and when the maitre d' asked, she said, "McKendrick for 6 pm?"

He bowed the little maitre d' bow and escorted us into the restaurant to a booth while Bev enjoyed the looks from the other patrons. With her tattoos, multiple piercings, and buzz cut hairstyle, she usually got looks. She was, of course, in her black leathers, and wearing an exquisite, soft yellow blouse under the jacket. The blouse was unbuttoned to her sternum, and it was obvious there was nothing but woman underneath—other than the surgical steel, of course. Beverly was gorgeous in her own vicious, animal way.

We had steaks—;the house specialty—;baked potatoes, and big, crunchy, green salads. Bev ordered a fruity red wine. We sat, ate, and talked like we had all the time in the world. Like we weren't spending the evening saying goodbye.

When the steaks had gone, like the salad and the wine, we ordered dessert. When the desserts had been ordered and eaten and the coffee drunk, we had to leave. Bev insisted on covering the check, "You're unemployed, remember?" she teased.

"Half-pay," I insisted, but she just shook her head.

We left the restaurant together and headed down the corridor, Beverly took me by the arm and we walked hip-to-hip back to the hotel. I flashed the lock and opened the door. She went in, shucked off her leather jacket, and kicked off her boots. The jacket went over the back of the couch before she turned to me. "Are you enjoying yourself?" she asked as she caught me admiring the way the black leather pants fit her.

"Oh, yes," I assured her. I could feel my chest tightening and my breath already beginning to quicken at the implication of her being there.

"Good," she said with a grin and held out her hand in invitation. "Then could I ask you to come over here and sit on the sofa and just hold me for a while?"

The request was so unexpected. I asked, "Are you okay?" out of reflex.

"Yes, indeed," she said with a soft sigh as we settled together. "It's just that I've wanted this for so long, I want to savor every moment."

That brought a pang as I realized what she had not said. We wrapped around each other and just held on. I was surprised at how soft her cropped hair felt on my cheek. I had expected it to be more bristly, although I didn't know why. I found myself stroking her head and loving the curve of her skull in my palm and the way her hair tickled between my fingers while being too short to grasp. Eventually there was gentle kissing—fingers, foreheads, ears, eyes, and, after a time, mouths. Later we moved to the other room and she walked to the bed, while unbuckling her belt and slipping the leather pants down her legs, and at last, kicked them off. She dove face first onto the mattress, just bouncing on it slightly. The tails of her yellow blouse flipped up exposing lacy white briefs stretched deliciously across her backside. "Ooh," she cooed. "Somebody could get very, very naughty here."

She rolled over to her back and propped up on her elbows to look at me. "I'm sorry," she growled low in the back of her throat, "but it really does seem like you better get in here." Her blouse had pulled down from her right shoulder, and while it revealed nothing more than tattoos and a smoothly rounded shoulder, it only needed another few centimeters to expose considerably more. She drew up her left knee, allowing her thighs to open the tiniest amount in invitation, her briefs painting a pale target against her flesh.

A very long time later, after several rounds of sobbing, laughing, moaning and sighing—some of it Bev's—we fell asleep with only a sheet over us to keep in some of the warmth.

The feeling of something wet, tickling down my ribs woke me after a time. Bev's head rested on my chest, one arm thrown up and over my shoulder and her breasts on either side of my upper arm. She had fallen asleep with her mouth open and drooled on me. It was such a child-like, innocent thing to see after the long evening of deliciously depraved behavior, that I started to laugh. It caught in my throat and came out as a sob when I remembered that she would be gone soon—probably forever.

The movement of my chest as much as the sound woke her and her mouth closed. She raised her head a little, looking down to see what she was lying in. I saw memory flash across her face as she turned those fiercely beautiful eyes in my direction and she let out a small chuckle.

"Sorry about that," she said, as she used the edge of the sheet to wipe my chest and then her cheek.

I could not say anything just then, so I just hugged her head back down to my chest. I held her like that for a while and we fell asleep again.

The sound of the shower woke me and I found myself alone in the bed. The chrono on the nightstand read 0730. Good, I thought, she must not have the watch.

Bev came out of the bathroom wearing a pair of black briefs and a turtle-neck pullover clinging to her torso. I wondered, briefly, where she had gotten fresh clothes but she climbed onto the bed and distracted me for several ticks without doing anything too naughty.

She wasn't exactly innocent, but she pulled back before things got too heated and pointed toward the bathroom. "Shower now, you tomcat!" she said trying to be stern. "You smell like me. I want breakfast and I want it soon. Be quick." She lost the effect by laughing.

It wasn't long before we were sitting down to breakfast and, compared to the leisurely meal of the night before, breakfast was all business. We went. We ate. We left. Outside the restaurant, Bev turned to me. "Will you be okay on your own for a few stans? I have some business to take care of back on the ship. Pip will be along shortly and you two boys will undoubtedly find plenty of mischief to get into."

"Would it make any difference if I said no?"

She shook her head with a grin.

"You're coming back, though, right?"

"Yes. I'll be back later today. And I'll be at the party tonight." She kissed me playfully on the nose and turned toward the lift, hips swinging loosely as she walked. I was not the only one watching her go. I noticed several men and at least two women tracking on her as she sashayed by.

I went back to my room and took stock. I was still wearing the clothes I had left the ship in, other than the change of briefs. I wondered again, what I might need for clothes on the trip to Port Newmar. There was nothing I could do about that except wait for Pip. Yawning and smiling, I crawled back into the rumpled sheets and fell asleep, smelling the scent of Bev's hair on the pillow.

Pip was as good as his word and showed up at 1330 with his kit. "Nice digs!" he said as he walked in. "We paying for this?"

"Lois paid the bill in advance through the twenty-first. The *Bad Penny* is due to dock tomorrow so we've got another couple of days of living the high life. Do you know how long we'll have after they get here?"

"Naw. They'll clear customs and cargoes before they get too carried away with planning. We got plenty of time, though. I think as long as we leave here by the twenty-seventh, we'll be fine." He started poking about and stuck his head into the sleeping room. "Nice. And well used, I see." He winked at me. He surprised me by walking to the other end of the sitting room and opening a door on that end. "Ah!" he said, and disappeared through it.

I hadn't even noticed it, let alone considered it. I started to follow him but he came back out without his kit and said, "Good, I'll just take that one then." He pointed at the portable still set up on the table. "That was pretty clever thinking. The peeda just doesn't compare after you've had a tablet, does it?"

"No kidding. So what's the deal with shipsuits?"

"Aunt P and Uncle Q don't require them, but they're a hell of a lot more practical than civvies underway. The big companies all provide them, but indies just buy their own. Kinda like having your own tools. Come on, we need to stock up."

He took me down to the oh-one level. Orbital stations were all the same. The oh-one was one deck down from the docks. Typically the upper decks were residential, tourist, and retail. Below was commercial. It was the first time I had visited the oh-one. While the oh-two level had entertainment catering to the Deep Dark crowd, the oh-one was all business. Consultants, import/export brokers, repair brokers, cargo brokers, even a tailor and a barber shop. Everything the well-heeled spacer might need, including a chandlery selling anything you might want for a ship—from deck paint to fiber optics. Crew supplies had a whole wing onto itself. Duffel bags, shipsuits, environmental soft suits, hygiene gear, even blankets, sheets, and towels in standard ship sizes.

"We only need to get the minimum to get by for the next couple of months," he told me. "All this stuff will come around again when we hit the academy and they'll want us to buy theirs." He pointed to the racks of suits, "Find your size, you'll need two, and three sets of ship-tee and boxers."

"Any particular color?" I asked. The suits were in all colors of the rainbow.

"Gray, or light brown. Doesn't matter really, but I always feel like I'm glowing in those brighter shades." He already had two suits and a packet of ship-tees and boxers in his size.

I followed his lead. We picked up some Depil, deodorant and tooth gel, then headed for the checkout. My bundle came to just a bit under twenty creds. Pip was grinning as we rode the lift back to the suite. "You're enjoying this, aren't ya?" I said.

"You have no idea how much," he agreed.

"Aren't you sad to be leaving the *Lois*?"

"Oh, some, sure. But the *Lois* is just the latest step on a path that will have many more in it before I'm done. Look ahead, not back. That's my motto." Pip seemed very chipper.

"I thought your motto was 'Enjoy the ride.'"

"That too," he agreed.

After that we were at loose ends. We wandered back to the room and I stowed the new gear in the bottom of my duffel. Of course that meant I had to take everything out first. The downside of these bags is that when you want to pack, you almost always have to dump it all out and start again. By the time I came back to the common room, Pip was scrolling through the list of ship arrivals.

"Anything new?" I asked.

"Naw, just looking."

"What'll we do now?" I asked. "It's 1530 and the party isn't until 2000."

"Sleep. We may not get much later."

I wasn't sure I could sleep, but I woke up to find Pip speaking to me from the door. "Hey! It's 1830 and I wanna eat before we go."

I blinked up from a deep sleep as his voice echoed inside my ears for a bit. "Yeah. Good. Food before drinking. Yes." I sat up in my bed and grinned. "I need a fast splash and some clothes and I'll be ready to go. Find something cheap to eat."

He grinned and left while I clambered off the bed. After sleeping for two years on a narrow bunk, that hotel bed seemed big and empty. I grabbed a shower and fresh clothes—the pink shirt—and was ready for food. Pip waited in the common room and by 1845 we were tucking into large, grilled sandwiches with fried potatoes and salads on the side.

"Long time since breakfast?" he asked with a grin as I practically inhaled the first half of the sandwich.

"Forgot to get lunch," I said with a sheepish grin.

Pip insisted we eat slowly and then take a turn around the level to settle dinner before going down to *Jump!* "Wouldn't want to arrive too early. We need to give them a chance to get it together before the guests of honor show up."

When we finally got down there, the party was still tuning up. Pip led me back to the same corner we had been in over a year before. I marveled that so much time could have passed yet the memories were so clear. On the wall above *our* tables a banner read: Congratulations, Cadets. That was the extent of the decoration, for which I was grateful.

Lee von Ickles walked up to me and handed me a drink—gin and tonic—and said, "We'll talk in a bit. Have fun." He was gone again before I could thank him.

Tabitha Rondita sashayed up to me and all but mugged me right there. I was feeling delightfully rumpled by the time she finished. There was more than enough catcalling and encouragement to go around, I thought, but nobody asked me. I came up for air grinning. Pip got a dose from Jennifer Agotto. I grinned to hear her mother cheering her on. I grabbed a quick swig of my drink while I still could, because Sandy Belterson and Rebecca Saltzman were both heading in my direction. I had the distinct impression I was about to be double teamed. I was right. Rebecca held me while Sandy helped herself to a kiss so deep I thought I better get my tonsils checked. To be honest, I offered no struggle. At least not more than necessary for Rebecca to make a good show of holding me. For her part, the kiss she gave me was gentle and sweet and she whispered, "Good luck, Ish," in my ear as she gave me a hug before letting go. She was not so gentle with Pip and when he came up for air, he seemed dazed.

After that, the party cooled down and well-wishers surrounded us. They came to shake or hug or kiss, sometimes all three. At least four of the women who came to wish me luck were not members of the *Lois's* crew but I pretended not to notice. I kept trying to see Bev or Brill but couldn't spot them. CC and Emile were both there so that meant Diane had the watch. Perhaps that's why she had said good-bye on the mess deck. I grinned a little at the memory.

I was startled by Mr. Maxwell, who stepped up beside me to shake my hand. "Best wishes, Ishmael. The captain sends her compliments. She wishes she could attend but the obligations of command prevent it."

"Thank you for everything, Mr. Maxwell. You've been great to serve under."

"Please don't let that get around, Mr. Wang," he said with a grin and a twinkle in his eye. "I have a reputation to protect."

Before I could answer he pulled an envelope from his inner pocket and slipped it into my jacket. "A little something personal from the officers to help you on your way. You'll do us proud." He smiled at me then and winked. He was gone before I could even thank him.

Mr. Kelley and Mr. Cotton came up together while I was still looking to see where Mr. Maxwell had gone. They smiled and clapped me on the shoulders. Mr. Cotton even gave me a hug. They wished me well. "Thank you, both," I told them. They just smiled and took their exit cue. I realized then that the officers were clearing the decks for the crew to have a serious party.

Ms Avril was next in line and she leaned in to speak softly in my ear. "Alicia was my roommate at the academy. She sends her love," she said. Then she kissed me on the ear, flicking her tongue delightfully across the lobe. "Good luck, Ishmael," she said with a smoldering look and I suddenly had the image of her and Alicia Alvarez practicing that same look on each other at the academy.

"Thank you, and if you can let me know how those astrogation enhancements work?"

"I'll do that," she said, and brushed my mouth with her lips. "That's from me," she said with a wink. Before she joined the parade of officers leaving the party.

Lee was the last of the officers there and he stepped up next with a small flat box in his hand. He handed it to me. "When you go to the academy, they make you buy a tablet—one of theirs. When I heard the captain finally got you to apply, I ordered one for you and it was waiting for us here when we got in. It's not much, but from one systems guy to another, best wishes and use it well. Drop me a line now and again to let me know how you're doing."

I was speechless. I had no idea how much they cost, but it was an extravagant gift. "You shouldn't have," I said at last.

"Probably not. But I only ordered it. I didn't pay for it, so it's okay."

"Lois?" I asked.

"Who else?"

"Lois is being awfully nice to me."

He looked at me for a long moment. "You earned it."

"Thank Lois for me. She gave me a home when I needed one." It was all I could say without losing it again.

Lee seemed to realize that, and clapped me on the shoulder. "Maybe we'll have time to grab a quiet beer before you leave. Message me," he said, nodding at the package in my hands. Then he, too, headed out of the bar.

I looked around and Bev and Brill had arrived amid a swirl of shipmates so I just took a deep breath and a swig of my drink. I looked around and saw Pip at the center of another group of women, at least half of whom weren't from the *Lois*. He caught me looking in his direction and smiled. I grinned back and raised my glass. We hadn't been there a full stan yet, but the party had already started to warm up. The band finished setting up, the officers were gone, and the place was beginning to fill.

Salina Matteo came up to me then and gave me a kiss. It was not the lose a tonsil kind of kiss but still warm enough from a married lady with two kids, one of whom was watching with amusement. "Well," she said softly, "now I understand." Then she winked at me and stepped back. "Jennifer," she called to her daughter, "you might want to try this one. Just to see if you like it." She turned back to me and said, "I certainly did." I'm pretty sure I blushed then and she backed off a little. "You're a good man, Ishmael. You're going to make a great officer. The Agotto Trader's co-op is always looking for good officers to handle their business." She said it so salaciously that I had to laugh. It made me wonder what business needed handling.

"Mother, he's young enough to be your son!" Jennifer complained, but she did step up and give me a peck on the lips and then a longer, smoochy kiss. "Keep your hands off my mother, you home wrecker!" she said with a grin. "Maybe you'd like to keep them on me, instead?" She arched her body into me while her mother laughed.

"Jennifer, stop teasing him," she scolded, playfully.

"Who's teasing?" she asked, looking straight in my eyes. "You're the one who said he was a good kisser. Can I help it if you're right?" She winked at me on the side away from her mother and kissed me again.

Salina just huffed. "Well, I never!" she said with a grin.

Jennifer pulled back from me then with a smile and said, "You have had too. At least twice, unless you're claiming immaculate conception."

"You'll pay for that, young lady!"

Jennifer pouted a little. "I suppose I better behave. Being grounded has a special meaning in our family." We all laughed and she said, "Good luck, Ish. Take care." Then they wandered off and I was left alone again.

The band started up for real then and the whole group moved out to the dance floor. I drained my drink and left the empty on a table before joining the group myself. I was still a member in good standing in this tribe. I took my place among them one last time.

For the next couple of stans we danced together, all of us, the past and present crew of the *Lois McKendrick*. We danced together

242

and we danced with the crews of the other vessels in port. I had been on that dance floor before but not really part of the dance the way I was that night—it felt good.

At some point in the evening, Pip disappeared. I was pretty sure I knew where to find him, but also knew why he had taken the other bedroom in the suite. As time went on more and more people faded from the floor and paired off according to the rules they had set for themselves. Eventually the band shut down and with it a lot of the patrons shut down as well. They left in small groups, occasional pairs and, even rarer, alone. The night was winding down and it was time to head back to the room. I looked around to see if I could spot either Bev or Brill, and no sooner had the thought of them hit me, that they were there.

"Shall we sit awhile?" I asked.

"We can if you want," Bev said. "Personally, I'm ready for bed."

Brill looked at her then and asked, "Did you have any particular bed in mind?"

"Why yes, I know of a lovely full sized bed up on level seven. I was thinking of that one."

"Well, might wanna see if there's anybody using it at the moment," Brill observed.

Bev turned her predatory eyes on me, and if she hadn't been smiling warmly, I might have felt a bit more afraid. "I don't think he's there, yet," she said to Brill while looking straight into my eyes.

Brill grinned and leaned over to kiss me. "You guys take care. See you soon."

My heart lay heavy in my chest. I tried to remember to breathe as I watched that magnificent woman turn and sail out of my life forever.

Bev nudged me and took my arm. "Come on, sailor. I've got some plans for you that don't include mooning over your ex-boss." She said it with a softness in her voice that told me she understood.

I couldn't ignore the offer.

It was one of those nights that lives in your heart and warms you in the cold times. We sailed into my room and managed to get the door closed and locked behind us before clothes started flying. Then we were on the bed, giggling and rolling around in a pile like puppies—stroking, and licking—kissing and even nipping. Skin, everywhere skin, soft and smooth, some with downy pelt, some delightfully naked. Some of it tattooed and some of it pierced with steel, gold, or silver. Eventually, all of it got wet and slippery. The giggles and squeals eventually gave way to gasps and moans and, much later, cries and sighs. Eventually the night won over and we fell asleep in a satisfied and quivering heap.

Pip woke me by pounding on the door. "Hey! Anybody still alive in there?"

Bev answered, "No," before I was fully awake.

Pip pounded on the door again. "If you people don't get out here and help me eat this food, I'm going to send it back to the kitchen."

"Food?" she asked.

"Breakfast. Should be enough if there's only one army in there."

Bev was out of bed first and for an instant I thought she was going to go as she was, that is naked, barring the odd patch of sweat and her tattoos. But she went to the closet and pulled out a fluffy robe, threw it over herself, and then another one was coming my way. I had a mental overlay of the suit drill months before, when she had opened the locker and handed out environmental suits clad in her ship-tee and boxers.

Even before Pip had stepped all the way back from the door, Bev flung it open and said, "Good morning, Pip." She gave him a kiss on the cheek and headed for breakfast, still tying her robe. She left me standing there, still half tangled in mine.

Pip stuck his head in the door and grinned at me. "You need me to show you how to put that on?" he asked and managed to duck before the pillow I threw at him arrived.

I got the robe on and wandered out to find Pip and Bev loading plates from a mobile buffet cart that had been wheeled into the suite. I also found Rebecca Saltzman looking very seriously pleased with herself and dressed in the same clothes I'd seen her in the night before. "Morning, Bev. Hi, Ish," she said in her growly purr. It sounded even a little more like a purr than normal and judging from the look on Pip's face, he'd had quite a night himself.

"Good morning, Rebecca," Bev said, but wasted no more time on chit-chat before loading a plate with meat, eggs, potatoes and what looked like a spicy red salsa.

"Hi, Rebecca," I said. The day was off to a great start. Who was I to complain?

We made short work of the food. From the way Bev was looking around for more, I thought maybe we should call for another cart. "You want some more breakfast, Bev?" I asked with a smile.

"Oh no, I'm fine. Just didn't want any to go to waste."

"I think we ate everything but the plates," Pip said. "And I'm not sure we didn't eat one of those." He made a show of counting them. "Anybody notice something real crunchy?"

We all chuckled and Rebecca stood up. "Well, I have to get back to work."

I glanced at the chrono by the bar, 0730. "You're kinda late for watch, aren't you?"

"Co-op duty. I'm breaking in a new manager this morning, Sarah Krugg. I said I'd help out, but that woman needs no help when it comes to selling. She could sell water to a drowning man."

We all laughed again. Rebecca went around the room and kissed everybody. On her way out the door she said, "Safe voyage. See ya round the docks." Then she left.

My portable gave the little bee-boop sound it made when a new message arrived and I went to see who it was. I should have known it was Aunt P.

"They're at the inner marker, Pip. Aunt P says they'll be docked by 1000 and clear of customs by noon." The last line caught me off guard. "She also says she wants to leave by tomorrow afternoon."

Pip grinned. "I told ya she'd have a hot cargo lined up. We'll go down and meet 'em when they clear customs." He turned to Bev. "You wanna come say hi?"

She shrugged. "I'm off today. Why not?"

My dream of taking her back to bed evaporated, but I was in no position to complain. "Maybe we should get cleaned up and dressed first?" I suggested.

"Dibs on the shower," Bev called and bolted for the other room. She had the robe half off before clearing the door. Pip blinked, it was quite an eyeful.

"No false modesty in her family, huh?" I said.

Pip grinned, "Actually, I think her family are nudists. She's the least self-conscious when she's naked."

"Now you tell me," I groaned. "I've been bunking with a gorgeous and repressed nudist for two stanyers and you wait until now to tell me?"

"Sorry, but it's probably just as well you didn't know."

"Good point."

We were silent for a moment before he asked, "You okay, Ish?"

"Yeah," I said but paused for a few heartbeats."No, not really. I thought we'd have a little more time."

He shrugged at that. "When the boat leaves, you gotta be on it. What can I say?"

"Yeah, I know, but it's just—" I started but then I couldn't finish.

"I know. I know." He slapped his thighs with both hands and said, "Still we have the suite for the night and we'd have to check out tomorrow anyway. Some breaks probably are best made quickly."

I rubbed my face with my hands. "Yeah, but being right doesn't make it hurt any less."

"You got that right, brother," he said then sighed. "I better get my own act together here." He headed for his room and presumably a shower.

I looked at the chronometer, 0800, and thought, *What am I going to do with that animal in my shower?* The realization of what had just run through my head hit me and I hurried to the bathroom myself. At the very least I was going to watch.

The morning went too quickly, but we made it to the dock by noon, dressed and presentable to the public. Just strolling the corridors with Bev felt decadent. Watching other people's reactions was priceless. Just before we got to the lock, we met Brill and invited her along.

"Sure, I'd love to see the ship!" she said, and fell into step with Bev and me.

Something had happened when I wasn't looking. For the first time I noticed that Brill didn't walk with her stoop. What's more, people no longer regarded her with the same kind of derision I had grown used to ignoring. Seeing her stride along with Bev, I could see why. She was awe inspiring. Bev held station on her port side and I took up my position on the starboard. We strode the corridors together, invincible, if only for a few more stans. Pip walked slightly ahead of us and I could see his smile in the reflections in the shop windows as we passed.

The *Bad Penny's* telltale showed clear when we got there and Pip rang. Cousin Roger opened up. His eyes bugged out slightly when Brill and Beverly stepped in with us but I couldn't blame him. They had that effect on a lot of people—me among them.

Roger led us through the living room and into a cozy galley. There was no mess deck, per se, but a table large enough to seat twelve comfortably was there. It felt warm and welcoming, like I had just come home.

Aunt P beamed when she saw us and came over to hug. "How good to see you all!"

Bev and Brill stepped up and returned her embrace and I thought Brill said something to her, but Pip asked, "What's the big rush? I thought we were gonna hang around for a few days."

Roger said, "Cargo deadline. Extra fifty kilocreds if we deliver on time."

Pip gave me a *I-told-ya-so* look.

Aunt P patted Brill on the cheek before turning to me. "I'm so glad you're going with Pip. His father wasn't nearly as upset as I thought he'd be."

"He knew all along, Aunt P," Pip said. "We ran into him on Umber."

"Well, I should hope so. That's where we sent him. And here you are. Are you excited?" she asked Pip.

"Excited isn't the word, really, Aunt P, it's more of a, 'yes, it's time I went, so let's get on with it' kind of feeling.

"What about you, Ishmael? Are you excited?"

"Yes and no," I told her. "The *Lois* was like my family after my mother died and now I'm leaving her. It's the right thing to do, but I hate going."

"Well, it's not permanent and we're a small community. You're bound to meet up again."

"Ain't that the truth," Bev said with a shuttle full of irony that flew right past me.

Aunt P gave us the short tour of the ship. It was really impressive. I could see every part of the ship was built for efficiency, compared to the *Lois* everything was very compact. The staterooms were nice. Besides the captain's cabin, there were two singles, four doubles and a big one with four bunks. There was even a small work out area with exercise equipment and, in lieu of a sauna, a hot tub that looked like about ten people could fit in.

As we went back to the living room, I said, "This is so nice! I wish we had more than just a few weeks!"

"Wait until those few weeks are over, then see if you'll be saying that," Roger put in with a low chuckle. "It can get pretty cramped."

I allowed that was possibly true, but it still looked good to me.

"Well, who's up for some lunch?" Aunt P asked. "Quent's gone to deal with the cargo but Roger and I were just heading up to a little place we like on level five. You kids wanna join us?"

We had a ball at lunch but it was so unfair. Bev, Brill, and Aunt P got on like gang busters. We had such a good time and I tried to stay in the moment and ignore the pending break in my heart. I succeeded but only because everybody was having such fun. It was easier to ignore while I was distracted.

As lunch wrapped up, Aunt P said, "Well, I expect you young people will have things to do this evening, but everybody needs to be aboard by 0900 for a 1200 pull out. Normally, it's less but the Confederation is being persnickety about it."

"Okay, Aunt P," Pip said. "We'll be there. And thanks for giving us a ride."

"Oh, you know me. I'm always willing to fly half way across the galaxy to turn a profit." She grinned, then took Roger's arm and sauntered back toward the lift.

Bev said, "We've got some stuff to do too."

Brill agreed. "You know how it is. Always something needing doing."

I looked at Bev. "You don't have watch tonight?"

She shook her head. "Normally I would but they're breaking Tabitha in on it."

Brill broke in with, "We'll meet you back at the suite at about 1800?" She looked at Bev who nodded in confirmation.

I wanted to spend every last remaining moment with them, but all I could do was say, "See you soon."

They linked arms and followed in the wake of Aunt P and Roger.

"Those two are up to something," I said.

"Why do you say that?"

"I don't know. Something's up, and with that pair it could be anything," I said admiring the view until they passed out of sight.

"You may be right," he said. "We'll find out when they're darn good and ready to tell us, though, so it's no good speculating."

I chuckled in agreement. "So? What'll we do for,"—I checked my chrono—"three stans?"

"I'm thinking sleep. I didn't get much last night and judging from the sounds, you didn't either."

"I like your idea better than any I could come up with."

When I woke up it was 1815 and the women were sitting and talking in the common room. They had changed clothes and looked ready for a night out. "You didn't come wake me?" I asked.

Bev said, "I was pretty rough on ya last night, and I suspect you needed the nap."

Brill added, "Yes, and she intends on keeping you awake tonight, too, so it's probably a good thing."

That was both good and bad. Good for what it promised. Bad for what it meant for the next day.

Pip came out of his room, dressed and ready to go. "So what

are we doing?"

"Dinner and dancing?" Bev suggested.

Brill added, "Dinner anyway. We need to feed."

"Last night in port," Pip noted. "Any preferences for dinner?"

I had some but they involved smearing various tasty morsels across an amazing array of anatomy. I didn't mention them, instead I said, "I'm open to almost anything."

There was a knock on the door and Pip said, "Ah, my date!"

He went to open it and Rhon Scham launched herself at him, pinning him to the wall, and kissing him very thoroughly.

She came up for air and looked over at us, "Oh, hi! You kids about ready for dinner?" Then she went back for a second helping of Pip before any of us could summon sufficient wit to reply.

When she surfaced the second time, Pip looked like he might have died right there, but he shook himself and came back to us. "Hi, Rhon. Good to see you."

She grinned at him, "You too." She kissed him on the tip of his nose before releasing the lapels of his jacket. She came into the room and flopped down on the sofa. "So? What are we doing for dinner? I'm famished."

"We're just trying to decide. You have any preferences?" I asked her.

"I'm pretty sure I know what I'm having for dessert," she said with a nakedly wanton glance in Pip's direction. "But I think I'd like a nice steak as entree. You kids know of any good steak places?"

"Yeah," Bev said, "There's one just down to starboard a couple hundred meters."

"Oh, good," Rhon said. "Close by."

It was a side of Rhon I'd never seen before and I laughed along with everybody else. In less than ten ticks we had adjourned to the restaurant and the maitre d' seemed happy to find us a quiet corner.

When I sat down, I thought, so this is our last dinner together. I remembered all the dinners I had shared with Brill and Bev—starting with Maurice's on Gugara, and including all the mess deck meals we had shared out in the Deep Dark, eating Cookie's excellent meals. Luckily, Rhon's antics soon distracted me from that morose contemplation and we started having fun. We were there until nearly 2100, eating, drinking a little, telling stories, and laughing together. For a little while I was able to forget that in just a few stans, I'd be leaving Bev and Brill on the wrong side of the galaxy.

After we finished the third bottle of wine, we settled up and headed back to the suite. Rhon practically dragged Pip into his bedroom and with a cheerful little, "Night, now! You kids have fun!" closed the door. I heard her turn the bolt and I wondered if it was to keep us out or Pip in.

Bev and Brill looked at each other. "He's in for a hell of a night, isn't he." Brill said.

"Yeah," Bev said. With a grin she added, "So's Pip."

Brill turned to me and said, "You take care of yourself. I'll see ya around the docks." Before I knew what had happened, she had slipped out of the suite and the door latch clicked shut behind her.

Bev took my arm and led me to the bedroom, stopping at the door to look up at me as if to make sure I was actually there. She looked anxiously from one eye to the other until I managed a little smile. She took me the rest of the way into the room, closing the door behind us.

We didn't rip our clothes off and attack. It was more deliberate, more loving. The sheets had been changed again, but we saw no reason not to make as much of a mess of this new set as we had the last ones. We were in no hurry and we took our time with each other. It was by turns: tender, hilarious, wanton, and gentle. Bodies intertwined—fingers, tongues, arms, legs, feet, ears. In many cases, napes of necks were favored. There was so much skin to kiss, hold, and cry on. We fell asleep, completely sated before midnight and woke again at 0300 to have another round before finally sleeping for good.

Bev kissed me awake at 0730. "You need to get cleaned up and get out of here. Grab the shower quick and get your clothes on. If you hurry you can grab breakfast on the way down to the docks." She kissed me again and kicked me unceremoniously out of bed and onto the floor.

I crawled reluctantly to my feet and into the shower. It only took a few moments to wash up and clean my teeth. I skipped the Depil. My beard didn't grow that fast.

Bev was still in bed watching me move about and get dressed. She followed me with her eyes as I packed my things, getting ready to leave her. She didn't look as sad as I felt. Perhaps her feelings were something I had built up in my own mind and I was making more of it than I should. I sat beside her on the bed and took her in my arms one last time, kissing her gently on her eyes and nose and mouth. "Thank you, Beverly Arith. You are a she-wolf, you know."

She grinned lazily up at me, stretching sensuously in my arms. "You're not so bad yourself," she growled at me. She reached up and kissed me tenderly, putting her hand around my head and stroking the back of my skull.

I heard Pip stirring about in the common room, so I knew it

was time to go. I let Bev go with a final peck on the cheek, and crossed to the connecting door. Before I opened it, I turned back and said, "I love you, you know. Thank you for all you've done for me." I slipped out and closed the door behind me without waiting for a reply.

Pip waited with his duffel packed and fully dressed. "Ready?" he asked.

I shrugged, not trusting myself to speak and headed for the door. I didn't have a lot to say on the way down to the docks and Pip didn't press. Remembering how long it had taken me to recover from Alvarez, I wondered how long it would take to get over Bev. I chuckled to myself, at that. Did you ever get over being loved by a she-wolf?

I turned to Pip. "Do you wanna grab some breakfast?"

"Can you eat?" he asked.

"Probably not, but—" I shrugged. "Gotta try."

We slipped into a spacer diner just off the docks and ordered the standard egg, bacon, and potato breakfast. Pip said it was good and I ate mine, but I didn't taste it. By the time we finished and settled up, it was already pushing 0845. We had to hustle to make it to the docks. Cousin Roger waited with the lock open and grinned when he saw us.

"Welcome aboard," he said. "You can drop your duffels in the living room, Mom and Dad are in the galley and the coffee's hot."

It is going to be okay, I thought. This was so homey. I could recover here and be, if not whole, then at least mostly healed by the time we hit Port Newmar. Pip and I dropped our bags in the corner of the living room and went on to find Aunt P and Uncle Q sitting at one end of the big table.

Aunt P pointed to a coffee pot— a real coffee pot—not a utility sized urn. "Help yourself, boys. Mugs are in the cabinet above."

Uncle Q said, "Welcome aboard, guys. You timed it well."

Aunt P looked at the chrono, "Yeah, now if the others make it on time, we'll be shaking the dust off right on schedule."

I took my coffee over and sat across from them at the table. I figured we'd be sharing a few meals. I wondered who would be cooking. "Others, Aunt P?" I asked curiously.

"Yeah, we got a couple more cadets needing a ride. Figured we could get you all in the same trip and save some time." She kept her eye on the chrono and waited.

We all heard the lock start to close as the chrono read 0855. Aunt P punched a button on her tablet. "There! Now the port authorities know we're buttoned up on time. They'll be happy."

"I didn't know there would be other passengers. How about you

Pip?" I asked.

He was studying his coffee but I could see a grin. I heard voices in the living room, then steps in the passage, and finally Brill and Bev walked into the kitchen.

"You girls cut that a bit close, didn't you?" Aunt P asked.

"We got caught in traffic," Brill said.

Bev just grinned and I realized that everybody was looking at me.

"You all knew!" I said. "Cadets?"

Brill said, "Yeah, when I heard you'd applied, I went to Mr. Kelley and told him I wanted to go. He'd been after me for two stanyers to head there so he was delighted."

Bev added, "I'm number thirty-five on the captain's hit parade. That filled out application with the stack of recommendations on it is a very effective tactic." She turned to Aunt P. "Thank you for your recommendation as well, Captain."

"I'm Penny when I'm at home, dear. and I'm glad to help Alys out whenever I can. How did your father take the news, Brill?"

"He was overjoyed. I thought he was going to fly out himself."

"Any problems from the co-op, Bev?" Aunt P asked.

"Nope, they're tickled that another one of us is going."

"Are you going to have to serve your time there?"

"No, Mom and Dad have been investing just for this. They're going to do everything they can to help me out. I got a nice financial aid package. It's gonna work out."

Bev and Brill settled at the table with us all and it felt so amazingly right. Aunt P and Uncle Q beamed at us and Aunt P said, "You four are the craziest, luckiest, and least likely team I think I've ever met. You watch out for each other at Port Newmar and you'll all do just fine. Now let's go get you settled."

We all trooped back to the living room and picked up duffels. I still had no idea how they'd pulled it off, and I wasn't going to ask. I just counted my blessings. Aunt P led us down to the cabins and turned to Pip. "You want your old cabin?" she asked.

"Sure," he said, and peeled off into one of the singles.

Aunt P looked at us then. "You three can have any combination that you want," she said with a devilish little grin.

Brill chuckled, pointed at one of the singles, and said, "Dibs! I don't remember the last time I had a room to myself!"

We took a couple of ticks, divvying up the rooms and figuring out where to stash duffel bags. We changed into shipsuits and it amused me when Brill showed up in a suit in midnight black, while Bev wore blood-red. I felt under dressed in my gray. All told it took us close to a stan to get out of our civvies, into the shipsuits, and finally make our way to the kitchen for coffee.

When we got close to departure, Pip led us up to the bridge. Because it was so small I felt like I was standing in space, surrounded by stars. There was even a skylight in the overhead and I could look up the see the orbital from where I stood at the back of the bridge. It would be a very romantic setting out in the Deep Dark with stars all around and the ship sailing through the ever-night. The bridge had three consoles along with two mismatched sofas and a pair of over-stuffed chairs.

We heard Aunt P giggling as she came up the ladder to the bridge and Uncle Q was very close behind her. I wondered what he had been doing to make her laugh like that. The thought made me grin.

Aunt P took the center seat, Uncle Q sat to her right. She waved Bev over to take the seat on her left. "You stood helm watch, didn't you, Bev?" she asked.

"Of course," Bev said.

If getting the *Lois McKendrick* underway was a ballet, leaving on the *Bad Penny* was a jam session. I stood at the back of the bridge so I could watch. Brill stood beside me, close enough I could feel the heat of her but not quite touching. Pip sprawled on one of the couches, possibly dozing.

Aunt P. keyed a mic and asked, "You ready, Roger?"

"We're ready to rumble, Mom," his voice came back from a speaker on the console.

"Mother may I?" she said to Quent.

He keyed a systems command and said, "Clearance requested." A moment later he said, "Clearance granted."

Aunt P ran a few commands through her board and I felt the docking clamps release with a small thump. In a moment we were sliding backwards under our own power. "Just keep us pointing at the orbital, dear," she said to Bev. "We'll slide out for a half a stan or so and then come about to our exit vector."

Bev's console was live and she grinned as she watched her screens and the ports all at once. "After the *Lois*, this is like driving a flitter!"

"If you think this is good, wait until we get the sails up," Aunt P said. "You may need a towel."

"A towel?" she asked.

Aunt P nodded. "Yeah. To sit on," she said with a wink.

Uncle Q sat back in his chair and smiled at his wife. She did not seem to be looking in his direction, but she reached over and patted his thigh. Brill must have seen the gesture because she shifted her weight so she was leaning against me. Or maybe I shifted mine. It didn't matter. As long as I could feel her, I felt at peace. I had the same sensation looking over at Bev on helm. Just looking at her made me feel whole.

I could see Aunt P getting ready on her board and glancing out the ports as if she could actually eyeball the positions. She keyed her mic once more and said, "Stand by, Roger. Another tick and we'll be coming about."

"Okay, Mom," Rogers voice came back.

Aunt P turned to Bev and asked, "Could you bring her around about sixty-five degrees to port with a fifteen degree up angle at the bow, please, Bev?"

"Sixty-five degrees port and fifteen degrees up, aye, Captain," Bev said automatically, then she squealed in delight as the view outside the ports shifted.

Aunt P laughed. "I shoulda mentioned that. She's a bit ticklish. Now watch her, I'm gonna bring up the kickers."

Bev just grinned.

Aunt P ran up the engines. I could feel them come on-line through the frame of the ship. Our vector shifted and we pulled away.

"Did you log us out, honey?" P asked Q.

"Yes, dear. On the mark at 1200 and leaving orbital space at 1235."

She patted his thigh again and left her hand resting there for a long moment.

In what seemed like no time at all, we were clear of the proximity markers and Aunt P keyed her mic, "Okay, Roger, we're out. See you in the galley."

"What do you want for lunch?" he asked.

I hadn't thought about food, but as soon as he said the word lunch, my stomach reminded me. Apparently Aunt P heard it too because she said, "I think we need something quick, hon. How about sandwiches, for now."

"You got it, Mom. See ya in the galley."

I looked over my shoulder and out the aft port where the planet was almost visibly falling astern. I turned back to the woman I loved and who seemed to love me in return. I smiled. I knew it couldn't last. Demands of school and, later, career would drag us apart. We'd grow along our separate paths and maybe come to need things we couldn't give each other. But still, I remembered the way P's hand had rested on Q's thigh. The loving familiarity of long association in the touch and the thought gave me hope for some day, perhaps in a ship like this. I dreamed that it might be with this wonderful woman, but I also knew that not all dreams come true. Most evaporate in the light of waking, disappearing—never to be seen again.

Of course, when you are really fortunate, others come to take their places.

Aunt P ran the engines down and secured them before glancing at Bev. "I'm bringing up the sails. You ready?"

Bev said, "I think so."

Aunt P grinned and keyed up the field generators that unfurled sails to the solar winds.

I could see Bev's hands on the controls actually loosen and relax as the sails filled and the *Penny* began clawing up out of the gravity well. "Oh, my, you can almost feel them."

"Yup," Aunt P said.

After just a few ticks running out like that Aunt P stood up and stretched. "Well, I want some lunch. You guys coming?"

Pip was on his feet instantly and heading for the door. "Last one to the galley does the dishes."

Uncle Q was right behind him.

Aunt P stepped over and gave Bev a pat on the back, "You don't need to sit here," she said. "The autopilot works perfectly well."

"Is it okay if I stay for a while?" Bev asked.

Aunt P leaned down and gave her a peck on the cheek, "Of course, dear. I sail her myself sometimes. The autopilot has the course. Anytime you're ready, just engage it with that control." She pointed to a broad button at the upper edge of the console.

As Aunt P stepped off the bridge, she paused at the door and looked out of the forward port with a happy little smile. "First star on the right, Ms. Arith. Straight on til morning."

Bev grinned at that and answered, "Aye, aye, Captain, straight on til morning."

Nathan Lowell

The Golden Age of the Solar Clipper

Quarter Share

Half Share

Full Share

Double Share

Captains Share

Owners Share

South Coast

Tanyth Fairport Adventures

Ravenwood

Zypherias Call

Awards

2011 Parsec Award Winner for Best Speculative Fiction
(Long Form) for *Owners Share*

2010 Parsec Award Winner for Best Speculative Fiction
(Long Form) for *Captains Share*

2009 Podiobooks Founders Choice Award for Captains Share

2009 Parsec Award Finalist for Best Speculative Fiction
(Long Form) for *Double Share*

2008 Podiobooks Founders Choice Award for *Double Share*

2008 Parsec Award Finalist for Best Speculative Fiction
(Long Form) for *Full Share*

2008 Parsec Award Finalist for Best Speculative Fiction
(Long Form) for *South Coast*

Contact

Website: nathanlowell.com
Twitter: twitter.com/nlowell
Email: nathan.lowell@gmail.com

About The Author

Nathan Lowell first entered the literary world by podcasting his novels. The Golden Age of the Solar Clipper grew from his life-long fascination with space opera and his own experiences shipboard in the United States Coast Guard. Unlike most works which focus on a larger-than-life hero, Nathan centers on the people behind the scenes—ordinary men and women trying to make a living in the depths of interstellar space. In his novels, there are no bug-eyed monsters, or galactic space battles, instead he paints a richly vivid and realistic world where the hero uses hard work and his own innate talents to improve his station and the lives of those of his community.

Dr. Nathan Lowell holds a Ph.D. in Educational Technology with specializations in Distance Education and Instructional Design. He also holds an M.A. in Educational Technology and a BS in Business Administration. He grew up on the south coast of Maine and is strongly rooted in the maritime heritage of the sea-farer. He served in the USCG from 1970 to 1975, seeing duty aboard a cutter on hurricane patrol in the North Atlantic and at a communications station in Kodiak, Alaska. He currently lives on the plains east of the Rocky Mountains with his wife and two daughters.

78069374R00147

Made in the USA
Lexington, KY
06 January 2018